THE ELEMENTAL

T. B. WIESE

1

———

RAELYN

A CHILL TINGLES down my spine, causing me to shiver despite the late afternoon sun stinging my skin. A dizzying mix of dread and excitement fills me as I glance in the reflection of a store window spying the male trailing me several yards back. Tension forms a knot behind my right shoulder blade.

Detouring away from the entrance to the grocery store, I keep my pace casual, wishing I hadn't worn sandals today, and head toward the airport road loop trail. I need to get him away from the busy street.

Rust-colored spires of rock catch my eye. Perfect. Red Rock Country. It's not as secluded an area as I would like for our confrontation, but it will do. My steps are even and unhurried as I head down the street toward the trailhead.

I like Sedona more than I've liked any place I've lived in a long while. And now I'm going to have to move. Again.

Because of him. A tiny voice whispers in my head, *Stop running. It's time to stop running.*

I wish I knew how. It's all I've known.

I haven't seen Asheraht in … I'm not sure how long. Was it Russia 1852 right before the first Crimean War? No, no, we had that brief encounter in France in 1868. I feel my face curl into a scowl remembering how enraged I was to see him. I had just gifted Rodolphe Julian a large sum of money to open her arts school, which would be the first of its kind to admit women.

My scowl melts into a small smile as I recall standing with Rodolphe, our hands clasped together watching the groundbreaking. My chest was tight with pride and excitement for my friend. She was a kindred spirit, and the fact she was willing to champion womens' right to education, especially in the time of history she was born, made her a fast friend of mine. We were going to take France by storm. We were going to enact real change.

She did.

I couldn't.

Because Asheraht showed up.

How many times have I run from him—picked up my life and just ran? I have long lost count. Mesopotamia was a bad one. Then, China—though I guess I should be grateful for that one—he did technically get me out of prison. Then there was Greece, followed by Rome, where Ash and I might have been responsible for the fire that burned a significant portion of the city down. Those fires, born of Ash's fae fire, burned for four days. *Oops.*

Pompeii was shortly after that.

Memories flash past my mind's eye of the great clouds of ash and gas engulfing that beautiful city, my beautiful life.

Then it was China again, Scandinavia, Sumatra, France, Japan ... on and on and on.

My toe catches on the edge of an uneven section of pavement, tripping me up and snapping me out of my thoughts.

Glancing at the window of a shop to my left, I notice Ash is still trailing me, staying back, trying to hide in small groups walking the loop road, but the day is getting late, the sun is setting, and the air is turning cool, so pedestrian traffic is thinning out.

My hand flexes, aching for the feel of my bow. The tips of my fingers still tingle from the pull of the bowstring during practice this morning. But my bow is in my car, so I shake out my hands, focusing on getting Ash away from town.

The sound of my sandals hitting the ground changes from the clop of pavement to the crunch of dirt as I hit the rust-colored rock, dirt, and sand of Red Rock.

I stop. The trail ahead is empty of pedestrians. My muscles tense, and my heart rate picks up as adrenaline courses through my blood. I lie to myself, telling myself the adrenaline is in anticipation of the coming fight, not in seeing Asheraht again.

Turning, my gaze locks onto Ash's brown eyes, and his eyebrows rise. I grin. His lips form the curse, and just as he clenches his fists and leans forward, I spin and run. I always run.

Holding back my natural fae speed, at least for now, I aim for the larger scrub and ravines out in the center of Red Rock. Ash's boots crunch and scrape across the dirt as he pursues me.

My feet are already sore from the sand and pebbles tumbling through my sandals. I want to use my magic, but I hold back. The sun is setting fast, but I can't chance a human seeing me use my power. A shiver of fear tightens my shoulders. I know first-hand what the humans will do if they find out what Ash and I are. I flex my right hand, grateful for the movement in all my fingers. Even after all this time, the fear, the pain, the agony from my past flares up unwanted.

A small throwing knife sails over my right shoulder, the blade flashing in the dying light of the day. I snort at the wide throw.

Grabbing the knife off the ground where it fell before me, I keep running while fighting to keep a smile from my face. This is the game we play.

My fingernails scrape the stone of a rock outcropping as I spin to a stop at a large boulder. Turning, I gulp down a few deep breaths, knife gripped firmly in my hand as Ash catches up.

Ash's muscled chest heaves with his breaths, but annoyingly, he's not breathing quite as hard as I am. His short wavy brown hair, barely brushing his ears, has a slight red tinge to it from all the dust I kicked up. Even in his human form, he looks good. I have missed him, and how sick is that? He was hired to kill me. He's been chasing me across this ever-changing planet for thousands of years ... but he is the only other fae on Earth, my only connection to Attolyn, to home.

"Hey, Rae." His grin shows off his straight, white teeth against tanned, olive skin. He stands just under six feet, muscled but not bulky, lean. The face he wears is one that would make you say, do I know you from somewhere? And you would place him around his mid-to-late thirties, same as me, though we fae are immortal. His fae features are glamoured into the perfect blend of 'human average,' which makes him the perfect assassin. He was known as one of the best in the New Moon Guild back home.

But I know his fae form, his true appearance. It's been a long time since I've seen him as he truly is, but I recall him being taller with a broader chest and back. I find myself aching to see the sharp curve of his ears, and with that ache comes the desire to drop my glamour to reveal my own fae features. But I shake it off, realizing I've been looking him over, and I sneer at him to cover my embarrassment. "Only my friends get to call me Rae."

His grin widens. "Hello, your Highness, Lady Raelyn of Attolyn." He mocks a fraction of a bow, and I grind my teeth together at my formal title—the title of Princess of the Seelie Fae.

"Raelyn, it's just Raelyn. And you know that, *Asheraht*."

His lips pull back in a grimace at his full name, and I whip my arm around, unleashing the knife at his head. I telegraphed the throw, and he doesn't even glance at the knife as he simply steps to the side, letting the blade clatter against the boulder behind him before it thuds into the red dirt. His smiling gaze never leaves my face. "And you know I prefer Ash."

I step to my right as he steps to his right. Our slow dance begins.

"How long has it been, Raelyn? France?"

I nod as we circle each other. His body is tense, but his eyes seem almost soft as he looks me over, smirking at my dirty feet.

We complete one full circle before his eyes come back to mine. "You look good. How have you been?"

I stop and plant my right foot behind me. He does the same. Despite the kick in my heart at his compliment, at his attempt at friendly words, I force myself to pull up the anger

I know I should feel toward him. "We're not doing the banter thing, Ash. Let's just do this. The sooner I kick your ass, the sooner I can get on with my life."

I pause, grinning at him, but there is no joy behind my smile. I bury the small seed of worry that tries to take root in my chest—the worry that this time he will actually kill me. Instead, I fill my voice with dangerous promise. "You will never fulfill your contract, assassin."

A fraction of the tension in his muscles releases, his lips turn down, and his brows pinch together. "Raelyn, I—"

"No!" I can't let him keep talking. I can't let his deep voice draw me in. I fight to hold on to my anger, dredging up memories of those early years on Earth when purpose and fire fueled his attempts on my life. Oh, his fire, his power pitted against my air magic. I recall the heat of his flames tearing through the tornado I created in Mesopotamia. There were several attempts on my life in Egypt—poisoned food, venomous snakes, even a near miss when a boulder fell from the top of my temple while it was under construction. It wasn't until my rooms were set on fire while I slept that I realized it was Ash. Then more fire in Greece, so much fire. He even glamoured himself and befriended me as a comrade in the French army in the early 1400's only to attack me after nearly a month of serving together. Ass.

On and on, I pull up the memories. Yet the rage I feel is not directed at Ash, but aimed at whomever had the gall to hire an assassin against me. I let that fury fill me until I'm trembling with it. I clench my fists, focusing on the pain of my nails digging into my palms.

"Okay, Rae." My nickname on his lips makes my stomach flutter uncomfortably, so I grind my teeth and hiss at him, reminding him—and myself—he is the enemy. But he continues to circle, ignoring my snarl. Finally, he raises his arms slightly and cocks his head at me. "Shall we? I've come all this way."

The sun dips behind the horizon, bruising the rocks and dirt around us into shades of purple and black. Like taking a deep, cleansing breath, I draw up my magic with a thought. It rises to my call, like a dog eager to do my bidding. I hold my magic within me, waiting for the full darkness of night to hide my power, just in case. In today's world, it feels as if someone is always watching with their phones at the ready. I can't chance someone seeing. I won't. Not after what happened in China.

We continue circling each other like a pair of sharks, and I grin, not able to tamp down the anticipation. "I wouldn't want your trip to be wasted."

I charge.

Ash runs at me, and I dip as he throws a punch. Sweeping out a leg, I spin on my heel as he jumps, lands, and turns in one fluid motion. I stand, seeing the glint of steel as he produces another blade from somewhere on his body. My vision goes wide, following the movement of the knife, his foot patterns, the bunch of muscles in his shoulders, where his eyes are tracking ... I take it all in, evading his every half-hearted thrust, slash, and stab.

We dance as the final streaks of deep violet sky bleeds into black.

His movements begin to streak, like waving a torch and watching the light trail through the air. I speed up, matching his pace as we move with our natural fae speed, and we blur. If anyone were to see us, we would be but a stream of misty movement, yet I catch every twitch of muscle he makes.

A sheen of sweat sticks my shirt to my skin, and red dust is everywhere, coating my body. I breathe it in with every inhale and taste the earth on my tongue. I don't slow. I don't falter. I roll my shoulders and match him move for move.

I jump to my left as he swipes the blade at my stomach, which brings me right over the blade I threw earlier. Grabbing it without pausing, two long strides have me toe-to-toe with Ash.

We clash, each gripping the other's knife arm by the wrist. He grunts as he struggles to keep my knife from piercing his cheek, and my muscles shake as I strain to keep his blade from sliding between my ribs. My feet scrabble in the dirt and pebbles. He gains another inch closer to my side as he pushes my knife hand back from his face.

He's stronger than this. He's holding back. And he confirms it by smiling down at me, easily holding me in place.

My lips twitch with the desire to smile back.

I spin, tearing myself out of his hold and stepping out of his reach before I turn to face him. My arm burns, and I glance down, noticing a long, thin line of blood welling up on my forearm where his blade sliced me.

First blood.

The air is cooling faster, and the moon is new, so we are well hidden. My power, sitting in my chest like a held breath, expands at my will, and I unleash my magic—the magic of who I am at my core—an Air Fae. I create a bubble of pressurized air around his body, not quite pinning him in place but slowing him down.

He swears under the weight of my magic. Gritting his teeth, he grunts, "Okay. So magic is now in play."

Shit.

I drop my assault, pulling my magic to me. The pressure pops my ears when I solidify a shield of air in front of me as he throws a bolt of fire at my chest. It thuds against my shield, embers falling to the dirt and dying like tiny shooting stars.

Taking a chance, I drop my shield and gather currents to create a mini whirlwind, spinning a red dust devil around Ash. Faster and faster, it throws dust and rock into his face, and I take the few seconds he's distracted to move in toward him. He knows most of my moves by now, so I'm shocked that I catch him by surprise.

For a moment, he's open. I have him. I could stab my blade between his ribs and into his heart. But my own heart betrays me with a pang of panic at the thought of Ash dead. I can't be locked away here on this planet, alone. I can't.

Ash spins toward me with blade in hand, so I shift, slashing my knife across his thigh and take the momentum of the upward swing to slice the edge of the blade across his bicep. Both cuts are shallow but oh so satisfying. Two points for me.

He hisses in pain and throws a ball of fire at me. It hits high, landing with a sizzling thud on my shoulder. I stumble back, clenching my teeth against the pain that feels like steam blasting against my skin.

My concentration falters, and my magic sputters, giving him another straight shot. I drop to my knees as he launches himself at me, but surprisingly he uses his knife instead of his fire. I manage to duck the slash of his blade, but his other hand hooks around my waist, pulling me with him as he sails over me. We roll and it's like the desert attacks me. My hip slams into a large rock, blooming pain up my side. Our momentum tumbles me onto my back, where tiny pebbles grate my skin through my shirt. As we roll, sand grinds into the sensitive skin of my burnt shoulder, and my cheek glances off another sharp rock. By the time we come to a stop, I'm bruised, filthy, and pissed.

My knee kicks up, aimed for his groin, but lands on his inner thigh. He chuckles, actually chuckles. "Low blow, Rae."

His smirk makes my blood boil. "Don't call me that!"

Before I can break his hold, he rolls again, and when we stop once more, he's holding my back against his front, pinning my arms to my sides. I struggle to break his hold and hope there are a few sharp rocks digging into his back, but he squeezes so tight I have to put all my effort into drawing in breath.

"Rae." I snap my head back, missing his nose but clipping his chin. "Damn it, Raelyn. Stop!"

"No." I manage to grab his pinky finger, and I yank. Just before it snaps, he lets go and pushes me up and away from him. I grab a sharp rock in my free hand as I gain my feet and turn. And, of course, he's already standing.

My magic swirls, kicking dust into his eyes once again. Sprinting to my left, I throw the rock with my air magic behind it, and it crashes into the side of his face, knocking him back a few steps. He falters, staggering slightly as blood drips down his temple.

I still have the knife, and hold it before me, dropping my magic for a moment, breathing hard.

He swipes at the blood, smearing it into his hair. "You know, I'm actually quite charming and fun if you'd just give me a chance."

He waggles his eyebrows at me, and I press my lips into a tight line, hiding the fact that I am, in fact, amused by him. I keep the knife pointed at him, my muscles still tense, ready to pounce. "Fine, here's your chance. Answer me this. Why do you keep coming after me? Even if you ... fulfill your contract and kill me, it's not like you can return home and collect the remainder of your fee."

He pauses, dropping his arms, and tilts his head at me. His shoulders slump slightly. He opens his mouth, snaps it shut, and opens it again before closing it. It's almost comical, watching him struggle for words, but his eyes are too intent on mine. I swallow, resisting the urge to shift under his gaze and continued silence, but I force myself to stand still.

The silence builds, and the tension between us crackles through the air like an electrical storm. The stillness becomes too much—too charged. Finally, he sighs, drops his eyes to his boots, and whispers, "I can't seem to stay away, Raelyn." His eyes climb back to mine. "I can only go so long before I need to find you."

That simple admission sends a crack through my chest, weakening my knees. For 7200 years, the portals of Earth have been sealed. We have been stuck on Earth, unable to return home, and ... I understand. I only wish he had said something sooner, not that I've ever really given him a chance. My jaw clenches so tightly I'm afraid I might crack a tooth.

How many times have I wished to have someone to talk to about Attolyn, the Seelie realm, about my home? How often have I sat with an ever-growing pressure in my chest from missing my family? I've spent millennia yearning to unburden my loneliness with someone.

Can I trust his words? Or is he using my desolation against me? I mentally shake my head. I can't let him get to me, so I bury my conflicting feelings.

Angrier at myself than him, I raise the blade. Shoving my magic at him, I rip the air from his lungs and seal off his airways. His eyes go wide, and his mouth forms a silent "O" as he tries and fails to take a breath.

His lips start to turn blue, and I see it in his eyes when he realizes I'm not going to release him. His magic erupts, and I scream as my clothes catch fire. I'm forced to pull my magic back to snuff out the flames with a pop of low-pressure air.

I don't notice the flick of his wrist in time.

His knife hits me high, above my right collar bone on the opposite side of where his fire hit me earlier. I spin with the momentum of the impact, knowing in the back of my mind that he could have landed a killing blow at that moment. Without pausing, I grab the hilt, ripping it free of my flesh, grunting in pain. Turning to him, clothes singed, body bruised and bleeding, I lift both blades now in my possession.

But of course, he has produced yet another knife from somewhere.

"How many of these things do you have on you?" I ask, stalling to catch my breath, every exhale coming out in little hisses of pain.

He grins, lifting his arms from his sides. "You are welcome to search me and find out. You'll have to be very thorough to find them all."

I snort, ignoring the stupid flutter in my chest, and grip the knives tighter, bracing to rush him. My muscles bunch, and I lean forward. He does the same, the both of us ready to charge.

I freeze, and all my senses tingle.

No. They *scream* at me. Every hair stands on end along my arms and down my neck, a zap of electricity pulsing through my blood. Every instinct is telling me Ash and I are not alone.

Ash frowns as I whip my head around, looking, searching for anyone who might be out here with us.

"Raelyn, what is—?"

The glint of the steel tip of an arrow catches the corner

of my vision. Using my air magic to shove me forward, adding to my fae speed, I slam into Ash's chest. He exhales a startled "Oomph" as an arrow flies through the strands of my blowing hair, nearly grazing my temple. We hit the ground a fraction of a second before the arrow sinks into the rock behind where Ash's head was a moment before.

He stares up and back at the still trembling arrow as I turn my head toward where the arrow came from. Even in the dark of night, my fae eyes catch a flash of black hair and dark clothing as the assailant runs off, quickly swallowed by the shadows of the desert.

I shift to push off Ash, ready to give chase, but his arm tightens around my waist. I attempt to elbow him in the ribs, but his hold makes the maneuver impossible. "Ash, let me go. He's getting aw—"

"Rae, look."

I crane my neck to follow his gaze, still staring at the arrow above our heads. My eyes widen as I notice the distinctive whorls in the steel of the arrow sticking out of the rock, the dragon-scale design carved into the wooden shaft, and the tell-tale dragon hair fletching. This is an arrow of the Dragon Lords from The Realm of the Crimson Plains.

But ... how? The seal on the portals has barred the way from all the realms. My mind stalls at the implication. Does this mean the doorways are open?

Can I go home?

My world narrows to that arrow as my mind spins. Dragon Lords, at least one, are here on Earth.

Holy shit! I could go home. I could see my brothers again. My parents. I could walk the shining halls of the palace and enjoy my first fae meal in millennia, where the food and water are truly clean, beyond anything "organic" here on Earth could deliver. I could breathe the air of

Attolyn once again. What does the fae realm smell like? I cannot recall, but excitement speeds my heartbeat to an erratic pace.

I'm ripped from my dizzying thoughts as Ash's other arm snakes around my waist. His hand splays across my lower back—very low, and presses me into the hard length of him. My gaze snaps from the arrow to meet his intense eyes that are watching my face, seemingly no longer concerned with the arrow.

When did I drop both knives? I have a fistful of Ash's shirt in one hand, and the other grips his bicep in what I'm sure is a painful vice. One by one, I pull my fingers from his arm, releasing my nails from his skin, leaving behind little half-moon indentations in his arm.

Our faces are a whisper apart. His breath feathers across my face, and as the corner of his lips lift in a half-smile, revealing a rare sighting of the dimple in his left cheek, our noses actually brush together.

I seem to have lost the ability to think or speak, but he has no such problem as his deep voice rumbles against my chest. "Raelyn, you just saved my life."

2

———————

RAELYN

Ash's words break me from my momentary stupor. Snapping my arms out to the side, I break his hold while digging my knee into his gut. I land a swift kick to his ribs, and he grunts. His fingers brush against my skin as he tries to grab my ankle, but I jump away from his grasp and sprint off in the direction I saw the supposed Dragon Lord run.

All I can think is that I need to find him. Questions ping around my brain like a pinball machine. Why is a Dragon Lord after Asheraht? Because that arrow was definitely intended for Ash. And are the doorways open? Are they all open? Just certain doorways? Only one?

I cross out of the park and into urban Sedona. I weave through the streets and alleys, hunting for the tell-tale scent of sulfur that Dragon Lords carry with them. I listen for any indication that Ash is trailing me, but there's no sign of him.

My shoulders pinch together as I recall the first time I saw Ash. A week after I arrived on Earth, I went back to the portal I had arrived through, waiting for the shimmer of power to dance across my skin as it recognized my fae blood, but nothing happened. The door was sealed, and Ash was there.

I recognized the black clothing and headscarf of the famed Assassin's Guild, and when he charged at me with a blade in one hand and a ball of fire in the other, I couldn't believe someone had actually taken a contract out on my life. In my stupor, I barely managed to escape him that day, and it took me two weeks of pushing my fae speed to the limit to get to the Kalahari City—now lost to humanity— only to find the doorway there sealed as well. One by one I tried every doorway on Earth that I could get to. It took centuries simply because there was no way to travel the great seas and oceans. And Ash trailed me across the globe.

Every single portal was sealed.

Here in Sedona, there are three doorways. The humans call them vortexes, and those who know of these sites believe them to hold strong energies. If only they knew their real power. But doorways don't work for humans.

If a portal is open—and at least one has to be, how else could the Dragon Lord get here—I could be home tonight. I'm tempted to just jump in my car and go to the nearest one, but the Dragon Lord's presence is a question I want answered. For a Dragon Lord to be on the hunt; something very serious is going on.

The red dust boot print trail has faded. Doors to businesses and restaurants are open to the cool evening air, spilling laughter and conversation into the night. Dim streetlights dot the road with soft pools of light. The sweet and bitter scent of chocolate wafts from a confectionary. The savory, mouth-watering spice of Spanish food hits me next. My senses are overloaded as I turn down another street hunting for the scent of sulfur, but instead, the salty aromas of a Japanese restaurant hit me, and then the garlic and onion flavors from an Italian restaurant work its way down my nose, practically coating my tongue.

Millenia spent on this rock, and I'm still not used to the overpowering variety of scents and foods here. My fae senses are always bombarded when I come into any urban area, and I have to fight to keep my focus.

I huff in frustration as I comb my fingers through my hair then stand with hands-on-hips looking up and down the busy street. People weave around me, staring a little too long, before moving on.

I glance down at myself. I'm filthy. Red dirt covers my skin, and my clothes have singe marks all over them. I'm bleeding from multiple areas, and bruises dot my arms. I'm drawing too much attention, and I doubt I will pick up the Lord's trail here.

I bite my lip, looking around once more before turning toward where I left my car. I need to get off the street before someone calls the cops. Sighing, I make my decision. I'll go to my house, clean up, and grab a few things. I'll do one more sweep through town to see if I can find the Dragon Lord, but if not, I'm going to find out if the way home is open.

It will bug me, like a worm in my brain, to leave the Dragon Lord's presence unanswered, but I can't help the fluttering of nervous excitement that stirs, like a thousand butterflies just took flight in my stomach. I might be going home to Attolyn.

And if the doorways are still sealed, I will draw Ash out. It shouldn't be that hard. I can use him as bait to lure out the Dragon Lord since he seems to be after Ash, and demand to know how he got here. But, thoughts of trading Ash for information has my lips turning down in a frown.

After a few blocks traveled in silent thought, I stop on a quiet street. Modest stucco houses line one side, and a small park spreads out on the other.

With a sigh, I run a hand through my hair again before shoving it back over my shoulder. Though all Seelie fae have silver hair, I don't have to glamour my hair. No, I was born with hair that is not only completely brown, it's dark brown, almost black—almost the hair color of the Unseelie Fae.

I grab my keys from the gas compartment of my old BMW and run my hands over the chipped blue paint. Walking around the car, I open the door before sliding in, flicking the crystal hanging from the rearview mirror with my finger. I catch my reflection, frowning at my hair, memories of my family swimming through my mind.

I did not spend all that much time in the presence of my parents, the King and Queen of the Seelie fae, which was fine with me. I had nannies, teachers, and stewards, all of whom I ditched whenever possible to shadow my older brother.

How I've missed Garin. A soft chuckle floats from my lips as I try to imagine my older brother folding his large frame into my small car. His nose would probably wrinkle, but there'd be a smile behind his eyes, humoring me. He was always humoring me.

He was well educated, charismatic, and a great warrior. As far as I'm concerned, Garin hung the moon. Three hundred years my senior, he was my hero and the champion of my free spirit. To this day, I strive to be like him, brave and strong and confident. I love him and miss him so much my heart feels like it will rip apart every time I think about him. Yes, even after all this time.

I glance down. I vacuumed the floor mats and seats just

yesterday, and the amount of dust and blood I'm tracking in my car pisses me off. But then I remember I might actually be going home, and I smile at the mess, starting the car.

The desert stretches all around, the headlights reaching desperately but finding nothing but the dark of night. Technically, I don't need the headlights, but I do many unnecessary things to avoid confrontation with the law.

We fae have excellent sight and hearing and are fairly hard to kill. Our bodies can sustain quite a bit of damage and keep going, which is both a blessing and a curse. Yes, we can survive what mortals cannot. But surviving usually means pain, a lot of pain.

A very long time ago, I spent many, many years in a Chinese prison. My arm twitches, and I wince at the phantom pains as memories flash through my mind. Once my captors realized I healed faster than normal, the testing began. Once they realized I was not aging, the experiments really ramped up. Since then, I vowed to keep myself above board as much as possible, not that I did what I was accused of. But no amount of begging would convince them of my innocence. So now I avoid anything that would chance my capture or arrest.

I drive for about twenty minutes heading away from civilization into the open, desert area to the west of Sedona. The car sways as I turn onto a small road. My body goes on autopilot as I drive home, and my mind wanders.

In all my many millennia on Earth, in all the places I lived, I always tried to 'settle' near a portal site. Of course, that made it a bit easier for Ash to narrow down where I might be, but there are many doorways on this planet.

I first came through the Cradle of Life doorway in South Africa 7200 years ago. Portal sites emit strong power, magic that even humans can sense—to a point—and as such, monuments usually end up near the doors. There are portals near Stonehenge, The Pyramids, Easter Island, the Mayan temples, Matchu Pitchu ... and many more, including the Cradle, where human civilization began.

There are plenty of planets, worlds, galaxies, and realms to explore, and growing up, I loved them all. But when my older brother came to me with tales of an evolving species on a planet called Earth, I couldn't resist. I loved this feral, dangerous planet. Earth was a wild place, humans trying to claw their way up the food chain. It was exhilarating, and I was interested to see if the humans would come out on top.

My mother tried again and again to tame me into a proper princess, but as a young royal trying to escape the boredom of court and the responsibility of the crown, the 'newness' of other worlds was intoxicating to me. The danger was a thrill—one my older brother, Garin, encouraged. Garin understood my need for freedom, to explore, to learn through experience, through travel.

The last time I saw Garin, our mother had wrapped her slender hand around my arm, sending the arrows in my quiver clattering softly as she halted my steps toward the portal outside the palace gardens. The warm spring with white flowers along its bank, bubbled around the portal. The doorway was originally within the walled boundary of the castle grounds but was later decided to be too much of a security risk, so it was separated from the main grounds by an additional stone wall.

I remember the feel of my mother's skin, soft and smooth, perfectly manicured nails digging into my arm. Her grip was firm, matching the strength behind her voice. "Raelyn, you cannot run off to Fates know where. You have duties, responsibilities."

That fateful day, I ripped my arm from my mother's grip,

seething like a spoiled child, which I was at only five centuries old. It seems to be the fatal flaw of youths, regardless of what realm they grow up in, to believe they know what's best for their lives. And I was no exception.

I glared at my mother. "What does it matter if I miss a boring meeting on food distribution?"

"Magic regulation," Garin mumbled under his breath near my ear, a small smile on his lips.

I huffed at him but kept my eyes on my mother. "Magic regulation, whatever. We all know you and father are going to pass the crown to Garin."

"Raelyn." My older brother's voice held reproach, but there was pity under his tone as well. I didn't care. I didn't want the crown. Still don't.

I frowned at him. "No, Garin, The Fates know mother would give the crown to Alek before she let father give it to me."

My younger brother, Alek, was quiet, shy, practically living in the library. I don't recall him ever speaking above a whisper, with his eyes usually cast down or spearing hate-filled looks at our older brother. Mother doted on Alek, but she knew the mantle of the crown would crush him. No, the crown would go to Garin, not because he is the firstborn, that is not how the Fae rule. It is passed to the heir who proves they are strong enough, virtuous enough, to lead our people.

But Garin was more than worthy.

My mother pursed her lips in disapproval at my words. "No, as much as I love Alek, he is not meant to rule, which is why you need to stay, Raelyn. Garin will need your council and your support when that day comes."

I opened my mouth to throw another barb at her, but Garin stepped forward, placing his large, calloused hand on our mother's shoulder. "Mother, Raelyn will be of great service with her knowledge of the many races throughout the universe. Her travels gain us first-hand accounts of what is happening beyond our realm. Her experiences are important."

My mother clucked her tongue at him, and I did my best to hold back my smile, knowing she would relent—she always did when it came to Garin. With a sigh, she smoothed her skirts, which were always impeccable and needed no such attention, and looked back at me. "Be sure to be back in a week to help prepare for the Gathering."

Barely holding back an eye roll, I nodded. The Gathering was important. Once a year, the royal Fae families from across the realms meet, and that year it was happening in Attolyn. I despised the seemingly endless meetings, courts settling disputes, trades, alliances ... but I adored the parties. A small smile played at my lips as I thought of the gowns I would wear and the fae wine that would flow freely. "I promise I'll be back in time."

That day, I turned, smiling my thanks to Garin, and he winked with a grin of his own as I ran off, fingers clutching the familiar curve of my bow, all too eager to get through that doorway. Always running.

But I broke my promise. I never made it back. I'm sure my mother was furious. How long did she stew in anger before it turned to concern? How long did my family search for me?

I try but cannot recall what my mother looks like other than the one feature that ties us together—the single brown streak in her silver hair. She kept herself glamoured or styled her hair to hide what she considered an embarrassment to her otherwise flawless appearance.

I'm pulled from my memories as the car goes over the

bump at the top of my driveway. The headlights find my small, modern house. Stucco squares on squares, each painted the colors of the desert: sand beige, brown stone, red rock. Large windows create sharp, dark squares within the stucco, and the flat roof holds a low profile against the landscape. There are no other houses as far as the eye can see, even with my fae sight. This is the perfect place of quiet and solitude—a place for me to be Fae.

I park to the left of the house, grab my bow and quiver, and get out.

Back home in Attolyn, I trained with the royal soldiers with blade and bow and am deadly with both. While I've been stuck here on Earth, I've kept up my weapons training and am proficient in every type of bow I could get my hands on over the millennia. I've trained with bows made of everything from wood, animal horn, intestines, and stone, to aluminum and carbon. Longbows, recurves, and compound bows. I love them all.

The carbon of this bow sits slightly cool in my hand as I drop my glamour. Hiding my fae features to appear human is second nature at this point, well, mostly. I can still feel the glamour, though not as much as I used to. Glamour has always felt like I am wearing a formal dress with a too-tight corset. It's uncomfortable and not at all me. The more features I glamour, the tighter my skin feels. But I've gotten used to it. I've had to.

My shoulder spasms again with phantom pain, and I shudder trying to block the unwanted memories of opium induced nightmares and never-ending agony.

I could probably get away with dropping my glamour these days, what with body modifications, special effects, and comic con and such, but I don't like drawing undue attention to myself, so I've kept the glamour, kept my human appearance, only letting it drop when I'm at my house and I'm sure I'm alone.

As I approach my house, I run my finger over my right ear, smiling at the sensitive point, and I catch my reflection in the window to the right of the door. My fae eyes glow like an animal caught in light at night.

My keys clinking together seem overly loud in the quiet of the desert night as I separate the correct one. The door unlocks with a soft snick. I push it open to reveal the dark interior and step across the threshold.

My eyes water as the scent of brimstone hits me a second before the door slams and locks. An unnaturally warm hand grabs my arm, and black nails that are more like claws dig into my skin, reminding me of the talons of the beasts from this man's realm.

My eyes snap up, meeting black eyes with flaming ember centers—the eyes of the Dragon Lord.

3

———————

ASHERAHT

I AM in love with my mark.

And isn't that just classic? From the first day at guild training, two things were drilled into us over and over and over. One, do your research. And two, eliminate feelings, emotions, and attachments.

I was never very good at number two, but I am good at projecting what people want to see. Wearing personalities like masks, I have always easily slid from one to the next.

Until Rae.

Folding my hands behind my head, I stare at the stars, relaxing back into the hard ground beneath me. I should be worried about the Dragon Lord, but I smile. Finally, something different. Over the millennia, my only other source of excitement has been whenever I've managed to track Rae down. Every time I see her, my world becomes sharper, more vivid, more … everything.

My thoughts tumble back to my second clash with her, back in … hmm … must have been around 3400 BC. We both ended up in Sumer in the Middle East—or Mesopotamia at the time, and for years neither of us was aware the other was there.

We had been on Earth for 2000 years already at that point, and I was bored and frustrated. So bored, I 'invented' a form of writing, giving the humans a little nudge toward furthering civilization. It quickly spread across the continent to Egypt and into Asia, thus giving me a way to send and receive messages—granted, they were on slabs of rock, torn cloth, even palm fronds. But I wasn't picky. I was just glad I had a way to track down the whereabouts of where a woman of Rae's appearance would be.

All that effort, and she was right there in Sumer.

The day she spotted me in a trading market, the rage shooting from her eyes made me take a step back. She shook with it. I think that was the one time *I* ran from her. I turned and fled from her narrowed eyes and clenched hands. Her magic was already swirling around her, lifting her dark hair around her face. I had to use my fae speed to keep her from tackling me right there in the market.

Skidding to a stop at the edge of the Tigris river, rocks and dust kicked up around my sandaled feet, and her voice screamed across the distance between us. "How did you do it, Asheraht? Open them! Open them right now!"

Confusion had me tilting my head at her red face until I realized she thought I somehow closed the portals, that I was keeping her from going home. It did make sense. The sealed doorways confined her to one planet, and I didn't have to chase her all over the universe. But it was not me, and I said as much.

"I did not seal them. I'm as stuck on this world as you."

"LIAR!" She sprang at me, unleashing her magic, the air pinning me in place with a great weight pressing onto my body. My head bounced off the dirt, and my vision blurred for a second as she tackled me. When I could once again see straight, Rae was kneeling on top of me, fists pummeling my face over and over as her air magic nearly crushed my ribs.

Her voice ripped from her throat, raw and angry. "Who hired you? How did you seal the doors?" Her knuckles split against the bones of my cheeks, and as her next swing dove for my eye, I finally found the breath to summon my magic.

The edges of her tunic caught fire. She screamed, leaping up, patting herself down to extinguish the flames, and I jumped to my feet, muscles aching from the assault of her magic and fists.

With flames still licking my hands, I wiped blood and dirt from my face and spat a bloody tooth into the dirt at my feet. Staring Rae down, I let my fire fade and said, "If you must know, a man named Valna hired me. I doubt that was his real name, and I had never met him before."

She shoved me with a blast of air which felt like a troll had slammed into my body. "Why would you even take a contract on me? Taking out a member of the royal family is risky at best, deadly at worst. Or was the money just that good?"

"Honestly?"

She rolled her eyes.

"I didn't know you were my mark. Valna instructed me to go through a doorway and look for the only other Fae present and eliminate her." Her air magic shoved me again, and I teetered on the edge of the riverbank. "Raelyn, I tried to go back as soon as I realized, but the portal was already sealed."

"So you thought, what the hell—I'll kill her anyway?"

I shrugged, still wearing the mask of the arrogant assassin. "I have nothing else to do." Smiling at her and crossing my arms over my chest, was the wrong move.

Instead of shoving me again toward the river, her magic pushed me from behind. My face smacked into the ground, exploding pain through my already split cheek. I barely managed to roll over before her magic crashed into me. The ground beneath me started to crack, and I sank inch by inch into the dirt as my bones groaned and my muscles protested. My vision began to close in, and in a panic, my magic exploded from me.

Rae stumbled back a few steps, the pressure around me released, and I pushed to my feet. I must have had a death wish that day because I grinned again. "A contract is a contract, Rae. And I like a challenge."

She clenched her hands, throwing her magic back at me, but that time I was prepared and threw up a wall of fire as she screamed, "You don't get to call me Rae!"

"Fine, your Highness," I yelled back as my flames grew, climbing up into the sky. The river at my back started to steam, and as I stepped forward, a cracking sound drew my gaze. The sand at my feet shimmered and turned to glass as I stalked Rae. She surrounded herself with a whirlwind, holding the flames back, but they spread around her and flew into the air on the whirling currents of her magic.

Our powers clashed, pushing against each other, vying for dominance. Our battle that day became the basis for many stories of gods and plagues. I think we were even obscurely mentioned in the Bible.

All I could think of was how tired I was of being on this primitive planet—if only I knew then how terribly long we'd be stuck here—and how I just wanted to finish the job and find a way home.

I pushed my fire against her air, grunting, "Maybe if I kill you, Raelyn, the doorways will open again. It's worth a try." Her eyes widened, and she tried to suck the oxygen away from my fire to smother the flames, but my magic overpowered hers. She was born with strong air magic and is well trained, but my magic is stronger. I am older, just by a few centuries, but it's enough to give me an edge. With a roar, the air around her caught fire.

Luckily, Raelyn kept a shred of awareness around her, noticing the raging flames, by then caught on the natural winds of the desert, heading right to Sumer. She closed in on me, pushing her air magic ahead of her. Digging her sandals into the ground, she struggled one step forward, then another until her wall of wind pressed against my wall of fire in a display of spitting, raging power.

Fire needs oxygen to live. But if allowed, air will carry and feed the flames. So like Rae and me. We have the magic to utterly destroy the other or enhance the other's power. It's beautiful. It's exhilarating.

She was sweating, her face red from heat and exertion, and her dark hair whipped around her beautiful face as she screamed over the roaring of our magic. "Ash! Stop! Sumer will be destroyed, all those people!"

I refused to care, to stop. An assassin doesn't feel, and she saw that in my eyes.

She bellowed with her own fury, "No!" And with one tremendous push, her magic shoved me backward, and I let it. I let the blast of wind take me away from her rage, and I landed with a sizzling splash in the river. Before the fast currents swept me away, I saw her standing on the bank, hands on knees, breathing hard, coughs racking her body. Tears streamed down her soot-stained cheeks, as she watched me disappear around a turn in the river.

It was a few thousand years before I found her again in

Egypt. She was a Pharaoh, and trying to kill a Pharaoh who's actually a fae is extremely hard and lots of fun.

I'm drawn out of my memories as I shift, attempting to dislodge a small rock that's digging into my back. I chuckle, realizing I've been acting like a little boy pulling on the hair of the girl he likes because he can't figure out how to express himself properly.

I can do better.

A sigh hums in my chest. Tonight, when I whispered those words, I saw the disbelief in her eyes when I told her I couldn't stay away from her. And why should she believe me? She will always see me as the man hired to kill her. I can't even offer her the reason behind the contract on her life. I don't know—it's not the place of an assassin to ask the why behind their contracts.

With a grunt, I push myself to a seated position and pull my phone from my back pocket. A few swipes open the encrypted app, and a little red dot appears. It blinks at me, stationary.

There's Rae. The bug I planted on the waist of her jeans when she landed on top of me is broadcasting her location.

It took me a long time to find her this time. Too long. Over a thousand years. Throughout the millennia, I've spent so much time searching for her and trying to fill the void. And each time I find her, I spend more and more time trailing her, learning her patterns, observing her behaviors before I reveal myself to her. I tell myself I'm just doing my research—rule one. But if I were honest with myself, I just enjoy watching her, being close to her. Sure, she is the only other fae on Earth and provides a connection to our home, but over the years I've learned she is kind, empathetic, funny, fierce, and smart. She's wormed her way into my heart, and I'm more than happy to leave her there.

After she ran from me in France, back in 1868, I allowed myself a distraction. I have had relationships with a few people over the years simply to stave off the endless loneliness. After France, I spent a couple decades with a fetching, intelligent women in Norway. It was a nice relationship, but it wasn't love—at least not for me.

And like all things on this Earth, the situation with the Scandinavian woman could not last. While I can't quite recall her features, I remember kissing her at the docks. Her lips were cold, and there were tears in her blue eyes. Running a finger down her cheek in a gesture of reassurance, I promised to send for her as soon as I established a home for us in the new world, America. I knew damn well she would never be joining me. Instead, she received a letter, informing her that I died at sea due to an illness that claimed many lives on that boat.

After what felt like centuries on that stinking ship, we docked in New York, and my search for Raelyn began once again.

This planet is small compared to Attolyn, but the humans have spread like wildfire. You would think with all the technologies available this day and age, I would have found her easily. But the sheer amount of humanity on this rock makes it harder than one might think, especially when someone like Rae does not want to be found.

Pushing myself up off the ground, I head back to town and turn down a side street leading to a primarily residential area where I left my rental car. Very little light reaches the sidewalk from the windows of the homes tucked back away from the road. There are no streetlights here, and I remember reading Sedona has some sort of light pollution ordinance in place. My mind snaps back to Attolyn and the magic orbs that dotted our paths and streets with a pure white light that danced with undertones of shimmering purples and blues.

Fates, I miss it.

Light pollution. The humans have created quite a mess of their home. I've been sent all through the realms on different jobs and seen all manner of planets and lifeforms, but never have I seen a planet ravaged so quickly by a species. And they don't seem to care. Sure, some do, but not enough. Earth was once wild and beautiful, vast and dangerous. There are still a few wild places left, but they are shrinking at a rate that shocks even me. This planet is headed to ruin, and I've been preparing myself to see its end.

But maybe now I won't have to.

I fold myself into the Honda Accord, prop my phone in a cup holder, and head toward the blinking red light. Picking up speed, I watch that light with one eye as I watch the road with the other.

Rae's clothes were practically ruined with scorch marks. I glance down at my own clothing, noticing I'm covered in dust, sweat, and bloodstains, but it's not all that bad. Rae was much worse off.

She's likely to clean herself up and head right back out tonight to try and find the Dragon Lord, or a portal, or both. Once she changes out of her clothes—the thought of Rae naked has me clenching the steering wheel so hard, it creaks—I won't be able to track her.

I could lay in wait at her apartment or house or wherever she's living these days, but I don't like the thought of her out there hunting down the Dragon Lord on her own. Whoever wants me dead really wants me dead if they have gone to the Dragon Lords. I grin at the new challenge.

I just have to get to Rae before she finds him—or leaves

this planet. At that thought, my mind twists and turns with scenarios, none of them great.

Turning down a secluded road, I turn off my headlights as I get closer to the red blinking light. I stop while I'm still a half-mile away. Silently exiting the car, I keep my distance as I circle where the dot indicates until a modern house comes into view. My footsteps are light, my body just another shadow in the moonless night. I shiver as the darkness seems to press in on my skin, and I recognize where the feeling of unease comes from.

There are no night sounds. The desert is silent.

Keeping alert, I approach her house. It's nice, nicer than anything I've seen her buy before. I wonder how long she's been here? And now that I am here, she will move, run, pick up her life and make a new one somewhere else. Guilt pinches my shoulders, but then I remember the portals may be open, and she may be going home.

Her house is the only structure out here in the desert and boasts an impressive view of the mountains in the distance. The soft scratch of scrub brush slides across my pants as I pass in and out of the shadows of boulders and rock outcroppings that dot the desert around her house. I duck behind a large rock and watch.

A smile lifts my cheeks as a cool breeze of desert air combs through my hair, and I look around. This place reminds me of Mesopotamia. Plant a large river on the edge of town, and I would forget I am on the American continent.

The glass of the large windows cut squares out of the smooth stucco of her house. No interior lights are on, but with her Fae sight, she wouldn't need them. Seeing a car parked outside, I assume she's still home. Thank the Fates for small mercies.

I could easily find a way in through a window or door

and demand she let me handle the Dragon Lord. The very idea of her facing off against a Dragon Lord makes the breath stutter in my lungs. I'll restrain her if necessary.

Running my hands through my hair, I think it will probably be necessary.

As the wind shifts, my back stiffens, and my skin pebbles. Sulfur. The Dragon Lord is here.

I keep still, my eyes scanning the open space around Rae's house, looking for any sign of movement, no matter how slight. After a few minutes, I use my fae speed to blur to a large shrub a little closer to the house and immediately freeze again, waiting to see if my movement draws out the Lord.

I hold my breath. Nothing.

I'm still at least fifty yards from the house, approaching from the side, and it remains dark other than the light illuminating the front door and the landscape lighting that spotlights the cacti lining the sides of the house and the desert plants bordering her back patio. There are no sounds around me other than the wind. No desert bugs singing to the stars. No night birds calling out to each other. No scurrying of mice or desert lizards on the hunt for food. Now the silence makes sense. The creatures sense the Dragon Lord.

I chance moving closer to the house with another blur of motion, skidding to a stop behind a tall, granite fountain bubbling in Rae's backyard. The smell of brimstone is much stronger, and my chest constricts as I realize he's inside the house. Inside with Rae.

What is going on in there? It's too quiet, and all I can think of is how Raelyn knocked me clear of that arrow. She put herself in harm's way, for me. She could have been killed—not by me but for me.

I flick a throwing knife into my left hand as I creep

toward the house, skirting to a window. Peering inside, I see a bedroom, neat and sparsely furnished, and there is a door open to an ensuite bathroom. I try the window and find it locked. "Good girl," I whisper as I check for alarms.

Finding none, I fit the thin blade between the panes and snick back the lock. The window slides up silently as I push, straining my fae senses for any sounds within.

A second before I lift myself onto the sill, I hear Rae's voice, and it freezes me for a moment. It's quiet, almost shaky. Whatever the Dragon Lord has done or said has scared her.

Anger bubbles up in my chest as I catch what she's saying, "No. No. You're wrong. You're lying. I don't believe you. I ... I ..."

The absolute despair in her voice has my magic boiling to the surface, and my vision turns red. I silently haul myself into her bedroom. Her scent, the smell of linens dried in the sun, calms me slightly, clears my head enough to keep me from storming into her living room.

The Dragon Lord's deep, rumbling voice fills the house. "It does not matter if you believe me. I have two jobs here on this planet. Asheraht and you."

Rage fills me again. I shake with it. Is he threatening her? My fire magic will do shit-all against a Dragon Lord, but I don't care. I need a distraction to get Rae out of here.

A fireball explodes from my hand as I stride through the bedroom door into the living room. It slams into the Dragon Lord, and satisfaction puffs my chest as his dark, burning eyes widen in surprise.

Raelyn's eyes snap to me. She's white as a sheet, her hands are trembling, and her voice quivers. "Ash—"

Fireball after fireball slams into the Lord's chest, doing absolutely no damage but keeps him from moving across the room. Embers and sparks spill down to the cool, tiled floor around his feet.

He grins at me, showing off elongating fangs.

Reaching Rae, I grab her wrist and yank her to my side. It's a testament to just how shaken she is that she doesn't resist as I run to the front door.

Thick smoke curls around us as we burst outside, and the rumble of the angered dragon has me blurring us to her car. I shove her into the passenger seat, and a half-second later am behind the wheel. "Keys."

Her wide, glazed eyes turn to me. "What?"

Burning ember eyes appear in the doorway, and as the Lord steps through the door the shadows around him expand, swallowing him. His form melts, and the shadows form wings that stretch until they reach beyond the walls of the house.

"Shit." I rip out the panel under the steering wheel and yank on the wires. A few cuts and two quick sparks later, the car roars to life, and I throw it in reverse. Dust and rocks spew into the air as I execute a J-turn and punch the old Beamer down the dark road.

A roar like thunder screams from the front yard, and a column of fire shoots after us, growing in the rearview mirror. I may be a fire fae, but Dragon fire will kill me just like anyone else.

We barely outrun it, but a blast of air lurches against the car, almost lifting the back wheels off the road as the dark, shadowy form of the dragon shoots into the sky.

We are not going to survive this.

4

———————

RAELYN

My mind is churning, unable to land on a solid thought. I swallow back tears and grit my teeth to keep myself from screaming. This is too much. I feel like I might implode as the Dragon Lord's words press in, suffocating me.

Pain sparks down the side of my face when my head hits the glass of my car window as we take a sharp turn. "Ow."

"Sorry." The gruff word turns my attention to the driver. Ash. Turning in my seat, I see nothing but dark, deserted desert behind us, but Ash is driving like the hounds of hell are following us. I spin and grab him by the arm. "Ash, stop."

"Hell no."

"We can't outrun a Dragon Lord, and besides—"

There's the sound of the flap of giant wings followed by a woosh of air. Ash throws out his arm across my chest as the wheels on the driver's side lift off the road, and the car slams on its side, skidding to a stop. I hit my head again against the side window, and the glass cracks, cutting into my temple. The warm trickle of blood runs down my face and drips onto the shattered window, slowly painting it red like a blood-soaked spider web.

"Are you okay?" Ash's voice sounds slightly panicked as he kicks open his door. With a grip on my arm, he hauls me up and out behind him.

As soon as my feet hit pavement, I wrench my arm from his large, calloused hand. "What are you doing?"

"Saving you." I raise an eyebrow, and he reaches for me again, but I step back, and he huffs. "Fine, returning the favor. A life for a life. But we need to go, he's—"

The earth shakes under our feet, and a gust of wind and dust kicks into our faces. I have to brace myself to keep from stumbling back as the giant beast lands mere feet from us.

The black dragon's scales shimmer even in the deep dark of the night, and his belly and eyes glow red with the embers of his inner fire. With his every exhale, the scent of brimstone claws its way down my throat. Shadows swarm around the dragon, and he begins to shrink into the inky darkness. His smoky wings fold in and disappear.

Ash steps in front of me, and I slap his back, stepping back around to stand at his side. He just snorts, keeping his eyes on the Dragon Lord who now stands before us in his human form. At six and a half feet tall, he towers over us. His black skin is smooth and his hair, woven into locs, has a few silvery-grey streaks in them, mirrored in his close-cut beard. Still, he doesn't look that much older than Ash, early forties at most. But all three of us are immortal, so who knows how old the Dragon Lord is?

Though he looks like us, I know his dark skin is as hard and impenetrable as his dragon scales. His black nails can claw as deeply as his dragon talons, and fire will erupt from his mouth at the slightest provocation.

His gravelly voice fills the night air as he takes a single step toward us. "Step away, your Highness. I will finish *this* one for you." He nods to Ash, who is so tense I fear his muscles will snap, but he stands his ground nonetheless. "Then I will take you home. The Seelie need you."

Again, for reasons I don't care to examine, I step in front of Ash, shaking my head. "No. You're lying."

Ash whispers my name on an exhaled warning, and the Dragon Lord stands a bit taller, pressing his lips together in a sharp line. "Dragon Lords do not lie. We have no need to."

I straighten to my full five foot six inches, still dwarfed by the Dragon Lord. "Then your 'truth,' your information, is wrong."

Ash steps back to my side, folding his arms across his chest. "Okay, will someone tell me what's going on? If my life is forfeit, I might as well know why."

The Dragon Lord scoffs at his words. "You are deserved no explanation, just the death I was sent here to deal."

The Lord's eyes glow a little brighter, and smoke curls from his nostrils. I place my hands on my hips, feigning a strength I do not feel. "No. Asheraht's death is mine."

Ash whips his head towards me, but I stare up at the Dragon Lord who looks between Ash and me with a puzzled look before he nods. "If you wish it, his death is yours. I will escort you both through the doorway, unless you wish to dispose of him here and now."

So the portals are open, at least one anyway. Sighing, I rub my temples, feeling the adrenaline seeping out of me, leaving me tired and on the edge of exhaustion. Every cut and bruise from the day throbs in protest. "I can't." The Dragon Lord opens his mouth to protest, but I push on. "I want to. The Fates know I want to go home. But I can't." Taking another single step forward, I tilt my head up to stare into the Dragon Lord's eyes. I'm so close the heat from his body wraps around me, causing sweat to drip down my back and between my breasts. "There are too many unknowns."

I can tell Ash has questions as he shifts back and forth. But I can't explain. I can't repeat what the Dragon Lord told me. If I say it out loud, I might crack and fall apart. So, I lift my chin, donning my 'princess' persona. My mother would be equally proud and appalled as I dare to command the Dragon Lord. "Bring me proof."

Ash gasps, and the Lord's eyes widen at my command. I'm not about to die due to my arrogance, especially with home so close, so I tag on, "Please."

His eyes flit between Ash and me again before nodding once. "I will return in twenty-four Earth hours. Use that time wisely. Prepare yourself to face the truth and be ready to go back to Attolyn." He turns his burning gaze over my shoulder to Ash. "And you, Asheraht, have a choice. Run from Raelyn, avoid your death, and stay here on this planet, or return to your home and see Attolyn once more before you meet your end."

I release some of my tension on an exhale as shadows swirl around the Dragon Lord's body. His eyes stay on my face, and there's something in his expression ... like he's intrigued by me, like he knows me beyond our brief meeting tonight.

I don't stop to think as I hold out a hand, amazed at my audacity as my palm rests on his forearm. He seems as shocked at the contact as me because his eyes go wide, and the shadows melt back into his skin. I'm shaking, and I know he can feel it, but I force myself to hold his gaze. "What's your name?"

His mouth parts, and I don't think he's going to answer as his eyes skate across my face, but he says, "Kemremir is my dragon name, but you may call me Kem, your Highness."

I nod, swallowing down my fear, and manage a smile as the shadows once again peel away from him. I step back, and he vanishes into darkness, the burning embers of his eyes, the last piece of him to fade.

Ash's low whistle is loud behind me. "I didn't know they could do that."

I don't turn around, but answer, "Me either."

His boots crunch on the glass from my smashed-up car as he comes back to my side. "Are you going to tell me what's going on?"

The concern in his voice sends an ache through my heart, but I can't manage to form the words to tell him. I stare into the darkness, searching for the courage to speak, but I remain silent for too long.

He steps back, shaking his head, and hurt and disappointment flashes through his eyes. "Fine. But I'm not sticking around for you to take your 'owed' death." He turns but stops, looking over his shoulder. "Congratulations. You are the only one to survive a contract of mine. You'll be famous. Have a nice life, princess."

I want to tell him to wait, to stay, to come home to Attolyn, but the words sit like lead on my tongue, and panic grips my chest at the thought that I might never see him again.

"Ash!"

But he's gone, his fae speed whisking him from my sight, and my shout dies on the desert air.

I sigh, rounding my car and bend to grip the frame through the broken passenger window. With a heave of my magic, the air currents help me rock the car back and forth until I get it back on all four wheels. Wrenching open the driver's side door, I swallow the tears that threaten to fall. I get behind the wheel, leaning down to hotwire my car, then turning the wheel sharply, I make a slow U-turn. Shattered glass crunches under the tires, and I glance at the scorch mark where Kem landed.

I have no recollection of the drive home, but the next thing I know, I'm sitting in front of my house, having killed the car, and just stare at the open front door.

Managing to haul myself from the car, my limbs feel numb, and I can't feel my injuries, though I know they should hurt like hell. Shock. I think I'm in shock.

I walk past the large wood front door, kicking it closed behind me as the smell of sulfur still lingering in the house greets me. My eyes dart to where Kem stood. Where he told those lies.

They were lies. They had to be.

I pad across the living room, into my bedroom, and stop by my bed, glancing at the open window where Ash must have come in. I clench my hands, digging my nails into my palms against the insistent tears clawing at my throat. I can smell Asheraht here, in my bedroom, and it feels ... intimate. His scent wraps around me, the scent of pine and fresh grass, and I find myself inhaling deeply.

I shake my head and shed my clothes on the way to the bathroom. Turning the shower on, I keep the water cool to wash the burn on my shoulder first, but upon inspection, I realize it's not as bad as I thought. My skin is just a bit pink where Ash's fire hit me. I swear his magic hit me straight on. I should be blistered and burnt.

Shrugging it off, I set the spray to its hottest setting, needing the scalding water to wash away this day. As I step into the shower, the spray hits my head, and the pebbled floor massages my feet. I let the hot water run down my back, my shoulders, my chest. Turning my face up, the spray stings my cheeks and washes the blood and dirt away.

My hot tears blend with the water, but I ignore them, telling myself there are no tears, that I am not so weak as to cry in the shower.

I grab the bar of soap and work it from head to toe, twice. Rinsing my hair, I stare at the dark strands. The sight of it dripping wet, almost black under the water, buckles my knees, and I sit on the shower floor, letting the scalding water continue its assault over my head and down my curled-up body.

My hands shake as I wrap them around my shins and rest my chin on my knees. Where could I possibly run to escape this pain?

My gaze unfocuses as I fall into my memories, reaching for a happy one.

I was only five when Magda, the owner of my favorite sweet shop in the capital city of Attolyn, walked around the spotless counter displaying her beautiful confections. Jewel bright drops I knew would taste of exotic fruits from around the realm, dark, shiny chocolate dusted with cinnamon and cayenne, tarts that would fill my tiny hand glazed with glistening sugar, and much more.

But instead of a special treat she usually had for me, that day she held a wriggling puppy with a light brown coat and dark tiger-like stripes that I would later learn was called brindle.

Magda smiled down at me, lines creasing her face showing just how very old she was, even for a fae. She insisted every princess needed a loyal companion, and I'm sure my eyes were wide as saucers as I reached for the small dog. He squirmed wildly in my arms, causing me almost to drop him, but I held tight. Giggles built in my chest and bubbled from my lips as the pup licked my face, tail whipping back and forth in the air. I stared at him in wonder, noticing his one bright blue eye and one a golden brown.

I thanked her, promising that we would watch out for each other as I set the pup down, my dark hair falling in my face. Even at such a young age, I knew how to unravel the glamour my mother put on my hair every morning. My dark complexion may have been an embarrassment to my family, and most fae in the city were quick to look away at the sight of my brown hair, but I hated the painful pressure against my scalp caused by the glamour to turn my hair a shiny silver.

Naming the puppy Sidere after Attolyn's brightest star, his big paws thumped along, almost tripping him as he scrambled to keep up with me as I ran home.

As we approached the castle, we were both breathing hard, his pink tongue hanging from his mouth in a goofy grin. Sweat stuck my hair to my neck. I stopped in the long shadow of the glittering castle of white stone, gleaming glass, and shiny gold, and Sidere plopped his butt down at my feet.

Knowing mother would never approve, I shushed the pup, but only made it a few steps into the hallway when a familiar deep voice froze me in my tracks. I looked up at Garin who knelt to scratch the pup behind his ears. I remember as my eldest brother looked up at me through his long lashes, his silver hair looked almost pastel blue under the shimmering fae light illuminating the hall.

For a moment, I was afraid he would make me take Sidere back, but he simply told me to make sure I trained my new companion well, and that he would handle mother.

I nodded with such enthusiasm I was sure my head would bob right off my neck. Garin chuckled at me before standing, towering over me before turning down a side hall, his long strides quickly taking him around a corner.

As I spun to leave with a smile on my face, I spotted movement to my left. There, down the hall, was my younger brother, Alek, staring after Garin with a look that held fear and hate—a look I never understood.

Alek was only a year younger than me, but he was my complete opposite. Quiet where I was always sure to be heard. Gentle where I preferred to show off my strength. Content where I always craved ... more.

That day in the hall, Alek's wide, green eyes bounced between me and Sidere, who was sniffing the ground in circles around my feet. Shooting a stern look at Alek, I quietly begged him to keep my secret until Garin had the chance to smooth things over with mother.

Though Alek's frown deepened, he nodded.

I never knew what Garin told my mother, but she never said a thing about Sidere, who hardly left my side for the next fifteen years. Oh sure, she would shoot me her patented look of disapproval when Sidere would sit at my side during court proceedings or at the dining table during special events. But Garin always had a kind word and a pat on the head for Sidere, telling me what a good job I did in training the dog.

And that was just one of the hundreds of times Garin stood between me and my mother.

Garin understood me. He was my champion. Alek was ... an afterthought, my odd brother I often forgot even existed.

I unclench my hands, forcing myself out of my memories

What if what Kem said was true? What if ... ?

My breath hitches, and my fingers dig into my legs. I'll need to be prepared before I go through the portal ... if ...

5

____

ASHERHAT

I MAKE it a mile before I skid to a stop, breathing heavily, not from the run, but from the emotion roiling through my heart, making my skin feel too tight.

So many millennia spent on this planet chasing after Rae, I just now realize I assumed we would be trapped here forever, just the two of us. I assumed I would have the time to change what we are to each other.

I waited too long. I've fallen victim to the 'curse of the fae.' With almost limitless time stretching before us, we wait, we plan, we scheme, we get bored. We are rarely a race of action.

Turning toward Rae's house, I run my hands through my short hair, knowing it's probably sticking out in all directions and drop my glamour. Hands-on-hips, I turn away from the direction of Rae's house and look toward the airport. With a sigh, I drop my arms to my sides and turn back toward Rae's, then clench my fists and pivot away.

Over and over, I swivel back and forth, sure I look ridiculous. Finally, I tilt my head back and shout into the darkness, "Stop!" Without the light of the moon, the stars glitter like jewels, and a shooting star zips across the velvet sky, quickly chased by another—like I have been chasing Rae for all these many years.

Now I'm faced with two options: run or go home and die at Rae's hand, or her family's, or the Guild's.

But maybe there's a third option. Perhaps I can convince Rae I'm actually on her side. If I can get her to explain what in The Fates is going on, I'm sure I can help.

Raking a hand back through my hair, I groan before dropping my arms to my sides. I can't leave her. Even a death sentence seems less painful than spending eternity without her.

Rae's house looms before me, and I walk on silent feet to the still open window of her bedroom. Her scent, the scent of a sun-warmed breeze drifts through the window, and the sound of running water comes from the open door of the bathroom.

My shoulders slump, and I bite the inside of my cheek as the soft sound of her sobs reaches my too-sensitive fae hearing. Whatever is going on, whatever Kemremir told her, it must be bad.

I take a deep inhale, trying to ignore her intoxicating scent, and let my breath out slowly, counting to ten. Then I grip the windowsill to haul myself up and into her room but pause. What do I say? How can I make her believe me?

I turn, frustrated with myself, and press my back to the stucco wall of her house, sliding down, legs bending into my chest. I fold my arms over my knees and listen to the sounds of the desert night. Now that the Dragon Lord is gone, the crickets have resumed their songs. The night birds are trilling to the stars, and all manner of lizards and mice scurry in the scrub.

I am such a fool. I allowed myself to care. I allowed myself to fall for her, and now my idiot heart belongs to her.

I listen to Raelyn. Her tears slow and stop, and a few minutes later, the shower spray turns off, and I catch the soft sound of a towel brushing over skin. Her bare footsteps bring her into her bedroom right on the other side of the open window above my head. Will she scent me here?

I hold my breath, waiting for her to come flying through the window with a knife or some weapon in hand, ready to end me. But she just moves away from the window and crosses her room. My keen fae hearing follows her, painting a picture in my mind. The towel drops to the floor with a whisper of sound, and I swallow. The rustle of a garment being pulled over her head is followed by the faint sound of her fingers running through her damp hair. I imagine my fingers combing through her dark tresses like silk across my skin. A shiver steals down my spine.

I listen as she sinks onto the bed. She tosses and turns, trying to sleep until her breathing evens out and the slow rhythm indicates she has finally drifted off. Yet her quiet sleep only lasts for forty minutes before she jerks awake. Her ragged inhales scrape down her throat as she tries to calm herself from whatever nightmare woke her.

I dig my fingers into the hard-packed ground to keep myself from going to her to offer comfort. The sound of her throwing the blankets back wisps in the quiet night, and she paces around the room, bare feet padding with more force than usual. I can hear the anger in her footsteps.

I listen as she dresses, leaves the room before grabbing

her keys and storming out her front door. Standing, I walk around the side of the house, keeping to the shadows.

Her car is a wreck, all smashed up on the passenger side and a dent protruding from the driver's door where I kicked it open from the inside. She starts the car and slowly goes down the long driveway to the empty road.

I follow.

Her path takes us north. She turns onto Dry Creek Rd, and as soon as I see the sign for Boynton Canyon, I know where she's headed, so I peel off and cut through the desert where her car cannot go.

I get to the portal well before her, where I hide, watch, and wait. I settle into the darkness of the shadows of the red rock around me. My muscles relax as I find a comfortable position. This is the life of an assassin, the waiting, the watching, the planning. And I have logged more hours watching Rae than the total of all my prior marks. She is ingrained in my mind, and I know there will be no getting her out.

It's not long before I hear the crunch of her boots on the rock of the path, and then there she is.

Still without her glamour, and now that the blood and dirt has been washed away, she is radiant. I glance up, double-checking that no moon shines tonight—that's how luminescent her skin is. Her shimmering green eyes stare across the empty space before her where the magic of the portal pulses gently, and she halts a few paces away.

Worrying at her bottom lip, she shifts her weight from foot to foot, over and over. She even goes so far as to take another step forward before stepping back again.

"I know you're there, Ash. Come out. I'm not going to kill you."

I let a smile curve my lips, adding a little swagger to hide my uncertainty, my apprehension. My palms are sweaty, and it feels like my heart is trying to leap out of my chest. I need to tread carefully. I need to make this count.

Stepping from the deep shadows of the rock outcropping, I tilt my head at her. "How did you know?"

"Your scent."

She hasn't turned toward me, still staring toward the portal, and absurdly, I puff up a bit at the knowledge she knows my scent. I mean, of course she does. Prey always marks the scents of predators ... but still.

I draw up next to her, following her gaze. The portal is not something you can see, not even with our fae eyes, but fae can always feel a doorway, and this one is open. My mouth goes dry at the thought of home. It's right there.

Emotions rush over me like a wave crashing over the breakers. Excitement, trepidation, homesickness, anticipation, wariness, joy ... I have to swallow a few times before I'm able to speak. "Why are you waiting? It's open, can't you feel it?"

She nods, hugging one arm around her waist. The other bends, and she starts chewing on a nail.

I look down at her, momentarily shocked at how small she seems. It's been a long, long time since I've dropped my glamour, and now I'm almost a foot taller than her. She shifts from one foot to another yet again, so I ask, "Do you want to talk about it?"

"What are you doing here?"

"Making sure you're okay."

She snorts, finally turning her head toward me with narrowed eyes and a snarl on her lips. "That's rich."

I shrug, hiding the pain her remark claws into my chest.

She holds out a hand, waving it through the air, and I know what she feels because I've felt it so many times. I've dreamed of the feeling of a portal touching my skin once more—the feeling like saltwater over sunburned skin. "Ash?"

"Yes?"

"Why are you here?"

"I told you." I reach out my own hand, and my heart skips at the power.

Rae drops her hand and turns fully toward me. "To check on me?" Sarcasm drips from her words, and I open my mouth to respond, but she pushes on. "It's over Ash. Whatever weird, sick dance we've been dancing all these years. It's over." My mouth snaps shut as her voice raises. "I know you could have fulfilled your contract years ago, several times over, but you didn't."

I plant my hands on my hips, trying to look indignant. But I'm not sure what to say, so I say nothing.

She huffs at my silence. "You stalked me, and I allowed it. I should hate you. I used to live in fear of seeing your face, but then I started craving it. I allowed it to go on because I told myself it was okay to want to see you, to fight with you, because you are the only other fae here, and I needed something to tie me to home. I too could have killed you several times, including at least twice today." Her fists ball up and her arms shake. "But I didn't because of what this"—she waves her hand between us—"has become."

One of her small hands rakes through her still slightly damp hair that falls in waves just past her shoulders. Then her green, glittering eyes meet mine, and my breath leaves me in a whoosh. She is breathtaking.

Her voice drops lower. "I'm so angry at you, Ash." I think she's angry at both of us for wildly different reasons. She takes a step toward me, and I hold my ground. "We could have found a way to exist together." Another step brings her closer, and I notice her hands are still shaking, but I snap my eyes back to hers at her terrifyingly quiet words. "I should hate you. I definitely hate myself. I should kill you right now."

I see the pain in her eyes, pain I put there, pain we both caused, and my traitorous heart cracks. I palm one of my many knives and hold it out, hilt first. "Then do it. You're right. I should not have strung this out. Once I realized I no longer desired to fulfill my contract, I should have told you. I should have—"

Her snort cuts me off. "I can't lay all the blame at your feet. I wouldn't have listened."

"All the same. I am sorry. So, here ..." Her eyes flit between the knife in my hand and my face, and I take a step closer. "I treated your life as a game, and I lied to myself, telling myself that we were both playing—you running, me chasing. It's become an obsession with finding you, to see you again, to battle with you. You were the only thing keeping me sane on this crazy, crowded, too-loud planet."

I take a final step, my outstretched hand almost brushing the fabric of her flannel shirt. "So do it. Take your vengeance." Her hand wraps around the hilt of the knife, our fingers brushing as I release it. "Take your owed death."

She just holds it there, staring at the blade, her luminescent eyes reflecting in the sharp steel. I take a tiny step until the tip of the blade presses to my chest, and I look down at the knife. My face is so close to her down-turned head it would take a whisper of movement for my lips to press to her hair. Her chest rises and falls in great, deep breaths, and she presses the knife a little harder, piercing my shirt and breaking my skin. My whisper flutters against her hair. "Go home, princess. Go see your family."

As that last word leaves my lips, her eyes snap to mine, almost slamming her head into my nose. Her eyes have slightly narrowed, teeth gritted in pain or anger or both, and her hand clenches the knife so hard it's shaking.

I almost back away but manage to hold my ground.

It's her that steps back, spinning on her heel before pacing across the stony ground. "You don't get to come here and act the martyr at the final hour, Ash! I had to start over every time you showed up out of fear that you would grow tired or bored and decide to actually take my life. My only goal all these years has been to survive seeing you, both physically and emotionally."

Her hair is mostly dry now, and the ends curl and float around her face with every turn of her continued pacing. "Do you realize what I had to do, what I had to endure as an immortal woman on this backward planet?"

Thoughts of China flit through my mind, and I wince as she goes on, her voice rising as she releases her thousands of years' worth of pent-up anger and frustration. "I got Socrates killed with a simple explanation of the basics of this galaxy. It was a drop of knowledge. He deserved to know, and I was happy to help him understand a small part of how his world worked in the universe. And the humans killed him. I lived disguised as a man for years in Sumata and again in Japan just to be able to live some semblance of a normal life because being a single woman was unacceptable."

She flings her arm forward, and the knife sinks into the sand at my feet, trembling at the force of impact. "I've been constantly harassed, asked where my husband is, told to fetch my older brother or an uncle that can claim me, control me. For great stretches of my life, I couldn't be seen traveling alone as a woman. I couldn't buy property. I couldn't have a life unless I was a man."

She stops her pacing, facing away from me, her hands clenched tight at her sides. "And when I did find some peace, some thread of happiness, there you'd be! Your presence tore me apart every time you found me. I hated you, feared you, but craved you. And you kept coming, kept fighting me, and I kept running. Fates, I ran and ran, trying to save my life and my heart. Egypt, Greece, Rome, Pompeii ..."

At the mention of Pompei, her shoulders slump, and she sighs. Staring at her boots, she toes the ground, the fire of her rant extinguished. I hold myself still, eyes glued to her. "Raelyn, I—" She lifts her hand to silence me, and I press my lips together before whispering, "Was it all bad?"

Her fidgeting stops, and she lifts her eyes to mine. The anger is gone, replaced with sadness and regret. "You know it wasn't." Her voice is quiet. "I never thanked you for trying to save Camilia." She clasps her hands, looking uncomfortable with what she's about to say. "So, thank you." She shifts, dropping her gaze again, whispering, "Will you tell me about it? What happened that day?"

My fingers twitch with the urge to take her hand. This is a hard story. The year was 79 AD, and I had finally tracked Rae down in Rome. Glancing at her, I take a breath. "I'd been following you for a few weeks, learning your patterns, learning your life. I liked the name you chose. Ravinia suited you."

She shrugs, keeping her eyes downcast, and I give in to the desire to touch her, placing my hand on her shoulder. "Camilia was beautiful." And she was. She had an arched roman nose with bright pale green eyes and golden hair, which always seemed to fall in perfect shoulder-length waves. Her skin was bronzed, kissed by the sun.

Rae smiles, and I squeeze her arm before letting my hand fall away. "Every time I saw her, she was smiling, usually at you. The first time I saw the two of you kiss and witnessed the love between you, I decided to leave."

Rae's eyes lift to mine in surprise, and I shrug. "You deserved the slice of joy you had found. I understand, Rae. I'm the *only* one who understands. This planet, these humans, move so fast. They are gone in a blink, and our existence is ... ongoing. If we come across happiness, we have to grasp it, or go mad."

Rae bites the inside of her cheek, nodding with sadness pooling in her eyes.

"That morning, I watched you kiss Camilia, long and slow. What a kiss." I raise my eyebrows. "I mean, damn." Finally, she laughs with a blush. "Then you headed out to the country with a smile and a promise to return home to her by dinner."

"And where were you?"

"On a rooftop two houses down, three houses over." It's cliché, but I remember it like it was yesterday. "I left, heading north, not realizing my path would cross with yours just outside of the city. I saw you crest a hill, and for a split second, I considered approaching you, but I turned, ready to head in the opposite direction, to leave you to your life."

I realize my hands are shaking, so I shove them in my pockets. "But then the great rumble of the ground shoved my heart in my throat, and the earth exploded. I saw the fire and ash and knew what was coming. Pompei, the neighboring cities, and towns were about to be decimated."

Rae is once again staring off into the night, and her voice

trembles as she says, "It was the most horrible sound I've ever heard. It was like the entire planet was coming apart."

I nod, remembering how I stood there shocked and horrified as Mount Vesuvius violently expelled a deadly cloud of super-heated tephra and gas that climbed over twenty miles into the sky. Molten rock, pulverized pumice, and hot ash rained down like the wrath of an angry god. The deadly wave of thermal energy nearly knocked me to my knees. I know a little something about fire, and this was like nothing I had ever witnessed.

I continue, "The sky was raining literal fire and rock, but you turned. Your eyes were wide with horror as you sprinted toward the city, into danger, toward Camilia."

I grip my hands into fists in my pockets, trying my best to keep the roiling emotion out of my voice. "The ash and gas were already choking. I knew you would hurt yourself trying to get to Camilia, maybe even get yourself killed, and I ..."

Rae looks up at my pause. "What?"

I don't say it. I don't tell her that was the moment my heart shifted—when my obsession melted into love. Instead, I barrel on with my story. "I knew you still hadn't seen me, so I blurred, and well ... you know."

She lifts her hand, rubbing the side of her face. "You punched me. You knocked me out."

"I'm a fire fae, Rae. I could take it. You would have died."

I recall the moment my knuckles cracked against her temple; the sound drowned out by the chaos around us. The feel of her flesh splitting under my fist still replays in my nightmares.

"I blurred you as far as I could run, getting you out from under the ash cloud, far to the northeast. I left you there."

"And you went after her, after my Camilia."

I shrug. "I was never so glad to be a fire fae as I blurred back into Pompei. It was chaos." My words are quiet, and I swallow the lump of grief in my throat. I still feel those deaths in my heart and experience them in my dreams, like a piece of my soul is coated and preserved in the ash of my memories.

"Bodies littered the streets and doorways, already suffocated." I tried to dodge the plummeting, smoldering rocks, but there were too many. The impacts hurt, bruised, and cut, even as my magic kept the spitting volcanic embers from burning my skin. "I had little hope I would find Camilia alive, but I pushed on. Crashing through the door of your house, I called out and almost tripped over my feet when I heard a weak voice answer from below."

I see it all in my mind, my memories taking me back to one of the worst days I've experienced on this planet. I dropped to my knees, the hot ash covering my legs, burning the edges of my toga. Sweeping the ash and rubble aside with my forearms, praying I wouldn't be too late.

I can't meet Rae's eyes as I go on. "I found the latch in your floor and ripped it open." I had heard the sizzle against my skin, but thankfully I didn't feel it. "She was there." I remember how terror widened her eyes, and ash covered her face. Her lips trembled, and she was gasping for breath.

Rae wraps her arms around her middle.

I clear my throat, but it doesn't help, my voice still wavers. "I reached down, and on instinct she reached up, even though she didn't know me. I yanked her up, holding her close to my body, I tried my best to shield her as I blurred us out of the city."

I recall the acrid air and the panic that raced through my heart that day. Camilia's breathing became more labored, and I gritted my teeth against the pain of my flagging strength, knowing every second under that ash cloud brought her closer to death.

I look toward Rae. "But I made it. I thought I made it. I thought she was okay."

Rae's glowing eyes stare at me as she shakes her head.

No. I remember nearly dropping Camilia to the ground as I stumbled to a stop where Rae still lay unconscious. Coughing through the ash and smoke in my lungs, I looked at Camilia and managed to choke out instructions for her to find water, to keep moving north. I told her to keep going and don't stop until the ash cloud was no longer visible. She nodded, her eyes red, tears streaming down her face, coughs hacking from her chest. She held Rae so tightly, pressing her lips to her hair.

I almost take a step toward Rae but hold myself still. "I thought you both would get out. I ran."

My chest is as tight as it was that day as I fight back the tears and nausea that threaten to rise with the memories. I ran, witnessing the entire city die in a matter of moments. The waters of the far-off coasts started to boil, and the people trying to escape over the sea started screaming. Their small wooden boats cracked and smoked in the bubbling waters. Their screams of pain tore through me as they sunk and were boiled alive by the waters that until just a moment ago were their livelihood. The grasses browned, then blackened and curled into the ash building up on the ground. Trees shook with the raging rumble of the mountain, their leaves dropping and turning to ash, their limbs petrifying as I watched in horror.

Rae places her hand on my forearm, breaking me free from the terrors in my mind. I stare at the gentle contact, whispering, "I've seen and experienced many horrible things since arriving here on Earth; war, famine, plague ..."

She nods in understanding. She's the only one who understands. "But it is Pompeii that haunts me." And China.

I left Rae behind that day, certain she and Camilia would have several happy years together. I didn't find Rae again until the year 100 in China where a whole new set of nightmares were burned into my mind.

I unclench my fists, lifting my right hand out of my pocket and place it over hers still resting on my arm. "Camilia didn't make it?"

Another tiny shake of her head sends her hair swaying across her back. "The damage from the ash, gas, and smoke had destroyed her lungs. She lasted a day."

"I'm so sorry, Rae. I tried. I—"

"Ash, it's okay. We got to say our goodbyes. So, thank you."

She slides her hand out from under mine, and I shrug. "I didn't realize you knew it was me."

"Who else could it have been? Besides, Camilia described you and the unnatural speed with which you whisked her to my side." Her voice is sad, low, almost a whisper, but there are no tears. I think thousands of years around these humans have stripped us both of our tears. "Thank you."

"You're welcome, Raelyn." I take a chance and step closer and slowly lift my hand, cupping her face, letting my thumb graze her cheek. "What did the Dragon Lord tell you?"

I swear it feels like she leans into my hand ever so slightly. Her piercing green eyes search mine, and she worries her bottom lip, drawing my gaze. I drop my hand. "Raelyn, I can help." I give her my most charming grin. "Despite all evidence to the contrary, I am an excellent assassin." She laughs at that, and the sound is pretty, even with the undertones of her sadness. "I didn't rise in the ranks of the New Moon Guild on luck, Raelyn. I'm very good at my job. I am a master."

She smirks, but my grin slides into a serious line. "I can help if you can allow yourself to trust me. I—" I almost say the words. I almost blurt out that I care for her, but I bite back the words. "I am a creature of death. If a little bit—or a lot—of violence will help solve whatever it is that has you tied up in knots, then let me help."

She starts chewing her bottom lip again, and I mentally slap away the urge to kiss those lips. I seem to have an unquenchable need to banish every frown from her face, so I grin. "And if that particular skill won't help, I have many others that are guaranteed to help you relax and forget your troubles." I waggle my eyebrows at her suggestively, hoping to earn another smile, and she obliges, rolling her eyes.

Her laugh spears through my heart, and I meet her eyes. "Talk to me, Raelyn." I gesture to my right. "Home is right there, but you hesitate, you're holding back. Why?"

She looks toward the portal then back at me. "Why haven't *you* run through it? You could return to Attolyn or go anywhere."

I squeeze her shoulder, not letting her evade me, not this time. "What did the Dragon Lord say?"

She sighs and turns, staring at the portal. "He said my older brother, Garin"—I nod at her pause, knowing well of her charismatic brother— "has been using dark magic."

My fingers tighten on her shoulder, and I fight to gentle my grip, maintaining contact as she goes on, her voice getting stronger. "Kemremir claims Garin is the one behind your contract." I drop my hand at those words, shock sending a myriad of thoughts swirling through my head. But Rae's not done. "Supposedly, my brother is the one responsible for sealing the doorways, locking me ... locking us here."

She crosses her arms over her chest, hugging herself. "Kem insists Garin has ... that he has ... he um ..." She pauses then lets the words rush from her as if she suspects that if she doesn't get them all out at once, she won't say them at all. "Garin killed my parents, seized the throne, and is allowing the Unseelie access to our kingdom."

6

RAELYN

Saying those words out loud, voicing those accusations, sounds absurd. Garin wouldn't do such a thing. Alek? Maybe. They say it's always the quiet ones, but ...

Ash is frozen, standing still as stone, no doubt trying to process what I just said. Well, good luck with that. I can't seem to wrap my mind around what Kemremir told me either.

A gentle breeze flutters Ash's silver hair that barely reaches the tips of his curved ears, and I just now realize he's released all his glamours. He towers over me, and his eyes, now more gold than brown, glow softly. He's just overall larger, broader than his human form that I'm so used to. His olive skin sets off the gold of his eyes, and his features are sharper. His jawline cuts across his profile, and his nose is a slash down his face.

I knew the members of the New Moon Guild are masters

of glamour, but I'd forgotten how well Ash uses our fae magic to make himself blend in. Glancing at Ash again from the corner of my eye—I wouldn't want him to think I'm staring—I take him in. Free of my own glamours, we stand silently in the dark of night, stars glittering overhead, night animals and bugs lending soft sounds to the darkness. It's freeing.

I release a deep sigh, and Ash looks down at me. "It's a lot to take in. I mean ..."

Keeping my eyes forward, I press my lips in a tight line. I can't think about this. Garin's not a murderer. My parents are fine. My mother will scold me for being gone so long before hugging me stiffly and sending me off to put on a proper dress. My father will cry, and Alek will hug me quickly before stepping back into the shadows where he won't be noticed.

I bite the inside of my cheek. Oh, Alek.

My breath is coming faster, and Ash must sense my panic because he shifts, and I feel his gaze travel down my body and back up again. "I'd forgotten how stunning you are without your glamours."

I blink several times before turning toward him. There's a slight smile on his lips, and I snort a laugh, grateful for the momentary distraction. I sigh again. "It does feel good to be ... myself. Don't you get tired of them? The glamours? You wear so many. Don't they wear you down?"

His right shoulder lifts absently along with the right corner of his lips in a half-smile. "Honestly, I hardly notice. After all this time, the glamours still bother you?"

"They don't bother me. They just make me feel restricted."

His hand lifts and fingers a strand of my dark hair. I

tense at the touch and resist the instinct to back away as he says, "At least here, you don't have to worry about your hair."

Yanking my head back, pulling my hair from his fingers, I take a step, then two away from him. My already tense muscles bunch tighter as his slight smile widens to a grin. "I didn't mean it like that. I like that your hair is different. That is one of the things I love about being sent to different realms, different worlds. I get to see such variety, especially here." He stuffs his hands in his pockets. "Here, silver hair is exotic. In Attolyn, it just ... is. It's boring."

I self-consciously twirl the strand of hair I had freed from Ash around my finger. "My mother would be scandalized to hear you say so."

Ash chuckles. "She made you glamour your hair?"

I nod, looking down at the lock of dark hair between my fingers. "If I refused, she'd slap a glamour on me. Her magic is strong, and it would take me hours to strip it off, but I hated it, more than the looks of fear or pity or even hate that I would receive every time I left the palace. Hell, even within the palace, if I was caught without the glamour on my hair, someone would inevitably go scurrying to my mother."

"Really?"

"Oh yes. There were always whispers carrying down the hallways or drifting out of rooms in the palace. The most popular theory was that I am actually Unseelie and was switched at birth. I couldn't blame them, though." He tilts his head at me, lips pressed together in annoyance, but I shake my head. "I resemble the dark fae. My appearance made people uncomfortable because seeing me reminded them of the Unseelie and their dependence on blood magic."

Ash's eyes narrow, and his jaw ticks. "Raelyn, it's not your job to forgive the cruelty of those people."

Clasping my hands in front of me, I smile, but it's sad. "Of course it is. The only way I could show them there was nothing to fear was to be kind." I don't go on to tell him that a lot of those whispers that unknowingly reached my ears spat out that I should be exiled, 'taken out' in a quiet hall or alcove of the palace, or just straight up hung in the streets. There's nothing quite like being terrified of walking the halls of your own home.

I look back at Ash and change the subject. "Was Valna, the man who hired you, a noble or someone from court?"

He shakes his head. "Valna, or whatever his real name is, didn't seem like someone who lived or even associated with people at court. But he had plenty of coin." I frown, and a single step brings him closer once again. "I'm sorry, Raelyn. I wish I could tell you more." A tentative smile lifts his face. "I'm not sorry for taking the contract, though. It brought me here, to you."

I turn away, shaking off the fleeting thought that Valna's coin might have come from Garin. And Ash's tone tells me he's thinking the same thing, but he's not saying it. Neither of us is willing to say the words.

Staring at the invisible doorway, the silence spreads between us like ink dropped in water. There are so many thoughts swirling through my brain, and I can't keep track.

After a long while, Ash runs a hand through his silver locks, causing them to stick out wildly. He gestures at the portal. "Well, if you're not going through, what's the plan?"

I hold out my arm, letting the tingle of the doorway's magic dance across my fingers, over my hand, and up my forearm. Attolyn is so close. I don't want to believe what the Dragon Lord said, but a part of me wonders, and that part of me is keeping me from going home.

"Ash, what if it's true?"

"That's a loaded question, but at this point, we'd just be throwing around suppositions." He places his hands on his hips, lifting an eyebrow. "Plus, you bravely, brashly, foolishly, demanded the Dragon Lord produce proof."

I huff. "Yes, I don't know what came over me. Being around the humans has definitely bolstered my ego. I'd forgotten we are not the strongest beings out here; we just happen to be at the top of the chain here on Earth. As soon as the words started leaving my mouth, I figured he would kill me."

Ash chuckled. "Luckily, we got a reasonable Dragon Lord." He pauses, staring intently at me, and even though the last 7200 years I've programmed myself to run from this man, I force myself to stand my ground. It's surreal that Ash and I are standing here, having a conversation like ... friends.

While I'm still wary around him, I find it nice to talk to him. We understand each other, and I have a feeling I'm going to need all the help I can get, even from unexpected places.

He does that little half-smile again and crosses his arms over his chest. "So, we have some time to kill." He takes a step closer to me. "Can you think of anything we can do to pass the time?"

His small smile grows to a full grin as I scowl at him. He takes another step toward me, and I panic, flustered at my body's response to his words, to his body being so close. There's too much to deal with right now. I can't deal with my mixed-up feelings toward Ash.

Before I know what I'm doing, I make a fist, plant my foot, tighten my core, and swing. Blood coats my knuckles as his head snaps back, and he takes two stumbling steps back.

"Ow." He wipes blood from the corner of his lips with the back of his hand then spits onto the ground.

"This"—I gesture between us—"whatever it is, is not that." No matter what my racing heart says.

He smiles, gold eyes glittering. "Not yet."

My heart stops, then skips into a frantic rhythm, so I growl at him, "Not ever." *Liar.*

He takes another step back. "Never say never. Isn't that what the humans say? Such a wonderful saying."

"Ugh!" Turning on my heel, I stomp back to my car, with Ash following. "I'm going home." I glance over my shoulder, holding in a gasp at the sight of him. I'm so used to the 'average human' Ash, that his fae form startles me again. "If you promise to behave, you can come with me to wait for Kemremir's return. As much as it pains me to say it, I may need your help."

Ash inhales sharply behind me, coming to a stop. I turn to see him clutching his chest, eyes wide. Rushing to stand before him, I grip his forearm. "What's wrong!"

"I think ... I think hell just froze over."

"Oh my god!" I punch his shoulder, hard, and storm off. He just laughs behind me, and the sound sends little flutters through my stomach.

The drive back to my house is silent, and Ash's presence next to me is imposing. He feels too large for my car, and I almost ask him to put his glamour back on. But I make it home gritting through my discomfort, knowing full well it's not just his true form that's affecting me.

"I like your house." Ash looks around as he passes through my front door, closing it softly behind him, locking it. He toes off his boots, leaving them by the door even though I've kept mine on, before turning and following me deeper into the house.

"Thanks. It is a favorite. Here and Greece have come the closest to feeling like a home and not just a place to live."

"Ah, yes, the Grecians loved you." Ash smiles at me, standing in my living room, running a hand over my tufted leather couch.

I can't help but smile as I cross the room and walk around the bartop into the kitchen. Opening the large double doors to the fridge, I root around, pulling out a pitcher of limeade. "Yes, they really did." Setting the pitcher on the grey and white granite counter, I sigh. "Oh, the parties, the tributes."

Ash laughs, and I turn from the sound, doing my best to ignore how his laugh tightens certain muscles low in my core. I'm finding it hard to relax. I'm having a casual conversation in my house with the assassin hired to kill me, and his presence is making me nervous, but not in the way he should be.

But honestly, at this point, Ash probably knows me better than anyone other than Garin. But even Garin doesn't know. He doesn't understand what it has been like here on Earth. Ash does. We have history. It's a messy, complicated history, but I can't help but hope that I can trust him and come out with my heart still intact.

Opening a cupboard, I grab a bottle of tequila as he says, "I'm sure it helped that the Greeks thought you were the goddess Galatea incarnate."

I smile at the memories of the clean, white temple, now in ruins, swallowed and reclaimed by the earth. The Greeks used crushed shells in the plaster, which made the walls shimmer in the sunlight and glow in the moonlight. It was beautiful. That wasn't the last time I posed as a deity, but it was the best.

That summer of 401 BC, a great storm surged over

Greece, pushing rising water into the streets of Athens. I knew the strength of the storm would greatly damage the city, the beautiful city that I actually liked, and I panicked, anger clawing against my insides that the seas would threaten my home, threaten these people.

Marching down to the coast, my bare feet slapped against the stones of the road, occasionally sinking ankle-deep into puddles. I drew up my magic, pushing the air currents against the storm surge, letting the slashing rain pelt me from behind. My muscles shook, and sweat dripped into my eyes as the storm fought against my magic—like it was a living thing that was angry at my presence. I raged right back. I would not let my home fall without a fight. I gritted my teeth but smiled at the thought, realizing the Greek's ideas on gods and goddesses were sinking into my psyche.

I needed to get deeper into the heart of the storm, so I wrapped a bubble of air around myself and walked into the sea, and in that moment, I felt every bit like an avenging goddess of the sea.

Pulling the air currents behind me, lashing them to my being, I pulled the seawater with me as I walked along the seafloor. It was exhilarating and terrifying as the angry push of currents pressed against my magic.

The water lit up around me in flashes of blue and white with every lightning strike from above. Dragging the seawater with me, I marched away from Athens, every nerve tingling. It had been a long time, millennia even, since I'd used that much magic, and I felt truly alive, buzzing with energy.

It could have been hours, or it could have been days that I stood in the sea, holding back the surge. I lost all sense of time. All manner of creatures swam up to check out the stranger in their underwater world. And still, I refused to let the sea go. It was mine.

Eventually, the currents lessened their pull on my magic, and the waters calmed. I turned, slowly walking back toward the shore. The rush of fighting a mighty battle and winning roared through my head. Forgetting myself, I emerged from the gentle waves, skin glowing softly from my power and my hair blowing around my face as my magic swirled around me. Power buzzed through my blood, holding back my exhaustion as people gathered at the shore and followed me into the city.

The air currents danced to the soundless tune of my magic, and whispers grew to shouts as my clothes dried and even the streets cleared of water as I passed by. I glanced up, and the wind answered to my magic, parting the clouds and revealing the sun. Warmth spilled onto the square where I stood surrounded by a large crowd. Smiling at the sun, head tilted back, I drank in my triumph.

A woman to my right gasped, claiming I was shining like a pearl

Her companion nodded, whispering that I had conquered Poseidon himself. On and on, the exclamations continued, saying I was god-touched, or that I was an actual goddess.

When one woman pointed at me, awe shaking her voice, calling me Galatea, I smiled and turned to the crowd. Riding the high of calling up so much magic, I proclaimed myself as the goddess Galatea. Thinking back, I might have laid it on a bit thick, but when in ancient Greece ...

After the cheers and bowing died down, I spirited myself away to my humble home, practically passing out. I slept for two whole days replenishing my body and magic. And while I slept, construction on my temple started. I was living very comfortably in my glittering accommodations soon after. It was quite the upgrade.

Another wistful sigh escapes my lips, and Ash laughs. "If I knew all it would take was a show of magical power to grant me godhood, I would have strode down the promenade, flames trailing behind me." Ash walks over, leaning his forearms on the bar counter.

I pass him a margarita and grin. "They probably would have named you Hades and demanded that I get rid of you."

He smirks. "True. It's tricky having magic that scares people."

He sips at the drink, giving me an air-cheers that I ignore. I have never really thought about Ash's power like that. Sure, my magic can create great destruction, but for the most part, air, wind, currents are all considered benign. To wield fire though ... Garin is a fire fae like Ash. But Garin's power is ... more. He might be the most powerful fire fae I know.

Oh Fates, what if Kemremir is telling the truth? What will I do? What *can* I do? Garin was so powerful, even back then, and if he's using blood magic ... bile stings my throat, and I take a few seconds to breathe through the nausea.

I cross the room, and the leather chair sighs as I sit and nod toward the matching tufted chair. "Sit."

He puts his drink down and gestures at himself. "I'm still a bit of a mess." My gaze snaps to the bruises on his face, and I'm sure there are matching ones around his ribs. "Mind if I grab a shower?"

Do I mind? Do I mind having a naked Ash in my house, in my shower? I hide my flush behind the glass as I take a big gulp before answering, "Sure, go ahead." I mentally congratulate myself on how even and nonchalant I sound.

I damn my fae hearing as the sounds of Ash shedding

his clothing reaches me, and I almost jump out of my seat when he yells from the bedroom, "Go ahead and feel free to let your imagination roam free on what is going on in here."

I can practically hear the grin on his face, and I fight against my own smirk. "That sounds incredibly boring," I yell back, lying through my teeth. I turn on the large screen tv to distract myself.

He just chuckles, and the sound of the shower turning on spills from the room. I turn up the tv, not noticing or caring what's on. I dive into a breathing technique I learned centuries ago in Japan. My muscles release one by one as I work my consciousness from the crown of my head all the way to my toes. My body goes liquid, and as I close my eyes, my world focuses down to the air filling and leaving my lungs.

Turning, I lay down with a hand on my stomach to feel my breaths. The day peels away, and my magic swirls through me, responding to my concentration on the air. I feel light, my breaths holding back the worries of what lies before me.

The scent of pine and wild grass wraps around me, and a soft, lightweight blanket settles over me. And just before I drift off to sleep, I think, how can a top assassin from the New Moon guild be so ... sweet.

7

———————

ASHERHAT

RAE IS SLEEPING, but I can't seem to settle. I slip out the back door and throw myself down on the large outdoor sofa on her patio. Folding one arm behind my head, I watch the sky melt from deep black velvet to shadowy purple, to soft blue. A hint of pink blushes the cloudless morning sky which quickly becomes a gilded gold as the sun grips the horizon and pulls itself over the edge. The warm rays peek into the world with some trepidation but then gain confidence as they climb the sky, sending out heat to chase away the chill of the night.

As soon as the sun hits my skin, I sigh, closing my eyes, watching the day get brighter behind my closed eyelids.

I drift off, but not for long because when I open my eyes again, the sunlight has only reached Rae's back door, spilling light into the living room where she still sleeps soundly. It gilds her brown hair, turning it bronze in places, and I clench my fists against the urge to run my hands through it. Her hair was so soft last night as I held that single strand between my fingers, and I hate that our people mistreated her. How frightening it must have been for her. How lonely.

Pushing off the surprisingly comfortable sofa, I skirt around the house, breathing in the desert air, admiring the sheer expanse of space out here. It suits Rae, this house, this place.

Folding myself into her car, I touch the two dangling wires together and slide the car into drive. I don't want to be gone long. I don't want Rae waking to find me gone and assume I've run off, so it's a painful twenty-minute drive to town, then another 25 minutes before I find a clothing store that's open this early.

A bell tinkles overhead as I push through the door, and a feminine voice calls from the back of the store. "Good morning! I'll be right with you."

"Morning. I won't take long."

"No, no. Please, take your time and let me know if—"

The woman's words abruptly stop as she emerges from the back room. Her mouth hangs open slightly before she snaps it shut and averts her eyes, moving behind the register. "Let me know if you need any help."

Shit. Stupid, dumb mistake. I've forgotten all about my glamours, or the lack thereof. My heart races, but I chuckle, bringing her eyes back to mine. Her tight jeans hug her curvy hips, and the front of her cream blouse is causally tucked in the way that looks effortless but probably took some styling. The low heels of her ankle boots click along the worn wood floor as she moves around her store. With a smile, I shrug. "My friends and I are going to a Renaissance Faire later today." The lie comes easily. Thank goodness for the human's love of dressing up and inaccurately celebrating the Renaissance. Ren Faires, comic cons, and even L.A.R.Ping are my go-to excuses when I don't feel like glamouring. Though, I've never forgotten to glamour before. Rae is really under my skin.

The woman smiles, tucking her shoulder-length blond hair behind her ear as she glances at my pointed ears. "Ah, well, that explains the get-up." Her eyes narrow on mine. "How do you get your eyes to glow like that?"

I frown, turning, pretending to look in a mirror to my right, and take the moment to glamour my eyes to their human brown. Looking back at her, I tilt my head. "What do you mean?"

She frowns, shaking her head. "Must have been a trick of the lights." She chuckles softly. "Sorry."

"No worries." I gesture at myself with a smile. "Silver hair and pointed ears. Glowing eyes would be pretty cool."

More at ease with my lie, she walks around the counter. "Is there anything I can help you find?"

"Well, I'm embarrassed to say I took a little tumble on a hike yesterday, and I don't have another change of clothes." I tug at the hem of my stained t-shirt, keeping my smile in place even though my brain is screaming, *grab some clothes, throw some money at this woman, and get the hell back to Rae.*

"They are quite a mess. Let me grab you a few things to try on."

I open my mouth to protest, but she has already rushed to the far side of the store, grabbing items off shelves and hangers. The store is small, cozy, but well-stocked and organized. It's just a matter of moments before she's back in front of me with a pile of folded clothing in her arms.

I take the offered pile and set them on a nearby table displaying expensive candles, some tasteful jewelry, and a small selection of shoes. Thumbing through the clothes she handed me, I set aside a pair of soft, medium-wash jeans and two t-shirts, one a bright teal, the other a burnt red. I add a lightweight long sleeve knit shirt in charcoal grey along with a pair of grey socks to the pile.

Picking up my selections, I nod to the woman. "Thank you. You have a keen eye. You are very good at what you do."

She blushes, making the motion of tucking her hair behind her ear again even though her hair is already in place.

"Thanks. Would you like to try those on? I can bring you additional pieces if any of that doesn't work."

I pass her my credit card. "These are fine. Actually, do you mind if I go ahead and change into these here while you ring me up? That will save me so much time. I don't want to be late meeting my friends."

She takes the card, letting her fingers brush mine and linger before she moves to the register. Blushing, she avoids my eyes as she rings up my sale. "Of course. The dressing room is right over there." Nodding to my right, she busies herself at the computer.

I change quickly, and when I emerge, she has an empty paper bag with the store's logo on the front in her hands. "For your other clothes."

"Thank you." I drop my old clothes in the bag and place the extra t-shirt on top. Taking my card and receipt from her, I avoid her second attempt to brush her fingers against mine.

I feel myself rushing toward the door but force myself to smile at her as she calls out, "Have fun at the faire."

As I pull back up to Rae's house, it's been almost two hours since I left, but I sigh and shed some of the tension from my shoulders as I slip in the backdoor to find her still sleeping.

I don't find coffee in her kitchen, but I do find an entire cabinet dedicated to tea, so I select a strong black tea with spice and brew two cups. As I pour the fragrant tea over ice and top it with frothed oat milk, Rae's sleepy voice calls out from the living room. "No, no. Go ahead and make yourself at home."

I chuckle, topping off the second cup.

A moment later, she huffs. "But that does smell good. I better get a cup."

My gut seizes, and my heart pinches with longing. Longing for this, with her. Lazy mornings. Sleepy conversations. Maybe a kiss good morning. Maybe more ...

She pads into her bedroom, and a few minutes later, she joins me in the kitchen, her face fresh and the soft scent of mint wafts from her breath as she leans over and takes a cup. "Thanks."

"You're welcome. Did you sleep well?"

She takes a sip, smiles, and takes another. "Mmm. That's good." I congratulate myself as a little spark of pride burns in my chest. "And yes, surprisingly, I slept very well. Did you sleep?"

I give a noncommittal shrug.

A slight frown turns down her lips but then quickly kicks back into a slight smile. "Regardless, you look better today."

"A hot shower and clean clothes will do that for a person." I mentally slap myself. Why mention the shower? Fantasies of the two of us tangled under the hot spray flashes across my mind, and I take a large sip of my iced tea latte, but it does little to cool my blood.

She nods and goes back to the living room, plopping

down in the same spot she vacated just a few minutes ago. I take the chair once again. "You'll never believe this. I forgot to glamour myself when I went into town."

I grip the cup a little too tightly and force myself to relax as her eyes go wide, and a huge grin lights up her face. "The great assassin, Asheraht, forgot to glamour? What happened? What'd you do?"

"Luckily, the only person I encountered was the shop owner, but the look on her face ..."

I chuckle, and Rae laughs. "What did you say?"

"That I was meeting friends at a Renaissance faire later today."

"Ha! You, at a Renaissance faire. I can't imagine it."

"Have you ever been?"

"I lived through the actual Renaissance. I don't need cheap entertainment to reminisce."

I smile at her. "Oh, you don't know what you're missing! They are wildly inaccurate but a fun time nonetheless."

She leans forward, setting her drink on the table and resting her hands on her knees. I glue my eyes to her face to keep from looking down her shirt as she smiles. "Wait, do you mean to tell me you've been to one?"

"Several."

She throws herself back into the sofa, laughing loudly. "I would have paid good money to be there."

"You would have gotten your money's worth. I won a jousting contest at the last one."

"Oh my god. You did not!"

"I surely did."

"Well, that was a bit unfair of you."

"What? Just because I was an actual knight long, long, long ago? I call that using my skills to my advantage."

I can't help but laugh with her, as her laughter peels

around the house. "And what did the great knight win at said Ren faire?"

"Bottomless mead. It was awful, just like the real stuff, but I made many fast friends that day, and we drank the day away. It was very nostalgic."

"I bet."

As our laughter dies to smiles, we sit in silence until a small frown pulls at Rae's lips once more. I lean forward, giving in to the urge to be closer to her, even just a little bit. "Are you okay?"

Her eyes lift to mine, and she shrugs. "I don't know. I can't stop thinking about my brothers and my parents." I nod, and she looks down at her hands where she has clasped them tightly in her lap. "And then there's you."

"Me?"

"Ash, what am I supposed to do with you?"

I lift an eyebrow. "Well ..."

She attempts a smile, but it doesn't reach her eyes. "I can't make sense of anything right now. I feel like my brain has stalled and is caught on a loop of frustrating thoughts without offering any solutions or explanations."

I frown at her words. "Well, as to the situation back home, we shall see tonight when Kemremir returns. Until then, there is nothing to be done. Unless you want to say, 'the hell with it' and run through that portal and see what's what? And if that's what you want to do, then I'm right behind you." I pause and wait until she looks up at me. "I've been chasing you for so long. I'm not chasing you now, I'm following your lead. I'm with you, Raelyn."

Her voice comes out in a whisper, but it's strong and even. "What about the Dragon Lord? He was sent to kill you."

"If that's how my story must end, then so be it. You deserve some peace. You deserve happiness, Raelyn."

The air tingles with ... something between us. My skin itches with tension, and she chews on her bottom lip. I think I might explode if I have to sit here for one more second without touching her, so I push up off the chair, grab our cups and rinse them in the kitchen, saying over my shoulder, "Well, I can't sit here the rest of the day waiting for Kemremir to return. I need a distraction. Lunch?"

It's still early, but I need to get out of this house before I do something foolish, like fist her hair and pull her into a kiss until her knees buckle.

"I'm not hungry just yet. Wanna go on a run? There's a nice route I take out here. The sun gets pretty brutal, but it's secluded." She smiles. "We can blur."

Maybe I'll be able to breathe better out in the open, but I doubt it. "Sure, but my old clothes are a mess, and I'd rather not get these new ones all sweaty."

She disappears into her bedroom and returns, throwing some clothes on the coffee table. "Try these."

I pick them up, finding a pair of men's terry cloth shorts and a men's large t-shirt. I lift an eyebrow in question, and she shrugs, blushing. "A 'friend' left them here a while ago."

"A 'friend?'"

"It was nothing, lasted a week, then I got bored. Whatever. It was ages ago. Do you want them or not?"

I definitely do not want to wear another man's clothes, especially a man that had been with Rae. What I want is to shred this man's clothes and burn them to ash, but instead, I force a smile to my face, knowing it's too tight to look sincere. "Okay, okay. Let me change."

Five minutes later, we're jogging through the desert, starting at a slow human pace. The sun is already baking my skin and sweat starts to stick the man's shirt to my chest. Rae starts to pick up the pace, and I make it another five minutes before I rip the shirt off and throw it on the ground.

At her scowl, I say, "I'll pick it up on the way back. It's too hot." Plus, the smell of the man was driving my temper to the boiling point.

"Lightweight." And with that, she takes off, blurring down the narrow path between scrub, boulders, and cacti. Now this, this is what I live for. I give chase, just as I have done for millennia.

We run and run and run. I see flashes of her dark hair before she sprints off. I hold back for a bit, enjoying the chase, but then I let loose, and as I pass, I lean over and whisper, "Your turn to chase."

I'm positive I see a little shiver steal down her spine before she grins, and I take off. I really let myself go, like I haven't done in ages. I don't know where I'm going, I just know that at this moment I'm free—and I'm having fun —with Rae.

I don't expect Rae to be so fast. She nearly catches me a few times, but I manage to stay ahead. I realize we have turned back toward her house, and I start calculating how long it will take to get there when her hands snap around my sweaty waist and her fingers dig into my skin. The weight of her body slamming into mine topples me over, and we just miss rolling into a mean-looking spiky bush.

Once we stop rolling, Rae is kneeling on top of me, sun streaming through her sweat-slicked hair. I can't catch my breath. Her chest is quickly rising and falling, and her skin is flushed. We have been here, in this position before many times, and usually, it ends with one or both of us beat up and bloody.

My heart skips a beat as she smiles down at me. "I win. I caught you."

Without my permission, my hand reaches up and trails a finger down her arm. "And what shall be your prize?"

She freezes, and her smile falters before she smirks and stands. Damn my greedy hands. "Nothing you're thinking of, I'm sure. I'll simply take an admission of defeat."

I stand, ignoring the little pang in my heart, and smile, bowing deeply. "Then you have it. I have been bested. The lady Raelyn has won this day."

She snorts a little laugh, and I relax.

Back inside, we take turns showering and get dressed. Rae slides a basic glamour over her cuts and bruises. I cross to her, tracing my finger over where the bruise on her temple hides under her magic. "Sorry."

She shrugs me off. "Don't. I'm fine."

I know she's had worse. I've seen it. But she's not fine. The knife wound above her collarbone is deep, and even with our fae ability to heal faster than humans, it's still fresh and looked painful.

Though, I wonder at her right shoulder where I hit her with my fire magic. It should be burnt and blistered. I hit her hard. But where the damage of my flames should be, there is just pink skin, like she took a too-hot shower. Maybe I didn't hit her as hard as I thought.

I shake it off, and once again, we head into town. She takes me to a small Italian restaurant with a green awning covering a patio and little bistro tables dotting the space inside and out. We share a late lunch of pasta, garlic bread, Italian soda, and salad. We exchange idle talk, mostly about what we were up to during the long stretches of time between our confrontations.

I knew some of her exploits but am shocked to learn she

had a hand in creating the first known form of paper in China. And she had no idea I was the one who designed and helped build the very first sewage system in Sumer, Mesopotamia.

She laughs at my admission. "Of course that was you. Can't live without your creature comforts."

"If having a semi-sanitary way to relieve myself is a creature comfort, then guilty."

"Okay, okay. I get it." She leans in. "Were you ever in London in the Seventeenth or Eighteenth century?"

I throw myself back in my chair dramatically. "Oh my god! Don't get me started. I couldn't get out of there fast enough. Never have I known a place dirtier or more dangerous."

"I know! I have no idea why humans have romanticized old London."

Rae fakes a shiver, and I grin, then pause. "Wait. When were you there?"

Her hair falls over her shoulder as she tilts her head to the side in thought. "Hmmm. Maybe around 1880-ish. I wasn't there very long. Five years at the most. No. No. It was only two years. I hightailed it to Canada."

"No way. I was in London around 1910. Just missed you."

We both laugh as, one by one, we reveal little morsels of our lives to each other as we eat.

A half hour passes as I listen to her talk about the history of archery. Normally, I couldn't care less about the subject, but seeing the excitement on her face pulls me in. When she starts talking about the advancements of the compound bow, I laugh, shaking my head. "Wait, you're telling me you knew Holless Wilbur Allen?"

She smiles, her cheeks flushing. "I didn't just know him, we worked together. Back in 1996 I helped him develop the first compound bow, though I made sure he didn't mention me in the patent or paperwork."

Of course she did, Raelyn can't help herself. She's a giver.

Two bottles of red wine later, we sit in silence, and I hold my breath as I reach across the table. My fingers brush over the soft skin of her hand, and when she doesn't snap it back, I curl my hand under hers, turning it over and threading our fingers together. She just stares at our joined hands for a few long seconds before looking up and meeting my gaze. My heart is in my throat, and I'm practically vibrating with tension. I'm pretty sure the whole world has stopped as I sit and stare into her bright, green eyes.

Finally, she lets out a little breath, a smile curves up her lips, and she squeezes my hand. I smile back, relief settling over me like a cool breeze. My thumb caresses over her skin, and she licks her lips. With her free hand, she lifts her glass of wine and drains it, maintaining eye contact the whole time. I want to kiss her. What would her lips taste like under the wine?

"Can I get you anything else?" The server's voice cuts through the moment, and my eyes snap to his face as Rae slides her hand from mine.

I fight the urge to punch the server in the face and instead toss my napkin on the table. "No. Just the check." He startles at my harsh tone, but it's the best I can manage right now.

He drops the slip of paper on the table, and Rae snatches it up. Handing her credit card to him, she smiles. "Thank you."

He hurries off, and she smirks at me. "You didn't have to be so harsh."

"He should know when and when not to approach a table."

"Aw. Are you upset he interrupted our little moment?"

Her lips are pulled up in a teasing smile, but I latch onto her words, grinning. "So it *was* a moment."

She blushes and fiddles with the napkin on her lap but doesn't respond. The nervous server returns her card, and she signs the slip. We stand to leave, and I place my hand on her lower back as we step outside. I tense, waiting for her to shrug me off, but she actually relaxes into my touch. Once outside, I slide my hand from her back and hold it out, not touching, not taking, just waiting, letting her lead. Her fingers curl around mine, and I can't stop my smile as we walk side-by-side to the car.

The drive back is silent as we each fall back into our own thoughts. Besides the burning desire to kiss Rae, my mind keeps clawing at my skull with one thought. What proof will Kemremir bring to Rae?

Once we're back inside the house, the silence fills the space, and tension thickens the air. The next few hours pass so slowly I keep checking the time to make sure we have not somehow gotten stuck in a frozen slice of time. But no, the second hand creeps along.

"Should I make us some tea?" I ask, hoping for something to do, but she shakes her head, wringing her hands together.

"I don't think I could eat or drink anything right now." Her eyes lift to mine, and they look a bit desperate. "Ash, what am I going to do?"

I cross the room in a few long strides and throw caution to the wind. She looks so lost, so scared, and my heart just can't take it. I gently grip her shoulders and lean in close, holding her gaze. "You will do what you must. You are strong, and you are smart. Let's not forget you're the only one to escape a contract of mine, and that's no small feat."

She laughs nervously. "That's only because you fell madly in love with me."

I know she's joking, trying to break the tension, but her words ring true. My gaze travels across her face, a face I know better than my own, even when glamoured. The teasing smile slides from her lips as I bring my gaze back to her beautiful green eyes. I take a half step closer, and her breath hitches. I smell the garlic and red wine. I smell the sun on her skin from our run earlier. And under all that, I smell her—the scent of the sun on a breeze.

My fingers trail down her cheek, so soft, so warm, and I whisper, "Maybe I have."

Her eyes are intent on mine, and I can see a myriad of emotions and questions flitting through her mind. I can't begin to know what she's thinking, but all I know is that she's not pulling away. Her lips part, and she licks them, sending a bolt of desire through every nerve ending. Her whisper is even softer than mine. "Ash?"

I move with agonizing slowness, bringing our lips closer, giving her plenty of time to come to her senses. Yet her gaze flits between my lips and my eyes, and my heart threatens to leap from my chest. Her eyes flutter closed, and I lean in to close the last fraction of space between us. I can't believe I'm here, that this is happening.

"What the hell is going on here?"

Rae leaps out of my arms like she was electrocuted, and we both turn toward the angry voice growling from the other side of the living room.

A tall fae, almost as tall as me, emerges from swirling shadows. He's slight, almost graceful looking with the palest silver hair I've ever seen, high cheekbones, long delicate fingers, and thin, pale lips that are pressed into a tight, angry line.

Kemremir's shadows curl around them until they melt into the Dragon Lord, solidifying his form. A smirk plays at Kem's lips as he looks between Rae and me. He crosses his arms over his chest, ready to watch whatever is going to happen.

Rae's voice is shaky, and her face has drained of all color as she stares at the newcomer. "Alek?"

8

____

RAELYN

ALEK IS HERE, in my house, on Earth. His pale, silver hair is so long now, hanging past his shoulders. He looks sharper, harsher than I remembered. High cheekbones cut across his face and his green eyes, the same color as mine, have an intensity behind them that wasn't there the last time I saw him. Granted, that was thousands of years ago.

He's tall, taller than me, but while I remember him being thin, almost delicate, now I'd describe him as lean. Muscle adds power to his narrow frame. His hands are still delicate though, the hands of the scholar I remember.

There's a moment of absolute longing on his face as he looks at me, and I want to run to him, but then his eyes cut to Ash. "Raelyn, what is he doing here?" Alek's voice is deeper and coarser than I've ever heard it. His lips curl back, not bothering to hide his disdain. Turning to Kem, he practically growls, "Why isn't he dead?"

Kem's face remains impassive, and his voice rumbles from his chest, his natural voice making a mockery of Alek's growl. "Her Highness claimed his death."

Ash smiles, more cruel than amused, as he crosses his arms over his chest. There's no kindness in his golden eyes as he stares at my younger brother with that infuriating grin on his face. Before Ash can say something sarcastic and set Alek off, I face my brother again. "Ash and I have come to an understanding."

A single silver eyebrow lifts on Alek's face as he clicks his tongue at me. That expression I remember well—the look of utter disappointment. The same look he gave me when I skipped our history lessons at Garin's prodding and ran off with my bow slung over my shoulder. The same look he gave me every time I complained that the library was too quiet and terribly boring. The same look I got whenever Garin made excuses for me.

He opens his mouth, I'm sure to admonish me, but I cut him off. "I know you disapprove. I don't care. He's here because I ... *we* will need all the help we can get if what Kemremir told me is true."

Mirroring Ash, Kem's arms cross over his chest. "As I told you, your Highness, Dragon Lords do not lie." His gravelly voice sends a shiver down my spine. I understand why the Dragon Lords are the most revered race in all the realms— just hearing them speak, with the rumble of their dragon behind their words, demands deference. Kem angles his head toward Alek, who's still frowning at me. "I have brought you the proof you asked for. Now, let us conclude this business."

"Eager to get back home to a hot date?" Ash leans back against the sofa as he meets Kem's gaze, but Kem does not rise to the bait. He simply smirks back and stays silent.

I take a step toward Alek on unsteady legs. I ache to go to him and wrap my arms around him, but his stiff posture and narrowed eyes hold me in place. My voice comes out softer than I intend. "Alek, what's going on?"

He seems to deflate a bit at my question. His shoulders slump, and he sighs as he combs back his hair with his long, thin fingers. I feel like I should console him, pat his hand or something, but it has always been awkward between us. There was love between us, but it's always been a love of obligation because we are siblings, not because we shared an actual bond. We were just so different. There were times when I completely forgot Alek even existed, especially when I was with Garin. I don't know how to act around my younger brother, and it's making me itchy.

His voice snaps me from my thoughts. "I'm sorry, Raelyn. What Kemremir told you is true. All of it."

A soul-deep trembling spreads to my limbs as I realize my entire world is about to shift. "How? What happened?"

Alek clasps his hands, worrying his fingers together, and the silence in the room is deafening. Finally, avoiding my gaze, he says, "Nothing *happened*. Nothing *changed*. Garin has always been greedy and cruel."

I flinch at his words, and he rolls his eyes, sighing in obvious frustration. "I know how you idolized Garin, and it pains me to take that from you, but I need you to reconstruct your memories of him. I need you to see him as he really was, not how he painted himself to be. Then you will understand the man who murdered our parents, used dark magic to lock you away, and allowed the Unseelie into our kingdom."

I'm pretty sure my legs are going to give out any moment. My heart feels like it has cracked open and is leaking enough pain and sorrow that it just might drown me.

Kem saves me from trying to find the correct words to respond by turning to Alek. "I will leave you to discuss these matters with your sister. Call me when you are ready to go back to Attolyn, my friend."

Alek nods, and shadows swirl around Kem, swallowing him. When the tendrils of darkness disperse, he's gone.

"I'd love to know how he does that." I didn't realize Ash moved up next to me, and I almost jump out of my skin at the nearness of his voice. His fingers gently wrap around my arm, and that simple, kind touch threatens to bring tears to my eyes, but I manage to hold them back. Barely.

I let him guide me to the couch, and I practically fall onto the cushion. Ash sits next to me, sliding his hand from my arm, and holds my hand. It's a simple comfort but one I'm grateful for even though Alek looks like he's about to leap on Ash and tear him to pieces. Ash looks toward Alek then nods his head toward the chairs opposite the couch. "Want to join us, or are you going to continue to brood by the door?"

Alek presses his lips together in a harsh line and narrows his eyes. Ash chuckles under his breath but adds, "Your Highness."

When Alek doesn't move, I sigh and roll my eyes at him. "Alek, come sit down." It's good to know the commanding voice of an older sister is not something you lose, even after millennia apart.

He keeps his lips pressed tight and lifts his chin a bit higher as he crosses the room and perches on the edge of the chair. I can't help but laugh. "Okay, Alek. Let's start with something simple. How did you get through the doorway? Or rather, how did you send Kem through?"

"Kemremir doesn't need a portal." My mouth drops open, but Alek presses on. "Unfortunately, how I got through is not the simple question you think it to be." I just stare at him until he continues. "In short, I used dark magic."

"Alek!"

My voice comes out too high and loud but is drowned out by Ash's exclamation, "What in The Fates were you thinking?"

Alek finally sits back, crossing an ankle over a knee and resting a hand on his thigh. "I will not be judged by either of you. I did what I had to do. It was either stain my soul to open the doorway and get to you or let Garin destroy Attolyn."

I don't want to know the details, but I feel I should. I need to go into this with my eyes wide open. "Whose blood did you spill to work the magic?"

He glances at Ash. "His name was Valna."

Ash and I both stiffen at the name, and Alek raises an eyebrow. "Asheraht told you who hired him?"

I nod, and Ash asks, "How did you find him?"

"Through patience and acquainting myself with lowlifes. It was a lucky bit of chance that I was walking through the lower city one day and happened to overhear a conversation drifting out from a tavern. A group of drunkards were talking about the missing assassin, Asheraht, from the New Moon Guild. The dates were too close to Raelyn's disappearance to be circumstantial, so I slowed and slid into the shadows between the buildings. There were whispers of the name Valna as they talked of a huge contract that would set you up for life. They assumed the job proved to be too great a task for you when you failed to return."

Ash chuckles, shrugging, but I stare at Alek. "So what, you tracked Valna down and tortured him until he revealed where I was?"

My voice drips with sarcasm, but I startle when Alek nods. "Precisely. I brought him close to death many times. He held out longer than I thought he would, but I knew he'd tell me the name of the world where he sent Asheraht sooner or later. And then I'd find you."

I glance at Ash who's watching Alek intently.

Turning back to my brother, I catch his small smirk at Alek. "That's where my well-practiced patience came in. I spent years creating new ways to inflict pain on Valna."

Alek's eyes never leave Ash's. His voice is calm, level, quiet ... terrifying.

"I embedded shards of shungite under his skin to lock away his magic. My earth magic built on the walls of his cell to close him in a little more each day until he couldn't move an inch in either direction. Once I let the walls retreat, I commanded the ground to swallow him, slowly crushing him for days at a time. I commanded the earth to redirect deep water flows to the ceiling of his cell, letting it rain in small, incessant drops for years, never letting him know a dry moment. On and on, I got more creative, inflicted more pain, both psychological and physical."

Alek brushes an imaginary piece of lint from his pants, and I shiver at the man he's become in his quest to find me. I know his detailed description is meant to intimidate Ash, for if Alek went that far with the man who hired the assassin, what would Alek do to the assassin?

Alek smiles at Ash, but his eyes are cold and filled with menace. "Finally, many, many years later, Valna broke. He gave me the name Earth, as he pleaded for death, but when I turned from his broken body, ready to go through the nearest portal, he yelled after me." A narrowing of his eyes and a twitching in his jaw is the only indication of the rage within Alek as he stares at Ash. "Valna begged for me to kill him, claiming he had more information to give if I would grant him death. I agreed. He told me Garin hired him to hire you and then killed a friend of his to seal the way to Earth with a dark spell."

Alek's hands clench in his lap. "I checked his story, trying to get to Earth and failing. So, I dragged Valna to the portal, slit his throat, and cast the spell to open the portal."

I wince at the emptiness in his voice as he describes murdering a man.

A grimace crawls over his face, and he shudders dramatically. "I came through, landing in a sea of people. The noise was deafening, the press of bodies so great, no one even noticed I simply appeared out of nowhere."

I tilt my head. "Where were you?" He glares at me, raising a shoulder with a little shake of his head, and I smirk. "Okay, what was around you?"

He cracks his neck side to side. "There was a great golden temple around a pool of water. The language was ... throaty, their heads were covered."

Ash and I nod at the same time. I smile. "Must have been at the Golden Temple of Amritsar in India." I have to swallow a giggle at the thought of Ash appearing in the great crowds of mostly Sikhs that pilgrimage there. Christ, I would have paid good money to see that.

Alek shakes his head. "I realized finding you on this chaotic planet among this crush of humanity, would be extremely time consuming—time I didn't have."

Ash snorts, mumbling under his breath, "Tell me about it."

I shoot a glare at Ash, but Alek ignores him. "I immediately returned home to devise a plan. But I must have tipped off Garin by traveling to Earth, because soon after, I discovered his soldiers were watching me."

I rub my palms over my thighs. "So why go to the Dragon Lords?"

His finger taps his knee, and the silence draws out until he shrugs. "They owed me a favor." My brows climb my forehead, my eyes go wide, but before I can ask a single question, Alek presses on. "I could not risk Garin's wrath before I succeeded in bringing you home. You were all that mattered. I needed Asheraht dead"—Ash tenses next to me—"and I needed you delivered home safely. The Dragon Lords guaranteed me both."

My back stiffens as Alek sneers at us. "Instead, Kemremir returns to me saying my impertinent sister will not return without proof. So, against my better judgment, I bow to my sister's wishes, and what do I find? Her in an intimate embrace with the assassin paid to kill her."

I blush, and Ash leans toward me slightly.

Alek snarls. "Sister, tell me you were getting close to him to kill him."

How easy it would be to excuse my behavior by agreeing, but I've never been one to take the easy way out. I wanted Ash to kiss me. My skin had tingled with the need. Even now, I feel a flush creeping up my cheeks as I recall the heat between us. I want to look at Ash, to see his reaction to Alek's words, but I hold my gaze to my brother's. "What you saw doesn't matter. We need Ash."

"And just sweep away the fact that he spent millennia hunting you like an animal?"

I narrow my eyes at Alek, letting my anger deepen my voice. "Don't presume to know what my life has been like while I've been stuck here. And my life, my choices are not up for discussion. I still don't understand how Garin could have done all this. He was a great man, a strong warrior, and a loving brother."

Alek eyes soften into sadness. "No. He wasn't." I frown, and my anger melts as he continues. "I did not grow up idolizing Garin as you did. I feared him. He wore his smiles and charm around you and mother, but around me, there was nothing but stone behind his eyes. I always did my best to avoid him, and he seemed inclined to avoid me as well."

I'm shaking my head, unable to reconcile the Garin I knew and the Garin he describes. Alek sighs again. "Think, Raelyn. Really think. You saw him as your champion, but what was he championing?"

My frown deepens, and my mind goes blank, unable to see Garin any other way than my adoring big brother. Ash shifts, almost imperceptibly, but just enough to press the side of his knee against mine. His hand is still wrapped around mine, and I hold onto him as my world slowly tilts.

Alek frowns. "He encouraged you to visit the wildest, untamed worlds."

"I wanted to go."

Alek rolls his eyes like I'm the younger sibling and I'm being difficult. "He challenged you to dangerous tasks." Thoughts of the Whiteval Falls come to my mind. It was my 300th birthday. Garin bet me I couldn't climb the treacherous falls. I did, though I almost slipped and fell to my death, twice.

"He told you you were strong enough to ride the untamed horses. How many bones did you break? That one concussion almost killed you."

"It wasn't that bad." He raises an eyebrow at me. Yeah, okay, it was that bad, but still.

Alek goes on. "He took you on the most dangerous hunts, not to mention, Stratna."

Ash goes ridged next to me. "What about Stratna?"

Alek tsks. "Our dear brother sent Raelyn into the woods on a dare."

I feel Ash's gaze on me, but I don't turn to face him. I don't want to see the doubt in his eyes. Instead, I frown, tilting my head as I recall Garin's grin as he issued the dare to spend a week in the Stratna woods that border our kingdom and the Unseelie kingdom of Morthryl. Many foul things, unnatural things born of dark magic, roam those woods, and it was a perilous week.

Had there been malice behind Garin's grin? Was he a bit eager to send me on my way? All I can seem to remember is the pride I felt as I pushed through the palace doors at the end of the week, bruised, bloody, and covered in mud. Garin's smile seemed genuine, and his approval lit me up from within.

Slowly, I raise my head, meeting Alek's gaze. "Garin—"

"No, Raelyn! No more excuses! Garin attacked you and called it training."

"Alek, it *was* training. It made me stronger!"

"He wanted you dead, Raelyn!"

The room goes silent as Alek and I stare at each other. Finally, with a slow exhale, Alek's shoulders slump slightly. "Fates, Raelyn, you made it so easy for him, and all I could do was cringe and watch, waiting for the day one of his challenges, one of his dares, would take you from me."

My heart squeezes, and I open my mouth to protest, but he pushes on. "You would not have listened had I said anything. You loved him so very much, and it tore me apart that your free spirit and blind loyalty would be the weapon Garin used to kill you."

"Why?"

Alek meets my gaze, leaning forward, elbows on knees. "Don't you see? Garin was threatened by you. He saw what I saw, what father saw. He feared your confidence, that wildness within you. None of us could hope to be so free and unconcerned with what others thought while also being kind and sincere, strong, funny, and tough."

My cheeks are wet with my tears, and I don't bother to wipe them away as Alek pushes on. "Garin feared you. He feared father would choose you to rule. Yes, Garin is strong and charismatic, and his magic is powerful. But he is also cruel, and his arrogance makes him brash. He looks down at the common fae, especially those without magic, and honestly, so did I, but I'm trying to be better, to be more like you."

I shift uncomfortably, but he goes on. "You loved being with the people. You never seemed to notice or care whether they were rich or poor, beautiful or plain. You treated everyone the same, even those that feared the color of your hair."

I flinch and brush said locks away from my face. Ash scowls. "She is not lesser because of her difference. It has made her stronger, kinder ... more."

My stomach flutters at the passion behind Ash's words, but Alek just shrugs. "Regardless, Garin assumed Raelyn's dark complexion would keep father from appointing her as the next Queen, but Garin was never one to leave things to chance." My palms sweat at those words. Me? Queen? "Garin wanted you out of the way, and you eagerly went wherever he pointed."

I have to swallow twice before I manage to say, "But mother, she—"

"It was father's place to pick the next ruler, and he was going to pick you."

My heart stops and sweat drips down my spine. The air around me sucks at my ears, and a tingling in my fingers warns me I'm about to pass out. Ash rubs his thumb over my hand, leaning in, bringing his pine and grass scent closer. "Breathe."

I inhale, my breath shuddering on the way in, but it grounds me slightly. My voice is barely a whisper as I ask, "Our parents?"

Pain bleeds from Alek's eyes. "They spent years looking for you, Raelyn. Centuries. But there are too many realms, too many places to search. After so much time, they had to assume you were lost or dead. Of course, now I know Garin knew, but he was very good at bringing us so-called 'leads' that kept us looking everywhere but Earth.

Alek rubs his temples. "Confident in his deception, Garin assumed the crown was his. Mother certainly fueled his ego, but Garin grew impatient. It was subtle at first. He would suggest our parents had worked long and hard enough to secure a peaceful and prosperous kingdom, and that they should pass on the crown and enjoy a more relaxed life into their elder years. Mother liked the idea, but father laughed it off, claiming he had many, many years yet to rule and that he wasn't ready to 'retire' just yet."

Alek's fingers comb through his hair before he drops them in his lap. Ash gets up in the silence, and there's some soft banging of kitchen cabinets and clinking of glasses before he returns, three glasses in hand. He passes one to Alek, who accepts it with a hard stare. Ash returns to the couch, sitting close once again and hands a glass to me, keeping one for himself. I sniff at the liquid. Whiskey. I take a sip, shudder with a grimace, then take another.

Alek downs half of his glass in one gulp. "As time passed, Garin's impatience grew. He argued with father at almost every dinner. He tried to lead council meetings only to be shut down. He was angry all the time. He started drinking too much and would often show up at the soldiers' training yard bellowing for sparring partners, only to beat them to unconsciousness. Even mother scolded him for his rough behavior."

The other half of the whiskey disappears down Alek's throat, and he coughs before his gaze goes distant. "About fifty years ago, I was walking from the library to my rooms. It was late, the very early hours of the morning, and the castle was quiet, calm. I remember concentrating on the soft sound of my bare feet hitting the cool stone floor when I heard voices coming from our parents' rooms. I slowed and hid in the shadows of the tapestry hanging in the hall."

Funny, I can picture that tapestry. I can't picture the details of my mother's face. I don't recall the exact color of my father's eyes. But I remember that tapestry. It hung from ceiling to floor, eighteen feet tall. I could spread my arms wide and not grasp the edges. A green valley spilled in the lower-left corner, split with a silver river. Hills turned to mountains that climbed up the right side of the tapestry. A golden-threaded sun spread warm colors across the landscape and gilded the shining castle woven into the side of the mountains. The gold threads made the tapestry shimmer.

Alek's voice pulls me from my thoughts. "I could hear mother speaking. Her voice had that tone, you know the one, where she's trying to keep everyone calm, but it just sounds condescending?"

I do know that voice. I know it very well, and I give Alek a half-hearted smile as he continues, "She told Garin she knew he was disappointed, and that she appreciated his patience. Gah, she was so weak when it came to him."

I'm shocked at the bitterness in Alek's voice and notice his hand gripping his leg, the other clenching the glass.

"She begged him to remain patient a while longer, that his time would come. But Father interrupted her. His voice carried easily into the hall where I hid as he told Garin he was concerned with his behavior, and that his actions in the pubs, pleasure houses, and training ring, were less than honorable."

Alek scoffs. "If only Father knew. He didn't know half of the things Garin was getting into."

With some effort, Alek loosens his grip on his leg. "But I digress. Father reminded him that we are fae, we are immortal, and we are patient. I hadn't heard that tone from Father in years, the tone he used on us as children when we would misbehave."

I knew that tone as well. It was a tone you wanted to avoid.

Alek sits back. "And then he said something I never thought I'd hear. He told Garin if his behavior didn't change, if Garin didn't start acting as a leader should, he would give the crown to me. Though he wished you were there to pass the crown to."

I startle again at those words. Gone for so long, and father wanted me to rule, even not knowing what I'd been through or who I'd become. Poor Alek. Always feeling like the last resort in our family, even from me. Shame washes over me. I need to do better, be better.

"Alek, I'm so sorry—"

He holds up a hand. "It's how it's always been. I know my own worth."

I shake my head, needing to give him more, but he sighs. "Anyway, back to the story. For a moment, our parent's room went silent, and it leaked into the hall. I'm not sure if they were holding their breath, but I was holding mine, waiting.

And then Garin's voice speared through the quiet with a single word, 'No'."

Alek's eyes unfocus, and his shoulders tense back up. "The room exploded in flames. Mother screamed, and Father bellowed. Even out in the hall, I was thrown to the ground."

I realize I'm gripping my glass so hard it's cracking, and as I set it down, I notice Alek's hand shaking around his empty glass. "Garin's attack was so violent, so powerful, they had no time to react, to protect themselves. The heat was so intense, the stone walls outside their room turned red, and the air shimmered. A few moments later, Garin strode from their room like a walking nightmare, wiping ash from his coat, a smile on his face, untouched by the wrath of his magic. The Fates were watching over me because he didn't see me there, or he surely would have killed me right there in that hall. I'm no match for Garin. As soon as he turned a corner, I called my earth magic and tried to suffocate the flames, but they consumed everything I threw at them. It was as if his anger fed the fire even long after he walked away. The entire west wing of the castle burned down before several fae joined me, and we were finally able to extinguish the blaze."

Alek shakes himself out of the memory, and bitterness seeps back into his voice. "The next morning, Garin addressed the kingdom, declaring a great accident took our King and Queen and that he would, with 'great grief and a humble heart', take on the mantle of the crown. I couldn't say anything. I knew Garin would kill me. My only option was to find you, no matter how long it took. I've put all my hope in that together, we could stop him."

I feel hollowed out as he sets his glass on the table. The sound, though tiny, seems overly loud in the silence of the living room. He grits his teeth. "The following week, the Unseelie showed up, Garin claiming it was past time to work through our differences and become a single fae nation. He started filling the guard and soldier ranks with Unseelie and gave them seats on the council. Blood magic is now legal."

Alek's pained eyes, creased at the edges, meet mine. "Our people are dying, Raelyn. They are being slaughtered for dark magic, and more and more Seelie are turning to dark magic to protect themselves, only to be consumed by the power. You know, less and less Seelie were being born with magic, and it's only gotten worse over the years. And now we are losing precious magicked fae to blood magic. Good people are turning violent, and we are on the brink of a civil war. We need you to come home. *I* need you. Garin does not know I'm here, and he can't know, not until we stop him. Surprise is our greatest advantage right now."

Tears fill his eyes, and one tracks down his cheek. "I've missed you so much. I loved you fiercely." Another tear drips from his chin. "I still do."

I'm across the room and in Alek's arms in a flash of movement. I hug him so tight, my tears wetting his shoulder, I'm afraid I'll crush him. But he holds me even tighter in an embrace thousands of years overdue. I never knew. I never knew how much he loved me, and the fault is my own. My emotions are bleeding me out, leaving me hollow as I shake in his embrace, feeling grief, horror, guilt, sorrow, love, and regret. But one thing I know for sure ... I'm tired of running. I just don't know if I'm strong enough to face this.

After a few minutes, I pull back, wiping my face. "Alek, what do we do? Is there hope of talking to Garin? Can't we reason with him?"

"Give me some credit, Raelyn. I've tried. I doubt you'd be so willing to talk with him if you had watched him murder our parents." His voice is harsh, and I jerk back. But he's right. I don't know what it's been like back home. I'm fairly powerful, but I'm no match for Garin's magic and strength.

Alek presses his lips into a firm line. "Together, we must face him together." He grimaces as he looks over my shoulder to Ash. "We don't need anyone else." His gaze comes back to mine. "We are enough, Raelyn. You and me."

I shake my head before Ash can say anything. "I know you hate him, Alek, but we may not be enough. It's not just about us. You said our people are suffering. Ash can help. And maybe he can bring additional help from the New Moon Guild."

Alek's voice is sharp. "No."

His tone makes me want to pull back, but I force myself to stay there, to stay with my brother to make him understand. "I won't go home without him."

Alek's jaw clenches, but I just stare up at him, letting him see the resolve in my eyes. Finally, he huffs a sharp breath. "I do not condone this, but very well, the assassin can return with us."

I turn, and Ash nods, eyes glued to me. "I cannot speak for the Guild, but I will do my best to convince them that yours is a fight worth involving themselves. But for now, I promise you my help."

I smile and nod at Ash before looking back at my brother. His eyes soften as he lightly grasps my shoulders. "We have to try, Raelyn. There's no one else to stand against him. The people are terrified. The soldiers who spoke out against him were either executed or are missing. Same with the council. We need to stop him."

Ash steps forward. "What about Kemremir? Will he help?"

"I cannot." We all jump as the Dragon Lord materializes

from an inky patch of shadows. "We do not involve ourselves in the politics of others. I pushed our code in even taking on this task for Alek, but he has long been a friend and ally to the Dragon Lords, and we owed him the favor of finding his sister. I will escort you back to your home. Beyond that, I cannot help."

I frown at him, but Ash and Alek quickly take him at his word, and Alek squeezes my shoulders. "This may not work. We could die."

I take a deep breath and nod even though my insides are quaking. "As you said, we have to try." I'm not even half as sure as I sound.

He nods. "Then we must hurry before Garin realizes I'm gone. We must return to Attolyn. Now."

9

———

RAELYN

THIS IS all happening terribly fast, and my brain feels glitchy. So much in so little time has been thrown at me that my mind is leaping from thought to thought like a skipping record. There's nothing to ground me in the chaos of my thoughts.

And now a new emotion has crashed the party, panic.

Thousands of years of wanting to go home is over. But anxiety is clawing at my every nerve. My kingdom awaits. Responsibility awaits. I'm going to have to face Garin. How am I going to face him? Plus, now that I can leave, there's a secret part of me, a part that I could never tell Alek doesn't want to go home. I like Earth. Living here has been a lot of things for me; frustrating, scary, dangerous, boring, exhilarating, heartbreaking, lonely, adventurous ... fun.

I think of the archery range outside of town. I've been going there for years. The day little seven-year-old Kylie walked in, hiding behind her father's legs, brown eyes wide and partially obscured by her black curls as she watched the line of archers losing their arrows, I felt a kinship.

Kylie was no natural, struggling with stance, posture, and strength. But she was determined. I can't count how many hours I've spent holding her little brown hand in mine, directing her fingers in the correct position, poking her back to make her stand straighter. Recalling her giggles brings a frown to my face. She's been practicing with me for three years, and in just two weeks, she is going to take the test to graduate to a larger bow and the more complex training range.

I don't want to miss it. I promised I would be there.

And ... I really don't want to face Garin.

I put on a brave face and straighten my spine. No matter how valid my excuses, I need to stop running from my responsibilities. I just ... need a moment.

I nod to my brother. "I need to gather a few things. It won't take long. I'll meet you at the doorway. Which one did you use?"

Kem, still stoic—a black shadow in the room even while in his solid, human form—frowns. "It would be best if I shadow us all to the doorway together. There's no need to split up."

Alek nods, about to agree, but Ash steps to my side. "Raelyn and I will meet you at the portal within the hour." His words are calmly spoken, but the set of his shoulders and the hardness to his eyes begs no argument.

Of course, that doesn't stop my brother. Alek tilts his head with a frown. "An hour? What could you possibly need an—"

Ash cuts him off with a grin while stretching to his full height, looking down at Alek, and crosses his arms over his chest. "An hour is but a moment. Time to use some of that famous patience of yours."

I've seen that exasperated look from Alek many times when we were children. He used to tell me I could argue the stubborn out of a mule, and right now, I'd wager he doesn't want to waste more time arguing.

Alek nods but steps toward Ash, narrowing his eyes. "One hour. If my sister fails to show up, if she's even one second late, I will kill you myself no matter what claims Raelyn has made on your life."

Ash stands solid, like stone, just glaring at my brother. I roll my eyes, so tired of the testosterone practically flooding my house. "Alek, I'll be there."

He peels his gaze from Ash. "All the doorways are open, so we'll meet at ..." He looks at Kem with a question in his eyes.

Kem looks at me. "Cathedral Rock. It's close but remote."

I nod, and Alek steps back toward Kem. "One hour, Raelyn."

I roll my eyes again, and from the corner of my eye, I think I see Kem's lips lift ever so slightly in the tiniest of smiles. I flash a smile at him as he steps forward, placing a hand on Alek's shoulder and envelopes them in wisps of shadow.

The smoky tendrils melt away, and Ash and I are once again alone. Ash sighs. "I was hoping to get to shadow travel. Damn."

I turn, meeting his smiling face. "You could have gone with them."

He shrugs, looking away. "I could tell this was all hitting you a bit hard. Hell, my brain feels like it's on overload. I figured we could both use a minute."

"Thank you."

I'm ready for some smart-ass remark, but he just flicks his eyes to mine, nods, then looks away again. A few moments go by, and the silence stretches, filling the room, the house, the entire Sedona desert. One by one, the events of the last two days slam into me, and my knees buckle. I barely make it to one of the leather chairs before I collapse, eyes wide, breath short, forearms on knees. My parents are gone. I'll never see my father's kind smile or hear the gentle swish of my mother's skirts as she glides through the halls of the castle. Tears rim my eyes, making the room go unfocused before I blink them back.

Ash looks over at me and frowns. "I'm sorry, Raelyn."

Looking up at him, the man I loved to hate, I see complete understanding in his soft eyes. Emotion scratches at my throat as I whisper, "I don't want to go back."

He nods, folding himself to sit on the floor in front of me. My hands are shaking, and no amount of concentration keeps them still. A single soft bark of laughter breaks from my lips. "I mean, I want to go home. The Fates know I want to go home. But now that I know what's waiting for me, I don't want to go back."

I run a trembling hand through my hair, then pull a handful forward, staring down at the dark brown strands. "Will our people accept me as their ruler? And that's even if I can ... if I'm able to ... if Garin ..."

Ash's warm fingers wrap around mine, pulling my hand from my hair and holding it gently in his. "Raelyn, I understand. This is a shit situation, not at all how you imagined returning home." Another sharp bark of laughter escapes even though I'm on the verge of tears. I feel like I'm being ripped in two. I meet Ash's gaze as he squeezes my hand. "We could stay. Alek can't force you to return. He can't force you to take the throne. He can't force you to confront Garin. We can stay."

I just stare at him, frozen with indecision. He's right. I could stay. I could refuse my brother and stay here on Earth —or go anywhere I like now that the doorways are open again. But if things are really so bad in Attolyn, I have a responsibility to ... Ash's words catch up to me. He said 'we' could stay. "Ash, you're free to go and do what you please. You don't have to stick around. You don't have to get involved."

His hand drops from mine, and anger tightens his features. "I don't have to get involved? Raelyn, you are the only person I have truly been involved with for the past seven millennia. I'm involved whether you want me or not."

My right leg starts bouncing on the ball of my foot. Ash places his warm palm on my knee, and I stare at his hand, gaze unfocused as I sigh. "Everything Alek said ... He's never been one with much of an imagination. This isn't something he'd make up. He wouldn't lie about this, and I can only imagine what he's been dealing with on his own. He's been alone and probably afraid. But ..."

"You still hold love for your older brother and hope Alek is lying."

I nod, hiding behind the curtain of my dark hair. "Even if it's true. Even if we ... if we fight Garin, I don't think I'm strong enough, emotionally, magically, or physically to do what is needed."

Ash's voice grounds me. "Alek said the two of you together could take him down." I just shrug with uncertainty. "And you'll have my help." I lift my gaze, meeting his glowing golden eyes. He smiles, revealing that elusive dimple in his left cheek. "I'm involved."

The right side of my mouth lifts in a half-smile. "So, we're going home."

He stands, pulling me up by the hand. "We're going home, your Majesty."

I grimace. "Not yet."

He chuckles. "Okay, your Highness."

I swallow, forcing myself to hold his gaze. "Rae, just Rae."

A bright smile lights up his face. "Rae." He's said my nickname countless times, much to my annoyance, but this time it's said like a prayer, a wish, a hope, and I can't help but smile back as he asks, "Is there anything you want to bring with you?"

That's a heavy question, and I bite my lower lip in thought. Thousands of human lifetimes spent on this planet, I have too many mementos to carry. I turn and enter my bedroom, bend down, and slide the heavy wood frame of my king-size bed to the side. Ash has followed me and watches from the doorway, his broad shoulder leaning on the door jam. I press my palm to the center of a large tile on the floor, and it pops up with a little click. I work my fingernails under the small crack and lift the tile, setting it aside, revealing a safe. Punching in the code and scanning my fingerprint, the lock clicks open with a mechanical whir of gears, and I reach inside.

My fingers brush against the golden cuff I wore during my time as Pharoah Sobekneferu, bringing a smile to my face, but I shove it to the side. The soft texture of the cloth that preserves the scrolls from Socrates caresses the palm of my hand as I lift them from the safe and gently set them aside. Even through the protective vellum and cloth, the musty smell of leather and paper tickles my nose as I stack the three books I managed to save from the Library of Alexandria.

I continue rifling through the many items in the safe. A clink of copper scrapping against the safe's metal draws my eye to the ring I used to wear on my right thumb. The ring Camilia gave me the day we moved into our house in Pompeii. I grab the jade pen that sits next to the ring. It was gifted to me by the emperor of China and sits just as cold in the palm of my hand today as the day I received it. I stare at the swirling greens and blacks of the valuable writing tool.

Setting it down next to the books, I continue my search. I push aside the gilded crown I wore as the Goddess Gna during my time spent with the Vikings and almost cut my finger on the golden dagger given to me by Joan of Arc. Another wrapped roll of paper joins the scroll, this one a map drawn and given to me by Marco Polo in Sumatra.

Finally, my hand wraps around the one item I want.

Standing, I face Ash, and his eyes drop to my hand. The long iron arrow is rough against my skin, and the decorative gold fletching and arrowhead reflect the light from the sconces on either side of my bed.

Ash tilts his head. "What's that?"

"This is the prize arrow from the Buddhist temple, Sanjusangendo." I run my fingers over the cold iron and smile. I was living in Japan in 1686–one of the places I lived that Ash never found me. I left when I could no longer hide that the passage of time was not affecting me.

"You lived at a Buddhist temple?"

I nod, my smile growing as I watch the light from my eyes reflect in the gold point of the arrow. "For a very long time. I did have to live glamoured as a male, but it was a peaceful time. I had strong, almost familial connections with my comrades there. It was a quiet life, simple." I hold out the arrow, and he takes it, turning it in his hand. "I won that the year I left. Every year they held a contest at the temple. The challenge was to fire more arrows down the entire length of the temple than anyone else. It was an arduous task, and we would practice all year. Of course, I never used my magic during the actual contest. I was among honorable men and treated their contest with respect. Plus, what good is a prize if you cheat to win it?"

I watch the light reflect off the gold arrow tip as Ash turns it in his hand. "The day of the contest, we each had 14,000 arrows stacked in multiple quivers." Ash's eyebrows lift, and my smile widens. "That was part of the challenge. Firing that many arrows fatigue the muscles. Many can't even finish the contest. And then, to actually get your arrows all the way across the temple for it to count ... was exhausting. It was a close race for the first few hours, but one-by-one the men tired, and fewer and fewer arrows crossed their mark."

I remember how my arms burned, and my core shook. Sweat poured down my face and back. Even my fingers were sweaty, making pulling the bowstring back harder each time. As the sun rose, it seemed to sear my eyes until my vision blurred. The arrows behind me seemed endless, and my mind shut off until it was just me, the bow, and the arrows. It was like a trance. It was beautiful.

"Out of my 14,000 arrows, only 8,133 made it across the temple, but I won by over 300 hundred arrows." Ash holds up the iron arrow, twirling it between his thumb and forefinger before handing it back. "This was my prize. They still hold that contest to this day, every February."

Shoving his hands in his pockets, Ash smiles, though there is a bit of sadness behind his eyes. "Out of everything, why take just this?"

I grip the iron shaft, feeling its weight in my hand. "Because I earned this. It wasn't a gift. I didn't get it because of my magic. I worked hard, and I won. Just me."

Ash nods. "A worthy token to take home."

I place the arrow in a leather, cylindrical tube that I strap to my back. "What are you bringing?" Ash looks embarrassed as he lifts one shoulder in a little shrug and quirks his lips to the side. I frown. "There must be something. Or maybe a lot of things. I'm happy to help carry things if you need. But remember, the doorways are open, we are free, so if ... if we survive, there is no reason you can't come back. You can continue your life here or collect whatever you want to bring home."

He shakes his head. "I'm good."

For some reason, that quiet admission makes me sad, and my heart squeezes a little. "Nothing?"

"I already have what I want to bring home."

I look him over. He doesn't wear any jewelry, and unless there is something very small in his pocket, he's not carrying anything. I cock my head to the side. "What?"

His head drops, looking at his boots before he tilts his eyes back to mine, looking at me from under his lashes. "You."

My lips fall open in a startled 'oh,' and he pushes off the door frame and sweeps an arm toward the front door. "Attolyn awaits."

I've gone all warm and gooshy inside at his words. I'm not sure what to say, so I say nothing. As we leave the house, I lock the front door out of habit. Maybe I'll come back one day.

I give my car a little pat on the hood before we blur toward Cathedral Rock. Our progress is quiet and tense. I can't get Ash's words out of my head. All he wants with him when he goes home is me. My heart stutters, and my palms are sweaty as I steal little glances at him.

Cathedral Rock comes into view through the darkness of night, and we aim for a hidden trail at the north side of the base of the great rock spearing up from the rocky, sandy ground.

Alek is there, pacing a short path in front of Kem, who's leaning back against the red rock. As Ash and I stop before them, Alek takes a big inhale and releases it in a rush of air.

Ash smirks, unable to help himself. "Worried we wouldn't show?"

Alek scowls, but Kem pushes off the rock and steps forward. "You all should go."

The four of us skirt around a lower tower of the rock formation, and immediately the power of the doorway tingles across my skin. I can't seem to catch my breath. Alek turns, and his voice sounds far away over the rush of blood pumping past my eardrums. "We are going through the doorway in the mountain pass behind the castle. I could not chance using the one outside the royal gardens, it's too public. The portal in the mountain pass is practically forgotten. It's the safest option. Once we're through, I'll sneak you into the castle. You can hide in my rooms while Asheraht returns to the New Moon Guild to see if the assassins can bring any further assistance."

He turns to Ash, his face grave, serious. "Time is not our friend right now. I cannot risk Garin finding out Raelyn is back. One day's cycle is all I can offer before we will move on our brother, with or without you."

Ash nods. "I will bring what aid I can, but at the very least, I will be there."

Alek inclines his chin a fraction of an inch, a tiny display of his gratitude, though his eyes and tense posture say he still doesn't trust Ash. Turning toward me, he frowns, taking both of my hands in his. They're cold and clammy. "I am sorry that this is to be your homecoming, Raelyn."

I don't respond. My body is slowly going numb as the realization of what I'm about to do crushes me. Alek's frown deepens. "Raelyn?"

I pull him to me, wrapping my arms around his waist, burying my face in his chest. "Thank you for finding me. Thank you for coming for me."

His hand strokes down my back in a calming gesture, his voice soft. "I love you, Rae. I never would have stopped looking." I tilt my head back, looking into his green eyes. "Never."

I burrow back into him, holding him tighter, and I feel his breath stutter with his inhale. I whisper into his chest, "I'm so sorry, Alek, for everything. I love you too."

His sigh breaks my heart as I feel some of the tension leave his body at my words. Have I never told him I love him?

Kem steps forward and places a hot hand on my back. "Alek needs to get back before he's missed. You all must go." I'm surprised at the contact from the Dragon Lord, but his powerful touch bolsters me slightly.

Alek releases me and with a small nod, takes three steps and disappears through the portal.

Ash takes my hand, squeezes it with a smile, then lets go and turns, but I reach out, grabbing his arm. He turns back to me, a question in his eyes. "Change your mind?"

I shake my head and take the single step that separates us. I don't stop to think. I just give his arm a little tug as I stand on my toes, bringing my lips to his. He tenses, and I pull back quickly, taking the feel of his soft lips with me. My pulse is racing, and my body is flushed from head to toe.

Ash's eyes have widened, and his mouth hangs open in what I imagine is shock. I'm shocked at myself.

I can feel Kem behind me, watching, but I don't care. I smile tentatively at Ash, and my heart sinks when he doesn't return my smile. He just runs a hand through his hair before turning back toward the portal.

I mentally slap myself in the forehead. Stupid! That's what I get for being impulsive. We were finally making strides toward friendship, and I go and kiss him. I'm such an idiot. Why would I—

My thoughts are shoved from my head as Ash spins around. With a single great stride, he bands an arm around my waist as his other hand wraps behind my head gripping my hair in his fist. Pulling me tight to his chest, he crushes his lips to mine, and my body explodes. If I were a fire fae, I would be engulfed in flames right now. As it is, a breeze of my magic lifts my hair and dances across my heated skin. I see stars behind my closed lids as he tilts his head farther, taking the kiss deeper. I lick his lips and slide my tongue over his.

A primal growl rumbles from his chest, and I moan against his mouth. His kiss sears me as we claim each other. Everything that has built up between us over the years pours into this kiss. Everything we are about to face fades under the taste of him on my tongue. He's like spice and crisp fall air. He's my anchor. I grip the front of his shirt, feeling the muscled chest beneath. His arm presses harder to my lower back, crushing me into him.

I don't want this to end. I want to kiss Ash under the night sky with the desert breeze licking our skin forever. But he lifts his head, lips red and glistening, breath a bit ragged, as is mine. I stare into his luminescent gold eyes and see my green eyes reflected there. His finger traces down my temple and across my cheek. My heart skips a beat as he smiles, and that left dimple makes an appearance. "Ready?"

No. But I nod. He leans down, pressing one more swift kiss to my lips, and I have to clench my hands at my sides to keep from grabbing him and keeping him from going through the doorway.

Three long strides, and he steps through. Seeing him disappear in a shimmer of air, like walking through heat shimmers rising from hot pavement, sends my heart into a panicked gallop. Kem steps back up behind me, returns his hand to my back, and places his other on my shoulder. He leans in behind me, the heat of him wrapping around me. I don't even notice the brimstone scent anymore. His gravelly voice is soft. "I am glad you had Asheraht. Being the only one of your kind, being alone even in a sea of people is not a fate I would wish on anyone, least of all you, your Highness."

I turn to face him. He drops his hand from my back but keeps a gentle grip on my shoulder. I look up into his face, and instead of feeling fear at the embers burning in his dark eyes, I feel comfort. "Thank you, Kem. I just wish we had not wasted so much time fighting."

"Some of the best relationships are born of the fiercest fire." His bright smile lights up his face. The shadow of his dark beard, dusted with a few silvery hairs, frames his white teeth. He's striking, imposing, but I sense a gentleness in him.

"I hope you're right." I place a hand on his arm, feeling so small standing this close to him, but I feel safe. "Thank you, Kem."

He nods, giving my shoulder a little squeeze. "You are very brave. I am glad to have finally met you, Raelyn."

The trembling in my limbs remains, but my breathing

slows, and the rush of blood pounding in my ears quiets slightly. This Dragon Lord thinks I'm brave. I lift my chin. But what does he mean, *finally*? I shake that off. "I am glad to have met you as well. I don't know the rules of the Dragon Lords, but I'd like to be your friend ... if that's allowed."

His smile widens, and then he chuckles a quick laugh. I have a feeling he does not laugh all that often, and that's a shame. It's a glorious sound—deep but somehow light. "I would like to be your friend, Raelyn."

I pat his arm. "Good." Turning, I face the doorway and swallow. "Well, thanks for coming to find me, Kem. I guess you have fulfilled your favor to Alek. Don't be a stranger, you know, if I survive."

I don't turn to see his reaction, and he doesn't answer. With a gentle push of his hand, I step forward and into the portal. There's a popping sensation like I walked into a giant soap bubble, and then I'm in a cave softly glowing with flickering fae light. I hold back a sob at the sight of the orbs of pure white light shimmering with iridescent blues and purples.

I'm home.

"Raelyn." Alek's voice draws my gaze across the cave. He's standing stock still a few paces away, flanked by two soldiers, one Seelie, one Unseelie. My eyes go wide at the sight of the dark fae. I whip my head around. Anger and despair wage war within my chest as I notice Ash to my right, where an Unseelie soldier wearing the armor of Attolyn digs a dagger into Ash's back. Around us, in a semicircle stand twenty soldiers, over half of which are Unseelie fae. Their faces are hard and impassive as they all stare at me.

And there, in the center, stands Garin.

He's so tall and handsome. And formidable. Pure happiness washes through me. My brother is here. After all this time, he's right here. But then I remember the Unseelie around us and all that Alek told me, and my joy is drowned in uncertainty and sorrow.

Garin's silver hair is short, revealing a scar across the right side of his head that wasn't there 7000 years ago. The simple gold crown of Attolyn sits atop his head, and my breath catches. That crown belongs on my father's head. My father wore that crown comfortably. The way Garin holds his head, almost stretching his neck, seems like he is showing it off. He angles his head with every slight movement, so the crown is always drawing attention.

I peel my eyes from the crown, and my gaze finds his dark eyes that glow like obsidian. I don't see evil there. I can't find any hint of scheming or deception. I just see ... him. His full lips lift in a smile, a smile I remember well, and I tremble with the desire to go to him. He holds out his arms toward me, and I fight to keep myself from running into his arms.

My heart twists, and my eyes burn with the threat of tears as Garin takes another step toward me, arms opening even wider. "Welcome home, Rae. I have missed you so much."

10

———

ASHERAHT

THAT KISS. My whole world shifted, and my head was in the clouds as I stepped through the portal. But as soon as my feet hit the stone floor of the cave, the silly boyish grin peeled from my face as I watched two soldiers haul Alek off to the side. They gripped his arms tightly, and one held a dagger to his side.

Rae's older brother made eye contact with me, and a cruel smile crawled across his handsome face.

A soldier leapt for me as I threw myself backward. The portal hummed over my skin, and I opened my mouth to shout a warning to Rae, but before I was able to slip through, the soldier wrapped his arms around my middle, and we both hit the ground with a grunt. He was heavy, his shining armor digging into my flesh, but I managed to elbow him in the face and flicked one of my small throwing knives into my other palm just as I felt the press of a dagger into my back. He pushed the blade through my shirt, breaking skin. He had me.

As he hauled me to my feet, I caught the black hair and eyes, recognizing him as Unseelie. It's still hard to believe what I'm seeing ... The dark fae are in Attolyn, and not just in the kingdom but in the king's service.

The dark fae holding me mumbled something I couldn't decipher before growling in my ear, "Hold still, or you die right here, right now." I froze as the Unseelie pulled the dagger from my back, and I almost sighed at the relief. But every muscle in my body went rigid, and the sour taste of bile coated my tongue as he lifted the dagger to his mouth and licked my blood from his blade. He sneered as he ran his tongue over his teeth, staining his mouth bright red. "There is decent power in you, boy. I'll enjoy drinking you dry." His fingers flickered with flames, and he smiled. "Yes, I think I'll enjoy your power very much."

He pierced me again and again, and I held back my groans of pain as he stabbed shallow cuts into my skin. I felt like a pin cushion, and my shirt was starting to stick to my back from the blood.

The king held out his hand, and the soldier extended the dagger toward him. Garin ran his finger down the black blade and touched his finger to his tongue, licking it clean. "Yes, there is a decent amount of magic in you, fire fae, but my fire is stronger." He returned the dark fae's dagger and nodded. The soldier stuck me again, and Garin grinned.

I had no idea what was delaying Rae, but I was glad she wasn't here.

The Unseelie's dagger found a particularly sensitive spot, twisting the blade deeper, causing me to grit my teeth. My back spasmed with pain just as Rae came through as if I had summoned her with my thoughts. Her eyes lit up with joy as she looked at the glowing orbs of fae light, the happiness of being home plain on her face.

I opened my mouth to shout a warning, but the dark fae at my back slapped his free hand over my mouth as he moved his dagger to my throat. His whisper slid like oil over my skin. "Uh, uh, uh. Let the king and his sister have their reunion."

The sneering, confident grin on Garin's face transformed into a soft, welcoming smile as he took a step toward Rae and held out his arms. "Welcome home, Rae. I have missed you so much." Garin's words dripped with longing, and I saw it as he opened his arms even wider. I saw the brother Rae loved as his eyes filled with adoration.

He's good, very good.

He stands, arms still open wide with such sincerity in his eyes that my heart breaks for Rae, and my chest constricts painfully. Gone is the man who delighted in licking my blood from his finger. In his place is a brother filled with overwhelming emotion at seeing his long-lost sister.

The cave seems to grow darker, and the fae lights flicker. I look around to see if anyone else notices, but Rae moves, and my attention snaps back to her.

I inwardly groan as she unloops the cylinder holding her prized arrow over her head, sets it down, and steps into Garin's arms, hugging him tight. Alek's eyes close in defeat, and the Unseelie at my back chuckles.

Rae's hands bunch in Garin's white and gold tunic, and she buries her face in his chest. His arms wrap around her, one hugging her tight, the other stroking her hair. He leans down and whispers, "I've missed you, my Rae of sunshine."

What I assume is a pet name for her sends her into tears, and Garin smiles, actually smiles over her head at Alek.

That arrogant prick! My body tenses with rage, and I

struggle against the Unseelie holding me tight. How dare Garin play with Rae like this? He knows damn well how much she loves him, and he's using that against her. I want to set him on fire. I want to stab my dagger through his eye.

But I force my breaths to slow down. *Wait, Asheraht. Be patient. You'll know when to strike.* I shake with the effort to hold myself back. Never. Never in my life have I hated anyone as much as I hate the king right now.

After a few moments, Garin takes Rae by the shoulders and pushes her back a step to look into her eyes. She sniffles and glances at the Unseelie surrounding us. "Garin, I don't understand."

A sharp, tsking noise clicks off his tongue as he releases Rae and walks around her, slowly moving toward Alek. "Brother, I am disappointed. Scheming behind my back. Sticking your nose into things you know nothing about. Spreading lies and trying to turn our sister against me."

Without breaking eye contact with his younger brother, Garin sweeps a hand out to the side where the invisible portal stands. "Who did you kill to open the door? What part of your soul did you have to sell to get to Earth?" He pauses, glancing at Rae before turning back to Alek. "I am grateful, of course, that you rescued our sister. But was it worth the stain on your soul? Do you scrub your hands at night, trying to clean them of the blood you spilled? Do you see their eyes when you sleep? Does the tang of their blood taint the taste of your food?"

He's putting on quite the show, and I find myself almost believing he's thankful to have Rae back, and that he's concerned for his younger brother's soul. But his eyes sparkle around the frown on his face. He's enjoying baiting his younger brother.

Garin tilts his head. "Or did you enjoy working the dark

magic? Do you find yourself craving to do it again? To feel that rush of power course through your blood?"

Alek lifts his chin. "You're one to talk of dark deeds." He jerks his head at the Unseelie standing armed and ready around the room.

Garin pauses, his beautiful face turning back to Rae. His dark eyes turn down slightly, and a sad frown pulls at his too-perfect lips. I almost believe Garin's pain is real as he says, "Rae, please allow me to explain. All I have done has been for the good of the kingdom. I did what was necessary after our parents' death."

Rae whimpers but stays rooted where she stands, eyes flicking between Garin and Alek. Garin presses his hand to his heart, playing the part of a grieving son to perfection. "I don't know what lies Alek has fed you, but I hope the love we had for each other and my continued love for you now will earn me the chance to explain everything."

She deflates at his words, shoulders sagging, and she wraps her arms around her waist as if she's trying to hold herself together. Her eyes dart wildly around the room, again skipping from Garin to Alek, back to Garin, then to the soldiers, and finally landing on me. Our gazes hold for a long moment.

She looks so lost, so sad, and anger courses through my body I grip my hands into tight fists and reach for my fire magic, but the Unseelie soldier presses his dagger into the skin of my throat, and a wet, hot trail of blood slides down my neck. My magic does not respond. I was too distracted earlier to realize his black dagger is made of shungite, the only material that nullifies magic.

Well, shit.

The few stabs he's inflicted would normally only affect me for a short time, but I suspect the mumbled words he spoke earlier was a spell to extend the effects. Who knows how long my magic will stay locked away?

Rae snaps her head back to her older brother. "Garin, there's no need for anyone to get hurt. I'm home. I'm okay. Let him go."

The king's eyes travel from her to me and back again. "Him? Don't worry about him, Raelyn. I know he was hired to kill you, and the New Moon Guild has paid the penalty for accepting that contract. He will be made to pay as well."

I stay stock-still even as my back spasms again, and my neck burns under the blade. Did the New Moon Guild survive Garin's wrath, or has he torn it apart and burned them all to ash? A worry for another time.

Rae's voice is a little stronger though her eyes are still too wide, and her breaths are a bit too shallow. She holds out a hand to him. "Garin, tell your soldiers to stand down. I'm eager to go home. You and I can talk. We can figure this out. Whatever you've done, it's not too late. Let me help you."

Garin cocks his head to the side, and a small smile curves up his lips, but it doesn't reach his eyes. "Help me?" He laughs, and Rae drops her hand, taking a step back. "Yes, Raelyn, we do have much to talk about." Turning back toward Alek, he starts to move again with slow purpose like a snake moving to a striking position. "There are many things I need to straighten out that I suspect our younger brother has misled you about."

"Garin."

The king ignores Rae's plea as he takes Alek by the shoulders. "Brother. What have you done?"

Alek meets his older brother's eyes and holds his gaze. "What I had to."

Garin stares back, and the muscles in his back tense ever so slightly. "What do you think you know?"

I have to give Alek credit. He stands tall though the king dwarfs him. "Everything, Garin. I know it all. And so does our sister."

Garin freezes, and the two men standoff. Then a too-wide smile curves up the king's face. "Ah, brother. You've lived with your nose buried in books for too long. You have convinced yourself there is a conspiracy that does not actually exist."

"Then how did you know Rae was stuck on Earth?"

"What?"

"How. Did you know. About Earth?"

Rae's eyes snap back and forth between her brothers, and she's so still I suspect she's holding her breath.

Garin presses his lips together, no doubt scrambling to come up with an explanation, and I want to cheer for Alek as he goes on. "How did you know the doorways were sealed? And how did you know they were sealed with dark magic?"

"I—"

Alek cuts him off. "And if you did know, why didn't you rush to Rae's aid as soon as you found out?" He gestures at the Unseelie around the room. "You obviously have access to dark magic. You could have opened the doorway and brought her home very easily."

Garin's grip on Alek's shoulders tightens to the point I hear the leather of Alek's jacket creek, and Rae takes a small step toward them. I try to tell her to back away, but my words are muffled and lost against the Unseelie's hand still pressed hard to my mouth. Alek winces under the crushing pressure of his brother's hold.

"Garin." Rae's voice floats around the room, but everyone ignores her.

The room grows darker again, and I know I didn't imagine it this time. But again, no one else seems to notice.

Alek's back goes stiff as the king leans down, whispering, "Oh, Alek. You were always the smartest of us."

Alek's eyes go wide with pain as Garin slides a dagger between his ribs. Rae's younger brother locks eyes with her and mouths, "*Run.*"

"ALEK!" Rae's scream echoes around the cave and down the passageways. I imagine the entire kingdom hears her cry of anguish.

The cave erupts in motion. I flick a throwing knife into each hand, punching one into the eye of the Unseelie behind me, dodging away from the blade at my throat. With his death, the spell to extend the effects of the shungite is broken. Now I just have to wait for the shungite to wear off.

I slice the throat of a soldier to my right. Blood sprays across my face as both men fall. Two more soldiers rush me, and time seems to slow down. As I release both knives, they find their marks in the throat of one and the eye of the other. I already have two more blades in my hands before they hit the floor, and I slice open the belly of another soldier.

The fae lights to my left go out. No, that's not right. They're swallowed. By shadows.

The soldiers pause at the sudden dimming within the cave but recover quickly. Several move in on me, and I calculate my attack while sneaking a look toward Rae. Tears run down her face as she stares at her younger brother, her grief closing her off from the chaos around her.

I swipe a sword from a dead soldier and sink it into the chest of the fae who lunges at me.

Alek's body slips to the floor in a heap, and the king turns toward Rae. She takes a step back, and he grins, finally showing her the cruelty behind his eyes. "I was hoping we wouldn't have to do this the hard way. So, Raelyn, what are you going to do?" He glances at the portal. "Will you run? You're very good at that, always running away from your problems."

A dagger slams high into my chest, missing everything vital but hurting like hell as I rip it out. I slice it across the face of one soldier, punch another between the eyes, and throw the dagger across the room at an Unseelie trying to work his way behind Rae.

The shadows seem to reach for her as she screams at the king, spit flinging from her lips. "I will kill you, Garin!"

I hiss in pain as a soldier slices his sword over my bicep, the same bicep Rae cut earlier. I throw a knife at him, but he deflects it. I swipe up another sword from the ground and block attacks now coming from two sides.

I have to get to Rae before Garin does.

Garin stalks toward her. "Not if I kill you first, *sister*."

He lunges, and I move to intercept, but a searing pain in my hand rips a scream from my lips. I drop the sword to cradle my hand against my chest.

Shadows whip out like black ribbons of silk and wrap themselves around Rae's body. In a blink, Rae is gone.

Garin skids to a stop with a blade in one hand, fire crackling in the other. He turns in a circle, and not finding her, he bellows to the ceiling of the cave. His magic erupts, scorching the ceiling, and burning the remaining soldiers to ash. It seems none of them were fire fae. Too bad, I smirk as the king's flames surround me but don't touch my skin.

Now. Here's my chance. I can do this for Rae. Bending down, I swipe up the tube holding Rae's arrow, throwing it over my shoulder and across my back before flicking my last two knives to my palms. I hiss as the steel presses to my injured hand. I still have no idea what happened to my hand, but I can't worry about that now.

Garin continues to scream his fury, and his fire swirls around the cave in a show of power, the likes of which I have never seen. It's impressive and horrifying. His magic is so intense that I start to feel the heat of his flames, and for the first time, I fear the fire of another fae. Sweat breaks out on my skin, and there's a painful tingling sensation that I'm unfamiliar with. I almost stumble when I realize it's the feeling of the fire against my skin. I don't have much time.

I scramble to remember the spell to fortify my magic and thus my protection against Garin's assault. I never used spells on Earth. I didn't need to. Thankfully, the correct words tumble from my lips, and the heat fades. I'll pay for that later when the act of spell casting drains my energy, but I won't worry about that now.

Both knives fly from my hands, and my aim is true as they fly toward Garin. But the king shifts to the side at the last moment, somehow sensing my attack. The knife aimed for his heart hits high, sinking into his chest with a thud. The knife aimed for his head slices a cut across his cheek before sailing past and clattering against the wall.

He rips the blade from his chest and runs at me. I know I'm no match against him, and I will be no good to Rae— wherever she is—if I die trying to kill her brother.

So, I run.

I blur down a passageway, hearing Garin close on my heels. My wounds are throbbing, and I'm starting to slow from blood loss. At the next turn, the tunnel begins climbing, and I notice the walls and ceilings are no longer smooth but made of haphazardly stacked rock, presumably pulled from the mountain.

With a prayer, I reach for my magic, and it flares like electricity through my blood.

Thank the Fates. The shungite should have kept my magic from me for much longer, but its effects have worn off faster with every drop of blood I shed.

I shoot a bolt of fire at the ceiling as I push my fae speed. Over and over, I slam my magic into the walls and ceiling as I run. Every burst of magic becomes harder than the last until it feels like I'm ripping out a piece of myself every time I unleash my magic. Finally, the passageway groans, and the ground trembles.

A fireball slams into my back, and I stumble but manage to stay on my feet. I throw a dagger of fire behind me, hearing it thud into Garin, but his pace does not slow.

I run, and my body burns. There's daylight ahead, and I cling to it like a drowning man reaching for the surface. I pull on my magic and hold it in my chest. I let it build until it feels like it's going to crack my skin and tear me apart. I gather even more. Gritting my teeth, I scream through my clenched jaw.

The opening yawns before me, and I don't simply release my magic, I expel it behind me. The force throws me forward, and I slam to the ground, cracking my face into the stony ground. Pain rattles against my skull.

Rock and dirt shower around me as the tunnel behind me collapses with Garin on the other side. I hear his muffled scream of rage.

I roll my eyes. Of course he survived the cave-in.

This is not the only way out of that cave system, and I know it won't take long for the King to find his way out, so I shove a few rocks off my body and struggle to my feet. Breathing is a chore, and my back won't stop spasming.

I emerge from the mountain and take big gulping

breaths of fresh Attolyn air. The castle nestles at the base of the mountain to my right, with the city sprawling beyond its gates. The forests spread beyond the city. The mountain range climbs up to my left, the tips dusted in snow. The sun has just crested the horizon, and the soft morning light blankets Attolyn before me.

I can't stop the smile that spreads across my face.

I'm home. I'm alive.

For now.

Now, I just have to find Rae and see if anyone in the Guild survived and would be willing to help me kill the King.

No problem.

I bark a laugh to the sky but wince as a fresh wave of pain sears across my palm. I limp away from the mouth of the tunnel and hold up my hand to see what the hell hurts so much.

I stop and almost trip and fall down the mountain as I see a message burned into the palm of my hand. It says, "Dorwe. Be ready."

The words are still glowing red, and as I bring my hand closer to my face, I smell sulfur. My hand feels like I plunged it into the fires of hell, but I smile. Rae is with Kemremir. He will keep her safe.

Dorwe is a collection of ruins of a long-abandoned religious temple in the far south of the kingdom, so I assume the Dragon Lord will bring her there.

I don't have the energy to blur to Dorwe, and without my fae speed, it will take a few weeks to get there. My back and arm are still bleeding so much that hot blood drips down my leg, soaking my sock inside my boot. Blood drips in a steady staccato from the fingers on my left hand, and I glance at my bicep. The cut is much deeper than I thought. I can see bone through the torn muscle, and my shoulder has gone numb.

The spell I cast to protect me from Garin's magic has worn off, and my entire body is shaking.

I need help before I pass out.

I look south toward the ruins of Dorwe that lie beyond my sight. "I'm coming, Rae. Hold on."

11

———

RAELYN

As soon as Kem's shadows unwrap themselves from my body, I fall to my hands and knees, landing in soft grass that is more blue than green. My eyes burn and not just from the seemingly endless stream of tears caused by the pain of seeing Alek's pained face over and over in my mind. The transition from the dim cave to blinding sunlight makes my eyes tear up for a completely new reason.

Blinking rapidly, I take a few shaky breaths. My heart is a riot of pain and anger. It's like I've thrown a giant rock in the pond of my soul, kicking up sediment that swirls through my entire body. My feelings are ugly and chaotic as grief, sorrow, and rage churn within me. It's hard to breathe around the image of Alek's face screwed up in pain, telling me to run. And Garin ... oh, Garin. How did I not see the darkness behind his smiles? How could I have been so wrong? How?

A soft breeze kisses my face, blowing my hair over my shoulders. Kem is a few paces away, his back to me.

My throat is raw from my screams, but I manage to choke out, "Where's Ash?"

Kem doesn't move, doesn't reply.

"Kem, you left him? Garin will kill him! How could you?" I take a few seconds to breathe through my anguish and panic before I plant one foot under me and rise on shaky legs. I grab his arm. "We need to go back. Take me back."

His only reaction is to look down and stare at my hand on his forearm.

"Kemremir!"

"I will not take you back. You are not yet ready to face your brother."

My hand is shaking where it grips his skin. "Then you go back. Go get Ash. Kem, please."

"I will not bring an assassin here."

My eyes snap up to meet his. "What—?"

He nods forward, and I look out to where he indicates.

We are on a small meadow on the side of a mountain. Even though the peak, which is not that far away, has snow dusting the rock and grass, I'm not cold. In fact, I'm quite comfortable. Bright yellow flowers dot the grass at our feet, and I follow their brilliant splash of color down the slopes of the mountain and the surrounding hills. A waterfall streaming down the rocks to my right creates a cloud of mist that holds a rainbow suspended in the air.

My gaze follows the slopes down to a valley where the grass melds from the bright blue/green of the mountains to a deep red. There are small houses of wood and thatch and vast fields containing all manner of colors of what I assume are crops. And far on the other end of the valley, there's a castle that I swear looks like it's made of crystal or glass.

Movement in the sky snares my attention. My mouth drops open, and all thought leaves my brain as I look out and up.

Dragons. Dragons in every color fly through the bright blue sky. A ruby red beast takes notice of Kem and me. It swoops, and I involuntarily duck as a blast of wind whips my hair around my face. It shoots back into the sky, climbing until it becomes a tiny red dot.

A silver dragon does a barrel spin as it sweeps into the valley, and I flinch, sure it's going to crash into the ground, but at the last second, the silver of its scales seem to melt like quicksilver, and a woman touches down to the soft grass. She runs a few steps to slow her landing then walks into the house on her left.

I turn to Kem, watching him watch the dragons. I swallow, wishing I had some water to cool my raw, scratchy throat. I swallow again and croak a whisper. "Kem. Where are we?"

His voice is quiet, reverent as he keeps his face turned up to the sky. "This is the Realm of the Crimson Plains."

I blink rapidly, not quite sure I heard him right. My mouth just hangs open, and I'm sure I look like a gasping fish as Kem turns toward me, a soft smile on his face. "Yes, Raelyn. You are in my home world."

"I ... It's ... I ..." Words fail me as my eyes jump from Kem to the dragons dotting the bright sky with their brilliant colors.

"It is not what you thought?"

I laugh, and the sound seems loud and harsh in this beautiful place. "Ah, no."

Not much is known about the Dragon Lord's realm.

Nothing actually. As far as anyone knows, there are no portal doorways to the Crimson Plains. Unless you are a dragon or in the company of one, you cannot get to this world. And no outsider has ever seen their world.

Until now.

Kem crosses his arms, stretching his black tunic over his muscled back and chest. "Let me guess. You thought it was volcanoes and lava, dark skies, and smoke clogging the air."

I bite my bottom lip, quirking my lips up in a little half-smile of embarrassment. I'm grateful for this distraction. If anything can keep the sight of Alek's lifeless body slumping to the floor from playing over and over in my mind, it's a sky full of dragons. "Maybe?"

He smiles and drops his arms to his sides before placing a large hand to my back, leading me closer to the edge of the little meadow. We both look over the valley. The sky slowly clears of dragons as they either dip down to the houses below or disappear over the crests of the mountains around us.

"Don't worry, most outsiders think the same of our realm, but as you can see, the Crimson Plains is a beautiful world full of life and color."

I side-eye him nervously. "Is my memory going to be wiped so I forget this place? I wring my hands and stare at the bright grass under my boots. "I mean, Kem, I can keep a secret better than most, but this?"

He chuckles. The sound is deep, dredging up thoughts of the earth rumbling seconds before an earthquake. His locs, tied back at his nape, sway across his shoulders as he turns to me. "No need to worry, your Highness. You are here under my permission and protection. You are safe."

My breath hitches, and my chest cracks open as I think

of Ash with Garin in that cave. "Kem, why did you bring me here?"

"The kingdom of Attolyn needs you. But your brother is too strong. You need training if you are to defeat him. It was foolish of Alek just to throw you into that situation. I was a fool to let him."

My back stiffens as I come to Alek's defense. "He thought we would have time."

A frown pulls at Kem's lips. "Alek knew how smart and devious Garin is. He should not have rushed you home."

I stand tall, crossing my arms over my chest. "He did what he thought was right." My voice waivers as emotion tightens my throat. "Alek was alone for so long."

I release my arms to hang at my sides as Kem places a hand on my shoulder. "You will avenge him. You will train here."

I open my mouth, but he stops me before I can interrupt. "Yes, you are already well versed in combat, but there is always more to be learned, to be perfected. Plus, it has been a very long time since you've fought someone with magic." He grins down at me, his teeth startlingly white against his smooth black skin. "Someone actually trying to kill you. Asheraht doesn't count."

I frown, and Kem chuckles. "Besides, you have never been trained by a Dragon Lord."

Before I can formulate a response, the edges of my vision start to tunnel, and for a second, I think I'm about to pass out from the traumas of the past few days. But then I feel Kem's shadows wrap around me, the sensation like mists rolling off a pond that tickle your skin.

One second I'm on the side of the mountain, the next, it feels like I've walked through a portal, but there's more of a sense of traveling within Kem's shadows. A moment of vertigo has my vision spinning before my surroundings sharpen. The shadows peel away, and crystal and marble surround me.

Without a word, Kem starts off down a long hallway, his black boots barely making any sound against the cream marble floor. The sunlight creates little prisms in the crystal walls as I rush to follow his long strides. We pass several doors, some shut, some wide open to various rooms, and I assume we are in the castle I saw from atop the mountain.

A woman steps into the hall from a room on our right. Her hair is sapphire blue and done up in an intricate braid that drapes over her shoulder, framing her pale face that has a very slight smoky-blue tinge to it. Her brilliant blue eyes drop to the floor as Kem passes her without a glance, but as she lifts her head and sees me, an audible gasp slides from her lips.

Kem stops and turns, looking from the woman to me and back again. She looks up at Kem with something like panic on her face. "My lord, an outsider?"

"She is my guest."

"But—"

Kem raises a single eyebrow, silencing the woman's protest, and he turns. Continuing his progress down the never-ending hall, the left side of which opens to a series of glass doors, I slow as we pass the most stunning landscaped gardens I have ever and probably will ever see. There's a wildness in the riot of colors within the carefully sculpted hedges, trees, paths, and flower beds.

Kem turns to the right, and I have to jog to catch up. As I follow, we pass a few more people. A male with short shaved dark sapphire-blue hair and matching blue eyes. Another male with violet hair that hangs in ringlets around his face. A woman with flame-red hair and eyes almost drops a vase of flowers when she sees me. The colors of the people, much like the realm around me, are brilliant. It's almost overwhelming. There's a subtle brush of power radiating from each person we pass, like the pins and needles you feel when your foot goes to sleep. But no one emits power stronger than Kem, and I'm not sure if he's doing it on purpose or if this is his natural state of being.

Each person we pass has the same reaction—a slight bow of the head to Kem and then startled panic, fear, or incredulity at my presence. But none question Kem about me.

My nerves are building to a snapping point.

Finally, after what feels like fifteen minutes of walking through a maze of crystal hallways, we approach a towering pair of carved wooden doors. Two armed women flank the doorway. One has shimmery copper hair and eyes with bronze skin that reminds me of cinnamon mixed with gold dust. The other has silver hair that brings tears to my eyes, reminding me of the mess back home—reminding me of Alek's silver hair floating around his face as he stared at me, breathing his last breath—reminding me of Ash's hair, rumpled and sticking out from running his hands through it so many times.

The guard has luminescent skin with a silvery sheen that reflects the light in the hall. The two guards pull the doors open in tandem, bowing with a whispered, "My Lord," as Kem walks through, and I follow on his heels, shivering at a low growl that rumbles from the silver female's chest. I'm positive that growl is meant for me.

I have a list of questions a mile long and can't wait to unleash my curiosity on Kem. The soft tap of my boots on marble goes silent as I cross onto a giant carpet that spans the vast room. The doors close quietly behind us, and Kem crosses the room, shrugs out of his jacket, and drapes it over a chair in front of a desk piled high with books and stacks of papers.

The ceilings are at least twenty feet high, if not higher, and the entire left wall is sparkling windows that look out over the valley. Being dragons, I'm sure they appreciate space, even in human form. A ridiculously large bed stands along the wall on my right, and a pair of doors close off whatever lies beyond the wall across the room. To my left, yet another door stands open, and I can barely make out another sitting area with a balcony stretching over the gardens.

Kem turns to me, rolling up his sleeves revealing thick forearms. I'm not quite sure what to do with myself, so I stuff my hands in my pockets. He looks comfortable here, like he belongs, and a tickle of a thought makes me want to fidget in place. I take in the room again, then look back at Kem. "Your rooms?"

He nods.

I wonder if all Dragon Lords live in the castle, but instead, I ask, "Is the people's hair and eye color their dragon's color?"

He tilts his head to the side in thought before answering, "It is more like their dragon's color transfers to their human form."

"Are—"

"I'm sure you have many questions, but they can wait."

I smirk to hide my desperation. I'm afraid if I stop talking, if I stop asking questions, I'll start thinking about how my entire world has crumbled. "Two more?"

He rolls his eyes and crosses to the wall of windows, throwing one open, letting in the mountain breeze that carries in the soft scent of lilac. He faces me, leaning against the frame of the open window, sliding his hands in his pockets, mirroring me.

He nods, and I smile. "Okay, so I assume not everyone is a Dragon Lord?" A single shake of his head is my answer. "So, how many Lords are there?"

"That is information I will not tell you."

"Fair enough. Okay. I get the feeling I'm not supposed to be here. Will my presence here cause you trouble?"

He lifts his hands from his pockets and pushes off from the window, striding across the room with more grace than a man that large has any right to have. He's not any taller than Ash, but he's broader. He stops a few feet from me. "You are safe, and you are no trouble to me. Word will travel that you are my guest. The rumor mill works just as fast here as in any realm." He grins, and I smile. "Though an outsider has never been to our realm, no one will question me."

"Your position is that powerful?"

"You are well over your two-question quota."

I smirk and he sighs, but there's a smile behind it. "I guess you will find out sooner or later, might as well be sooner. I am technically not a Dragon Lord." My eyebrows climb up my forehead, and I know I'm gawking. He presses his lips together before going on. "I am the King of the Dragons."

Luckily, the leather chair in front of his desk is just two steps away, so I drop into it, staring up at Kem. I think back on our interactions back on Earth and on the mountainside. I grimace, remembering how demanding I'd been with him. Ugh. But honestly, how was I supposed to know the King of the Dragons would come for me?

He shrugs, brushing right past that huge revelation. "I was planning to begin your training right away, but it has been a long couple of days for you. A few hours of rest will do you good. You will need it."

I clench my hands in my lap, twisting my fingers nervously. "Honestly, I don't know if I'll be able to sleep."

Kem nods his understanding. "You should try nonetheless. Are you hungry?"

I shake my head and push unsteadily to my feet, waiting for him to take me to a guest room or something, but he turns and starts to pull thick velvet curtains over the windows. "You can sleep here. There is a bathing suite through those doors." He jerks his head toward the double doors at the back of the room.

Darkness begins to close in around me as the curtains swish, and the closed-in space of the cave flashes through my mind.

Another tug from Kem's hand brings up the image of Alek's crumpled. But as the curtains close, all I see are the shadows of the cave and the stony faces of the Unseelie soldiers surrounding Garin.

Before Kem can pull the curtains any farther, I gasp through my building terror, "Please. Don't, your Majesty." He pauses. "Please. The dark. It's like the cave. I see his face enough as it is." I hate the panicky whine in my voice, but I can't help it.

Thankfully, Kem walks the curtains back open, letting the setting sun spill back into the room before turning to me. "Call me Kem."

I give him a small smile and nod before looking around the great room. I hug my arms around my waist. "You don't need to give up your rooms. I can take a guest room or something."

He shakes his head, sending his locs swaying like smoke-colored ropes. "You may be here under my protection, and I trust my court and the Dragon Council, but I do not want to take any chances. A stranger in their midst may rile all sorts of emotions. While we enjoy our human natures, we are, at our cores, always dragons. It is who we are. You will be safest here. Besides, I have some matters to attend. I will return in a few hours, and we will begin your training."

I nod, feeling small and alone in this vast room as Kem heads to the doors. He pauses with his hand on the knob, looking back at me. "Raelyn. I'm very sorry about Alek."

A sob bubbles up from my chest, burning like the embers glowing in Kem's eyes. I swallow it down as tears rim my eyes, making Kem's form swim before me.

Kem's voice drops to a low whisper. "He was an honorable man and spoke well of you. He loved you very much."

I have to look away from the sorrow in Kem's eyes, so I stare at my boots. Blinking back my tears, I refuse to let them fall. I wonder how my younger brother and the king of the Dragons became acquainted, but that is a question for another time. Instead, with my head still bowed, I say, "I thought the Dragons don't get involved."

He's silent for so long I think he might have left, but when I glance up, he's still there gripping the doorknob so hard I can hear the metal groaning. "We don't. Yet here we are."

"Why?"

"I owed Alek a debt and ..." His grip loosens on the handle. "And I think you are worth the risk of getting ... involved."

My throat closes with the emotion his words evoke; words so close to Ash's.

He quickly slips out the door before I can respond, and I'm left alone with nothing but my thoughts. Alek was right about everything, and now he's gone. My sweet, quiet, gentle brother is dead. And Garin ... it's like I've lost both brothers today on top of the knowledge that I will never see my parents again. My entire family has been taken from me in one way or another. And Ash ... I feel hollowed out with nothing but pain and sorrow scraping at my insides.

Dragging myself out of the chair, I shed my clothes, leaving them in a pile on the pristine marble floor, and take a long, hot shower. The water makes a pretty tinkling sound against the crystal walls and floor of the shower, and I'm soothed by the melody.

There's a gigantic walk-in closet off the back of the wash-room, but I don't have the energy to try and find something to wear, so I crawl naked into the massive bed, the mattress sinking and molding to my body as I curl onto my side, angling myself so I can see out the wall of windows. Pulling the soft, cotton-like comforter up to my chin, I let the tears that I've been holding back fall as I recall the image of Alek mouthing the word 'run' right before his body crumpled to the floor.

Garin's cruel grin flashes across my mind, and I shake my head, trying to shake his image from my brain, but my memories of him are starting to shift. Every time I came back from one of Garin's dares or challenges, whenever I returned from a new world Garin told me about, Alek was always the one to offer to patch me up, to help apply a salve or stitch up a wound. And I always turned him down, tending to myself as I believed Garin would want me to.

My breath comes faster, and my brows pinch together as I search through my memories of Garin, one after the other, desperate to find one moment where he showed concern, one moment where he offered comfort in some way.

A tear slips down my face, and I dash it away angrily. Not once? I must be missing something. It's been so many years, and I'm tired and confused ... I'm sure something, some kindness, will come to mind.

Memories take over my mind, like a movie montage, every reel highlighting Garin's indifference. I can't take it any longer. I'm drowning in my pain and loss, I need a distraction so I focus on Ash.

I have to believe he's alive. I can't accept the alternative. Somehow, Ash made it out of that cave. I press my fingers to my lips, reliving our kiss.

I gasp as a giant black dragon flies past the windows, scales shimmering like obsidian in the rays of the setting sun. As Kem dives, shadows trail his wings like curls of smoke. He skims over the valley before spearing into the sky, circling the castle.

I relax into the mattress as I watch him catch the currents, wings spread, holding him in a gentle spiral. A few other dragons dot the sky, but none as large as Kem. I track his lazy flight across the valley, down and back.

Ash would love this.

The bed is huge and empty, and I can't think of any time in my long, long life where I've felt more alone.

I imagine Ash standing at the wall of windows, his shoulder propped against the wall, his eyes tracking the dragons. I imagine him smiling at me over his shoulder, his silver hair falling around his pointed ears, telling me to get some rest—that he'll keep watch.

And surprisingly, when I close my eyes, taking Ash's smile with me, I fall asleep with the feel of the setting sun's rays on my face.

$$12$$

12

———

RAELYN

GARIN SMILES AT ME, *pulling me into his arms. His arms band tightly around me, and he smells like I remember, leather and charred wood. I sigh as his hand strokes down my hair as he whispers, "My Rae of sunshine."*

I burrow deeper into his chest. "I missed you."

His grip tightens slightly. "Why did you come back?"

I try to pull back, but he's practically crushing me against him. "Garin, what do you mean? Let me go. I had to come home." But why was it so urgent for me to come back? I can't remember. It's right at the edge of my mind, but it floats away before I can grasp it.

"It's okay, Rae. Everything will be okay. I'll fix it."

"What—?" He squeezes me tighter, cutting off my words. I struggle against him, confused as to why he's holding me so tight. He's hurting me. It feels like my ribs are going to snap. "Garin." His name slides from my lips on a strangled exhale.

Panic is clawing at my chest, and I plant my feet to attempt to pull myself from his grip, but my feet slip, and I fall further into Garin. Glancing down, I see bright red blood coating the floor.

My feet scrabble and slip again as I try to find my footing. Garin tries to soothe me with shushing noise. "Calm yourself, Rae. It'll all be okay." But I can't peel my eyes from the growing pool of blood at my feet. Garin's voice grows insistent. "Look at me, Rae. I'll fix everything."

Something isn't right. There's something I'm forgetting. It's right there, and I struggle harder against Garin's hold... and then I freeze. Alek lays at our feet, his sightless eyes stare at me as an impossible amount of blood pours from his side. He's pale, and there's no rise or fall of his chest.

"Alek! Garin, help him!"

My eyes snap to my older brother's face only to find him smiling at me. "Rae, Alek is fine. Everything is fine."

"No! Garin, please." Alek's blood coats my boots and creeps up to my ankles as blood continues to gush from his wound. Every struggling move I make creates a squelching sound that threatens to make me vomit. "He needs our help. Garin, please."

Alek's body jerks, and his dead eyes snap to mine. His voice echoes loudly through my head. "Run, Raelyn. Run!"

I scream as a knife plunges into my back, and Garin twists the blade with a smile. "There now, my Rae of sunshine. All better."

I'm wrenched from sleep with my scream dying on my lips. My legs are tangled in the sheets, and I kick wildly to free myself, both from the bedding and my nightmare.

I swing my legs over the side of the bed and breathe deeply. The details of the dream are quickly fading, but the terror remains. I roll my shoulders, releasing tension as I stare at my feet.

I take a deep inhale, hold it, then slowly release it. Again. And again. A charged calm settles over me, and I bite my bottom lip in thought. With a shaking hand, I trace my fingers over my lips and let the memory of Ash's searing kiss banish the remnants of the nightmare.

Yes, I'd much rather think about this.

The kiss had been desperate and passionate and electric and ... everything I always thought it would be. I can still feel his hand at the back of my head, fingers twined through my hair. As I recall the memory of his tongue sliding over my lips, my pulse begins to beat between my thighs.

I give in to the distraction, to these feelings, desperate to leave my dark dream behind. Laying back, I trace my fingers over the swell of my breasts, imagining Ash's touch, his olive skin and golden eyes framed by his shimmering silver hair. While I continue to trail my fingernails over my breasts, my other hand slides down my stomach. A finger hits the apex between my thighs, and I rub small circles around my pulsing clit. I bite my lip to keep my moan from escaping.

I cup first one breast, then the other. Scraping my nails over my pebbled nipples, I slide a finger inside my folds and squeeze my thighs together.

Closing my eyes, I visualize Ash looming over me, his features tight with pleasure. I stroke myself, keeping pressure on my throbbing clit as my breaths start to come out in desperate pants.

My head falls to the side as I imagine Ash threading his hand tighter through my hair, gripping a handful to hold me in place as he scrapes his teeth over my neck and up my jaw before flicking his hot tongue over the sensitive curve of my ear.

I insert a second finger, picking up the pace of my strokes as I pinch my nipple, then glide my hand up my neck to caress the curve of my ear. The pressure is building, and I can practically hear Ash's panting breaths synchronizing with mine. My back arches, my thighs tremble as they flex, and my palm rubs my clit as my fingers curl deep inside me.

The remembered possessive sensation of Ash's lips crashing to mine sends me over the edge, and I shatter. My inner muscles pulse around my fingers as my hips pump into my hand until my muscles relax into the bed.

With a sigh, I chuckle softly. *Well, that's one way to distract myself.*

Slowly, I pad to the bathroom to relieve myself and clean up. Coming back into the bedroom, I look at the pile of folded clothing on the chair by the bed. They were not here last night, and it's unnerving knowing someone came in the room while I slept without me knowing. There's also a platter of breads, cheeses, and fruit on the nearby table, but I have no appetite.

I pick up the clothes and get dressed. Everything fits, even the underwear, and I'm not sure how I feel about that. But I'm grateful to have clean clothes. The black pants are thick but stretchy, and the short-sleeved tunic is soft, form-fitting, but gives me freedom of movement. It's black as well but has silvery-green threads that match my eyes woven around the short collar and down the front. I lace up my boots and stride to the double doors.

The same two females flank the doors. The silver woman scowls at me before snapping her eyes straight forward. The female with the bronze hair greets me with a nod. "Lord Kemremir is on the south lawn."

I smile, determined that as the first outsider allowed in the Dragon's realm to be as gracious an ambassador as I can be. "Could you help me? I have absolutely no idea where the south lawn is. I almost got lost between the bed and the bathroom."

Her lips twitch, and I think she might be holding back a smile, but the one with the silver hair hisses under her breath, and I realize she does not like the idea that I was in her King's rooms. I need to walk carefully here.

The copper Dragon sweeps her hand down the hall. "I will take you. His Majesty does not want you walking the grounds on your own."

I bristle at that even though I understand the wisdom behind Kem's order. Leaving behind the grumpy silver Dragon, I fall into step next to my escort. I glance at her. "What's your name?"

"I am Syphe."

"Nice to meet you, Syphe. I'm Raelyn, or Rae if you like."

She keeps her gaze forward but nods. "Nice to meet you, Raelyn."

I smile, pleased at her friendly demeanor. That smile rips from my face, and I nearly jump out of my skin as an emerald Dragon screams out of the sky, shifting into a woman at the last moment. Her momentum carries her through the open doors on my right. She stops in front of us, hands on hips, her almond-shaped emerald eyes narrowed at me, shimmering green hair tied up in a high ponytail. Despite the anger radiating from her, I can't help but think how beautiful she is. Even in her rage, she glides rather than walks, and her every move is powerful yet graceful.

Syphe steps forward, placing herself between us, and the woman scoffs. "So, it's true."

"Ziza, she is here with the King's permission."

The emerald woman eyes me from head to toe. "I hope he knows what he's doing. Former kings have been challenged over much less."

My palms sweat at her words, and Syphe takes another step forward. "Is that a threat against our King?"

Fear flashes through Ziza's eyes before she straightens her spine. "Of course not."

Syphe keeps her eyes on Ziza, extending an arm back toward me, and I step forward. Her warm hand presses to the middle of my back, and I note it's nothing like the heat of Kem's hand. She steers us around Ziza, who pivots to watch us pass. Her voice spits after us. "Be careful, Syphe. Bringing an outsider here was brash, and many of us are not happy with Kemremir's actions."

Syphe stops so suddenly I end up a few paces beyond her. Turning back, Syphe's voice rumbles, and scales crawl across her skin. "Lord Kemremir is our King by champion of challenge, and you will refer to him by his title. And if anything should happen to Lady Raelyn while she is here, you will be the first one I hunt down."

Ziza's eyes burn, and I start looking for a place to hide if these two should start fighting, but she backs down, spinning on her heel before briskly walking away.

The scales on Syphe's skin melt away, and she turns back to me. "Sorry about that."

We continue on our way, and I force a smile to my face. "I suspect my presence is spicing things up around here."

"Indeed." She laughs, and I mentally high-five myself. It seems I may have at least one friend here. That's a good start. She leads me through a pair of glass doors onto a wide stone patio overlooking a long stretch of red grass. Tall trees line the lawn, and Kem's dark form stands at the far end, talking to a group of three.

Syphe holds out her hand, indicating I should make my way down the stone steps onto the grass. "Have fun." She winks at me, and I smile.

I take my time, letting Kem finish his conversation, hoping the three Dragons will be gone by the time I reach him. I'm not up for another hostile confrontation right now.

My fingers trail over the soft petals of white flowers that cover a hedge spanning between the trees. Taking a deep breath, I wonder again at the sweet scent in the air. I think that is the thing I'm most surprised by. I was sure the air here would be choked with the smell of brimstone, yet all I smell is lilac and fresh mountain air.

Ash would love it here. He has as much of an adventurer's heart as I do. I can picture him asking one of the dragons if he could ride it. The image brings a smile to my face as well as a pang of loss.

I release a breath as the three Dragons walk off while I'm still a few feet away, but they cast uncertain looks at me over their shoulders.

Kem turns to me, nodding. "Did you get any rest?"

"Some."

"Did you eat?"

"No. I can't seem to find my appetite."

He nods again. "You will be. Do not complain when your energy starts to fail."

I smile, cocking a hip to the side. "Me, complain? Never."

He tilts his head, looking me over before saying, "Okay. Shield yourself."

"Right here?"

He nods, approaching.

Right to it then. Okay. The air around me solidifies with my magic. He holds out his hand, and it slowly turns a glowing red, like watching a kettle heat up. Running his hand over my shield, the heat from his skin spits and sputters everywhere it touches my magic. The push of his power against my magic feels like building pressure that I'm sure will turn into a headache. He walks a slow circle around me, testing my shield from every angle, and when he comes back in front of me, he pushes toward my chest, and the pressure intensifies.

The air in front of me shimmers like a mirage in the desert. He pushes a little harder, and sweat beads my skin from the heat.

"Reinforce your shield."

I add another layer of air, and the heat lessens.

"Hold it."

I have a split second of warning as he draws his hand back. Sliding my right foot back a few inches, I brace, pulling all my magic in front of me, abandoning my back. His hand slams into my shield, and I feel the impact in my teeth. His fist burns brighter, and he strikes again.

My magic shatters, throwing me to the ground.

Kem leans down, holding out his hand that is no longer smoldering. I take it, letting him haul me to my feet. "Two strikes. That's all it took for you to break through my magic. And that was all I had. I wasn't even shielding my entire body. I was focusing on where you were striking."

He releases my hand and steps back. "You did better than I thought. I expected to break through on the first strike."

I smirk but preen at the compliment. The smile quickly fades as Kem's entire arm glows like iron in a forge. "Shit!" I throw out my arms, shoving a blast of air at him to create resistance against his incoming punch before I snap up my shield. I manage to slow him down enough that when his punch lands against my shield, it only throws me back three steps. And my shield holds.

"Good." He comes at me again.

For three hours, Kem tests my shielding ability, getting

through more times than not. I grow more frustrated every time I fail to stop him, but thoughts of home keep me going.

As many times as Kem breaks through my shields, his attacks never touch me. He always stops short of hurting me. I can't help but think of the many times, in the name of training, Garin would throw bolts of his fire at me while I tried to hit the target with my arrows. His strikes hit me, hard. More often than not, I'd end up in my rooms treating the burns, cuts, and bruises with gritted teeth. I should have let Alek help me. I should have done a lot of things.

Here, under Kem's training, a pang of longing pinches my shoulders together. Kemremir's care only highlights what I didn't have with Garin, and that knowledge hurts. A lot.

By the time Kem declares it's time for a break, I'm sweating and am covered in red grass stains. Instead of heading to go back inside, he leads us down a packed gravel path into another section of the gardens. Colors riot around us, seeming all the more brilliant against the dark clothes we both wear and the shadows that curl around his skin.

"Why don't the other Dragons have the shadow, smoke thing?"

He glances down at me, not breaking his stride. "Shadow, smoke thing?"

"You know what I mean." I gesture broadly at him.

"It's a trait of the black Dragons."

I realize I have not seen any other black dragons. But before I can ask, he says, "Yes, I am the only one. I am unaware of my lineage, and I do not know where the shadows come from."

I fall silent at the slight tinge of grief I hear behind his words. I recall his earlier words back in Arizona when he spoke of being glad I was not alone on Earth—that I was not the only one of my kind. I sneak a glance at him from the corner of my eye, but he seems as stoic as ever. Regardless, my heart hurts for him.

We turn a corner, and all other questions empty from my mind as a table piled high with food stands before us. He smiles down at me as my stomach grumbles. "Hungry?"

"Yes."

He directs me to sit then joins me. With a nod from him, I dig in, starting with herbed roast potatoes. The fragrant rosemary, salt, pepper, and cumin dance on my tongue with every bite. A few minutes in, I look at Kem, who's eating what smells like roast lamb. I swallow and set my fork down, staring at the meat on his fork.

He lifts an eyebrow at me. "You have a question."

I feel a blush color my cheeks. "I don't want this to sound disrespectful, but why do you eat cooked food? Why do you bother to be in human form at all?"

"We enjoy the duality of our lives. And yes, some do prefer to live solely in their dragon form up in the mountains, but most of us appreciate both aspects of our being. In dragon form, we are powerful and closer to our baser natures. In human form, we enjoy greater comforts and can form a more social community than if we were to stay in our dragon form." He holds up his fork with the skewered piece of meat. "When I am human, I crave the flavors of spice and salt and fat. When I am my dragon, no spice can compare to the hot taste of blood and raw meat." He pulls the piece of lamb off his fork with his teeth and chews. "Does that answer your question?"

"Thoroughly." He smiles at me, and I can't help but smile back before dropping my gaze to the napkin in my lap. "I appreciate the help, Kem, but don't feel like you need to babysit me. I'm sure you have many important 'kingly' things to do."

"Kingly?" The tease in his voice has me looking back up. His grin is wide, and his black eyes sparkle with amusement like obsidian under moonlight—so much like Garin's, but Kem's eyes hold ... affection? I can't be sure. I can't trust my instincts. He takes another bite. "A King must eat as well."

I smile but press my point, thinking of the confrontation with Ziza. "That's good to know, but still. I don't want to distract you from your duties. Training me is one thing ... socializing with me is another."

His fork clinks against his plate as he sets it down. "What happened?"

"What do you—"

"Raelyn, what happened?"

"Nothing really. A green woman named Ziza was not all that pleased that I'm here. She seems to think my presence could be cause for a challenge?" A quick tightening of his lips is his only reaction. "Kem, are you in danger because of me?"

"I am always in danger. Dragons are a temperamental race. You will probably be used as an excuse for a few who have had their eye on the throne."

I throw my napkin on the table, but before I can say anything, he holds up a hand. "Raelyn, I appreciate the concern, but I have been challenged many times. Obviously, I have never lost." Crossing my arms, I try to look stern, but he grins. "Welcome to the Dragon realm."

I can't help but smile back.

He pushes back from the table, standing, and I follow. "Back to training, then there are some 'kingly' matters I should get to."

I snort, following him into another section of the

gardens. Tall stone statues of dragons stand in a circle of gravel surrounded by high hedges. Each statue stands at least a head taller than me, striking fierce poses with wings flared or tucked, fangs bared in a snarl or open in a wide roar. Some stand on their hind legs, while others crouch on all fours.

I look up at Kem with a question plainly on my face.

"Now it is time to work on making weapons out of air."

A full grin lifts my cheeks. "I'm fairly good with weaponizing air."

He rolls up his sleeves. "I don't want you to weaponize it, though that is a good skill. I want you to turn air into a weapon ... a knife, a dagger, a sword, an arrow, a mace ... whatever you choose."

I practically dance on the balls of my feet as Kem sets me up in the middle of the gravel circle and starts walking me through how to create weapons.

It's much harder than I thought. I'm good at fashioning the air around me into shields or concentrated bursts, but now I'm asking the air to solidify into the point of a dagger. It requires all my concentration. The tighter I compress the air, the more it pushes against my power, like the air I've displaced to create a weapon needs a place to go, and it presses against me.

After an hour, I've failed to keep an air weapon solid long enough to inflict any kind of damage to any of the statues.

"No," Kem says for what seems like the hundredth time. "You are dropping your concentration right before it hits. You are focusing on the statue and not your weapon."

I release my magic, taking a break, ignoring the shaking in my muscles from the strain. I tighten the tie in my hair, my arms aching with even that small motion. I glance at the sky, noticing a small, puffy cloud drifting by. "You know, I could strike any of the statues with a bolt of lightning. No weapon needed."

He tilts his head at me, considering. "How quickly?"

I raise an eyebrow, silently asking permission, and he nods. I encourage the natural charge in the cloud above us to increase. The negative fields in the lower portion of the cloud collide with the positive fields closer to the top. It's a small, loosely formed cloud, and the charge is weak, but my will behind my magic ramps it up. My focus turns to the statue closest to me—a dragon crouching with wings spread as if about to take to the skies. Sweat beads on my forehead, and the lack of solid sleep has dots dancing in my vision.

The hairs on my arms rise, and my teeth ache, telling me it's time. I clasp my magic around the air in the cloud like snapping my fist closed, and the charge cracks, arcing to the ground. A spear of white lightning slams down, hitting the statue square on the head with a great peal of sound. I'm blinded and deafened for a second, and when it clears, I smile at Kem.

He at the statue, now cracked down the center, stone scorched. "Good. Very good." I preen at his compliment, but it's short lived. "But your target was stationary, and it took 194 seconds to call that lightning."

I frown. He timed me? Of course he did. He clasps his hands behind his back. "It is a good skill, and you executed it well, but we need to work on your speed. And if you have to wait for a cloud, well ... we will go back to weapons tomorrow in the morning and work on your lightning summoning in the evening."

I roll my shoulders, trying to work out some of the stiffness. Day one, and I'm already sore.

Syphe walks up, bowing to Kem and winking at me. I

smile back. I hold my arms up and command the air to form resistance as if I held a bow. I create an arrow from the air around me. I pull it back, feeling the wisps of air brush my cheek a second before I release the tension and aim the arrow-shaped air current at the statue to my right. The sneering face of the stone dragon transforms into Garin's face in my mind, and the arrow falls apart before it gets halfway there. "Shit."

Kem unrolls his sleeves and shrugs into his tunic. "Keep practicing. I must leave, but Syphe will stay with you."

He doesn't say Syphe is here to protect me, but I know that's why the bronze dragon is here.

"Your task is to take a single chip of stone out of any of these statues using an air weapon." He gestures at the statues that taunt me with their unmoving sneers. I puff out a breath and turn back to the statue closest to me.

Kem whispers something to Syphe, who whispers something back. I block them out as I concentrate on breaking stone with air. If Ash were here, he'd be taunting me at every turn. He would probably have sunk a blade of fire through one of these statues within the first few tries.

Syphe steps forward, unsheathing her sword, swinging it with ease. "Take a break from that. Let's spar. You need to turn off your brain for a bit."

I smile, sighing softly as I release my magic. Shrugging, I lift my arms. "I don't have a—"

Syphe reaches back, unsheathing a second sword and tosses it to me. I snatch the hilt out of the air and give it a few practice swings to learn its weight. Syphe raises an eyebrow. "Good?"

I nod, and we step together, falling into an easy rhythm of strikes and blocks. We dance, easily finding each other's patterns. And she was right, my mind turns off, and my body moves in response to hers.

After about half an hour, Syphe sheathes both swords, nodding at me with a smile. "That was fun. Maybe next time we can add in a little hand-to-hand."

I grin, rolling my shoulders. "Can't wait. Thank you, Syphe."

She tilts her head toward the statues. "Better get back to it."

I scowl, and she laughs as I turn back to my stone nemeses.

Hours pass, and I forget Syphe's standing off to the side, watching my increasing frustration. My world narrows down to the stupid dragon statues and their pristine forms, though time and again, I see Garin's face as I attack the statues. He is the one I am training to kill, and he is the one who is holding me back.

How am I going to move past this?

I'm startled by Kem's voice, and as I turn, I realize the sun is setting, and the shadows have grown long. His gaze takes in all the statues, still intact, but says nothing about my failure. Instead, he places a hand on my shoulder. "Enough for today, Raelyn. Dinner is in an hour. There is time to clean up, and I'm sure a hot shower will feel good after your long day."

I glance down, noticing my grass-stained clothes and how my tunic is dark with sweat. "That sounds heavenly."

Syphe falls into stride at my back as I follow Kem to the castle where they both leave me in Kem's rooms. I have no idea where Kem goes, but after my shower and finding yet another set of clothes waiting for me on the bed, there's a knock on the door before Kem comes in. "Kem, you shouldn't have to knock to come into your own rooms."

He ignores my comment, leading me to the balcony off his sitting room. There's a small feast on the table, and Kem holds out a chair for me. "I was going to take you to dine in the hall but ..."

"Ziza is not the only one upset by my presence?" I guess aloud.

He lifts a glass of champagne. "I prefer this anyway. No formalities. Just good food and good company."

I clink my glass to his with a smile. "Well, I still feel bad for causing so much trouble. But I agree. This is nice."

Though, I miss Ash, and I worry that he didn't make it out of that cave ... that he ... No. He made it. He's alive. Sure, I spent centuries at a time, millennia even, without seeing Ash on Earth, but this is different. Ash is out of my reach while I'm in the Dragon realm.

Once we've finished our meal, I lean forward. "Can you go to Attolyn?"

He tilts his head. "Of course."

"Can you ..." I pause for several long seconds, trying to figure out how to word my question.

"What is it you want, Raelyn?"

"I want to know if Ash made it—if he's alive."

His eyes narrow slightly, and he remains silent for a long moment. "I will not bring him here."

"I'm not asking you to."

I hold my breath as he considers me. His shadows lift from his skin like dark steam before they envelop him. He disappears for several agonizing minutes, and then he is once again sitting before me. I realize I'm still holding my breath as my lungs ache in protest, so I release a slow exhale as Kem speaks. "The cave looks to have been incinerated, and one of the tunnels leading out has collapsed. But I did not see Asheraht's body. I believe either he was captured, or he made it out."

I twine my fingers together, a pit of worry in my gut. But at least he's alive ... or at the very least, he didn't die in that cave. "Thank you."

His lips are pressed tight, but he nods. "Send for me if you need me, otherwise, I will meet you at the statues in the morning." And with that, he leaves me alone in his rooms with a quiet click of the doors.

13

———

ASHERAHT

I MANAGE to stumble down the mountain, my injuries, blood loss, and spell casting draining my energy. My eyelids are heavy, and my arms and legs feel like they are lined with lead, but I press on.

I skirt the castle, and my boots drag lines through the dirt path that leads me to the city. As soon as I hit the cobblestone streets, I pause, leaning against the plaster wall of a house, its neighbor pressing close, hiding me in shadow.

Every breath sends sharp pains down my back where the Unseelie's shungite blade had pierced me over and over. A spasm grips the muscles in my back, and I grit my teeth with a great inhale.

Scents of roasting meat and ale, balanced with the soft scent of rose water, float down the city streets and alleys. And under those smells of everyday life lingers the aroma of

Attolyn, of the fae realm—heliotrope, sage, and salt. It's clean and fresh, and tears fall unbidden down my face. I'm so happy to be home, but my joy mixes uncomfortably with anger and sadness. Rae should be luxuriating in a hot bath, enjoying a sensuous meal, and breathing in the air of Attolyn. Instead, she's on the run from the brother she loved and idolized, again unable to return to the home she has been exiled from for millennia.

My chest aches like my inner fire is pressing against my ribs, trying to get out. I take another deep breath, wiping my face clean of tears, and straighten, pushing myself out from between the houses and into the street. The morning sun has begun its journey across the city, banishing all but the darkest of shadowy corners.

The pressure in my chest lessens, and a small smile turns up my lips as I move deeper into the city. There is the tailor's shop. She never asked questions about the many cloaks and outfits I commissioned for my jobs as an assassin with the New Moon Guild. She was expensive, but worth every penny.

It still looks the same as I pass with my head down, wondering if the same woman still runs the shop. The fashion displayed in the front window has changed, but the store remains the same.

My limping stride strikes an unsteady rhythm through the streets, ducking in and out of shadows as I navigate the familiar turns. I pass the baker's shop where there's a line already down the street with fae waiting for baked goods. I startle at the few dark-haired fae standing in line. The Seelie leave large gaps around where the Unseelie stand, and uneasy glances slide from fae to fae. As I pass, I see a female Unseelie bare her blood-stained teeth at the Seelie standing in front of her, who hunches his shoulders and steps to the side to let the Unseelie step forward. A few chuckles ripple down the line.

As I move into the residential area, I pick up my pace. I recognize a few New Moon Guild members' houses, several of which look dark, abandoned, neglected.

What has Garin done to the Guild?

I keep my pace steady but make a sharp right turn at the sight of several Unseelie walking my way. They stride with purpose, backs straight, eyes forward, not at all afraid or worried at freely walking the streets of the great capital city of Attolyn.

Listening sharply for any signs they have followed me, I release the painful tension in my back when the sounds of their footfalls continue past. I glance up, trying to figure out where I am, and there, three blocks down on my left stands the white facade of the New Moon Guild. Its great black steel door is closed. The streets are still fairly empty, not yet packed with the bustle of the day to come, but those few on the street seem to press themselves to the other side of the road, staying as far from the Guild's doors as possible.

Should I attempt to go to the Guild now? See what has become of ... well they aren't my friends. Not exactly. Any one of the Guild members wouldn't hesitate to take another member out to gain higher standing. The higher your standing, the better the jobs, the better the pay. But I guess, in a way, they were my family. Besides the manipulations within the Guild, we protected each other from outsiders.

As I lean against the wall of the Arcane building across the street, I notice no one has gone in or out of the New Moon building. I push off the stone wall but immediately press my hand back onto the cool plaster when my vision tunnels and my legs threaten to give out.

I need help. If the Guild is still operational and if a

healer is in house, I can get patched up and, in the process, find out what's going on and see if anyone would be willing to aid Raelyn against the King.

Thoughts of Rae have my heart racing, which I know is not great for my continued blood loss, but the reminder of her lips on mine heats my already fevered skin. She was so tentative with that first kiss, shocking me into utter stillness. It was over before I fully registered what happened, and I knew she took my stunned response as a rejection, and there was no way I could let her spend another second thinking I did not want her. So, I had closed the space between us and kissed her. I kissed her like my life depended on it, and she kissed me back.

It was magic. So much more powerful than the fire magic that runs through my veins. Rae's kiss shifted the ground beneath my feet, birthed stars in my eyes, and seared her essence onto my heart.

Pressing my hand to my heart, I silently swear I will do what I can to see her on the throne because I love her, I need her. Attolyn needs her too.

To prove my point, an Unseelie turns onto the street a block down from the Guild. She's wearing the armor of the royal soldiers and is moving slowly in my direction, her gaze sweeping the street, the windows, the buildings, the roofs.

My hand glides down the rough wall, leading me deeper into the shadowed space between the buildings. Finding the darkest shadows, where even a noonday sun would not reach, I hunch down, folding into my clothes. I clench my fists and grind my teeth together to keep from groaning in pain as I shift so my bleeding wounds fall within the folds of my clothing and not against the cobblestones at my feet. My breath slows, and my focus sharpens. The guard draws

Only the desperate come to us anymore, and often with very little to offer in the way of payment. The New Moon Guild is on the edge of ruin, Asheraht. And you are that ruin's architect."

She's now right before me, her gaze traveling down then back up my body. "I—" Another spasm tears through my back, stealing my words. A few seconds go by in agony as Nyira just stares at me. "I didn't kill her. Rae is coming back."

Her eyes go wide, and her heart-shaped lips drop open. I realize my mistake too late, and Nyira scoffs. "Oh, Asheraht, what a fool you are."

I finally give in to the weakness of my body, dropping to one knee then falling to my ass, somehow remaining in a seated position, propped with one hand. Staring at Nyira's boots, I sigh. "Maybe, but her Highness, lady Raelyn, needs my help. She needs our help."

She remains silent, so I go on. "Gar—" Nyira hisses so I correct myself. "*The King* is obviously a poison in our kingdom. The princess wants to return us to the Attolyn of old."

Her eyes widen a fraction before she can catch herself. "She means to take the throne?" I don't answer, and she tilts her head at me. "And where is our supposed savior now?"

"I cannot tell you, but I give you my word. She is coming."

Nyira laughs, and I drop to my forearm as darkness claws at the edges of my vision. I wish they were Kem's shadows come to take me to wherever Rae is, but I know they are just unconsciousness come to claim me. "Asheraht, 'she is coming,' does nothing for us. We are fae. We are eternal. Is she coming tomorrow? Next season? Next millennia? We will not survive while waiting for your princess."

The last of my energy leaks out of me, and I fall to my

back, the leather tube across my back arching my spine awkwardly. I barely register the pain, which I know is a bad sign. Staring up at the ruined dome, a whisper passes my lips. "She will come as soon as she is able. She's worth it, Nyira. She is the Queen we need." I know Rae struggles with the thought of ruling, but I've seen her do it before, on Earth. She was a leader in Egypt, Greece, and Scandinavia. And she did each time with grace and benevolence, finding the balance between being firm but fair. Plus, she has the template of her father to work from. He was a good King, and Attolyn had prospered under his rule. Rae will be just fine.

I close my eyes as I hear Nyira step closer to loom over me, and consciousness leaves me.

I jerk awake as pain shoots down my body. I'm being moved. More specifically, I'm being dragged by two people with a grip on my shoulders. The hallway is dark, but I know where I'm being taken. The healers' room. Thank the Fates, because I don't know how much longer I can hold on.

Another spasm squeezes my back as I'm hauled through the door into the grey granite room. My vision is blurring again as we pass two granite slabs already occupied with patients, both quiet and still in slumber.

A scream rips from my chest but comes out as a moan when I'm placed onto one of the stone tables. Darkness takes me again, and I gratefully fall into the dreams of oblivion brought on by being back in this place.

Greer, a fellow guild member, comes barreling through the black doors of the Guild, stumbling into the gleaming foyer, moonlight spilling through the glittering glass dome, highlighting the marble floor making it glow.

I recognize the memory.

Greer's hands desperately hold his stomach together. Blood soaks the front of his clothes, and his skin is pale. This is not the first time a member has stumbled into the Guild headquarters, bloody and on the brink of death, so his presence does not send us into frenzied alarm. Instead, we move with practiced calm.

I grab Greer around his upper arm, helping him through the marbled foyer, the sounds of his grunts of pain echoing off the domed ceiling. Another member grabs his other arm, and we work on getting Greer down the long hallway, not at all concerned with the trail of blood we're leaving in our wake.

Greer passes out before we make it to the large room at the end of the hall, and I hoist his shoulders as the other Guild member grabs his feet. The room is cold, all grey granite from floor to ceiling that is easily cleaned and sterilized. We haul him onto one of the ten granite tables, one of which is already occupied by another injured member.

I glance at the body on the slab and recognize myself as the past and present bleed together in my fevered memories.

I ignore myself as our healer comes over, immediately cutting Greer's clothes from his body, revealing a deep gash in his gut that exposes his intestines. The female who helped me bring Greer in hisses at the sight, and I gag as we help the healer get Greer's boots off. The sound of his boots hitting the granite floor bounces around the room.

Without looking my way, the healer thrusts out his arm, a small bottle in his hand, following protocol. I take the bottle, its cold glass smears with Greer's blood that coats my hands, and I yank out the stopper to hold it to Greer's nose. The sharp stench makes my eyes water, and Greer coughs to consciousness, spraying blood into the air, which I barely dodge.

As the healer begins his work, a strangled scream rips from Greer's lips. I lean down and hold Greer's face roughly in my free hand. Anger bubbles in my chest, but I keep it leashed, waiting. "Who did this?"

His eyes roll back, and blood shoots from his wound, staining the healer's clothes and half his face. I shake Greer violently, earning a scowl from the healer, but I need Greer to focus. "Who. Did. This!"

I need a name before he passes out again, or dies. I glance over as two more members come into the room, looking to me for answers, waiting for the name or names of those we will hunt tonight.

It takes another few minutes, but Greer manages to grunt out a name, one we all know well. A client who has used our services often. He's a seedy merchant who runs several businesses in the darker parts of the city. His dealings often land him in hot water, which then brings him to us. The Guild does not care about circumstance, only gold. But to attack as assassin of the Guild, that is a fool's mistake.

I stalk from the cold room, turning my back on the screaming Greer with the other members on my heels. We don our black leathers and cloaks, strapping all manner of weapons to our bodies, and go out into the night.

The merchant screams his excuses, and it's like a song to my ears. Then he whimpers for mercy, and we smile at him. Then begs for death. And oh, the sweet sound of someone who has reached their limit. Our task is complete.

I wipe off my hands before reaching into the inner pocket of my cloak. Pulling out a stark white card with nothing on it but a jagged outline of a circle drawn with thick, black ink, I place it on his chest, and his blood stains the edges. Come morning, everyone will know the merchant crossed the New Moon Guild ... and lost.

My comrades and I slink into the shadows, and as I make my way down a side street, I stumble over a loose stone ...

I startle awake, and pain greets me. I haven't been out long, maybe only a few minutes, because rough hands are still settling me on the cold, stone table, and the healer has only just begun cutting away my clothes. I grip the strap of the tube holding Rae's arrow as Nyira looms over me, her face impassive.

I close my eyes against the pain and her relentless stare. "The princess. Please, Nyira."

I feel myself fading again, but before I pass out, I hear Nyira's voice. "Hmm. We shall see, Asheraht."

14

ASHERAHT

THE FIRST THING I'm aware of is a dull pain in my back. Not as bad as it was before, but small spasms tighten my muscles as my mind climbs up from the dark pit of unconsciousness. My eyes feel like they're filled with sand as I lift my heavy eyelids. Even the soft grey light sends tears down my cheeks.

The grey stone ceiling of the healing chamber in the New Moon Guild stares back at me. The room is silent, and I let my head fall to the side, noticing I'm alone, the door to the room closed. I'm naked and covered only in a white sheet atop this stone slab of a table. Fae light glows softly from each corner of the square room, and the healer's grey stone desk is vacant.

I grip the sheet, glancing down at my arm where the Unseelie's blade had sliced me to the bone. It's raw and red but sealed and mending due to the healer's attention. Propping myself on my forearm, I strain my fae senses, listening for anyone lurking on the other side of the door or anywhere near the healing room. There's nothing.

I fall back, sending my awareness down my body, assessing. There's still some pain, but it's manageable. My fingers rise unconsciously to my lips, wishing I could still taste Rae there. My fever has broken, but my skin heats as I recall her body pressed against mine as we kissed before ... everything.

I bite my lip as the sheet tents with my growing desire from the memory. I'm aware someone might walk in right now, but I can't seem to care as the memory of Rae's lips on mine has my hand dipping under the sheet, and I spread the bead of pre-cum over the crown of my cock. A quick glance at the healer's station reveals all sorts of bottles, tins, and jars, but I'm not about to lube myself with a strange substance.

Propping myself up on my forearm, I roll my tongue around my mouth, working up the saliva before I spit in my hand. Giving my cock another firm stroke, I repeat the process until my fist glides up and down my length imagining it's Rae's hand stroking me.

Fates, I crave her.

I'm thankful Kemremir burned his message in my right hand since I'm a lefty, but I clench my right hand, adding that bite of pain to the pleasure, and I exhale softly at the combined sensations.

My mind paints an image of Rae's green eyes looking up at me before she wraps her luscious lips around my shaft. I groan as I pump my fist. My balls tighten, the pleasure builds, and my thighs start shaking. I imagine Rae rising over me, her dark hair spilling around her shoulders as she slides onto my cock, taking me deep into her wet heat. Her imagined smile as she throws her head back with pleasure has another groan tearing from my throat.

Too fast, the pressure is building, pleasure tingles down my spine to my toes. I imagine Rae's breasts bouncing as she rides me, and I can almost smell her clean, sunshine scent. My thighs flex, and my abs curl as my other hand grips the base of my cock and squeezes while I pump into my other hand. With a strangled moan, I come, hips jerking off the table in an uneven rhythm.

Finally, I relax my grip, sighing softly as I use the sheet to clean myself up.

Holding the now damp sheet around my waist, I sit up, annoyed that the room spins for a few seconds. Once I feel settled, I push to my feet, holding the table for support before I shuffle to the built-in granite shelves next to the healer's desk. I toss the sheet into the bin and grab a clean one, wrapping it around my waist.

I cross the room with the intention of finding someone. I have no idea how long I've been out, and I need to see if Nyira will help. And if not … regardless, I need to get to Dorwe.

There's a soft click and a soft hiss of pressure as the door slowly opens.

"Asheraht, you need to lie down. You need more rest." The healer rushes into the room, blocking my exit, trying to push me back down onto the table. And damn it all, she almost succeeds.

"I thank you for your services, but I cannot afford more rest." Her practiced healer's scowl almost has me laying back down, but I grin. "Might I borrow some clothes?"

"Can you pay for them?" Nyira's voice bounces around the stone room from where she stands in the doorway, and the healer slinks away to scratch some notes in one of her journals. Nyira looks me up and down, and I catch her pause where my hand grips the sheet low around my hips, reminding me I'm still very naked, which brings to mind something else.

"The case I was carrying, where is it?"

I don't mean for my words to come out panicked, but Nyira catches it and smirks. "Don't worry your pretty head." Her drop to my hand gripping the sheet even tighter before crawling back up to my eyes. "I have it stashed safely in my room. Figured it was important if you lugged it all the way here. Plus, you had a pretty tight hold on the strap even after you passed out."

She licks her lips, a single eyebrow lifting suggestively, and I fight to keep my face blank. I'm glad I 'took care' of myself, otherwise, Nyira would have thought my state of arousal was for her. And before, it would have been—before I left for Earth, before all ... this—I would have led Nyira to an empty room and let the sheet slip from my grip. I would have peeled those dark robes from her toned brown skin, and we would have enjoyed each other for a long while, even with my healing injuries.

And now, even after all this time, I see it in her eyes, the longing. Her face is flushed, and her breaths are a bit shallower. She is beautiful. Her silver hair is bright in this dull room. Her almond-shaped eyes are dark, holding all sorts of promises. And she is deadly. I've been on the receiving end of her carnal pleasures several times.

Yet, despite all that, all I want is Rae's lips back on mine. I'm desperate for the feel of her hand threading through my hair, the scent of her breath against my face.

I keep my face passive. "Will you hold onto to it for me?" She purses her lips, but nods. I know she'll keep it safe until I can retrieve it. "And as for the clothes, you know I'm good for it, though I haven't been to my house, so I don't know how much remains. I assume Garin's soldiers ransacked my home and holdings?"

Nyira stiffens for a split second, and I catch the fleeting surprise in her eyes that I didn't move to her, that I didn't kiss her. But it's gone in a flash. "I hope you had some hidden—very well hidden—assets because the King burned everything. Anything tied to you is gone."

Well, damn. That's a kick in the balls. I have some hidden stores I'll have to check, or I will have to chance going back to Earth to collect what gold and weapons I have there. I have considerable assets on Earth, but their currency means nothing here, except precious metals and gems, of which I have a good holding. But Fates be damned if I'll be forced back there right now, at least not without Rae.

"I'm good for it."

Nyira lifts a dark eyebrow but nods.

"And I need weapons."

She doesn't respond as she leaves the room, and I follow. My hand trails along the stone wall to keep the vertigo at bay. My energy is already flagging. I keep stumbling over the long sheet trailing around my legs but manage to keep up with Nyira's fast strides.

"I assume Garin doesn't know I'm here. How long have I been out?"

She doesn't turn, but her back stiffens at the mention of Garin. "No, the King does not know you're here, but he's searching. We had to stash you in one of the hidden rooms when a full contingent of soldiers showed up."

Fantastic. Another line-item to add to the list of things I owe Nyira. Though I am grateful she's helping me at all. Her hand presses to the storeroom door, but I lightly grip her arm and feel her lean muscle tense under my hand. I meet her hopeful eyes but refuse her what she wants from me, instead saying, "Thank you, Nyira."

For long seconds she just stares at me before she takes a step closer, licking her lips. I feel the heat of her, and my body remembers the way we fit together. She whispers, "I have missed you, Asheraht. I was sure you were dead." She shuffles closer so we are but a breath apart, and I smell the herbal scent of the soap she uses on her hair. She runs her fingers down my arm, careful of the still-healing wound, and she watches with a small smile as my skin pebbles under her touch. "The Fates have brought you back to me."

Her lips brush against mine in the teasing way we used to have with each other before she presses against me and slides her tongue over the seam of my lips. The curves of her body are familiar, and I know they would be soft with corded muscle beneath if I were to pull her against me. But she's not Raelyn. Now that I have tasted Rae, held her, Nyira feels ... wrong pressed against me.

I step back, physically holding her at arm's length, bracing against the hurt of rejection I see in her eyes. She stares at me, wiping her lips with her hand before saying, "The Fates have returned you, but it would seem, not for me."

"Nyira, I—"

She cuts me off with a raised hand and pushes into the storeroom. It's still as well organized as I remembered. The large, rectangular room, about fifteen paces wide and ten paces deep, is lined with lockers and chests. Three long tables stand parallel to each other down the center of the room. A pair of black pants, form fitting but with several pockets and straps, as well as a black linen shirt hit me square in the chest, and I drop the sheet to catch them.

Nyira is rummaging through a locker of shoes, her back to me, so I slip into the offered clothes just in time to catch a pair of black-leather boots she tosses at me.

As I lace them up, she says, "You have only been out for two cycles."

Two days. It's not great, but it is what it is.

She places a set of knives on a table, each making a metallic thudding sound against the wood. I grab a sheath and a thin baldric, strapping the knives to the leg sheath and on the baldric across my chest. A quick rummage through a locker awards me a leather jacket that I shrug into.

In the space on the table where she had set the knives, she places two small silver vials with the New Moon Guild symbol sealed in wax over the lid. Poison. I tuck both into the inner pockets of my jacket and face Nyira once again.

"Will you help Raelyn? Will the New Moon Guild stand against Garin when it is time?"

A sad frown pulls at her lips, but it morphs into a wary smile as she walks around the table and stands before me. "I will speak with the Guild. I will not order them to move against the King, but ..."

"And you?" My voice drops to a silken whisper. "Will you help?"

She stares at me for a few long moments, her shoulders tensing. With a sigh, she nods.

That's good enough for me. I don't need to know her reasons, though I suspect at least one reason she's helping me is because of our past. The sex was really good. "Thank you, Nyira. I will get you payment for the healer's services, the clothes, and the weapons as soon as I can."

"And the cleaners. You left a great mess in the foyer when you passed out."

I smirk at her, remembering the charred and broken state of the foyer. My blood probably livened up the space. I nod. "And the cleaners."

Feeling a bit more like myself now that I have proper attire and am weaponed up, I turn and make my way down the dim halls, lit softly with glowing fae orbs. I grip the hidden handle in the wall that opens a passage to the alley behind the Guild when Nyira's voice stops me.

"Be careful, Asheraht. The King is furious with you, and the Unseelie are relentless and ruthless." I nod, tension gripping the muscles between my shoulder blades, and I hold back a wince as my lower back spasms with a twinge of pain. That damned shungite blade sure did a number on me. Nyira's intense gold eyes meet mine. "I can't promise any help beyond my own at this point, Asheraht, but I will do what I can."

"I will find a way to keep in touch. Thank you, Nyira. The Guild is in great hands."

"It should have been yours."

I grip her shoulder, looking into her sad eyes. I was Kade's third, and I did have my eyes on leading the Guild one day. "Maybe once, I wanted to be the head of the guild, but that was a long time ago." I give her a little squeeze. "What *we* had was a long time ago. If my very presence here didn't threaten the existence of the Guild, I would be honored to serve under you."

The self-deprecating, playful grin on my face coaxes out a small smile from her before she says, "Wait here."

"Nyira, every moment I linger is dangerous—"

She's already jogging down the hall, so I stand in the silence. No matter how many people lived and worked here, the New Moon Guild was always a quiet place, the assassins preferring to live under their practiced silence. Nyira and I used to bet each other who could sneak up and steal a single knife from the most members before dinner. Sometimes we would show up empty-handed with a black eye or bruised hand, other times we would spread dozens of knives on the table in my room. I smile at the memories until I remember the Guild is now a shadow of what it once was, because of me. If what Nyira told me is true, that less than half remain, that would mean our numbers are down to under forty people.

I see Nyira round the corner before I hear her, a testament to her training. She has a length of black fabric draped over her elbow and is holding a sword in a black scabbard. She holds it out, and I take it, careful to avoid touching her fingers. This was Kade's blade, the blade of the head of the Guild. I don't know why Nyira isn't wielding it, but I take it without a word. With a soft snick, the blade slides from its scabbard as I pull on the hilt. The hammered steel glimmers in the soft fae light, and I quickly slide it back into its home. Once, my goal had been to wield this sword as the leader of the Guild. I expected it to feel heavy with responsibility or that the sound of the metal sliding from the scabbard would sing with purpose. But now, holding it in this dim hallway, it just feels like a normal sword. It's almost disappointing.

She holds out her arm, holding the long length of fabric. I take the cloak of the assassins, tilting my head. "Are you sure?"

She crosses her arms over her chest. "Just take it."

I smile, wrapping the length of fabric around my shoulders so it hangs down my back. The folds bunch around my neck, ready to pull up over my face and over my head if needed. I finger the red stitching along the hem, tracing the shapes of the phases of the moon that travel down the length of the fabric.

Slinging the sword over my back, nothing more is said between us as I crack the hidden door open, peer down the alley, and seeing it clear, disappear into the shadows of the night.

My boots are silent on the stones of the alleys and streets as I weave my way through the city. I haven't been walking for more than five minutes before I hear multiple footsteps. This time of night that can't be good, so I quickly alter my direction. A short while later, a pair of soldiers turn down the street, and I duck down an alley and haul myself onto a roof via the cold iron of a ladder bolted into the side of the building.

I travel by rooftop for a few blocks until the space between buildings becomes too great to leap across. Sliding back to the street, I finally make it out of the city, and a glance at the night sky tells me there are still a few hours before dawn.

I'm itching to get to Dorwe. What if Rae is already there? What if she thinks I'm dead, or worse, that I'm not coming? But I tamp down my concern and impatience with gritted teeth.

I can't hedge all my bets with Nyira and the Guild. I was a highly sought-after member of the Guild for two millennia before I got stuck on Earth, and there are several favors I'm about to call in.

From my hiding spot in the shadows, I watch the house across the street. This is the home of my very first client, and he used my services more than any other client over the years. I have tortured and killed for him, all for exorbitant fees, but I know every skeleton in this man's closet. I created them.

As soon as the way is clear, I casually walk across the street and silently climb the white limestone steps. My knuckles rap against the solid wood door, and I wait. It is the middle of the night, after all. I'll give Endra a few moments to answer before I find my way into his luxurious home.

I count off the seconds, and just as I start casing the windows, I hear bare feet slapping against the marble floor, and the door cracks open. Endra's mouth drops open, and his eyes go wide with fear. "Asheraht, you cannot be here. The King is hunting for you. I will not subject myself to his wrath for you."

The heavy door starts to close, but I stomp my boot into his foyer, halting the door, and I step inside. The door clicks shut behind me, and Endra fidgets uncomfortably, his eyes darting between me and the door like he's afraid soldiers might break it down any second. And I guess that is a legitimate fear.

I stay rooted where I stand and cross my arms over my chest. The muscles in my back flex painfully, but the movement brings his attention to the blade strapped there. "I need your contact at the mine."

I didn't think his eyes could get any wider, but they just about pop out of his head at my words. "I don't ... how do you ... I ... I'm not that man anymore. I've changed."

The mine, an underground operation that extracts and sells raw shungite, is only spoken of in whispers. A smirk lifts my lips, and I let the old me, the ruthless assassin, shutter over my eyes.

I shrug. "Even if I were to believe you have turned over a new leaf" —I look around at his expensive house— "which I don't ... you still have the name I need. You will tell me where I can find him. Now." I glance around the foyer and wave a casual hand at the gilded walls, the plush rug, and the crystal chandelier that glows with pure fae light. "Or do you want me to let slip how you really came into your wealth?"

His already pale skin blanches at my words, and a muscle in his jaw twitches. "You wouldn't dare."

I lift a single eyebrow and let my magic flare just enough to lick flames along my fingertips. I stare him down until he sighs. It's weak men like him that make the best clients. They do not have the strength to do the dirty work, so they pay well for others to do it for them. And Endra has paid me very well over the years. His hands shake as he combs back his wispy silver hair over his pale, balding head. "Fine."

He crosses the foyer and walks into a sitting room decorated in creams, golds, and dark blue accents. I follow, letting go of my magic and stop in the center of the room, boots sinking into yet another plush rug, this one a cream color with floral blues and greens curling across the expensive weave. Endra leans over a mahogany desk and opens a drawer, pulling out a piece of paper.

Before he's able to take up the ebony pen standing erect in its holder on the corner of the desk, I stop him. "No. Don't write it down. No trail. Just tell me."

His hand pauses mid-reach before he pulls it back and stands upright. "Okay. But after this, I don't want to see you again. Please, I don't want trouble."

I just stare at him, crossing my arms over my chest. He sighs, giving me a name and an address on the far north side of the country, and my gut clenches. That is in the complete opposite direction of Dorwe. *Shit, shit, shit.* Endra puts his hands on his hips, trying to look stern. "Now leave."

"Know that if I have need of your position, money, or contacts, I will call again. You know I can find you. And I'll expect immediate compliance."

His shoulders slump, and his wispy hair falls back into

his face as he nods. I turn, and once at the front door, I stop with my hand on the knob, throwing over my shoulder, "Don't leave the capital unless you want to return to an empty home and even emptier bank accounts." I narrow my eyes until he shifts uncomfortably. "And if this address is incorrect ..."

His feet shift his weight back and forth as he continues to worry his fingers together. "The information is good."

As I slip out of his house and into the night, I melt into the shadows. This is the most dangerous game I've ever played—moving against a powerful, clever, conniving King. I unclench my fist and flex my fingers to release some of my built-up stress.

Two blocks over, I approach another client's house. I take a deep breath. This is for Raelyn, for Attolyn.

I hope she's okay, wherever she is. She has to be.

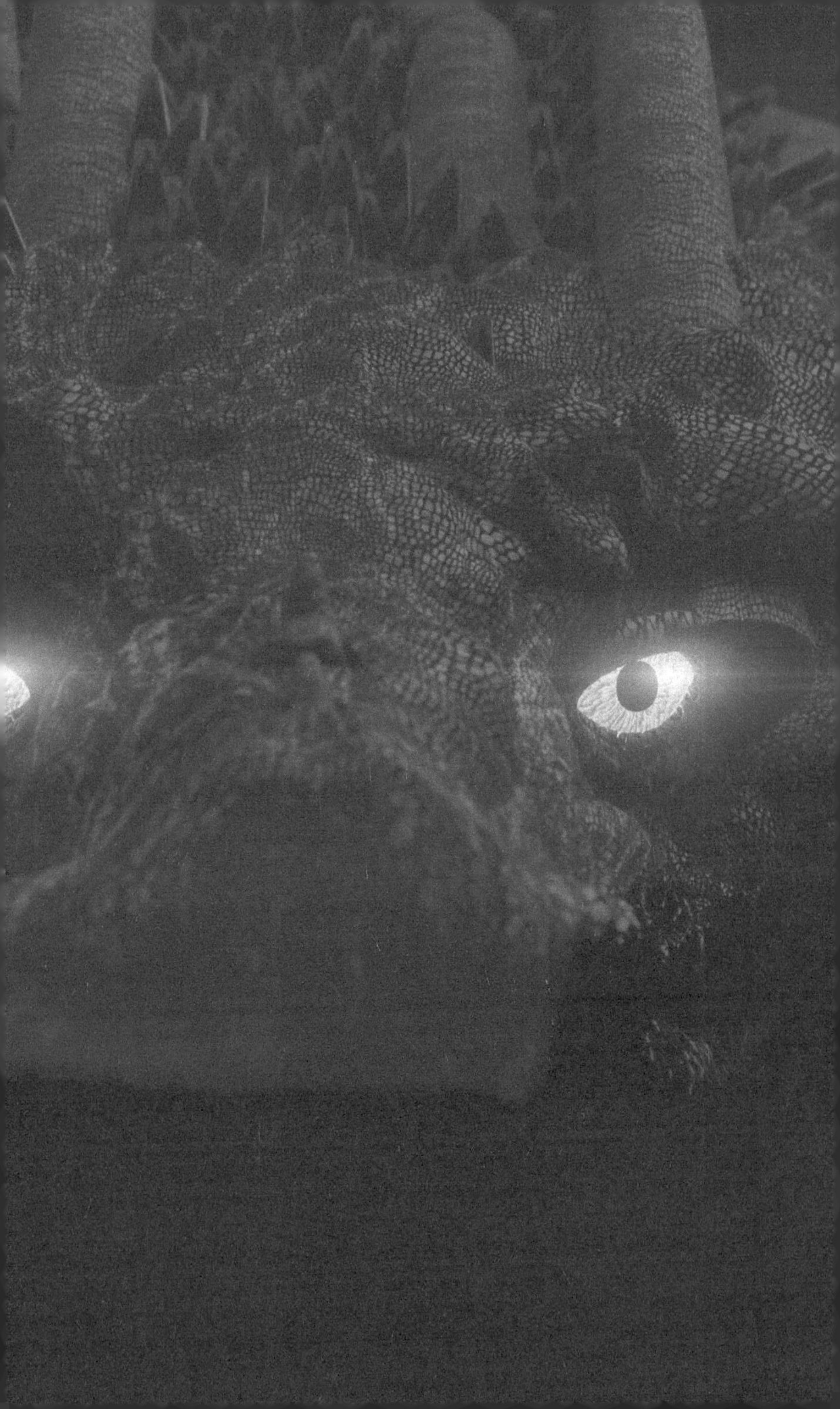

15

RAELYN

One day follows another, and one week bleeds into three. Most of my injuries from my fight with Ash in the desert have healed. That night seems so long ago now, and my chest aches with missing him. Sometimes the ache turns to anguish, keeping me up at night, tears soaking my pillow. Other nights, the ache turns to desperation, and I stroke myself to increasingly graphic fantasies of Ash until I'm whimpering his name with my climax.

My waking hours have fallen into a pattern of training, eating, and talking with any dragons who will speak with me.

As long as it doesn't interfere with training, Kem has allowed me to go into the small nearby village in the valley with Syphe. The first time I was met with looks of shock and a few of anger, but some had a smile and a warm welcome for me. The second time Syphe and I walked into the village, a man with short sunflower yellow hair styled neatly away from his face, gripped my hand in welcome with a wide smile on his face.

With a nod of encouragement from Syphe, I had allowed him to lead me along the road, my hand tucked into the crook of his arm. He welcomed me into his shop with a grin of pride, where he presented me with a host of mouth-watering confections. My smile grew with every bite as he filled the silence with stories and village gossip. He reminded me so much of Magda, the baker I visited as a child and who gave me Sidere, I immediately felt at home with him. His shop became my first stop every time Syphe brought me back to the village.

Today, Syphe and I walk the wide, worn path toward the weaver's house to pick up something Syphe had ordered. My skin warms under the rays of the sun, but it's tempered by the cool breeze that kisses my face, bringing with the light scent of lilac and snow.

I lick my lips, still tasting the almond and chocolate from the pastry I ate earlier.

Syphe pushes open the door to the weaver's, calling out, "Afternoon, Annra."

I follow Syphe into the house, blinking a few times to adjust to the dimmer light. A disembodied voice comes from the rear of the house. "Ah, Syphe. Good afternoon. I'll be right out."

"No rush, take your time." Syphe moves through the room, flopping into an overstuffed chair in the corner.

My boots thud softly on the worn wood floor of the open space. I trace a fingertip over the edge of a well-used loom, a colorful piece in the early stage of creation held tight on the front beam. Spools of every type of fiber in every imaginable color hang from the walls, fill baskets, and spill from shelves.

I cross the room toward Syphe, my attention glued to the wall behind where she sits. It's painted a bright cream, contrasting with the dark wood of the rest of the space. Beautiful tapestries hang on display lit with strategically placed lights. Some display dragons evenly spaced over a mountainous background, and I quickly realize they are family trees. A large tapestry in the center of the wall is a landscape, intricately woven to depict the valley, village, and castle.

At the end of the wall, built into the corner, is a tall row of shelves. My fingers brush soft fabric as I thumb through neat stacks of sweaters, cloaks, wraps, and other clothing items.

"See anything you like?"

I snap my hand back, turning toward the voice as a woman comes through a door from the back. Before the door closes behind her, I catch a glimpse of a cozy sitting area and a tidy kitchen beyond.

"Everything." Annra smiles, her dark, rich hair on the edge of red and orange, sways over her shoulder in a thick braid. I can't help but return her smile. "Your shop is lovely."

"Thank you, dear."

She hands Syphe two wrapped bundles, and Syphe nods. "Thank you." She sets them on the floor, settling deeper into the chair. Seems we're staying for a bit.

Annra flicks a hand at the vacant chair next to Syphe and I sit, sinking farther than I anticipated as the chair swallows me.

Syphe chuckles. "Annra refuses to get rid of that chair. I swear, someone is going to get sucked into it one day and be lost forever."

I laugh, and Annra tsks at us as she pushes back through

the door to her living space. "It still has plenty of life left in it."

Returning a few moments later balancing a tray with three glasses and what smells like sweet bread, Annra joins us taking the third chair which seems much more stable than mine.

Taking the glass she holds out to me, my fingers brush against her burnt-red nails. Mint, orange, and spice slides down my throat as I take a sip of the iced drink. "Delicious. Thank you."

She smiles at me, and Syphe leans over, slicing off herself a piece of the bread before sitting back and taking a small bite. I watch the two women while they talk quietly, catching up, asking after family and chatting about the weather.

When a lull in the conversation settles over them, I sit up as much as I can in the squishy chair, setting my empty glass on the floor at my feet. Glancing at Syphe, I ask, "How did you come to be one of Kemremir's guards?"

Syphe takes a sip of her drink. "I fought with him in the last civil war. Then once he won the challenge against our previous king, he asked me to join his court. I agreed, but only if I could serve as his guard."

"Why did Kemremir challenge the last king?"

Annra swallows her mouthful of bread before raising her glass in salute. "He saved us from that monster. He was the only one strong enough. Many dragons died in Challenge against our former king."

I shift in my seat, trying to figure out what to ask next, but Annra chuckles. "I see those wheels turning in your head. Let's just say his Majesty's predecessor was a dragon full of violence and brutality and ruled with an iron fist. He kept us oppressed under heavy taxes and strict laws about shifting."

Her eyes go distant, and a small frown pulls at her lips, mirrored on Syphe's face. "He declared it punishable by death for us to shift out of our human forms without permission from the King himself, effectively completely controlling us by keeping us from our dragons."

Annra shivers, and Syphe shakes her head, taking up the story. "Anyway, Lord Kemremir won the crown in Challenge, freeing us. That's why, to this day, several of the dragons choose to live solely in their dragon forms having been deprived of it for so long."

I run my nails over the arm of the chair, scratching against the worn fabric. "What happened at the challenge?"

Syphe presses her lips together, her brows pinching, and Annra slaps her hands on her thighs. "There's no need to talk of such dark things. I have work to do." She looks at me with a smile. "And you, my Lady, need to get to training."

I roll my eyes with a smile. It seems the entire village knows of my every move. My training up at the castle has become hot gossip.

We all stand, Annra collecting the glasses, and Syphe gathering her packages before we're lovingly pushed out the door back into the warm sunlight.

I tilt my head back, watching a few dragons fly overhead as Syphe and I walk down a side path between a few tightly packed homes. Their thatched roofs almost overlap each other, hiding the small space between the buildings in shadow. I pause to admire the bright, almost fluorescent blue blooms of a flowering vine that clings to the stone of one of the houses. I don't think I've ever seen a blue so ... blue.

Hushed voices reach my ears, but I keep my eyes on the flowers.

"Have you seen the outsider?"

"Yes, you?"

"Not yet."

I bite my lip.

"If the King is willing to bring her here, maybe it's time to bring him our requests again."

The voice is deep and rumbling, and a lighter one answers. "Perhaps. Though he was pretty adamant the last time we brought it up."

I fight to keep from wringing my hands together as a third voice joins in. "And he was right. We are safer with our borders closed. It's not like he's keeping us from leaving. We can travel where we please. I think the King is right in keeping our realm closed to outsiders. He should not have brought her here."

Before I can hear more, Syphe takes my arm and leads me down the road, away from the whispers. I sigh, and Syphe glances at me with a frown. "I do not envy King Kemremir the burdens of ruling."

I smile, though I don't feel it. "He is walking the tightrope between keeping his people safe and keeping them happy. It's a hard line to walk, and one I'll have to learn to walk as well if I become Queen."

"When you become Queen."

Her words yank my smile from my face, so I drop my gaze to my boots.

I ruled, several times, on Earth, but it didn't feel real. Each time was a blink in my existence. While I tried my best to take care of those under my rule, I knew, no matter what, they would all be gone within a century or so. Ruling

Attolyn will be ... hard. But if Ash is with me, if he wants to be with me, it might be a little easier.

As we round a corner, Syphe grabs my arm, halting my steps. I look at her and follow her gaze, finding a group of three people before us. The two men are literally snarling at me, their teeth bared, and the woman's hands have shifted into claws.

There's a brief standoff. I know I'm staring, but I'm trying to come up with the correct words to calm tensions. Syphe glares at the group, holding her ground, and effectively holding me in place as well.

Finally, after what feels like five minutes but I'm sure is only a few seconds, the three shift into their dragon forms and fly away with growls rumbling from their chests.

Syphe keeps a sharp eye on the skies as we continue toward the castle. I've been here for three weeks now, and this isn't the first time we've come across some hostile emotions, but so far, that's all it's been. No one has actually bothered me.

Once we reach the castle grounds, Syphe leaves me in the sculpture garden and before long, I'm sweating, my clothes sticking to my skin as I alternate throwing blades and shooting arrows of air at the stone dragons, doing my best to block Garin's face from my mind.

With a yell that tears from my throat, I focus on the blade I have created and watch it fly end-over-end as I release it. The blade slices through the air, creating shimmering currents, and as I focus on the dagger, I force my magic to the tip of the blade a split second before it slams into the throat of the stone dragon. I'm so startled, a grin lifts my face, and I'm ready to celebrate, but the dagger dissolves, leaving the statue scratched, but whole.

"Enough." I whip around at Kem's tone. He has shed his

tunic and his shirt. His skin seems to absorb the sunlight as he stalks toward me. "This is not a game, Raelyn."

"I know that."

"Do you?"

"Of course! I watched one of my brothers kill the other. I know what's at stake." Of course, I know. But I also know I'm holding back. As much as I want to let go, I still love Garin.

"I thought you did, but your heart is not in this. You are afraid."

His fist swings for my face, and I duck. "Yes! I'm afraid!"

I throw up a shield of air, shocked at the power behind his next punch. Kem's not holding back. He means to hit me. "Don't just defend. Strike me, Raelyn."

"I can't! I'm not strong enough." I scream the words, frustrated at the double meaning. I'm not strong enough to hit Kem ... I'm not strong enough to kill my brother. But Kem keeps coming, and I keep ducking and deflecting with my shield. I dodge a left hook, realizing too late it's a diversion. His right fist slams into my thigh, and my leg gives out, sending me to one knee.

I form a small knife with my magic and throw it at him, but he knocks it aside with his hand. He snarls at me. "Your people need you to be their Queen." He unleashes a ball of dragon fire at me, and it breaks against my shield. "You will do what you must for your people, for your kingdom." Before I can get up, he lands another hit, this time kicking through my shield, connecting with my hip. "As I did for my people." I grunt in pain and throw another air-knife at him that he swats away. "Let go of your fear, Raelyn. Hit me!"

This is too reminiscent of my training sessions with Garin, but instead of the self-pity that's been sitting on my shoulders, I feel anger. And it feels good. A sword of air solidifies in my hand, and I stab it toward his gut, but it's like scraping against a rock. Kem moves back a few steps. "My skin is dragon hide. You're going to have to do better than that."

He throws another fireball at me, and I fling a shield up just in time to deflect most of it. A few embers singe the edges of my tunic. One after the other, Kem hurls fire at me until all I can see is red flame and smoke. My shield cracks then shatters, and the next fireball hits my shoulder, burning through my clothes and bubbling my skin. Another hit lands on my forearm, and I scream as my flesh burns.

His next one is aimed right at my chest, and my anger turns to rage. Rage at Garin. Rage at my parents. Rage at Ash. But mostly I'm furious at myself.

My magic solidifies into another shield, scattering the flames, but I'm not satisfied. I revel in my seething emotions. This is better than the pain.

Alek was taken from me, and I was too stupid to accept his version of love.

I mentally lift my shield.

Ash was wounded, and I left him behind.

I turn my shield on its side like a large disc.

My parents were murdered, and I wasn't there to pick up the pieces. If I had been there, maybe I could have saved them. Maybe.

I press the shield's edge to a razor-sharp rim.

My own brother is trying to kill me, and I've been so blind!

I hurl the shield at Kem, thrusting my arms out, putting all my intent behind my magic. He stumbles back at the impact, and both of our eyes look down at his stomach. There is a fine line slicing up from his right hip to the top of the left side of his ribs. A thin trickle of blood drips down his torso from the shallow cut.

"Oh, Fates, Kem. I'm so sorry."

He just grins at me. "Well done. You actually pierced dragon flesh. That blow on anyone else would have sliced them in half."

I chew at my bottom lip, guilt at hurting him coiling in my gut. Kem reaches for his shirt, still smiling. "I am fine, Raelyn. You did well."

As he shrugs into his tunic, he crosses to me, holding out his hand. "Let me see your burns and where I struck you."

I shake my head, stepping back and hugging my arms around my middle. "I'll be okay. Fae heal fast. It's all part of training."

He frowns, following me with a step in my direction, hand still raised. "And part of training is making sure you're okay to train the next day."

I frown but hold still as his hand hovers over the burn marks on my arm. I keep my eyes on his hand so I don't have to look at him. How many times had I wished Garin would check on me after a particularly hard training session? How many times did I send Alek away when he offered his help?

Kem's hand shimmers with shadows before he gently skims his palm over my skin. I flinch at the pain, but it quickly subsides, the blisters peeling away, and the red skin turning pink. He moves his touch to my hip where he kicked me. The ache melts away and he steps back. "Better?"

I nod, finding the courage to look at him. "Yes. Thank you. I didn't realize you had healing power."

He nods. "Some. Enough to take the edge off."

We both turn at the sound of boots crunching on gravel, and the silver dragon that usually stands guard at Kem's rooms comes around a tall hedge with a smirk on her face as her eyes meet mine.

Kem steps in front of me, glaring at the intrusion. "What is it, Arvun?"

The dragon bows and takes a small step to her right, but when she lifts her head, her lips curl up in a small smile, eyes on me while speaking to her King. "A Challenge has been issued."

I gasp. Kem doesn't react at all, his face impassive as he asks, "Who issued the Challenge?"

"Ziza." I recall the stunning woman with the green hair and eyes filled with scorn all aimed at me.

Kem frowns. "That is uncharacteristically brash of her. Her power is nowhere strong enough to best mine. I will give her the chance to withdraw."

The silver dragon's smile widens, eyes still on me. "She did not Challenge you, my King."

My eyes go wide at her insinuation. Kem barks, "No. We do not Challenge outsiders."

"We also don't bring outsiders to our realm, ... your Majesty."

Kem stands stock still, the clenching of his jaw muscles the only indication of his anger. After a few long, silent minutes, he turns to me, and I see it in his eyes.

From my time in the village, I've learned that the rite of Challenge is a tradition that goes back to the beginning of the dragon people's history.

I think I'm going to have to fight a dragon.

16

RAELYN

KEM GLANCES over his shoulder then turns back to me. "I'll be right back."

He storms off toward the castle, and I fidget in place for a few minutes that turn into half an hour. I can't stay here. Alone. I feel exposed. Raw.

I turn away from the castle. Picking up my pace, I practically jog through the gardens, barely registering the light scent of the blue and yellow flowers lining the path. The soft buzz of insects hums through the air, competing with the hum of adrenaline coursing through my body.

My boots leave the crunch of the gravel behind and fall silent against the thick red grass now underfoot as I leave the castle grounds. Climbing a small rise, I stop, wrapping my arms around my middle.

"Raelyn!" I close my eyes as Syphe jogs up behind me,

stopping at my side. She's silent for a moment before asking, "Are you okay?"

I shrug. "I have to be, don't I?"

"Raelyn, I—"

"Any tips on how to keep Ziza from killing me?"

I catch her frown from the corner of my eye. "Kill her first."

My heart skips a beat, but I smirk to hide my utter lack of confidence in myself. "Sure."

She faces me, but I avoid eye contact. Instead, I look forward, watching as grey clouds slowly move in with the scent of rain. Syphe reaches out, grabbing my arm to turn me toward her. "I'm serious, Raelyn. You have to kill her, and as quickly as possible. She is stronger than you, and she'll wear you down. She'll play with you, make an example of you."

I hear it in her voice, the sadness. She knows I can't win. So do I, so I don't respond.

The village is just over the slight ridge in front of us, and the top half of the castle peeks over the hill behind us. Rain starts to fall, and the scales of the few dragons flying overhead shimmer, making their colors more intense, more alive. One by one, the dragons fly off, leaving the sky a depressing grey without their bright colors. But a single dragon remains. It's bright red, and I imagine it's dancing in the rain as it circles, loops, and dives above us.

We stand there for several minutes in silence when I notice the red dragon is coming closer. I expect it to veer toward the village or the castle, but its course doesn't shift, and Syphe tenses.

She wraps an arm around my waist and shifts me behind her, just as the red dragon lands before us. The ground shakes like an avalanche at its impact, and a gust of wind from its wings sends me back a step. Its molten eyes bore into us, and Syphe's back stiffens, her hands spread like claws, and her bronze nails rend the air at her sides.

The red dragon flicks its tail, and I'm thrown to the side as Syphe shoves me. I land hard, a rock digging into my hip, and I mutter, "I just can't catch a break."

The dragon's tail slams against the ground where I was just standing, tearing grass from the earth. When I pick myself up, I find myself staring at two dragons. Syphe has shifted, and her copper-scaled body glimmers in the rain, her arched wings spread to shield me. Smoke curls from her nostrils, and her talons shred deep grooves in the ground. Her voice rumbles from her glowing chest, and it's much deeper and older sounding than her human voice. "Orsun, you would dare attack a guest of the King?"

The red dragon's forked tongue flicks between his razor-sharp teeth, and a smile curves up his long snout revealing even more of those teeth. "The King dared bring an outsider into our realm."

"You court death with your actions."

"You betray your kind by standing with this ... fae." Orsun locks eyes with Syphe. "Besides, I'm not here for her, I am here for you, traitor. You parade her around the castle and our village." He nods his massive head in my direction. "You protect *her*."

My magic fills me. My skin prickles with the power, and my hair starts to lift and blow softly. Anger, hot and trembling, courses through me, and I feed it, relishing the power of rage. Syphe was my first friend here, and I will not let this dragon hurt her on my account.

Syphe holds her ground, and Orsun sneers, the sound a long, steamy hiss. "Your fae friend thinks to use her paltry magic to help you." A grin that's more snarl than smile lifts the red dragon's lips. "I will teach you a lesson, Syphe, then I'll take care of this ... intruder."

I clench my fists, taking one shaking step toward Orsun, drawing the dragon's gaze to me. "We'll see." It is a stupid thing to say, but I see Alek's face and how much he believed in me. I see Garin's cruel smile and the sneers of the Unseelie soldiers. I remember Kem's words, 'You are worth the risk'. And I see Ash's face a breath away from mine, his eyes asking, hoping that I will see him and not just the assassin. I feel his lips on mine, desperate, hopeful.

Orsun lunges, and Syphe leaps on the red dragon. I dive to the side to avoid Orsun's tail as it swings at my head. I roll and crawl out of the way as they claw and snap at each other. The noise is deafening. Syphe rips her talons down Orsun's back, and four red lines tear across his scales, revealing blood and muscle. Orsun bellows and unleashes his dragon fire. It hits Syphe along her right side, like lava hitting earth, it smokes and spits, dripping from her scales. Dragon fire darkens and chars her hide as the flames slide to the ground, burning the grass and scorching the dirt. The air fills with the acrid scent of brimstone, and I back up even farther, wrapping a shield of air around myself. This is like nothing I've ever witnessed.

As I watch, Orsun sinks his talons into Syphe's hip, holding her down. Syphe screams, and Orsun pushes her back, slamming his back claws into Syphe's gut. Blood and fire leak from the wounds as Syphe struggles. Her great tail lashes out, striking Orsun so hard in the head, the red dragon is thrown back, and his talons rip from Syphe's hide.

Syphe rises, barely holding weight on her back leg. I can't hold a shield around myself and help Syphe at the same time, so I release my shield and concentrate on her wounds, sealing the cuts and tears with a solid layer of air and bracing her leg as much as I can.

Syphe glances at me with a quick nod of thanks, but that small mistake leaves her open to Orsun, who snaps his powerful jaws around Syphe's neck. I scream at Syphe's roar of pain, and my magic explodes from me in an angry torrent of freezing air. The rain turns to ice, and the sharp shards ping against the dragons' scales.

Orsun's jaw tightens, and Syphe's eyes widen in pain as she scrambles to find purchase on Orsun's hide to push him off. My magic swells and grows until it fills the air around us. My heartbeat slows, and my skin tingles. My magic feels wild, untamable, but I reach down inside myself and gather it, tighter and tighter, holding it within the fist of my control. It resists. It wants to rend and tear and destroy. I whisper to it, *Don't worry, I'm not caging you. I'm unleashing you*—I lift my gaze to Orsun and meet his red eyes—*at him*.

With my silent command, my magic hurls itself at Orsun, hungry and desperate. I throw my arms out, shoving my power down his throat and nostrils until my magic coats his insides. I hold it as I slowly stride toward the two dragons. I will not let Orsun kill my friend. I will not die here today. My first kiss with Ash will not be my last.

Syphe stills. Her breathing is shallow, but her eyes track me as I face Orsun. I look up and up and up until I meet Orsun's ruby eyes, and I tighten that bubble of air I've lodged in his gut. Smoke coughs from his mouth, and when he tries to take a breath, it gets stuck. He releases Syphe and claws at his throat, but I just shrink that bubble of air and squeeze. His eyes go wide. He stumbles back and falls onto his hindquarters. Deep gashes tear through the grass as he claws at anything and everything in his panic to breathe.

I smile. Years of fighting Ash has taught me some valuable lessons. "You are a being of fire. You know what fire needs to survive?" Orsun's form collapses, shrinking until a man sits before me. His red hair sticks to his face with the sweat beading his skin. His red nails claw at his throat as he watches me approach. I lift a hand and twirl my fingers, sending a small current of air swirling around my face, lifting my hair off my shoulders. "Air. Fire needs air. And I've cut you off."

Smoke is now pouring from his mouth and nostrils and even leaks from his ears as I smother his dragon's flame. Panic widens his eyes until they are more white than red. Yes, I *am* powerful. I've brought this mighty, arrogant dragon to heel. He collapses onto his side, and his struggles weaken as the heart of his dragon slowly dies under the assault of my magic. I wonder if I kill the dragon in his soul, will the man die as well? I imagine so.

But then I make yet another stupid mistake. I smile at him, at his pain, at his panic.

His eyes narrow, and a single word gasps from his lips. "No."

With a growl that I feel all the way to my toes, his dragon form erupts, and a great clawed paw swipes at me, hitting me in the chest full force, rending a deep gash across my stomach and snapping several ribs. I'm sent flying through the air and land with a crushing thud, my head slamming into the ground. I see stars as Syphe cries out. The pain is intense, but when I draw in a breath to scream, the air stutters in my chest. I think one of my lungs has been punctured. My vision tunnels as Orson, now released from my magic, leaps at me. Syphe lunges between us and curls herself around me, baring her teeth and growling.

Everything goes dark, and a roar resounds around me, the sound so loud and fearsome it shakes the ground and rattles my teeth. There is a wet crunch close by, and then the darkness pulls back.

Every breath is a struggle, and pain threatens to drag me into unconsciousness, but the sight before me grounds me. A giant black dragon stands over us. He's so large he's practically blocking out the entire sky. Kemremir stands over Orsun's dragon body. The red dragon's neck has several deep puncture marks, and his head is tilted at an odd angle. Kem's ember eyes meet mine, and I try to stand but immediately fall back. A hand wraps around my upper arm, and Syphe is there, back in her human form, helping me to my feet. Her breaths are shallow, and pain pinches the edges of her eyes, but she whispers, "Are you okay?"

I glance at her, taking in the blood dripping from her wounds, coating her skin. "Are you?"

She's cut off from answering at Kem's deep voice. "I need to get Lady Raelyn back to the castle." And with that, before I can process what is happening, Kem folds his wings around Syphe and me like a giant cocoon, and his shadows tickle my skin. The sensation of being pulled forward tugs at my body, then we land in Kem's rooms, and as his shadows dissolve, he is back in his human form. He takes a step toward me, gently taking me from Syphe's grip.

Keeping his eyes on me, he says to Syphe, "I am sorry for what happened, my friend. Thank you for protecting her."

She grins at me despite her many wounds. "I was actually Orsun's target. He had me in his jaws. Lady Raelyn saved me."

Kem's eyes never leave me, assessing my injuries, which are becoming more painful by the second. He nods, seeing the pain in my eyes. "Then I thank you, Rae, for saving one of my own." He has only used my nickname a few times, but this time feels more.

Syphe bows, holding a hand to her side. "I will go to my rooms with your leave."

Kem looks her over. "I can call the healer for you. I want you looked after."

My heart squeezes at his desire to see someone in his service taken care of. He is fierce, protective, terrifying, strong, but kind, and gentle, and caring.

Syphe bows again. "I thank you, my King, but my mate has some healing ability. He will take care of me."

Kem nods, bringing his attention back to me as he dismisses her. "Thank you again, Syphe. Rest well."

The doors close softly behind her limping form, and Kem and I are alone. I realize how tired I am, and I go to take a deep breath but falter, my ribs stabbing pain through my chest, and Kem picks me up. His hold is gentle, but I still hiss in agony.

We leave the receiving area and pass into the bedroom, and though he is holding me as gently as possible, pain is still radiating through my entire body with every breath. I grip Kem's shirt as my stomach burns where Orsun's claw caught me.

Kem pauses. "Am I hurting you?"

"No. No. It's just. I'm a big ball of pain right now. I don't think it's possible for me not to hurt right now. But I'll be okay. I'll heal. In fact, if you point me in the direction of the healer's chamber, I'll deposit myself in their care."

His eyes skim over me again, and a frown pulls at his lips. "You are my responsibility. I will see that you are taken care of." My brows furrow in confusion, so he says, "I'm not comfortable allowing you around others right now."

I keep my breaths shallow as he carefully sets me on my feet. "Surely you trust your healer."

He nods, but a frown still pulls at his lips. "Yes, of course

I trust him, but right now, I'm finding it very hard to trust anyone with you." He helps me sit on the edge of the bed before stepping back and running a hand over his face. "My dragon is feeling very protective right now."

I curl my lips between my teeth before taking a short, painful breath. Two strides bring him back to me, and he kneels, placing his hands on the bed on either side of my hips. "I am so sorry for what happened."

There's such pain and guilt on his face. I grip his left hand. "It's not your fault."

"But it is. I should not have brought you here. I will find a suitable realm to take you to finish your training. You are not safe here."

"Why *did* you bring me here?"

"I knew Garin would not be able to follow."

My strength is failing, and I just want to lay down and sleep for days, but something in Kem's eyes makes me ask, "Why did you *really* bring me here?"

He's silent for a while, staring at our joined hands. "I wanted someone to know. I wanted someone to see the beauty of our realm. I just ... I wanted you to see my home."

His words, his trust in me, brings tears to my eyes, but I blink them back and nod. "Thank you. I'm honored. It is beautiful here."

He looks down at me, taking in my wounds. "The beauty of my lands has been marred by the violence committed against you. I am ashamed of my people."

I give his hand a squeeze. "It was one dragon." I think of Ziza and her challenge. "Okay, two." He frowns, but I attempt a smile. "I'm still glad you brought me here."

I can't hold back a wince as I take in another shaky breath. I glance down, taking in my torn and dirty clothing. I can't see the gash in my stomach, but I sure can feel it. "As much as I'd like to just pass out, I need to clean up."

Without a word, he carefully scoops me up and takes me to the bathing room. He holds me gently as he turns on the shower and sets out several towels. Kem sets me on a chair near the counter before placing his hand on mine where it rests on my thigh. "I'll be right back." The corner of his mouth lifts in a small smile. "Don't wander off this time."

I grin, nodding. He strides from the bathroom, returns with some clothes, and sets them next to the towels on the counter. One is a stretchy top, similar to a sports bra but looks like it wraps, so I won't have to pull it over my head. The other is a loose pair of silky-looking shorts.

He glances at me, his frown still in place, and I swallow my pain to smile at him. "Thank you. I'll manage."

"Let me see to your injuries. I'll heal what I can. Then you can shower as long as you'd like."

Kem helps me off the counter, and I manage to get my pants off, using the counter for support. The thought of lifting my arms to take off my shirt makes me weak in the knees. But I've been through worse. Images of the dungeon in China flit through my mind, and then I'm thinking of Ash. If he hadn't come for me, I would have died there.

Kem's deep voice rumbles through his chest. "Do you need help with the shirt?" I raise an eyebrow at him, and he blushes, actually blushes. I chuckle, which causes me to cough, and I almost black out.

My learned response, the one Garin hammered into my soul, is to do this on my own—prove that I am strong enough. But I sigh, wincing, then nod. "Yes, please."

He steps forward, and carefully, he slowly draws his nail down the front of my shirt. It rips smoothly, and when it hangs open, the large gash across my stomach is revealed.

I'm surprised my intestines are still inside my body. My skin is split from hip to ribs. The flesh hangs open, showing muscle and blood, so much blood. How am I still standing? How am I still conscious? The pain triples.

Kem hisses at the sight of the tear in my skin and the blood dripping down my body now that my shirt isn't soaking it up. With gentle efficiency, he pushes my shirt off my shoulders and down my arms until it pools on the floor at my feet. I turn around, giving him my back, and he hisses again. I try to look over my shoulder.

"What?"

"Were you struck from behind?"

Was I? I don't recall. Oh, wait. "I did land hard when Orsun hit me. Is it bad? It doesn't hurt."

"The fact that you can't feel it worries me."

I turn again, glimpsing my back in the mirror over the counter. Deep black and purple bruises have bloomed across my back, and there are several deep scrapes and cuts from where I must have skidded across the ground. "Well, yikes."

Kem shakes his head, and a small smile pulls at his lips. "Yikes indeed." His smile melts away, replaced by a frown of worry. "This looks internal. I will be as gentle as possible." I relax slightly as Kem's fingers brush against my back, his touch hot like a heating pad. "Hold still."

I tense at his words, but a second later, his warm touch presses a little harder to my back, working his way from my neck to my lower back then up again. The pain flares back, and I whimper before it starts to fade away again, and I sigh in relief.

He steps around me, and I have the vague thought that I should be embarrassed to be standing here in front of the

King of the Dragons in my underwear, but I'm in too much pain to care.

Kem's palms run over my temple, calming a bruise on the right side of my face that I didn't realize was there until he touched it. Then he kneels. The King of the Dragons kneels. I have to close my eyes to keep the tears from falling. My throat is tight, and it takes two tries to swallow. Garin would never have prostrated himself before me, even to help me.

Kem's hands feather over my stomach, and his warm heat seeps into my skin. Over and over, he runs his hand across the deep wound in my abdomen. The room is hot with the steam from the shower, and my skin is flushed from Kem's touch.

He leans back on his heels. "Is there anywhere I missed?"

I look down, and my eyes go wide when I see the shallow cut across my skin. It's still raw and tender, but it's now a mere scrape compared to the deep gash it was. I press my fingers to the cut, amazed that it's almost completely sealed and in place of the blinding pain is only a tugging ache. "That's amazing, Kem." I assess my body, feeling sore all over, but there are no deep twinges of pain. Even my ribs feel better, down to a dull ache instead of the stabbing pain from moments before. "I don't think you missed anything."

"You're sure?"

I roll my shoulders and smile. "Yes. Thank you."

He nods, handing me a bar of soap. "I'll stay close, just in case. I'll be right outside."

I exhale, and now able to move a bit better, I shed my underwear and step into the hot shower. I don't think a shower has ever felt so good, and a groan slides from my lips.

Kem calls out from the other side of the door. "Are you okay?"

I giggle. "Fine. It just feels good to get clean."

I hear his deep chuckle before the room goes quiet except for the tinkling of the water hitting the crystal walls of the shower.

Slowly cleaning the rest of the blood from my skin, I inhale the fresh, clean scent of the soap. The water runs red at my feet for a second before it turns pink, then clear. I wash my hair twice, and then just stand under the spray, letting the hot water stream from the crown of my head to my toes. When I turn off the water and step from the shower, I feel much more myself.

After drying off, I slip my arms through the wide straps of the top and wrap the soft fabric around my chest, tying it at the side. I pull on the silky shorts and step from the bathroom. I chance a glance in the mirror, noticing the dark grey color of the top and shorts makes my already too-pale skin much paler, but there is a healthy flush to my cheeks from the hot shower.

I step into the bedroom, and Kem's brows pinch slightly as his eyes sweep over me before nodding. "Better?"

"Much, thank you. I hope Syphe is okay."

Kem crosses the room and hands me a glass with a milky substance inside. "Syphe's wounds were deep, but her mate will tend to her. Syphe will be fine." When I sniff at the contents of the glass, he smiles. "It's for any lingering pain. It's best if you just down it in one go."

I lift the glass in a little salute and toss the liquid down my throat. I wince and shiver but manage to keep it down as it burns down my throat and coats my stomach. Kem takes the glass from my hand and sets it on a side table. "Syphe said you defended her, saved her."

I shrug. "He was about to kill her. I couldn't do nothing. Syphe is my friend. But I got cocky. I was sure I had the upper hand. I felt his dragon dying, and I forgot myself. I forgot what I was dealing with. I wasn't expecting his dragon to be strong enough to take back over."

"Our dragons will always lash out in death. We are more dragon than human, and the animal part of us will always win out in the end." I nod, frowning, but he takes another step toward me, and I meet his gaze. "You did well, Raelyn. You saved the life of my guard, my friend, and almost killed a dragon."

I shrug again and turn away, but his hand lightly grips my upper arm and turns me back to him. "It's no small thing what you did, Raelyn. Don't dismiss your power. You held your own against a dragon. And not just any dragon. Orsun was a Dragon Lord and quite a powerful one at that."

My eyes go wide at his words, and I feel myself start to shake. I stiffen my spine and look up into Kem's eyes. "But almost doesn't count. He had me." I pause, steeling myself for my next question. "Can I beat Ziza?"

His hand tightens slightly on my arm before he relaxes it back to his gentle hold. "You don't have to worry about that. I'll make sure you are gone from our realm before the Challenge arrives."

I step out of his grip and shake my head. "I can't keep running, Kem." I place my hands on my hips, trying to stand tall, to be brave.

"If you die here, Alek's death would have been for nothing."

I flinch at his words but shake my head again. "You brought me here to save me, even knowing the backlash you'd receive." I reach out, placing my hand on his forearm. "And I'm glad you brought me here, Kem."

He frowns. "My decision is proving to be ill-conceived."

"No, Kem." I squeeze him lightly. "You're a good friend." A single tear slides down my face, and he brushes it away with his finger. My breath hitches, my voice barely a whisper. "You are what Garin should have been."

He pulls me into his arms, holding me tight. My shoulders heave, and I just let go. I cry into Kem's chest, balling his shirt in my hands. "If I had seen him for who he was, this all might have been avoided."

My words are muffled against his body, and he rubs a hand down my back. "You loved your brother and wanted him to love you in return. There's nothing wrong with that Raelyn." I feel him tilt his head down until his breath feathers over my hair. "I'm here for you, Rae. No deceit, no catch. Whatever you need, I'm here."

I take a deep inhale, my breath shaking on the way in, but as I breathe out slowly, I do my best to find some sense of calm. Pushing away from him slightly, I smile. "Thank you, Kem. I can't leave though. If I can't stand up and defend my friends" —I look into his dark eyes—"my family, I don't deserve the crown. I ran from Ash for thousands of years. I ran from place to place on Earth because nowhere felt like home. I ran from Garin's rage in that cave." Kem opens his mouth to interrupt, but I barrel on. "I can't keep running. You were right. My people need me, and I won't run from my responsibilities. I think I know how to beat Ziza." Maybe. "I'm staying." A small smile curves my lips. "With your permission."

His eyes search mine, and it's like staring into the fires of a forge. "It is good to know I was right about you, Raelyn. You were worth the risk. You are strong and brave. You will be a glorious Queen."

My smile lifts my cheeks, and I feel lighter for the first

time in a long time, but a question bubbles to the surface of my brain. "Why *did* you take a risk on me? Before, at the portal on Earth, you said you were glad you finally got to meet me. What did that mean?"

He takes a step back, clasping his hands behind his back, stretching his tunic over his broad chest. "Alek talked of you often. He was very fond of you. He loved you very much." And just like that, the lightness is gone, replaced with a tightening in my chest. Kem continues. "He was a good man and a good judge of character. The way he spoke of you, the stories he told, made me eager to meet you. That's all."

That's all? I have no words to respond, and tears scratch at my throat, but I swallow them down. What tales did Alek share with Kem? How much does the King of the Dragons know about me?

His eyes search my face. "The medication will take effect soon. You should rest." He presses his hand to my lower back, leading me to the giant bed, but a knock on the doors halts him in place, and he actually growls. When I glance up, his eyes are more red than black, and I realize that while he's in his human form right now, his dragon is always simmering, ready to defend, ready to fight.

The knock sounds again, followed by a muffled, "My Lord?"

Kem growls again before peeling his hand from my back and crosses the room. He cracks open the door, says a few words that I can't make out, then closes it again. He strides back to me, and I tilt my head back to look up at him. "Is everything okay?"

He frowns. "A youngling was injured, and the healers are having a hard time setting his delicate wing. If they don't set it properly before they attempt to heal it, he might not be able to fly."

"The poor child! Kem, if you need to go, please." His jaw clenches. "I'm fine. I feel so much better, thanks to you. Go."

The red embers in his eyes flare brightly before dimming into the background. He takes a deep, calming breath, and I smile. Finally, he nods. "Send a guard if you need me. Get some rest." And with that, he spins on his heel and pushes through the door.

I sigh, and calling up a soft wind, I finish drying my hair just to feel the soft caress of my magic. This is the magic that I love. That vengeful rush of power that almost killed a dragon scared me more than I care to admit. My hand shakes as I hold it up, letting my magic swirl around and through my fingers. I prefer the gentle breezes and playful strokes of my air magic. But that doesn't mean I won't use the rage within my power. I'll have to.

I glance at the bed and feel the drugs in the medication start to muddle my mind, but it's not too bad, just a warm numbing to my aches and pains. Sinking into the bed, I stare at the ceiling, hoping Ash is having a better time than I am.

17

ASHERAHT

I'M TIRED, wet, sore, and frustrated.

Endra's source from the shungite mine was legit. However, the results were ... disappointing.

Warm blood coats my blade. I kneel and clean it on the pants of the man I just killed, his body lying face down on the damp, cold stone of the dark street. Someone will find him soon enough, but I'll be long gone by then. I can't wait to get out of these seedy docks, away from this fridge town. Dalnak, the northern seaport, has never been one of my favorite places in the kingdom.

A peel of obnoxious laughter and the sound of a bottle breaking spills from a tavern down the street as if to punctuate my dislike for this place.

Standing from where I kneel, I pocket the carefully wrapped Shungite shards. I was hoping for more, but I'll take what I can get. The black mineral is illegal unless you have the correct permits, which I don't, and this fae certainly did not. It took a lot of smooth-talking to get this man to give up his meager supply. But taking my money and then refusing to hand over the product was not the wisest move on his part.

Nor was trying to kill me.

I walk half a block when an odd shadow catches my eye. Focusing on the dark shape hanging outside a building, my teeth grind together, and bile climbs my throat. A woman hangs from the sign of an inn. Her body is decayed, and carrion birds have picked out her eyes, lips, and other soft flesh. She's been there so long, the rope is more than halfway through her rotted neck.

Anger pulses through my blood in time with my heartbeat. I'm practically shaking with rage. Why has everyone just left her there?

The smell is awful, and I try to breathe through my mouth, but it doesn't help. I think about sending my fire to her body and let her ashes float away on the mists, but I don't want to call that much attention to myself. So, I reach up, swallowing a gag as I touch the cold, slimy skin of her leg.

"I wouldn't do that."

I pause and slowly turn toward the voice. Putting my hands in my pockets, I try to ignore the sheen of damp that clings to every surface in this frigid town. A shadowed form stands in the darkened doorway two buildings down. No fae lamps light these streets, and only the smaller of the two moons crosses the sky tonight. The tiny sliver of a waning crescent provides very little light, of which I'm grateful.

"And why not?"

"The soldiers. They've threatened to kill anyone who takes her down. She is meant to be an example."

It takes a moment to place his voice. "An example?"

Taron steps from the building, his silver hair shining in the dim light, and his pale skin makes him look almost ghost-like. "This was her inn. All her rooms were rented, and the soldiers demanded she kick out her patrons to make room for them." He glances up at the woman hanging heavy from the sign of her inn. "She refused."

His eyes find mine, and he nods at the obvious anger radiating from my posture. "Don't worry, Asheraht. I'll bury her once she falls."

He tilts his head at me, and his eyes skirt to my pockets before coming back to my face. "Now, what could you possibly need raw Shungite for?"

Well, it seems Taron has been watching me for a while. "I'm sure I have no idea what you mean."

"Come now, Asheraht. Let's not play this game."

A grin lifts my lips. "But, I love games."

"Asheraht." He says my name like a warning, but my grin doesn't falter, and my stride brings me before him. His gaze rakes me from head to toe before a half-smile softens his sharp features, and he clasps my forearm.

"Taron, good to see you, old friend. What are you doing all the way up here? Are you on a job?" We release our grip, and he crosses his arms over his chest. I shove my hand back in my pocket, trying and failing to keep my fingers warm.

A quick shake of his head sends little drops of water flying from the ends of his wet hair, and I wonder how long he was standing there, watching. "I'm no longer in the Guild." He starts walking down the street, away from the dead bodies of my kill and the poor inn owner, and I fall into step at his side. "There are few left in the Guild these days." Glancing at me, there's a shadow of anger in his eyes before he drops his head to stare at his boots.

"Yeah, I heard." Anger and a decent amount of guilt tighten my shoulders as I'm reminded of what Garin did to the Guild, to my friends. "I'm glad you made it out."

"I was one of the lucky ones."

Remorse chokes me for a moment, stealing any words I might say. Every few blocks, Taron turns, weaving through the small town like we're being followed. We're not, but I imagine old habits die hard. Spending most of one's life looking over your shoulder tends to create obsessive behaviors.

I stretch my muscles going stiff from the damp cold of this town. The Guild's healer did a thorough job, and I only feel the slightest twinge in my back from the shungite wound.

After almost five minutes of walking in silence, he whispers, "You really took a contract on the princess?"

I nod, knowing he'll see the small movement even in the dark. "To be fair, I didn't know it was her until I landed on Earth."

"So that's where you've been all this time?" Again, a nod is my only answer. "Was the pay worth it at least?"

My lips quirk up in a small smile. "More than any contract I've ever had"—I listen to the soft echo of our footsteps on the street before I continue—"by triple at least. The down payment alone was more than I used to make on three or four jobs when I first started with the Guild."

Taron's glowing dark blue eyes widen, and a low whistle slides from his lips. "And you didn't think the price would reflect the difficulty of the target?"

When Valna offered me that large sum, my gut had screamed that it was not a job I wanted to get mixed up in, but that amount of gold was impossible to pass up. And if I hadn't taken it, someone else in the Guild would have, and

Rae might be dead because of it. So yeah, I might hold some responsibility for what happened to the Guild, but Raelyn is alive, so I can't regret it. Not all of it.

I grin. "It was a lot of gold. And you know I like a challenge."

A chuckle rumbles from his chest. "Yeah. That's why you were so good."

"Still am."

He snorts, and I huddle deeper into my cloak, trying to keep the damp mist from soaking me completely.

He pushes through the wood door of a house pinched between two others in a long line of cramped houses on this block. Their damp, black roofs almost touch each other as water drips into the narrow alleys. Even if I turned sideways, I wouldn't fit between the houses.

Inside, it smells of musty clothing, and when he kneels in front of a hearth and starts stacking wood, I wait until he's done and leans back for the flint hanging on the stone surround before I wave a hand, igniting the wood in a single rush of my magic.

Taron smiles, standing. "Thanks."

He shrugs out of his oiled jacket and drapes it over a chair close to the fire. I keep mine on. I'm not sure how long I'll be here. Crossing the room, his boots are loud on the wood floor as he goes to a small kitchen that is open to the living area. A small table and two chairs stand between us, and a pair of overstuffed tartan chairs flank the fireplace.

I move to stand before the flames, holding out my frozen fingers, skin tingling as feeling starts to come back. "So, what are you doing these days?"

Taron crosses back to me, two mugs in hand. Holding one out, I take it, sniff it, and down the whiskey in one shot. He presses his lips in a tight line, not drinking from his yet.

"I hire out my services at the docks to protect shipments, storehouses, cargo ..." Seems boring and a waste of his talent, but I keep quiet. "Are you going to tell me what you plan to do with the shungite?"

I stare at the dancing flames, seeing Rae's curves in the wisps of fire. I let the silence drag out for a few minutes, but we are both seasoned assassins and are comfortable with the quiet.

Finally, I take a breath, not brave enough to meet his eyes. I don't want to see disappointment, or amusement, or ... whatever. "I'm going after Garin." After a few heartbeats, I add, "With Raelyn."

"So, it's Raelyn, is it?"

No, it's Rae, but I don't say that. I just sigh at the insinuation behind his words. "Sorry, her Highness, Lady Raelyn is coming back to claim the throne, and I'm helping her."

He throws back his whiskey, and with his free hand, he runs his fingers through his damp hair, shaking it out. There's nothing more to say, so I let him think. I look around the room to keep myself busy. There is no art on the walls, and the cream paint is chipped in places. The fae lights in the kitchen are empty and dark, and as an earth fae, Taron wouldn't have been able to replenish the light once it went out. Fae lights are lit and replenished by fire fae, so there must not be one in this town, which is worrying.

I direct my magic to the empty orbs, and a small glow ignites in the center before slowly growing brighter. Taron nods his thanks, and I nod back. Not all fae have magic, and it seemed more and more fae were born without the spark of magic even before I left for Earth. From the looks of things, that trend has continued. How long before all magic is gone from our race?

I'm pulled from my thoughts as Taron turns to me.

"When is her Highness planning to return, and does she have an army? Because she'd need an army. A big one."

There is a layer of sarcasm in his tone, but I think there's also some hope there. "I'm sorry, but I don't know. I have a location but not a time. She could already be back. And no. No army."

"So it's just you and Lady Raelyn against the King and his soldiers?"

I shrug. "You wouldn't want to join us, would you? I promise it'll be a fun time ... until it isn't."

I grin, and he chuckles before his smile slides from his face. "I'm sorry, my friend. I wish you luck, but I don't see the point of sticking myself between the royals. Just let them duke it out if you ask me."

Disappointment skates through me for a moment, but I really didn't expect anything else. "It's okay, my friend. I understand. I've asked Nyira for help ... but who knows."

His eyebrows lift a fraction. "Indeed. I wouldn't expect much help from her. I'm surprised she didn't kill you on site."

"Me too. But she promised she would talk to the Guild. Beyond that, it's just me and Ra—Lady Raelyn."

"And his Highness, prince Alek? Where do you expect him to stand?"

I press my lips together to hold back my anger and sadness. I clench and unclench my fists in front of the fire. "He's dead."

Taron stumbles back, almost dropping his mug, fumbling for a second before setting it on a worn table by one of the chairs. "You know this for sure?

"I saw it with my own eyes. The King murdered him."

I can feel him staring at me, but I'm not ready to meet

his eyes. A sigh slides from his lips. "What have you gotten yourself involved with, Asheraht?"

Rae. I've gotten myself involved with Rae, and I'll follow her to the end.

Forcing my gaze to meet his, I frown. "I have to try. I have to try and make things right. Ra—damn it, Lady Raelyn, can make things better."

"I think the princess has gotten under your skin, and you are willing to die for a pair of pretty green eyes."

"Maybe. But you asked. I answered." My voice comes out harsh and louder than I intend. He holds up a placating hand before swiping up his mug and taking mine from where I sat it on the mantle. The ceramic clinks in the sink, and I turn, striding to the door. "Thank you for the hospitality, Taron. It was good to see you, my friend. I'm glad you got out, and I wish you the best of luck."

The handle is cold in my palm, and I grimace, thinking of the damp night air on the other side of this door. Before I open it, Taron's voice floats across the room in a sad whisper. "Be careful, Asheraht." There is pain and utter dejection on his face. His eyes meet mine, tears swimming in their edges but refusing to fall. "Be sure, Asheraht. Be absolutely sure that this is a battle you want to fight. Because you will most likely lose."

I nod, staying silent because he's right. I'm ready to die for a pair of brilliant green eyes and the heart behind them. I step into the fog and mists of the night, letting the door click shut behind me. I have one more stop to make in the next village over to see a source with more shungite, if I'm lucky. Hopefully, this deal will go more smoothly. Then I can finally make my way south to Dorwe, to Raelyn.

Loud laughter rings through the thick, damp air as two soldiers stumble from a tavern, the only place for blocks doing any business at this hour. One soldier playfully shoves the other, making a lude remark about a serving girl, going into great detail about what he plans to do with her once her shift is over. None of it sounds like it will be consensual, and the other soldier laughs, offering to hold her down as long as he gets a turn.

Anger, strong and familiar, rises and grips my muscles. I melt into the deeper shadows, slowing my breaths, letting adrenaline sharpen my vision and hearing. I follow them for two blocks, palming a throwing knife in my left hand, gripping the cool steel blade between my fingers as I grab the leather hilt of my dagger in my right in an underhand grip.

I stalk my prey and draw back my left arm, ready to unleash death.

Yes. This is what I was made for, what I excel at. The assassin consumes me. A cruel smile curves my lips, and my fire magic licks flames along my blades as I let them fly.

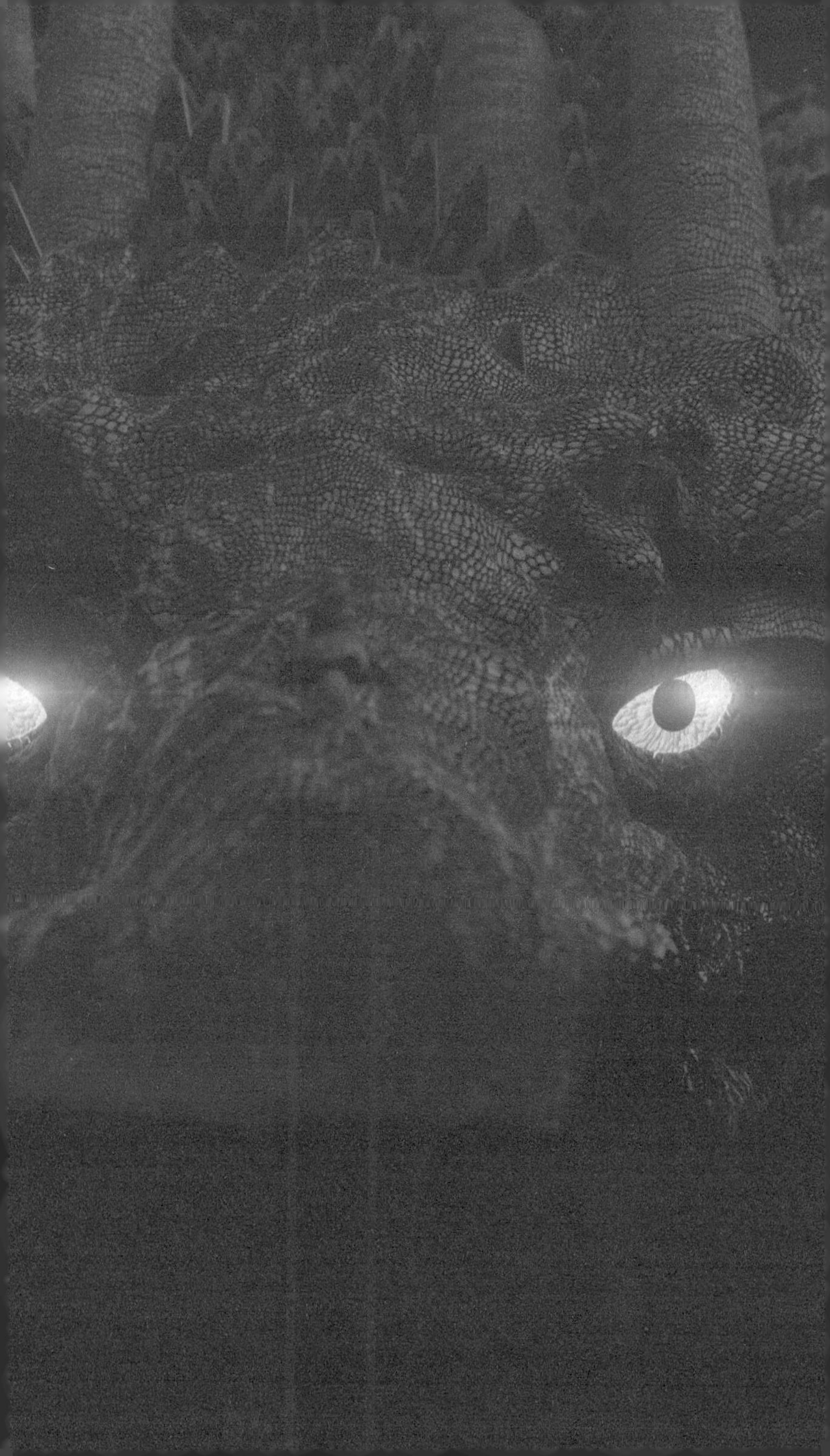

18

RAELYN

I STARE at the ceiling of Kem's bedroom, the silence pressing in on me like a second blanket. A heady mix of desire and worry for Ash keeps me awake, and now that the adrenaline has worn off from Orsun's attack, my stomach grumbles.

I cross to the closet and slip on a deep green, light-weight button-up shirt and a pair of black leggings. Slipping from the room, the silver guard, Arvun, growls at me, but I ignore her and hurry down the long hallway. I pass a few people along the way, some smiling and bowing slightly as I hurry by. Others frown or scowl, but I pay them no mind and continue on.

Entering the dining hall, I make my way across the vast room where at least thirty people mingle, eating at the long tables, or piling their plates with food at the buffet down the side wall. The muted sounds of conversation and the clinking of dinnerware slowly die until silence wraps around me.

I feel everyone's gaze pin to me, and I barely hold back a panic-induced giggle when the children's game, pin the tail on the donkey, springs to mind. But no one approaches me.

I hear Orsun's name whispered among the dragons. Word travels fast, and I wonder how many here side with what Orsun did?

My fingers wrap around the cool porcelain of a plate, and I step down the line. Everything looks delicious. My mouth is watering, and I take a little of everything. I'm so engrossed with trying to figure out what the dish before contains—it looks like mashed potatoes but is a bright pink and has an earthy smell—that I bump into the man next to me.

"So sorry." I lift my head to ask him what the dish is, but his scowl halts my words.

"What's the King's little pet doing here on her own?"

There're a few chuckles around the room, and I take a step back, bumping into the person behind me. My skin feels too tight, trapped between these dragon shifters, but the person behind me speaks softly, "The King's guest is obviously hungry."

The man before me peels back his lips, his growl growing louder, but the man behind me drowns him out with his own growl until the other man drops his gaze, turns, and stomps away.

Trying to calm my racing heart, I turn, backing up a step to face the tall man with a plate of food in his hand. His skin is a deep brown, like freshly turned soil, and his hair is a pale blue, the color of a clear sky. The room is still silent, and I swallow my nerves as he looks down at me, saying, "Is it true? You saved Syphe?"

His energy is confusing. I can't tell if this dragon is angry at me, or Orsun, or Kem. Or if he is angry at all. I nod. "She was defending me. I could not allow her to die if I could help it. I'm just sorry I couldn't keep her from getting hurt."

Mumbling spreads around the hall, like insects buzzing in the night desert air. He nods, and I'm surprised at the emotion on his face. Tears rim his eyes. His voice cracks as he presses a hand over his heart. "I give you my most sincere thanks. She is my mate."

I step toward him but catch myself and stop, not wanting to make any sudden moves in a room full of shifters. "Is she okay?"

He nods with a sweet smile on his face. "She is healing nicely." He holds up the heaping plate in his hand. "Once she has been fed, she will be able to rest." There is a teasing affection in his eyes, and it reminds me of Ash. Syphe's mate reaches toward me, and I fight to keep from backing up. I know he means me no harm, but still. He places his free hand on my shoulder with a soft smile. "Thank you, Lady Raelyn."

I feel a blush coloring my cheeks. "Please tell her I'm grateful for her protection, and I hope she heals quickly."

He nods. "I will see that she does."

I nod back with a small smile, and as I turn to find a seat, I catch a flash of emerald-green hair disappearing down a side hall. I glance at my plate longingly before setting it on the closest table, leaving the dining hall with ever-growing conversation building behind me.

I turn down yet another hallway, the cut on my stomach starting to burn, and my back aches with every step. Finally, I see another flash of that emerald green disappear through a doorway, and I pick up my pace. I'm about to push through the door to follow Ziza, when a strong hand grips my wrist, spinning me around.

Kem growls at me, but there's concern behind his eyes. "Where are you going, Raelyn? You need rest, and it's not smart wandering about on your own."

I glance over my shoulder. "I was hungry so I went to the dining hall, but then I saw Ziza and thought if I could just talk with her ..."

He shakes his head. "No. Ziza's mind won't be swayed."

"How can you be sure? I should at least tr—"

Kem holds up a hand. "I came to see if you were awake" —he smirks at me—"not at all surprised to find you gone." He tugs me back the way I came, practically dragging me down the hall at a fast clip. For a moment, shadows curl out from Kem's body, swirling around him for a few seconds before they seep back into his skin.

I jog to draw up next to him, my wrist still in his strong grip. "What was that?"

"I called the council. They will meet us in the council chambers."

My heels drop, and my weight shifts back. I skate along the floor before Kem stops, turning back to me. "The council? The dragon council? You want me to talk to the dragon council?"

"I may be king, but my words alone will not sway them to stop the Challenge, Raelyn. They need to see you, meet you. They need to understand what's at stake."

He tugs me forward, but I tense, holding my ground. "Kemremir, what am I supposed to say? Who's on the council? What if Ziza shows up? What if they punish you for bringing me here in the first place—"

Kem steps into my space, releasing my wrist before gently gripping my shoulders. My eyes catch movement over his shoulder as a man with creamy-white hair turns the corner at the end of the hall. Upon seeing us, his eyes widen, and he quickly turns back the way he came.

"Raelyn." Kem's voice draws my gaze back to his. "I will do the talking. I just need you there to put a face to the name. Ziza won't show up, it's a closed meeting." I bite my lip, and he squeezes my shoulder. "They might grumble and posture at trying to do something over my decision to bring you here, but unless someone wants to Challenge me outright, there's not much they can do."

"Kem—"

"Raelyn, the council can't touch me. It's you I'm worried about."

He nods his head over his shoulder down the hall before sliding his hand back down my arm. Instead of gripping my wrist again, he takes my hand, and my palm goes damp in his hot grip. "So, what's going to happen? Will there be a vote or something?"

"Yes. There are eight council members representing the eight regions of the Crimson Plains. But only seven will be there. The dragons of the mountains never come to the meetings unless they have a direct grievance. I will introduce you and plead our case."

"And if the vote doesn't go our way?"

His voice drops. It would be a whisper if it wasn't so gravely. "Let's just see what happens."

We approach a tall wood door, and Kem turns the handle, pulling me into the room beyond. The door closes quietly behind us, and I can't help the shiver that drives down my spine. The ceiling soars overhead, carved-marble tresses arching gracefully. The walls are the same beautiful cream marble with gold veining, and the floor is the same shimmering crystal as the rest of the castle.

Three males are already standing near the center of the room, talking in whispers—one a shiny silver, one a forest-green, and the last a bright spring-grass green. They look in our direction, and Kem leans down, raises an eyebrow in warning before whispering, "Stay here."

Gladly, though I miss his support the moment his hand leaves mine. He crosses the room, addressing the men, and as they nod and bow at each other, there's a quick rush of pressure that causes my ears to pop before two more people simply appear in the center of the room.

My mouth drops open, but I'm quick to snap it shut, taking in the newcomers—one a deep pink, and the other a golden yellow like a stalk of wheat. The yellow woman bows to Kem, but the pink male simply nods his head in a slight movement of deference.

Everyone's eyes keep shifting to me, but no one approaches or even addresses me.

It's not even a full minute later when that same snap of pressure hits me again in rapid succession. A bluish-grey woman appears, immediately followed by a deep purple male.

On some unspoken signal, the seven council members fan out, each standing on a different symbol carved into the crystal floor, one left empty. When they're all in place, they form a wide circle, and Kem paces in the center, hands clasped loosely behind his back.

The blue woman speaks, her voice soft, gentle. "Lord Kemremir, why have you called us here? And on such short notice?"

The light-green male gestures at me with a wave of his hand. "Isn't it obvious, Ambra? His little pet must have gotten herself in some trouble, and now the King asks us to intervene."

Despite the seriousness of the situation, I bristle at his words, my shoulders bunching and my teeth clenching at once again being called a pet.

The pink male crosses his arms over his chest, stretching his grey tunic over his muscled arms. "Is this true, Lord Kemremir?"

Kem pauses his pacing. "Lady Raelyn is not at fault." He turns slowly, meeting each member's gaze. "I am here to ask you to dissolve the Challenge issued against Lady Raelyn by Ziza Arafaren."

The blue female speaks again, her long, curly hair swaying. "You believe the Challenge was issued without cause?"

The dark-green male huffs, throwing his arms up in exasperation. "Of course there was cause. She's an outsider. Her very presence is against our law."

The light-green male glares at me. "The King himself breaks our law, then summons us the moment his pet is threatened."

Kem doesn't raise his voice, but it still echoes around the cavernous room. "Enough. I brought Lady Raelyn here to save her life. Prince Alek of Attolyn is dead at the hand of King Garin." Tension coils around the council members, and several gasps accompany uneasy shifting. Does everyone here know my brothers? Kem lets them settle before he continues. "Prince Alek asked for our help, and we agreed."

Well, that answers that, though I have so many new questions.

The silver male tsks. "We agreed to fetch the princess. Nothing was said about getting involved in the fae's politics. The dragons don't interfere in the petty political machinations of other realms."

Kem lifts an eyebrow, making another slow turn, staring

down each member. "So that is all Prince Alek's sacrifice is worth?"

The blue female clasps her hands in front of her. "I agree with Lord Kemremir. Prince Alek was owed our help, and in extension, his sister."

What did Alek do for the Dragons?

Kem glances at her but turns to hold the light-green male's gaze. "Our indifference to the suffering of the Seelie should not be the legacy of how we treat those who come to our aid."

The light-green male sneers, taking slow steps toward Kem. His smile reminds me of a cat stalking a bird, and I involuntarily step forward in defense of Kem, but pause, knowing I'd be more of a distraction than a help if something did actually happen.

The male stops two strides from Kem, crossing one arm around his waist, the other bent, finger tapping his smooth cheek. "I'd think you'd be happy about this Challenge, Lord Kemremir. Why not let this Ziza clean up your mess?" His eyes dart beyond Kem and land on me. I hold my head high, ignoring the slight shaking in my knees. "Defending your pet only makes you look weak."

Kem snarls, snapping the male's eyes back to him. "If you think me weak, Inchel, Challenge me."

Inchel's eyes widen a fraction, and he tries to hide his fear by taking another step toward Kem. "You think I won't?"

I can't see Kem's face, but I hear the smile in his voice. "No. No, I do not."

The council springs into a cacophony of noise as each member starts speaking simultaneously. There are shouts for Inchel to stand down, but Kem and the green dragon stand firm, their growls growing louder until my skin vibrates with the sound. The council members continue to argue, yelling over the snarling, growling males in the center of the circle. They debate my fate while I stand at the edge of room like the useless pet Inchel accused me of being.

I gasp as lime-green scales crawl across Inchel's skin, and his nails elongate into claws. Another rumble comes from Kem, and shadows begin to leak from his skin. His form seems to swell, and the form of giant wings begins to solidify within his shadows. The voices of the other council members rise even louder, like a rushing river.

The green shifter roars. "You were a fool to bring the fae here. Outsiders do not belong among us. We are superior. We do not need other's assistance and we bow to no one. We are not lowly human or fae. We are not simple wizards, or elves, or magi. We are not Druid, or pixie, or gargoyles, or Vashta Nerada. We are not Chitauri or Zenn-Lavians. We are ancient. We are Dragons! The council has been foolish to allow you—"

Kem bellows back even louder. "You allow me nothing! I am King! I killed king Ruenar. I have bested every Challenger." Black scales erupt across his body. "Go ahead, Inchel, speak the words. Challenge me."

Smoke pours from Inchel's mouth as he sneers at Kem. The dark green male steps up behind Inchel, his eyes burning, his nails lengthened into claws. The purple male steps to Inchel's other side, his body vibrating with the growls rising from his chest. Inchel smiles. "I am not the only one growing tired of you, Kemremir."

Kem throws his head back and laughs, the sound bouncing around the room, quieting the other councilors. "Go ahead. Do it. One Challenger or three"—his shadows explode from his skin, slamming into the walls, plunging the room into swirling chaos of blacks and greys—"the outcome will be the same ... your deaths."

The room is utterly silent, and I stand rigid, holding on to the wall at my back, waiting for the telltale sound of snapping teeth or rending claws, but nothing happens. The seconds draw out, and it's so quiet, I think everyone has left me standing alone like a doofus in a dark room.

But slowly, light seeps through the inky mists floating around me, and the council room returns to normal. The two shifters who backed Inchel have moved back to their positions in the circle, and while Inchel still stands before Kem, body tense, fists clenched, his head is bowed.

I have no idea if this is how council meetings typically go, and Kem did tell me to stay put, but my nerves are at a snapping point. Channeling the Queen that Alek wanted me to be, I stride forward, walking into the center of the circle. Inchel's scales recede as he takes several quick steps back, disgust on his face like he's afraid I might touch him.

Kem's shadows continue to swirl around him, and when I look up, his eyes are blazing, the molten core burning brightly. Smoke curls from his nostrils and between his clenched teeth. I lock down my muscles to try and hide my trembling as I place a hand on his forearm. He nods at me, but doesn't completely pull back his shadows.

I turn, facing the councilors before me, turning slowly to look at them each in turn. I'm met with some snarls and frowns, but there's also a few subtle nods of encouragement. Raising my chin and drawing my shoulders down my back, I beg my voice to come out stronger than I feel.

"I understand my presence in your realm is ... precarious, and I'm sorry for any trouble I have caused." Inchel snarls, and I force myself to meet his burning gaze. "But my kingdom needs me. My brother, Alek, believed in me, risking his life to find and bring me home to save our people."

The silver male waves a hand. "Then why aren't you there, saving your people?"

I refuse to wilt before him, though the trembling in my legs is growing worse. "My brother, Garin, is too strong. He would have killed me if not for your King. And if Garin is left to drive Attolyn into the depths of blood magic, the Seelie will be exterminated, and the balance between Light and Dark will crumble. The Unseelie will be unleashed upon the realms. They will spread unchecked, bleeding world after world for power."

The room has gone deathly silent. There's not even a rustling of clothes as every person in the room stands still, watching me. "How many worlds, how many realms will be consumed by dark magic before you intervene? Or will you lock yourselves away here on the Crimson Plains and let the universe fall around you?"

The silence stretches, pressing in on my ears until Inchel chuckles. "You overestimate your importance in keeping the Unseelie leashed."

I raise an eyebrow at him. "Do I?"

His smile slides into a frown, but before he says anything more, the blue woman speaks, her light voice like a balm on the tension in the room. "We will put the issue of the Challenge against Lady Raelyn to a vote, but I ask you all to remember what Prince Alek did for us."

I glance up at Kem, noticing his shadows are gone. There's worry behind his eyes, but he smiles at me with a small nod. I nod back with a tentative smile of my own, striding from the circle. Channeling my mother, I hold my posture tall as I settle back near the wall.

I wait.

Inchel looks across the room at me. "I vote for the Challenge to proceed."

Big shock there.

The forest-green male nods. "I vote to proceed."

The blue female nods at Kem. "I vote to dissolve the Challenge."

My heart rate is racing, and my palms are sweating as I fight to keep from cracking my neck.

The yellow woman lifts her chin. "Dissolve."

The purple male speaks next. "Proceed."

Shit, shit, shit. If there's one more vote to proceed … can I run? Kem offered to take me away. But I made that big speech about standing my ground. Well, joke's on me. I'm a fool.

No! *I need to be strong. I'm not ready. I need to be ready. I can't fight a dragon. I can't fight my brother. My people are suffering. I have help. I have to fight my brother. I have to kill … I can't. I must.*

My blood rushes through my ears so fast, I can't hear what's being said. The edges of my vision are turning grey, and my lungs can't seem to take in enough air.

Reaching behind me and to the right, my fingers scramble along the wall until I grip the cool metal of the doorknob. Gritting my teeth, I turn it slowly before inching the door open just enough for me to slip through. Inchel's eyes snap to mine. His cruel grin is the last thing I see as the door clicks shut.

I take a deep breath, but it doesn't help the burning in my chest.

Ashamed, but unable to stop myself, I run. Garin was right. I always run.

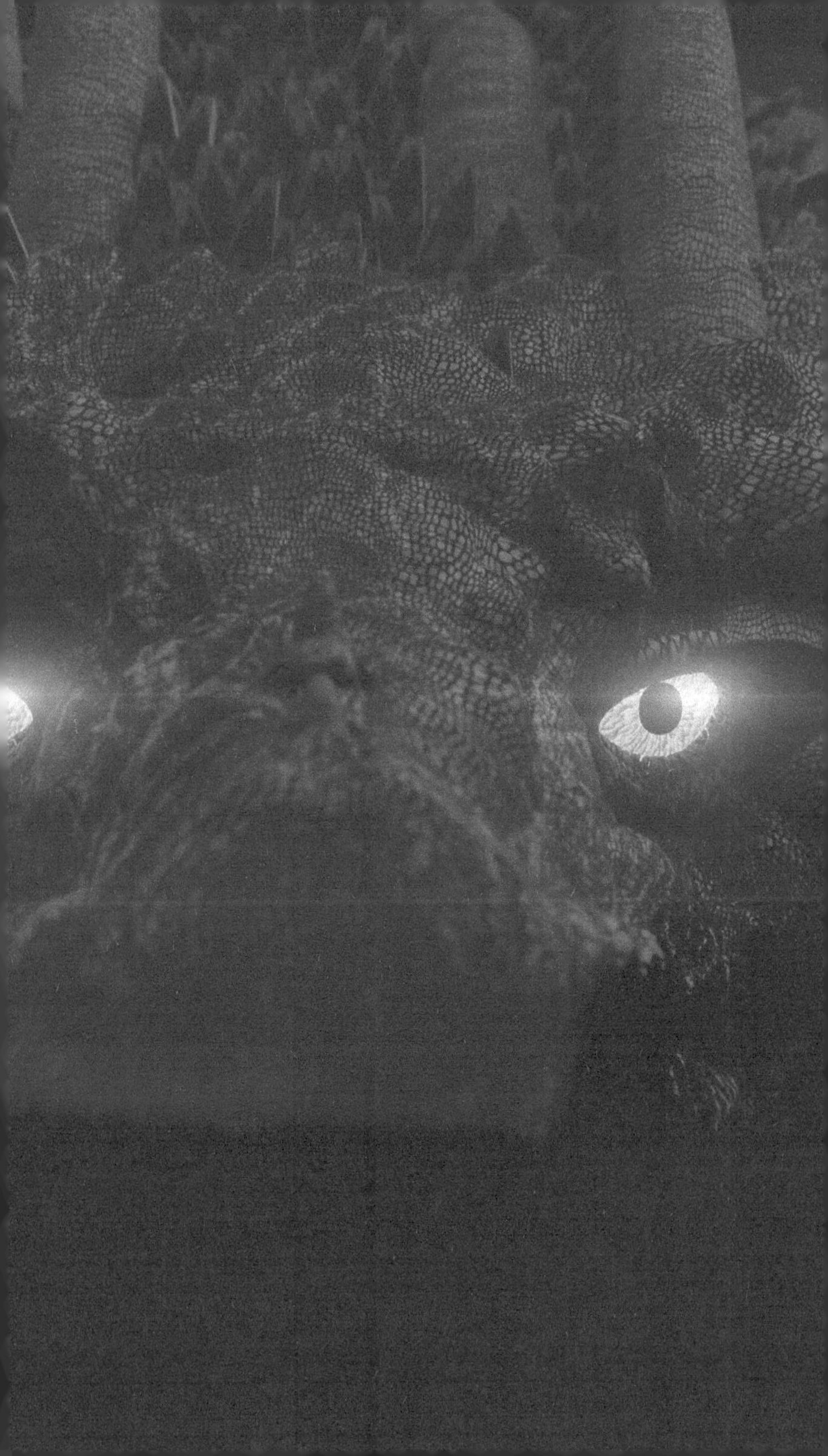

19

RAELYN

I MAKE it down two hallways and around the corner of a third before pressing my back to the cool, crystal wall and slide down. My knees fold into my chest, and I hug my shins, trying to catch my breath.

Magic swells within me as panic and anger swirl inside me. My hair blows around my face, and a shield of air snaps around me, closing me in its protective embrace. Alek's pained face flashes in my mind, and I close my eyes against the sorrow, but that doesn't help. His green eyes, eyes so like mine, still beg me to run. Garin's cruel laugh echoes through my ears, and rage pumps my blood faster through my veins. The air around me starts to spark with charged electrons against my skin. Images of the cruel sneers of the dark Unseelie in that cave, standing at Garin's side, have my hands curling into tight fists. The memory of Ash's blood on that soldier's blade makes my blood boil with fury.

My eyes pop open when the shield of air around me shimmers and creaks as it freezes, growing thicker and more solid with every passing second. My shield obscures the hall as magic keeps pulsing from me, trying to protect me from myself: my fears, pain, terror, and sorrow, my anger, rage, and wrath.

Images of Orsun's giant dragon jaws clamping around Syphe's neck have my breath coming out in short gasps. The ice around me thickens, but my skin is hot as the little electrical pulses continue to snap within my shield.

Ziza's smirk flashes in my mind, and I can't help but imagine her sharp fangs closing around my throat.

The stone floor beneath me ices over, and a boom resounds like thunder as a great crack tears up the wall at my back. An ancient tree in the gardens calls to me, and its roots rush through the dirt under the castle and push through the crack in the wall. They form a ball of tangled wood around me, and unnatural thorns sprout from the roots, adding another layer to my shield.

Alek's dead body, Garin's smile, Ash's blood, Orsun's roar, the Unseelie, Ziza's sneer, Garin's arms holding me tight, Alek's pained eyes, Syphe's cry of pain ... Like flashcards of misery, the images assault me.

Orange light flickers beyond my shield, and as I push to kneeling, flames lick my fingers. Thunder booms, and power builds inside me until it feels like it's too much to contain within my skin. The quaking in my chest has spread to the rest of my body. I feel like my bones are going to shatter with the anguish and anger threatening to tear me in half.

Air whirls around me with a deafening rush in my ears. The ground rumbles under the stone floor. The ice around me groans as it continues to expand, now almost a foot thick, and my magic rages within the ice cave I've created to protect myself. Mini lightning strikes flash from my skin, the orange glow of fire outside the shield grows brighter, and the flames on my hands turn the brilliant white of phosphorus.

It's so loud—both inside my head and all around me. I hear Ash's voice, asking me why I left him behind. I hear Alek asking why I didn't save him. I hear my parents asking why I never came back. I hear Ziza say she's going to kill me. I hear Kem saying he shouldn't have brought me here. And above it all, I hear Garin laughing at me.

I shove to my feet and close my eyes, surrounded by the riot of my magic, and I remember my father's crown on Garin's head.

Am I screaming? I think I'm screaming as Air, Water, Fire, and Earth rise to my inner call for vengeance.

But there's another voice shouting over mine.

"RAELYN!"

Someone's trying to get to me. Someone is trying to break down my defenses. Friend or foe? I open my eyes as a dark shape hits my shield and the icy walls shake.

"No!" My scream tears from my raw throat. The ice doubles, and the thorny roots punch through, creating a prickly wall of frozen water.

Over and over, something rams into my shield, into my magic, and I feel each strike to my bones. I draw more and more power, the elemental magics feeding off my rage. The wind is howling in the hallway beyond my ice shield, and the thorns have thickened and lengthened to the size of daggers. The glow of fire outside of my shield burns brighter as the tree's thick roots continue to try to pull the walls down. The dirt under the stone floor shifts and rumbles, threatening to swallow the entire castle.

I press a hand to my chest, trying and failing to take a full breath. The magic is not only feeding off my anger, it's consuming my energy, taking from me what I am pulling from the elements. It's wild, like an untamed horse, and I think I might lose myself to the power. But maybe I should let it. Maybe it will stop the pain.

Another crash hits my shield. With the next impact, a crack slashes through the ice. A bloody fist punches into the weak point once, twice, and on the third time, the ice shatters, falling in glittering chunks around me. The thorny roots splinter and scatter to the floor, and I stumble, hitting the wall at my back.

There are dozens of people in the hall, shielding their eyes from the whipping wind flinging ice shards and thorn debris around the chaotic hallway. I can't focus, and the walls tilt as a wave of dizziness hits me, but a deep voice reaches me. "Raelyn, let go of your magic. You are safe."

But I'm not safe. Garin wants me dead. Ash is on his own, probably being hunted by my brother if he's not already his prisoner. Attolyn is awash in dark magic, and if it's not stopped, the Seelie fae will be no more. My people will be wiped from the universe. Some of the dragons, maybe including those in this hall, want me dead. And my magic, whatever is happening with my power, feels like it is going to consume me.

I. Am. Not. Safe.

My body snaps tight, my head falls back as my arms thrust wide at my sides. My body erupts in flames. My air magic kicks the flames into a tornado of fire that licks the ceiling. The walls shake before the one down the hall crumbles, and part of the ceiling caves in. Several people try to run away, but the rubble blocks one end of the hall, and my fire tornado blocks the other.

Kem steps through the flames and grasps my shoulders. I struggle to focus on him as he leans down, bringing his dark eyes level with mine. "Raelyn."

My magic continues to pulse from me, and the hallway begins to go dark. I vaguely wonder if Kem is enclosing us in his shadows to get me away from his people, to protect them from me. His voice is nothing but a whisper that somehow carries through the raging fire and wind. "Rae. Let go."

I'm finally able to focus on his eyes. His hand slides down my arm and threads his fingers through mine. Giving me a little squeeze, he leans in, pressing a kiss to my forehead before moving his lips to my ear. "I'm here."

A sob bubbles up from my broken and bleeding heart, and I struggle to rein in my magic. It's like pulling a rug through mud, but finally, the power settles within me. All my rage and anger have burned away with my magic, leaving me exhausted. My body is one big ache. Everything hurts and darkness presses in. Kem leans back. There's worry behind his eyes, but there's a teasing smile on his lips. "Every time I turn around, you're showing off."

I try to laugh, but I only manage a weak smile. "You mean causing trouble."

He chuckles. "That too."

I feel myself falling forward.

The last thing I remember is Kem's warm arms wrapping around me.

20

ASHERAHT

MY HEELS DRAW lines in the dirt as the soldiers drag me to where their horses are tied up.

I was so close. Fifty more miles, and I would have reached the Dorwe Sanctuary. Yet here I am, failing Rae yet again. My forearms spasm painfully as the shungite cuffs dig into my wrists. The spikes inside the cuffs dig deep into my skin, cutting me off from my magic. Blood drips down my hands, leaving a trail between the tracks left by my boots.

When the soldiers erupted from the dense woods around me, I held my own for a while, but it was a numbers game, and there were too many of them—eleven, in fact. Glancing back to the treeline, I see the bodies of the four men I killed lying where they fell. Their comrades seem uninterested in retrieving the bodies as they haul me ever closer to their horses.

My shoulder slips from the grip of the man on my right, and my hip lands hard in the dirt, jostling my wrists, sending the spiked cuffs deeper into my skin. I bite my lip to keep my cry of pain contained as the man on my left swears. "Fates!"

He drops me, and as I fall back, I let my head thunk against the hard ground. My gaze meets the angry eyes of a silver-haired Seelie and a black-haired Unseelie. The Seelie draws his blade, pressing it to my chest with a scowl while speaking to the Unseelie. "Go get the horses and the rest of the party."

"It's not that much farther." The Unseelie reaches for my shoulder, and I involuntarily flinch. There's a wrongness in the touch of these dark fae. Obtaining magic through blood consumption and spells leaves a mark on your soul, and this fae emanates darkness. The Unseelie are called dark fae for more than just their black hair and eyes.

But the Seelie kicks me in the side, and if my rib isn't cracked, it's certainly bruised, and I cough a grunt of pain. "Just go get the horses. I'm not dragging him any farther. He's heavy, and my arm hurts."

I bet it does. I sliced him nearly to the bone before one of the soldiers struck me from behind. I smirk, unable to help myself. "I didn't peg you as a quitter. Give it another go. I'll even make it easier on you. I won't dig my heels into the ground anymore."

I watch the Unseelie walk off and miss the movement of the silver-haired fae standing next to me. His leg kicks out, landing a blow to my face. My cheek slams into the dirt, and my vision closes in for a few seconds. Unconsciousness is right there, and I will myself to slide into oblivion, but the darkness annoyingly recedes, and I'm left all too aware with a pounding headache. Just one more injury to add to the deep gash in my right thigh, my sprained left wrist, the slash across my upper back, and the many, many bruises across my face, arms, and torso. I'm proud of each one, telling the tale of the fight I put up.

As the Unseelie's footfalls grow quieter, the Seelie leans down, moving his sword from my chest to my side. His silver hair, streaked with blood from a gash I gave him along his hairline, falls over his face, and his ice-blue eyes glow with power and menace as his lips peel back in a sneer. There is also a dark bruise blooming along the lower half of his jaw, where I landed a right hook. I smile at his swollen face, and in response his hand wraps around my throat.

I'm surprised by the strength still left in his injured arm as he squeezes my windpipe. I force my smile to stay in place, enjoying his rage. Maybe he'll kill me. This is not how I wanted to go, but ...

He must see the resolve in my eyes because his grip lets up slightly, and he gives me a smile of his own.

Shit.

His voice slides between his lips in a harsh whisper. "You think you're so clever, assassin. But the King has plans for you, and no amount of taunting will drive us to disobey our King. You are to be brought in alive." He grins. "It's okay if you're broken, though."

Yeah, just as I thought. Garin wants to use me against Rae. And that, more than anything else, makes my heart race. I must find a way to either escape or make them kill me before we get back to the capital. I will not be used as a pawn, especially against Rae.

I let my anger pull my smile into a cruel grin as I completely relax into the ground, crossing one ankle over the other, ignoring the sting of the wound in my thigh.

"Garin really has you all on a tight leash, huh? How does it feel being a lap dog to a murderer and a coward?"

He holds back his anger for all of three seconds before his grip around my throat tightens once again. Bright points of light start to dance in front of my eyes. This is going to suck. I wish he would just stab me already.

"Really? Come on. Don't let him rile you. You know the King's orders." The Unseelie's voice breaks the tension, and as the Seelie stands, I roll my eyes. So close.

A chuckle has my ribs aching, but I ignore it. "The capital is far away. Think you can make it there without killing me? I promise to be a constant thorn in your side." They both scowl at me, and I laugh loudly, letting the pain wash over me. "This is going to be so much fun." I angle my head to look at the Unseelie. "By the way, when you strike with your right arm, you leave your left side open—you know, if you care about correct fighting technique."

His dark eyes go pensive for a moment before he shakes his head. "What do you know? You're on your back, unarmed, and our prisoner. It seems my technique is just fine."

"Yeah, well had it been just you ... eleven against one was a challenge, but I still managed to take out almost half of your party."

The Seelie sheaths his sword with a huff in the Unseelie's direction. "You do leave your left side open."

"I do not. And don't encourage him."

I smile at the sky, listening to the two bicker for a few minutes before the Seelie holds up a hand. "Whatever, it doesn't matter. Let's go." He bends down and grabs me under my shoulder. The Unseelie grabs a handful of my jacket, and the two haul me upright, though I don't make it easy for them. I go boneless, hanging heavy and limp in their arms, and they struggle to keep me upright. Every slight movement shoots pain through my body, but I relish the agony, I relish their frustration.

The remaining soldiers have joined us, three astride their horses, two more leading their mounts. A few chuckles ring through the air as the two struggle with me. One of the mounted soldiers laughs, his scruffy, silver beard almost hiding his lips. "Is it really taking the both of you to handle that single, bound fae?"

The Unseelie whips his head around. "Get off your ass and help us. There's no way we're going to get him on the horse. And until we get him mounted, we are stuck out here in the middle of—"

A six-pointed, metal star slams into the Unseelie's throat. His mouth gapes open, and I put my feet under me to steady myself, making sure I'm seeing what I think I'm seeing. Indeed, there in the center of the sharp star is a swirling circle design hammered into the metal.

Nyira is here.

The Seelie lets go of me as he steps back and unsheathes his sword again. Without either man holding me, I almost stumble and fall under my own weight, but I manage to stay on my feet.

The Unseelie staggers, reaching for the star still lodged in his throat, when an arrow made of fire slams into his chest. The blast sends him back a step, but the flames fall to the ground without causing any damage since he's a fire fae, which I learned during our fight.

But wait, Nyira is not a fire fae, she's an earth fae. She brought help.

The remaining soldiers erupt into action. The Seelie on my right grabs my arm and spins us in a tight circle, searching for where the attack is coming from, hoping to use me as a shield.

The three mounted soldiers jump to the ground, hiding behind their horses alongside the two who were already grounded. The Unseelie is fading fast as blood continues to pour from his neck, and flames coat his hands as his magic rises in a vain attempt to defend him. He drops to his knees, and the Seelie yanks me around. I watch the Unseelie grip the star, blood streaming between his fingers.

There's the clash of magic and steel behind us, but the Seelie has a tight hold on my cuffs, and I can't turn to see who's winning. His grip tightens, and for a second, I think he's been struck, but when I glance at his face, I see his eyes staring greedily at the dying Unseelie.

Oh no. Fates no.

I'm shoved forward and then kicked to my knees. An arrow lodges in my captor's shoulder, but he doesn't so much as wince. Yanking me forward, I grunt in pain as the Seelie uses me as a shield while he leans over the Unseelie, who's barely breathing at this point.

Bile stings my throat as the Seelie rips the star from the other man's throat. Blood spurts from the wound before it leaks down his neck, drenching his clothes. I want to tear my gaze away, but the silver-haired fae has a tight hold on me, and every effort to struggle away sends pain erupting up my arms. So, I watch with horror and disgust as the Seelie brings the star to his mouth and licks the blood.

His blue eyes flare and dilate before fire flickers along his fingers. A greedy smile lifts his lips, and my skin prickles. He pulls me closer on top of him, and in a quick, jarring motion, he latches onto the Unseelie's wound, drinking his blood. With every slurping swallow, the Unseelie's struggles weaken as his fire goes out and flames flare around the Seelie, drinking his power.

I swallow, again and again, trying to keep myself from vomiting. I manage to lift my head enough to peer over his shoulder. Three of the five soldiers are down. Two assassins, clothed in black, faces and hair covered with the New Moon Guild scarves approach the final two with slow, purposeful strides.

My gaze is ripped away from their lethal movements when the Seelie under me throws back his head with a final, satisfied swallow. The Unseelie is pale, unmoving, and fire covers the Seelie's body. Luckily, even though I can't call up my own fire, my innate fire magic protects me from the flames jumping from the Seelie's hands to the skin of my own hands and arms.

A crazed laugh rips from the Seelie as he shoves to his feet, dragging me with him. Fire blasts from him in every direction as he loses himself to his newly acquired power. Smoke billows up around us as the grass catches fire, and the horses start to scream as the flames get hotter. I peer through the raging fire, holding my breath. I may be immune to fire, but smoke inhalation is a rough way to die.

One of the assassins draws a blade across a soldier's neck, and the other throws a solidified, sharpened sword of air at the remaining soldier's head. There's a moment of shock and stillness before his head slides from his neck, thumping to the ground a second before his body joins it.

The Seelie holding me seems unaware of everything going on around us, so consumed is he by the rush of fire magic searing his veins. Good news, his magic is raging so hot, the metal chains between my cuffs are melting, though the shungite cuffs remain solid and unaffected, fortified by spells. He throws a stream of fire at the assassins who duck behind a shield of air, and the horses scatter, one trailing a stream of smoke behind it.

I grit my teeth and clench my upper back muscles as I rip my wrists apart, snapping the chain. The cuffs are still tight and digging into my skin, but at least I have independent movement of my arms again. I pull back my right arm and punch the flaming Seelie in the temple. He staggers but turns on me, actually growling. His fire rushes at me, the idiot too far gone to realize his fire is doing nothing to me. But I'd rather him direct his rage at me than the assassins.

I push through the heat and flame, choking as smoke pours down my throat. I duck under his flaming fist as he swings a left hook at me, and I grab his blade. I'll be damned if I die here, after all this. Swinging the blade hard overhead, I aim for the junction between his neck and shoulder but end up swinging at air.

I blink several times before I look down and see him clinging to the edge of a small chasm at my feet. A scream rips from his lips as the ground snaps closed, snuffing out his flames and squishing the fae like a roach.

I let my arm fall to my side, peering through the smoke as I stagger forward. There, emerging from the treeline, is Nyira. The New Moon Guild cloak and scarf cover her from head to boot, but I can tell it's her. I know her well—that confident sway of hips, the way her head is slightly tilted as she assesses everything around her.

The grass grows taller and turns a brighter shade of green as she walks toward me. A few flowers sprout and bloom in the wake of her footsteps. The residual energy of her earth magic makes her look like the fabled faeries in the children's books from Earth.

The air fae assassin smothers the remaining flames and sends a wind to carry away the last of the thick smoke. I take a few cleansing breaths while I fight to stay on my feet. I'm so tired. Everything hurts. Exhaustion weighs me down like heavy ropes looped around my shoulders and shackling my feet, making my steps heavy and uneven. But if I stop now, I'm not sure when I will get up again.

Nyira and the other two assassins stop in a semicircle around me. All three place their hands on their hips, and Nyira lifts a gloved hand to pull away the fabric covering her face. She smiles at me, cocking her hip to the side. "You've only been home a month, and I've had to save you twice. Earth really did make you soft."

I laugh, but it's cut short as pain tears through my bruised ribs. "It seems so."

One of the assassins tosses me a water orb—a thin membrane of fae magic that holds and preserves any liquid. I reach for it, but my forearms spasm painfully as the shungite spikes inside the cuffs dig into my skin. The orb falls and bounces along the ground, rolling to a stop at Nyira's feet.

She leans down, scoops up the orb, and steps forward, placing it in my hands. They shake as I bring it to my lips, and with a whispered word, "Elaxid," I'm able to bite through the membrane and drink down the cool water. It tastes like ambrosia, and I sigh, experiencing relief for the first time all day. As I finish the water, the membrane dissolves and floats away on the soft breeze.

I nod my thanks, and the assassin nods back. I still have no idea who the other two are, and I'm not going to ask. If they don't want to reveal themselves, that is their right within the assassin's code. Their identity is theirs to protect.

Nyira's voice draws my gaze back to her. "Any word on the princess?"

My stomach drops, and tension tightens my shoulders. "No."

"So, what next?"

I look at the other two. "You have decided to help?"

One shrugs, his voice revealing him to be male. "We are considering. Most of the Guild walked out as soon as Nyira mentioned your name." That's fair. It hurts my feelings more than I thought it would, but still. "But we"—he gestures to the other assassin standing still and silent, watching me—"are intrigued at the prospect of getting out from under the King's rule and the filthy Unseelie out of our kingdom." He kicks the drained Unseelie at our feet and sneers at the smear of goo on the ground—all that's left of the Seelie soldier—for emphasis.

Three assassins. That's all the help I'll get. It'll have to do. Now, do I take them to Dorwe? Rae might have already come back. And if she has, I can't imagine she would have hung out at the ruins for long. So hopefully, she would have left me some sort of message. If she has not come back, how long can I wait for her without drawing more soldiers to Dorwe? Apparently, Garin's soldiers are very good at tracking me down, and I can't lead Garin to Dorwe.

Nyira must see my indecision because she nods at my cuffs. "Well, first thing first, we need to get those off you. Then I suggest we check Dorwe before we make our next decision."

I open my mouth to ask her how she knew, but she nods again with a knowing smile at my hands, and I glance down. My palms are turned up, exposing the brand on my hand. Fates, I'm dumb. But I nod and take a step. My thigh spasms under me, and I almost fall to my knees, but lock my legs and stay upright.

Nyira frowns. "There's a small town ten miles northwest.

We can find a blacksmith to remove those cuffs. If you're lucky, there will be a halfway decent healer there as well."

I can only hope. It seems like ever since I landed back home, I've been constantly assaulted, beaten, bruised, cut, kicked ... things have to get better soon. Right? I nod up the road. "Lead the way."

The third assassin turns. "Our horses are half a mile through the woods to the east. We have an extra for you." She sounds young and sweet. But I know more than anyone that voices and appearances can be deceptive. I glance at the bodies of the soldiers she took down, looking over her handiwork as she turns, saying, "We will retrieve them. Rest. Catch your breath."

I nod my thanks as the two jog off into the woods, leaving Nyira with me. My legs shake more and more, and I struggle to stay upright. We remain silent until the assassins emerge with four horses in tow. I lean against the blue roan they brought for me and just breathe as I let the horse hold me up. On my third inhale, I feel the eyes of the assassins on my back, waiting for me, but I take my time gathering my strength before I heave myself into the saddle.

I will not fail you, Raelyn. I will not give up. I found you over and over on Earth, and we will find each other again.

With that vow to myself and to Rae, I turn my horse toward the waiting assassins. Nyira looks me over and must see through the pain into my resolve because she nods and turns her horse to the northwest.

They set a fast pace, maintaining a quick canter through the woods and breaking into a gallop in the open. Every hoofbeat is agony, and I almost fall from my horse twice when I start to blackout. But Rae's face, bright smile, glowing eyes, and delicately curved ears keep me going.

The three assassins are like mounted shadows, and I

smile. I'm not alone anymore. It's not as much help as I was hoping for, but it's something.

One step at a time, my path is leading me to war, and my magic tries to flare at the thought, held back by the cursed shungite cuffs. But even without my magic, I have ways to help Rae end Garin. The assassin within me, the part of my soul that I've trained and honed to thrive off secrets and death, won't hesitate to strike Garin's head from his shoulders.

I smile, thinking about the Seelie crown gleaming atop Raelyn's beautiful head.

21

RAELYN

AWARENESS COMES TO ME SLOWLY, like a winter sunrise trying to chase frost off a field. Wherever I am, it's quiet, but a faint rustling and the sound of soft, even breathing tells me there is at least one other person with me.

I take stock of my body, letting my mind travel from my toes to my head. Surprisingly, I feel okay—a little tired, and my limbs feel heavy, but the tearing pressure of my magic is gone.

Shit! My magic. What the hell was that?

Cracking open my eyelids, I immediately notice the sun's reflection off the crystal walls shimmering on the cream ceiling like light on rippling water. A slow, cautious inhale brings no additional pain, and I smell lilac and mountain breezes. So, I'm still in the Dragon's realm and back in Kem's rooms. I was afraid Kem was going to whisk me away.

"Good, you're awake." The concerned female voice

draws my head to the side. Syphe is sitting in a plush cream velvet chair. The sunlight gilds her bronze hair and eyes making her look like she's made of molten metal. Her lips are tight, and her eyes are pinched with worry as she looks me over.

There are a million questions tumbling through my mind like dead leaves on the wind. Each one seems more important and pressing than the last, and I'm not sure which one to grasp onto. Finally, I just blurt out, "When's the Challenge? Did I happen to sleep through it?" I smile, hoping if I joke around, it will push the pit of panic from my gut. "No. I know, the council voted in my favor. Oh, oh! Better yet, Ziza decided to call the whole thing off, and we're all having lunch together."

Syphe's lips attempt a smile, but her eyes dart to the floor, and my stomach plummets. Her eyes draw back to my face, and I can't help but notice the faint scars around her throat. Her mate may have healed her wounds, but apparently, she will carry the scars—because of me.

She notices my stare and leans forward, taking my hand. "I never got the chance to thank you, Raelyn. You saved me. I owe you my life."

I sit up, bringing the bed covers with me as I notice I'm completely naked. "The only reason you were attacked was because I'm here. I couldn't do nothing."

She squeezes my hand, and the warmth of her skin against mine is comforting. "Not all are as noble and true of heart as you." I blush at her words and fight to keep from fidgeting. The silence stretches between us for a few moments before she withdraws her hand and sits back, gripping the plush arms of her chair. "As to the Challenge, it's in an hour. I was about to wake you." She catches my panicked look and frowns. "I thought about waking you earlier but decided the extra rest would serve you better than having more time to stress."

"An hour? Fuck!" I throw my legs over the bed, standing as I wrap the sheet around my body. My skin prickles with tension, and my magic begins to claw at my skin. It feels crowded within my body. Where my air magic used to stir, there's now a swirling mass of powers just ... waiting.

My legs tremble as my eyes dart around the room, looking for clothes and weapons. Syphe grips my upper arm, and I go still. Her hand slides down my arm and takes my hand. With an awkward tug, she pulls my hand to her side, pressing my palm to the soft fabric of her tunic above her left hip. "Dragon's do have weaknesses, though it's against dragon law to speak of them." She pats my hand resting on the side of her stomach. "Raelyn, you can do this."

I step back, slightly unnerved by her actions, and Syphe releases me. What was that about?

I hug the sheet a little closer to my chest. Okay, an hour. Oomph. Okay. First things first. I hold up a hand, staring at my palm as I recall the crazy magic that assaulted me yesterday. "Do you know what happened? With my magic? Did I hurt anyone?"

Syphe doesn't answer. Instead, she backs up. "I'm going to get the King. He commanded that I notify him as soon as you woke. I should have gone as soon as you opened your eyes. He's been ... agitated."

"Isn't that normal? For dragons?"

She shrugs, but a small smile pulls at her lips. Crossing the room, her steps are silent on the thick rug. She opens the top drawer of a chest and pulls out several items. Coming back to where I'm still standing, she holds out an armful of folded clothes: undergarments, a black linen shirt, brown leather pants, and jacket. The leather is supple to allow for maximum movement, and tough leather reinforces the vital areas.

On top of the clothes rests a wrapped package. I glance at it with a frown. "What's this?"

"I got it for you the other day in the village, but never had a chance to give it to you."

Placing the clothes on the bed, my fingers tug at the string then peel back the simple brown paper. I gasp at the bright colors of a small tapestry no longer than my forearm. Despite its small size, it's highly detailed, and if I hadn't seen the weaver's work myself, I'd think it was machine made. There's a woman standing on a low rise of red grass, her head tilted back, her pointed ears peeking through her brown hair. Above her hovers a bronze dragon, the metallic threads shimmering through her spread wings.

My finger traces the outline of the dragon before I look up at Syphe with a wide grin on my face. "It's us."

She nods with what looks like embarrassment. "It's us."

I throw my arms around her, sinking into her warmth as she hugs me back. "Thank you, Syphe. I love it." She pulls back, holding my hand, her eyes shine with a confidence I wish I had. She nods, and without another word, Syphe leaves the room.

Just as I'm fastening the last buckle of the jacket, Kem stalks through the door. He is darkness, shadow, and power. As he crosses the room, his gaze travels from my head to my boots and back again. He stops an arm's distance from me, his voice is deep, resonating around the room, bouncing off the crystal walls. "How are you feeling?"

I look down at my body then hold my arms up away from my sides. "Okay, considering."

"Headache?"

I shake my head no.

"Nausea?"

"Nope."

"Is your vision clear?"

"I can clearly see you're annoying me." I grin, and he relaxes slightly, allowing a small smile to lift his lips. Tilting my head to the side, I plant my hands on my hips. "What happened with my magic?"

"You tapped into deeper power."

"Deeper?"

"Wild magic of the Elementals." He smiles down at me. "It's been a long, long time since I've met an Elemental." He shakes his head, chuckling softly. "Of course, it would be you."

My brain glitches. That can't be right. There hasn't been an Elemental in ... Fates, I don't know how long. And for a fae to not remember, it's been a while.

"You have strong magic, Raelyn, and with practice, the power of the four elements will aid you, delight you, and defend you."

I bite my lip. How could I possibly be an Elemental? My air magic sends soft currents swirling around me, and there, pressing against me from the inside, is ... more. That crowded feeling I noticed before intensifies as earth, water, and fire push at me. My body feels too warm, and I fight to keep the power contained.

Kem watches my hair dance in the breeze. "Breathe, Raelyn. I know this feels overwhelming right now, but you are a master of Air Magic." I fight to slow my breathing and focus on Kem's voice. "The other elements work and respond much the same way. You have the knowledge. You have the skill. You just need to apply what you know to four elements instead of one."

"Oh, is that all?" I'm trying to concentrate on my breaths, but the tangle of magics within me is distracting.

Kem's warm hand clasps my shoulder. "Raelyn, the magic wants to work with you, but if you don't maintain control, if you don't give it purpose, it will take over."

"Like in the hall."

He nods and takes a deep, slow inhale, and I breathe with him. The pressure fades, and my magic quiets. I look at Kem. "I'm an Elemental."

"You are an Elemental."

I frown. "What if I can't control it during the Challenge? What if I hurt a bystander?" I shift on my feet and lick my suddenly dry lips.

Kem steps back, sliding his hands in his pockets. "We can work on calling and controlling your new magic ... after the Challenge."

If I survive. Wait, after?

"Unfortunately"—Kem's shoulders bunch with tension—"the council decided you will not be able to use your magic during the Challenge."

"Excuse me?" Anger and fear tumble through my gut, and to keep my magic from rising, I start pacing the room. "I'm expected to fight a dragon with what, a blade?" My voice drips with sarcasm and no little amount of accusation.

"Ziza will not be allowed to shift. She will face you in her human form."

"Oh, phew." My voice is rising with every word. "I'll just face off against a woman who despises me and happens to have skin as tough as dragon's hide and nails as lethal as talons. But at least she can't shift. I feel so much better."

Kem's jaw ticks, and I have the impression he's holding back a smile. Damn it! This isn't funny. He's too calm, and it annoys me when his voice comes out strong and confident. "You are a good fighter, Rae."

"I guess we'll see." I snatch my daggers from the table by the bed and take small comfort that my hands are no longer shaking as I slip the blades into the sheaths strapped to my arm and thigh and slide a sword into place at my back.

"Raelyn." Kem's soft tone freezes me in place. "I would not let you fight if I didn't think you could win."

"The council voted. There's nothing you cou—"

"I would break all our laws and slay any dragon who defied me to keep you safe." My heart stutters, and I think I might melt under his intense gaze. "I believe in you, Raelyn. You can do this—and you can defeat Garin."

I break eye contact, shaking my head, and stare at my boots. I used to think Garin had faith in me, but now, with Kem, I realize what real support feels like. "I wish I believed in myself as much as you do." My voice lowers, and in a moment of weakness, I whisper, "What if I run? What if I ask you to take me somewhere, anywhere?"

"Is that what you want?"

"Yes ... No?" I huff a breath of frustration and meet Kem's burning gaze once more. "No. I'm tired of running." I'm angry. At myself, at Garin, at Ziza, at the mess of my life right now. "I'm done. No more running."

Nodding at Kem with a growing sense of determination, I cross the room toward the door. Just as I pass him, his arm shoots out and grabs my forearm. I'm pulled to a halt, and my eyes snap up to his face towering above me. "Give me a second."

Walking across the room, I marvel how quietly he moves for someone so big. Disappearing into the secondary bedroom, he returns a few seconds later holding a short sword in its scabbard. Stopping before me, he holds it out.

I take it, titling my head in question. He gestures at the sword. "Go ahead, draw it."

My hands wrap around the soft leather-wrapped hilt, and the sword glides silently from its home. The blade is light, astonishingly so. It fits my hand perfectly and is wonderfully balanced. The steel gleams in the soft sunlight, and as I tilt it, I see images crawling up the length. A diamond shape near the hilt for air. Four stacked wavy lines above that for water. A triangle for fire. And three stacked horizontal lines for earth. At the tip is a small crown—the fae crown, the crown Garin now wears.

My vision blurs as I look up at Kem, trying my best to hold back my tears. "This seems to be a day for gifts. It feels like my birthday."

His brows pinch in question, and I glance at the small tapestry laying on the bed. "From Syphe."

"It's beautiful."

"So is this sword, Kem. It's magnificent." I trace the elemental signs with a fingertip. "You just had this lying around?"

He shrugs. "I made it while you recovered. You need a blade fit for a Queen. A Queen who commands the elements. All it needs is a name."

The name shouts across my mind, and I smile. "It is called Sidere."

"After the brightest star on Attolyn?"

Nodding, I discard the blade strapped to my back and replace it with this one. "That was also my dog's name when I was a small girl. The star is bright and leads the way. My dog was a true companion with unquestioning loyalty."

"Leadership and loyalty. A worthy name for the blade."

Thank you, Kem." I close the distance between us, wrapping my arms around his waist, tucking my face into his chest. "Thank you."

Kem squeezes me tightly. "You're welcome."

I step back, breaking contact and walk to the door. I have a Challenge to win.

Kem is at my back, and Syphe draws up next to us, nodding at me with an encouraging smile. I nod back, trying to look confident, not sure if I succeed. My insides are starting to tremble.

Arvun, the silver dragon, stands at the doors with a sneer on her lips and mirth in her eyes. My fists clench. I've done nothing to this dragon. I've done nothing to any of them. I can't stop myself as I turn to Arvun, staring right into her silver eyes. "Are you going to come cheer me on, Arvun?"

Her sneer slips, and she looks baffled for a second before a low growl escapes between her clenched teeth.

"I'll take that as a no."

Syphe chuckles, and I toss her a smile as we march past Arvun. But my smile slides from my face as we turn a corner and pass through a pair of glass doors that lead to an open stretch of the gardens. We walk between the large trees on either side of the dirt path. Sunlight dapples the ground. Bees and butterflies flit from flower to flower in the blooming bushes. This place is too beautiful for what is about to happen.

A light breeze flutters through my hair, and I reach back to tie it into a tight ponytail. Glancing up, I see several dragons flying low and dipping behind the trees.

We leave the gardens with the next turn, and step on the red grass of a field with a few trees dotting the landscape. A lead ball of dread thunks into my stomach. People surround a large circle of pea gravel. Their hair creates a rainbow of color that I can't help but find beautiful as we approach. But I guess that is the essence of the realm of the Crimson Plains. It is a world of blinding beauty where beasts of immense power and violence live.

The sea of bodies part, and as I stride into the large circle, the sound of gravel crunching under my boots reminds me of the sound of Orsun's neck snapping under Kem's powerful jaws. I hold back my cringe, noticing Kem and Syphe are no longer behind me. They stopped at the edge of the crowd, and I feel their eyes on my back, especially Kem's.

The gorgeous woman in the center of the circle turns to face me. Her bright green hair is pulled back in a tight braid that weaves down her head and between her shoulder blades. Her emerald eyes take me in, and her skin shimmers with a light green iridescence. If she saw or heard about my little show of power yesterday, she is obviously not impressed or threatened. Her smile is cold, confident, and her eyes dance with arrogance.

A male steps into the circle and comes between us. His hair is a bright purple and is tied back in a small bun at the nape of his neck. His amethyst eyes flick between Ziza and me, nodding to each of us in turn. With a clear voice, he addresses the crowd. "Challenge has been issued and will be resolved this day." He turns to Ziza, and I find myself staring at his broad back. "Ziza will not shift to her dragon form during any point of the Challenge." Silence wraps around the clearing for what seems like an endless amount of seconds before Ziza nods.

The male turns to me, and I'm shocked to see kindness in his eyes as he once again addresses the crowd while holding my gaze. "Lady Raelyn will not use her magic during any point of the Challenge." I nod my agreement, and a small smile lifts his lips as he nods back before turning a small circle, speaking once again to the crowd. "No outside interference. This is a Challenge to the death. Once the Challenge is over, no recourse may be taken over the results."

With that, the male steps to the edge of the circle and shouts, "The Challenge is open."

Shouts, yells, and taunts erupt from the crowd as Ziza draws a wicked-looking blade from the scabbard at her hip. The sword Kem gave me is solid in my right hand as I unsheathe it, and I focus on the woman before me. I focus on her movements; how she moves, lowering her center of gravity, how she watches me, how she smirks and smiles in response to the calls of the dragons that surround us. That's good. Her attention is split. I ignore the crowd as I note how she holds her blade in her right hand, and her steps always lead with her left.

Years of training and sparring with the royal soldiers of Attolyn readies my body. And suddenly, I'm grateful for the thousands of years of fighting with Ash on Earth. A small smile lifts my lips, thinking through our many epic battles. He was the one who made my time on Earth bearable.

I won't let him down now.

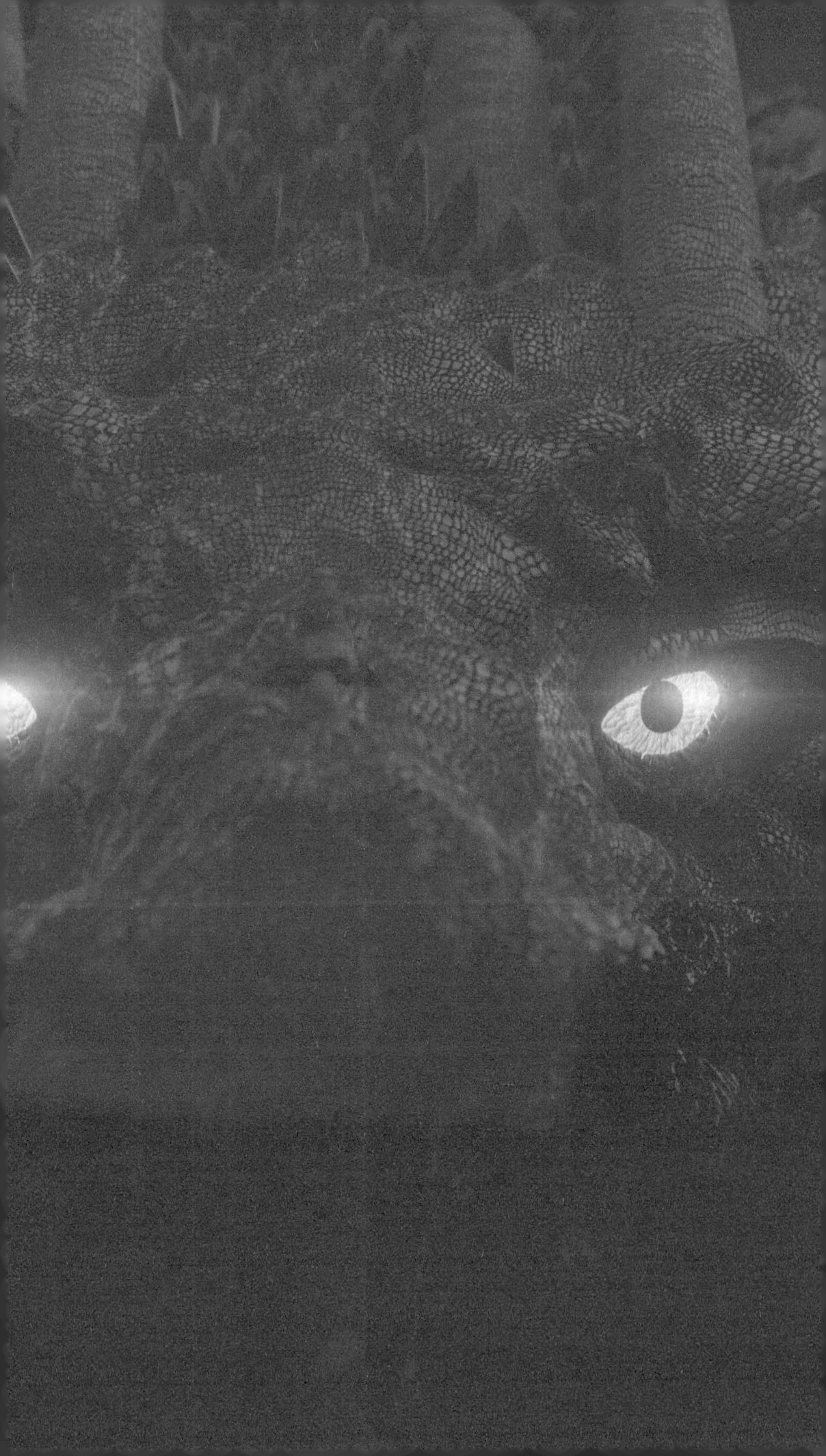

22

RAELYN

ZIZA CHARGES, and I brace for the first blow.

I drop and roll, barely clearing the vicious downward swipe of Ziza's blade. Gravel sticks to the side of my face as I push back to my feet. She's already swinging her blade again, and I throw up my sword arm, stopping her from slashing my head from my shoulders.

Great, three seconds in, and I'm already on the defensive. Just perfect.

It takes three more desperate deflections for me to realize I need to change tactics, or I'm going to die. I'm already sweating and regretting the leather jacket. Sure, it's offering me some level of protection from Ziza's seemingly endless assaults, but if I die from heatstroke, that will be eternally embarrassing.

Finally, I catch a break when Ziza's next swing takes her past me as I dodge. I'm able to turn quickly enough to step into her space, and for the first time, thrust my sword at her in an attack instead of a block. Surprisingly, I come fairly close to striking her—so close her tunic tears as my blade slices near her chest. But her sword clashes with mine, and my wrist barks with pain at the strength behind her block.

I keep a hold on my blade and step back, arching painfully to avoid losing my head as Ziza swings for my neck again. Sweat stings my eyes, and the buzz of the crowd is a loud distraction. There are cheers for Ziza and taunts aimed at me. "Teach the outsider a lesson! ... Cut her down! ... Tear her apart! ... Ziza doesn't need her talons or dragon fire to beat a lowly fae ..."

I suck in air, sweat running down my temple. Ziza's braided hair is neat, her face looks fresh, not a single bead of sweat mars her brow, and her breaths are even. I feel like I'm a mouse being toyed with by a mountain cat.

As she lunges again, blade thrusting right for my abdomen, I jump backward, but not fast enough. A cut opens along my stomach. I hiss, but if I look at it, it will hurt worse. The slice hits higher than the still-tender cut from Orsun's claws, but warm blood trickles down my skin, and sweat burns the wound.

I swing my sword, aiming for her shoulder. I make it past her block, and her tunic slices open as my blade cuts through the fabric. My sword slides right off her skin though, like I hit rock. Her damned dragon skin. My forward momentum brings me too close, and her free hand swipes out, her long, claw-like nails tear through my jacket, ripping open the skin on my shoulder. Pain zips down my arm.

I stay up. I keep fighting. I've tried to drown out the shouts around me, but the angry shouts keep worming their way into my consciousness. I'm tired, the muscles in my arms trembling a little more with each swing. My breaths come deep and fast. I haven't eaten in almost twenty-four hours—since I passed out from my magical outburst in the castle yesterday. My stomach tightens painfully, and for a second, all I can think about is food.

Dumbass who should be focusing on not dying right now, party of one, your table is ready.

I thrust, duck, pivot, and slash. Ziza grabs my sword arm, holding it out to the side, and punches me in the face. Stars dance in my vision for a second. Luckily, I don't need to see to reach for one of the small throwing knives I have strapped to my thigh.

The small blade slaps into my palm, and I stab it with all my strength into her hand. It actually sinks through the thick skin of her palm and out the back of her hand, drawing my own blood. She gives a yelp of pain, releases me, and as she steps back, I rip the knife from her hand.

I take a few seconds to catch my breath, surprised when I once again notice the shouts ringing out. They're not all against me. "You can do this, Lady Raelyn. Nice move, Raelyn. Her Highness is holding her own!"

I grip my weapons tighter as Ziza aims a roundhouse kick at my head, spraying gravel that pelts me in the face. I duck, stabbing my knife upward, glancing off her ankle without piercing her skin. I'm not so lucky as she plants her foot, using her momentum to slice her sword at my leg.

Jumping to the side, I manage to keep her from taking my leg off, instead earning a deep gash on my thigh. I stagger back, my legs wobbling with exhaustion. Though adrenaline is keeping most of the pain at bay, that won't last for much longer.

In the next few minutes, Ziza lands three more blows, and all I manage is a scrape across the skin of her collarbone. With every swing, my blade gets heavier, and my vision is starting to waiver with blood loss.

We end up tangled again with me gripping her sword arm by the wrist, straining against her massive strength. She has a crushing grip on my hand holding the throwing knife, and my wrist bones creak, about to snap. I do the only desperate thing I can think of. I head butt her.

Shit! Pain explodes between my eyes as we stumble apart, but satisfaction curls my lips in a half-smile as I see blood pouring from her nose, bruises already blooming across her eyes.

My small victory is short-lived as she growls at me, the sound deep and gravely from her dragon's belly. She's not allowed to shift, but she wants to—I can see it in her narrowed, enraged eyes.

A voice breaks through the deafening din, and I glance over Ziza's shoulder, seeing Syphe. Her eyes lock on mine, wide and intense. She shouts, exaggerating the movement of her lips in case I can't hear her. "Pay attention."

My first thought is, yeah, duh. But then I see her place her hand on her hip. No, not her hip. She presses her hand to her lower stomach right above her hip, where she pressed my hand earlier. I thought it weird at the time, and I could be reading into this—she could simply be resting her hand on her waist—but ... maybe. Dragons have weaknesses.

Fuck it. I take a chance. I pull back my arm and whip my sword end-over-end right at Ziza's lower stomach above her left hip. Before I see if my throw meets its mark, I'm running at her as I flick one, two, three, throwing knives at the same spot.

The crowd goes quiet, and I'm startled that I can once again hear bird song. I would have thought they would have all flown off at the ruckus. Ziza's face drops with shock as she looks down. My sword is sticking out of her stomach, still swaying slightly from the impact. Around the sword, in a small arc, my three throwing blades have sunk to the hilt into her skin like macabre popsicle sticks.

Before she registers what has happened, I'm on her. I grip the hilt of my sword and twist, tearing a scream from her throat. I kick the inside of her right knee, and she collapses, sinking into the bloody gravel. Kicking her sword from her hand, I shove her, pinning her back to the ground as I kneel on her chest with my knees holding her arms down. She bucks against me as I grip her hair, pulling her head back and exposing her neck. Leaning into her, I reach back, ripping one of the throwing knives from her stomach and press it to her neck. I brace against her and push my body weight behind the knife, and it starts to sink in, though it feels like I'm trying to push a knife through three-inch-thick leather.

Her eyes are wild as she stares at me, teeth bared, lips pulled back in a hateful sneer as she continues to buck against me. Sweat stings my eyes, and I grunt with effort as I push on the blade with both hands. Blood drips down her neck, and I grit out, "Yield."

A growl rumbles from her chest. "Kill me, or I will kill you."

I keep my eyes on hers as I press the blade deeper. She gurgles, and blood drips from her lips as she tries to say something but fails.

I raise my voice so the still-silent crowd can hear me. "I am not a dragon." My voice is strained as I continue to press all my strength into the blade. "I understand your anger at my presence in your world, but I will not fall victim to your ways. Not by dying here today, and not by letting you force me to kill another."

Another piece of who I want to be as a Queen snaps into place.

"I have bested Ziza, and that will be enough." I keep my full weight on the blade as I lift my gaze, once again searching for Kem, but I don't find him with my quick glance. So instead, my gaze flicks to the dragon who announced the start of the Challenge before I stare back down at Ziza with a growl of my own. "Declare it over."

The crowd starts to grumble which builds to shouts. "Finish it! ... End her ... Spill her blood ... Claim her death!" Yet more voices cry out, "Spare her ... Grant her mercy ... Raelyn has won ... Let it be done ... Raelyn has won!"

Finally, the officiant, or whoever he is, steps into the circle and raises his hand. It takes a few moments for the crowd to settle, but once they do, he says, "Her Lady Raelyn holds Ziza's life and has chosen not to take it. The Challenge is complete."

I release a shaky breath as groans, shouts, and cheers ring out around me. Keeping my eyes on Ziza, who has gone pale, blood coating her slender neck, I start to draw back, releasing some of the pressure against the hilt.

There are soft metallic sounds, and I vaguely realize people are exchanging gold coins. I have to swallow a laugh, or maybe it's a sob. People bet on this fight. A few gold pieces on whether I would live or die. How ... human.

Shadows peel away from the surrounding trees and coalesce at the edge of the circle. And there stands Kem. I'm relieved to see him. For a moment, I feared he didn't want to watch me fight, and lose, so he had left. A tiny smile pulls at his lips, and he nods at me. Fates, he's proud of me, and wow, does that feel good.

I'm still kneeling on Ziza as I yank the blade from her throat. As soon as it's free, her low whisper curls across my skin, raising goosebumps. "You should have killed me." My eyes snap to hers, and my heart leaps into double time. Smoke curls from her nostrils, and her chest is glowing red hot with her inner dragon fire. She bucks to the side, releasing her arm, now covered in green scales and tipped with the extended talons of her dragon. As I fall to the side, she swipes at me with her dragon claw, a grin on her face. "Garin sends his regards ... your Highness."

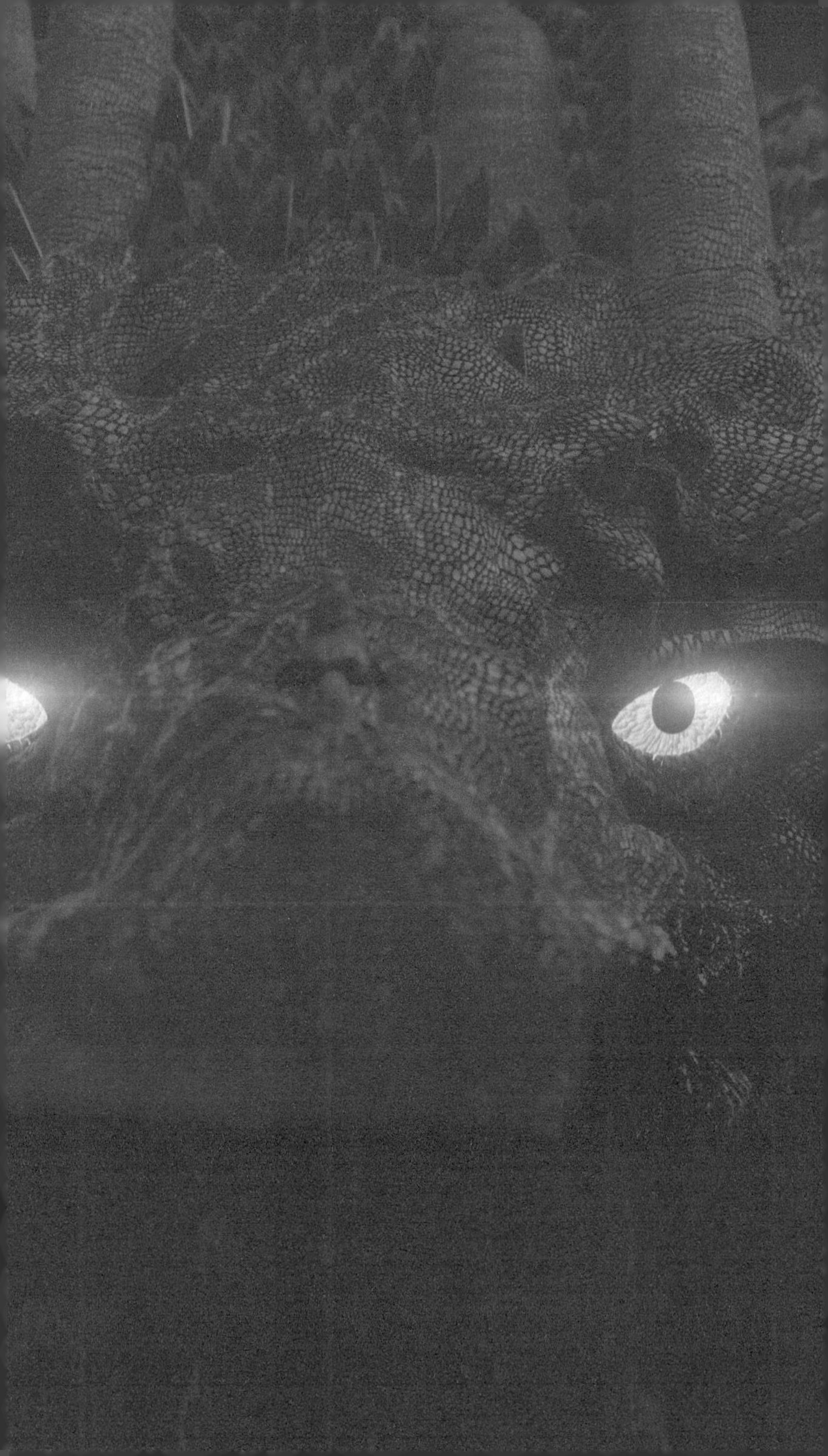

23

RAELYN

A GREAT ROAR erupts through the air. I ignore it, recognizing it as Kem's rage filled bellow. Instead, I leap to my feet, calling up my magic and shove it outward in a show of power that erupts from my very soul. A dome of solid air encases us, locking us away from the crowd. This is between Ziza and me.

I'm shaking with a potent mix of anger and fear, and my blood roars in my ears.

Molten fire erupts from Ziza's mouth, but her magma hits my magic and freezes mid-air, falling to the ground and shattering into a million dark shards at my feet. My air magic reaches into her chest and cuts off the oxygen to her inner fire. I squeeze, reveling in my power, enjoying the panicked look on her face.

My voice is deep, laced with cruel amusement. "You've

mistaken mercy with weakness. You've messed with the wrong fae."

The ground rumbles, roots burst through the gravel and wrap themselves around her legs, waist, neck, and head, yanking her to the ground, pinning her on her back.

A storm of emotions roils through me. I'm in awe of my magic, and I'm enjoying seeing Ziza squirm before me. I'm also angry that this woman is wasting my time when I should be concentrating on my brother.

Ugh. My brother. Rage and terror fill me like poison. Somehow, my brother is involved here. Somehow Garin has reached me—even here.

Fire licks at my hands and climbs up my arms as I lean down and grip the hilt of my sword, still lodged in her stomach. The blade heats under my flames, and it slides deeper, first one inch, then two, until I feel the tip of the blade punch through her back, pinning her to the ground like an insect on a display board.

She screams, and smoke puffs from her gasping mouth. I don't care. I lean closer, inhaling the scent of brimstone. Her eyes are wide and panicked, our lips almost touch as I whisper, "What was that about my brother?"

The roots wind tighter, pulling her harder against the ground, and my air magic increases the pressure on her chest, slowly crushing her. She whimpers, and I vaguely register the presence of the crowd outside the bubble of air. I think someone or several someones might be calling my name, but I can't be bothered with the distraction. Reinforcing my air shield, the noise is cut off, and silence snaps in around Ziza and me.

"I will snuff out your dragon's heart, your dragon fire." She's no longer struggling, and true fear spreads across her face. "I'll kill your dragon. Do you think you can survive that? I don't." I smile, feeding off her terror. "How do you know my brother?"

She tries to shake her head, but the roots hold her too tightly, blood running down her face where the roots have dug deep into her scalp. Her voice is shaky, and even as close as I am, I almost don't hear her strangled words. "He'll ... kill me."

My heart cracks open once again, and I wonder how many times you can put your heart back together before it refuses to be fixed. How did I so misjudge Garin?

I keep my face blank, and little sparks of electricity snap from my fingers. "I have no doubt. But right now"—I press my hand to her chest, and an electrical shock causes her body to jerk against the stranglehold of the roots—"I'm the one you should be worried about."

Her eyes are the only thing she can move, and they lower. She's scared. I can feel her trembling beneath my hands. Magic is coursing through me, around me, and it's hungry. Condensation puffs from my lips as the space around us starts to freeze. Pushing the cold inside her I coat her inner fire with ice crystals. She screams, blood coating the roots as she struggles against her bonds. Smoke pours from her mouth, nose, ears, and even her eyes.

Ziza's struggles are weakening, her screams turning to moans. Magic is buzzing through me, and I feel ... everything. The ground vibrates with the strength of my power causing the gravel to jump in a little dance. The air shield around us frosts over, and Ziza's hair turns white with ice crystals. I can't see the trees beyond the shield, but I can feel them. Their trunks expand and contract like they are breathing in my magic, and their branches reach toward me. I can feel the water bubbling in a nearby fountain, and I somehow understand the water comes from a spring that lies deep underground.

The air currents gather distant clouds, and the space within the shield falls into shadow as a storm gathers. The winds beyond our bubble start to circulate into a funnel, and the angry clouds overhead rumble with electrical charge.

I want to feel it. I want to feel my magic unleashed, so I drop the shield.

Shifters have backed away from the Challenge circle. Some crouch under trees and bushes. A few have shifted and are trying to fly away, but the erratic wind currents created by my magic quickly ground them.

I rip a lightning bolt from the sky, and it slams to the ground a few feet from Ziza's head. Everything turns white with the flash, and her scream is lost in the deafening crack of thunder.

"D-Don't ... kill m-me." There's desperation behind her voice. Her lips are blue, and the fire in her eyes is sputtering. On a weak wheeze, she stutters, "I ha-have in-informa ... tion." Her eyes are wide and desperate. "You'll ..." A cough sends chunks of frozen blood from her mouth. "Want ... to ... know." Her eyes roll back before she forces herself to focus back on me. "Please."

Wind whips my ponytail around my face, and little electrical pulses continue to snap along my skin, shocking Ziza over and over. Frost coats her skin, and the black smoke that was pouring from her is now weak, white vapor that puffs from her lips with every pained exhale.

I smile as I look down at Ziza's agonized face. "I already know my brother is a scheming liar." Saying those words out loud crushes my heart, and the thrill of conquering this dragon seeps away.

In its place is pity.

Did Alek feel gnawing guilt when he tortured the fae who hired Ash, or did he enjoy it? Did Garin's hands shake the first time he spilled another's blood and used dark magic, or did he thrill at it from the start? Maybe I am more like my brothers than I thought.

I swallow down bile, goosebumps spreading across my skin.

"No." Blood-coated ice vapor floats from Ziza's mouth as she coughs. Every word is a struggle. "No. Please don't."

"ENOUGH." Kem's voice cuts through her pleas, and he approaches from my right and steps up to us. I stand slowly, ignoring the pain of my wounds, letting my magic hold Ziza down.

Snow has started to drift from the angry clouds, and Kem's skin steams every time a large flake lands on him. I pull back my air magic, calming the whirlwinds but keeping pressure on Ziza. Kem's eyes sweep over me, and I catch what I think looks like relief on his face before he turns to Ziza. Rage tenses his muscles, and his shadows start to curl away from his body, reaching for Ziza like an angel of death.

His voice is low and calm, which makes it sound all the more deadly. "Your life is forfeit." His chest and stomach start glowing, the red-hot embers of his dragon burning away the front of his tunic until it hangs off him like a cloak.

His shadows lick at Ziza's boots, and she's frozen with literal ice and fear. Her wide eyes snap to me with a silent plea as a growl rumbles from Kem's chest. He inhales, and I know he means to incinerate her right here.

"No." Her cry is weak, but her nails claw the ground, desperate to save herself. Her eyes beg me, pleading.

Damn it.

Before I can think about it, I leap in front of her,

throwing up a shield just as the first splash of molten fire spews from Kem's mouth. The fire drips down my shield like a lava flow, and Kem takes a step back. For a moment, his eyes go wide with shock, but it's gone a second later, and his scowl returns. "Your Highness?"

Uh oh. We're back to 'your Highness.' I'm in trouble.

I lift my chin and stare him down, attempting to look like a Queen. "I spared Ziza's life. Your rules say you don't get to claim reprisal."

"She broke the rules of Challenge."

"Technically, the Challenge was declared over."

He just stares at me, a disapproving frown on his face. The seconds draw out as I stare right back. Peeling his eyes from me, he tilts his head and looks at Ziza, now laying limp in her bonds, every breath a struggle. "Speak."

"I—" That single word chokes from her lips, and frothy blood slides down her face. With a sigh, I release my earth magic, letting the roots slide back into the ground. The winds calm, and the clouds part allowing the sun to thaw Ziza's frozen body. With a roll of my tight shoulders, I let go of the hold I have on her inner fire, and her stomach glows as her dragon heart flares. She licks her lips, breathing slow and deep.

Leaning down, I grip the hilt of my sword, plant my feet, and yank. She grunts as the blade rips from her stomach, and I seal the wound with a patch of air. Her blood drips off my sword, splashing on the gravel in rhythmic drops.

Kem crosses his arms over his chest, and Ziza slowly pushes herself to a seated position. Bracing herself with one arm, she uses her other hand to pull the remaining two throwing knives from her stomach, letting them clatter to the bloody gravel. "I went to the King of the fae."

A low growl is Kem's only response, and I grip my sword

a little tighter at her words. She opens her mouth to continue, but Kem holds up a hand. Without looking away from her, his scowl deepening, he says, "The Challenge is over. Leave."

The adrenaline is slowly leaking from my body, and I think he's talking to me, but then the remainder of the crowd scatters, and I realize he was dismissing his people. Some quickly walk into the gardens, others shift and fly off with great flaps of colorful wings. No more than a minute later, it's just the three of us.

No. Wait. Off to my right, standing under a tree, dappled sunlight shimmering over her bronze hair, Syphe stands, arms crossed over her chest, eyes on me. I take a deep breath, and for the first time in a while, it fills my lungs completely. Biting my bottom lip, I nod at her. A small smile lifts her lips, and she nods back.

I look back at Kem. He's still staring daggers down at Ziza, and he lifts a single eyebrow.

She takes a deep breath and winces in pain. "I was so angry that you would break our laws"—her head bows, strands of emerald hair escaping her braid—"for her." It takes all my willpower to keep from fidgeting as she goes on. "For centuries, I and others have petitioned you to reconsider several of our laws." Kem's face is like granite, no emotion breaking through. How does he do that? "You know we wanted a doorway to our realm, we wanted to be more connected to the other realms. We wanted more freedom." There is such betrayal in her voice, I find I empathize with her. "And then you just show up, with her."

"I am King."

"Precisely. I realized if I ever wanted change, I would have to be Queen. But I'm not strong enough."

Kem smirks, but there's anger behind it. "No. You are not."

Ziza drops her gaze. "So, in my anger, I went to Garin and told him his sister was here." My palms start to sweat at the mention of my brother, and I widen my stance to keep my shaking legs from buckling. "I promised him I would kill Raelyn for him. In exchange, I would grant him access to our realm so he could bring his army of Seelie and Unseelie and"—she looks back up at her King, and I can't tell from her expression what she's thinking in this moment—"take care of you and those loyal to you."

Kem stands stoic and silent. He doesn't react to Ziza's admission, and my skin is itchy with tension. The silence draws out, and I can't help myself from asking her, "What made you think my brother could best Kemremir and the dragons? And if he did, what made you think he wouldn't claim this realm for himself?"

She frowns. "I ... I don't know. I was just so angry." She flicks her eyes to me before dropping her gaze to the ground. "It wasn't personal. You were a means to an end. I saw an opportunity, and I took it." She presses her lips together before licking them and taking a deep breath, wincing in pain. "For what it's worth, I'm sorry. I let my anger lead my actions."

I sigh, combing my fingers through my messy ponytail. I kneel next to the woman who just tried to kill me—for a crown. I move to sit, but with absolutely no grace, I fall onto my hip. Settling as much as I can, I sigh again. "I understand." I allow a small smile to curve up my lips. "I mean, I'm still pissed you challenged me, but I understand." Her pale face looks almost sickly against her green hair, which has dirt and gravel stuck in her messy braid, but she chuckles. I set my blade on the ground, crossing my ankles. I'm tired—of everything.

Ziza murmurs, "What now?"

I look up at Kem, and whatever he sees on my face causes him to sigh and uncross his arms to let them hang at his sides. His voice grumbles but is calm and quiet. "What would you do, Ziza, if our roles were reversed?"

The question surprises me and outright shocks Ziza. Her eyes widen, and her mouth drops open, but a second later, a frown pulls at her lips. "I'd kill you."

I open my mouth to protest, but Kem cuts me off. "I could just let the fae King take care of you. You were so eager to work with him, I could drop you in Attolyn, block your magic from being able to bring you back to our realm, and leave you with your new friend. I can't imagine he will be very happy with you when he learns you failed."

Ziza looks to me, not Kem. "Your brother will find no shortage of dragons willing to help him. I believed his promises of power and partnership. Others will too."

Kem's eyes narrow. His body goes rigid as he tilts his head toward the sky. Shadows peel from his skin and swirl around him in a dark dance of power. The edges of his body blur to the point where he seems more shadow than man. A few seconds pass before his body absorbs the shadows, and he solidifies. His gaze lands back on Ziza's, and his eyebrow lifts with a smirk on his face.

Ziza nods.

My gaze bounces between them. "What just happened?"

Kem doesn't move, and Ziza coughs, sending more blood dripping down her chin before saying, "His Majesty has blocked the magic that allows us to travel between realms."

"What?" I can't seem to keep up. I'm so tired, and my body and brain are trying to shut down.

Ziza looks at me. "The dragons have been grounded. We cannot leave The Crimson Plains until our King releases us."

My head snaps to Kem. "You can do that?"

He nods, and his arms flex as he reaches up to tie half of his locs away from his face. "Your brother will find no assistance here."

I kind of wish he had done that as soon as we first arrived here, but I understand wanting to allow your people as much freedom as possible. I mean, how could he have guessed one of his own would seek out Garin? You can't predict everything. And as someone who is fighting to be Queen, that's terrifying.

Kem's voice shifts to a harsh command. "Leave us." For a second, I once again think he's talking to me, but he's staring at Ziza. "Unless"—he looks down at me—"you have decided to claim her life as payment for her betrayal?"

I shake my head, exhaustion slumping my shoulders. The slashes in my skin from Ziza's claws are starting to burn with increasing pain as the adrenaline drains away. I have never felt less like a princess than I do right now. I'm so tired of fighting, and the real fight isn't even here yet.

Kem tilts his head. "Imprisonment then?"

I shake my head again and turn to Ziza. "I'd like to think you can get beyond your anger and see that my presence here can actually be seen as a good thing. I'd like to be your friend, Ziza."

Shock, then gratitude flits through her tired eyes. "I ... I'll think on that, Lady Raelyn."

She smiles, shifting, but I grip her hand before she can stand. "Don't make me regret this." Electrical sparks zip from my skin to hers before I rein in my magic. She hisses, and I let her go, holding her gaze. She nods and, avoiding Kem's eyes, quickly limps away.

"I don't know if that was wise." Kem sits on the ground next to me, his warmth comforting.

"Isn't that part of being a Queen? Making decisions and then questioning them?"

I smile up at him, and finally, a smile breaks his serious face. "I'm afraid so. And unfortunately, it doesn't get easier. Not for people like you." I frown at him, not sure how to take that. "You have a kind heart and a fierce spirit. Tenderness is hard to hold onto. The weight of the crown will always try to rip compassion from your heart."

"Wow. Thanks for that. I feel so much better."

He smiles, nudging my shoulder with his. "It was supposed to be a compliment."

I smile back. "I know."

His eyes flit over my body. "Are you in much pain?"

I look at my shoulder, pulling back the torn fabric of my ruined jacket and shirt. Deep gashes score across my chest and shoulder. The cut on my stomach burns, and the slash on my thigh is slowly seeping blood.

"I could lie, but yes. Everything hurts, and I honestly don't know how I'm still conscious."

He places a gentle hand on my shoulder, and the pain subsides. His other hand splays across my stomach, and there's a slight tremor to his touch. He holds his hand there for several minutes before sliding it down over my hip and over my thigh. After another few minutes, he pulls back and places his hands in the gravel behind him, leaning back slightly.

"Thanks."

"I'm appalled at the number of times I've had to heal you since you've been here."

He angles his head down toward me as I chuckle softly. "Well, don't go thinking you're special or something. I've always been exceptional at getting myself into trouble."

He laughs, letting his head fall back, and I do the same. Our laugher dies, and we sit in silence for a few seconds watching white wisps of clouds float lazily overhead.

I nearly jump out of my skin when Kem's raised voice cuts through the clearing. "Syphe, will you make sure my rooms are prepared for Lady Raelyn?"

She doesn't answer, but the crunch of gravel under boots tells me she's heading back to the castle. I keep my eyes on the sky, wishing I could drift away with the clouds. Kem lets me sit in silence for several long minutes before I sigh. "I guess I should go in and get cleaned up."

He sits up, pressing a hand to my forearm, so I settle back into the increasingly uncomfortable gravel. He opens his mouth to say something, closes it, and opens it again before looking down at where his hand rests on my arm. I can feel his warmth through the leather of my jacket, and even more of my pain leaks away.

He pulls his hand from my arm and drops his gaze to his lap. "Ask me, Raelyn."

He's avoiding my gaze, and he clasps his hands tightly, turning his knuckles white. I'm confused by his question. "Wha—"

"Ask me to kill Garin."

24

ASHERAHT

An eerie quiet settles in my ears as we move through the ruins of Dorwe. I feel the muscles of my horse's back bunch and tense under my thighs. Even he knows there's something off about this place.

It's not a large area, smaller than the tiny town we just left. Dorwe is the remains of a temple sanctuary from a long-lost religion that worshiped the stars. That religion fell out of favor when the temples of the Fates started to spread. And now, the number of those who still worship the Fates is dwindling, though I'm sure another religion will pop up. They always do.

I absently rub my wrists. It took the local blacksmith an hour of agonizing labor to get the cuffs off. Every strike of his iron, every run of his file over the shungite made the tiny spikes dig deeper into my flesh. The first half-hour or so, I was able to grit through the pain. But after a while, the spasms in my forearms started sending bolts of agony up my arms, across my shoulders, and down my back. Before the first cuff hit the ground, silent tears were streaming down my face, and I was shaking so badly, Nyira had to bring over a stool for me to sit on.

Once the first cuff came off, I just stared at the bloody spikes covered in pieces of my flesh, laying on the ground. I swore and almost resolved to just live with the other cuff. The thought of going through all that again was ...

But then my mind took me back to the palace dungeons in China, 570. The image of Rae chained to a stone table, drugged on opium—the drug keeping her magic buried— played through my mind. Her right arm was sliced open from shoulder to elbow, and the skin was pulled back with pins to reveal muscle and bone. Her face was pale and slick with sweat.

My heart had ripped apart as I called her name and received no response. Sure, I was sent to Earth to kill her, but the thought of those lowly humans hurting her, experimenting on her, drove me to near madness. It was an anger I blamed on indignation, not yet ready to admit she was getting under my skin and worming her way into my heart.

Her glassy eyes looked right through me. I had killed dozens of guards to get to her, and at that moment, I wanted nothing more than to raze the whole goddamn palace to the ground.

I melted the chains from the table with my fire magic and noted the scars along her torso. Some were long and thin, others were round and puckered like they had scooped pieces of flesh from her body over and over. Her left wrist was broken, several of her nails had been ripped clean off, there were needles sticking out of both her knees, and her feet were twisted at an odd angle. At the time, I had no idea how long she had been there, but from the state of her, I knew it must have been a while. I later learned she was there for years. She had been arrested under the suspicion of conspiring with the monks who smuggled silkworm eggs out of China to Byzantine back in 552.

Eighteen years. She was there for eighteen years.

She didn't moan or flinch as I scooped her off the table. Her head just fell back into my arms, and her limbs hung heavy. Drool dripped down her cheek, and her dark hair was almost black with sweat and dirt. I whispered her name over and over, hoping she could somehow hear me and know she was free from her nightmare. Chanting her name also kept me from erupting with fury.

That came later.

Once she was safe under the care of a medicine man deep in the mountains, I returned to the palace, leaving a trail of bodies until I had hunted down every person responsible for her torture. After, I set my fire free and burned the dungeons down, stone and all.

The memory of Raelyn's torture gave me the strength to push through the removal of my second cuff.

Now, as we finish yet another pass through the ruins, our horses walk under a half-crumbled stone archway. I stare at the puncture wounds on my wrists which are now angry scabs. The twinge of my bruised ribs has subsided to a dull ache. The swelling on my face has gone down, and my other cuts have closed. My wrists will be the last to heal. Shungite will do that to a fae. My back spasms just to prove my point as the dagger wound from the cave continues to flare. But the healer in that village was both skilled and powerful, a rarity for a town so small.

Nyira draws her horse to a stop, and we follow suit. She

dismounts, as do the other two. I'm a little slower to follow, looking around for any sign that Rae is or was here.

One of the assassins walks off. The other gathers both horse's reins and leads them to a small clearing. I still haven't learned either of their names. The female has short silver hair cut in what would be called a pixie cut on Earth. Her features are delicate with soft angles to her face and unique lavender eyes, but she rarely reveals her face, keeping her scarf secured most of the time.

The other assassin is male and has spoken a few times. He's slight but well-muscled with sharp features and deep-set eyes the color of moss. He makes quick work of the saddles, setting them aside before rubbing down the sweaty horse's backs. His arm muscles ripple with each stroke, revealing the power under his lithe form.

As I dismount, Nyira comes to my side, her glowing gold eyes assessing me. She gently lifts one of my wrists in her hand, running the pad of her thumb over the scabs. "Can you fight?"

I pull out of her grip. "Of course. The shungite has worn off enough so I can call up my magic, and the pain is not so bad that I can't wield a blade." My voice is a little harsher than I intended, and a flicker of hurt passes her eyes before she slaps a neutral expression on her face and steps back.

"We have been through the ruins twice, and there's no sign of Raelyn."

I don't answer. I'm not ready to give up. Not yet. This was my only connection to Rae, and if I leave here without her, or at least a clue where she will be, it'll be like losing her all over again.

The leather of my horse's reins is both rough and supple in my hand as I lead him to where the other horses are tied up. The male assassin takes my horse and begins to unsaddle him.

Turning, I stride a dozen yards away before sitting on a large flat stone once a part of the temple wall. I lean forward, resting my forearms on my thighs, letting my head hang heavy. The sun warms my back, and a soft breeze kicks a few leaves around my boots. The weather is so much milder down here in the south of the kingdom, and I'm happy to be out of the constant freezing mists and rains of Dalnak.

I let my magic spool through my blood, and flames lick at my fingers. Concentrating my power to my hands, I force my fire into a white-hot point of flame. I lean over and hold my hand over the side of the stone where I sit, burning a circle into its face. I've left these marks all around the ruins of Dorwe in hopes that when Rae shows up, she'll see the marks and know I'm with my Guild.

Nyira sighs where she stands at my side, and I don't bother to look up. I know she's frustrated and wants to move on. While it's true we assassins are trained in the art of endless patience, Nyira is ready to do something, anything.

I turn my hands over, back and forth, staring at the scabs ringing my wrists like a painful bracelet. "Once the horses are rested, we'll head back toward the capital." My chest constricts as I voice the words, but we can't stay here much longer. I can't chance leading Garin's soldiers to this place. "I'm not sure when Raelyn is coming back." Or if she's coming back. But I don't say that out loud. She has to come back. For so many reasons. "But I need time to scout the city streets and learn the soldiers' patterns to prepare for her return."

I lift my head and meet Nyira's golden eyes. "How often does Garin leave the castle?"

She places her hands on her hips, kicking out her left hip in her familiar stance. "Not often. But occasionally, he graces the city with his presence when a particularly disobedient citizen requires punishment. He likes to remind the people of how powerful his magic is. We've seen him burn people alive, crush people in the earth, strip the air from their lungs, and drown people with their own bodily fluids. The King steals magic daily and doesn't hesitate to show off his power. The rumors say his dungeons are filled with fae who possess magic. He doesn't drain them but keeps them alive and rotates through them, drinking their power."

Shit. So much blood magic. If those rumors are true, I have to be glad Garin's not killing those he's drinking from. Consuming blood gives you a piece of their power. Drinking them to death gives you a rush of immense magic—like what happened to the Seelie earlier.

I groan inwardly. How are we going to defeat him? I have fire, Nyira has earth, and Rae and the male assassin in our party have air magic. But Garin might have access to all the elements depending on how much dark magic he has consumed on any given day ... and he has an army of soldiers.

Nyira crosses her right arm over her waist, holding her hip. "Ash, I don't know if the King can be beaten. He might as well have midnight black hair and coal-black eyes for all the dark, blood magic he has used." She bites her bottom lip before continuing. "That fae back there who drained the Unseelie—" I shiver as I recall his cruel, power-hungry smile. "That was child's play compared to what the King has done."

I felt Garin's magic in that cave. Never have I felt the heat of flames before, but that night was the closest I've ever come to fearing fire, that and facing Kem's dragon. "I appreciate what you've done for me, Nyira, but you don't have to do this. You've already lost too much to him. The Guild needs you."

She crouches in front of me, taking my hands in hers. I want to pull away, but I let her hold me for now. She has a sad frown on her face as her thumb starts to trace small circles on the back of my hand. "What use will there be for a guild if our people are exterminated? Plus, you can't do this on your own." One of her hands stays clasped to mine as her calloused palm caresses my cheek. Our gazes meet, and I frown at her as she continues. "What if she doesn't come back?"

I flinch at her words, hating to hear her voice the doubt I've been trying to bury inside myself. I jerk out of her touch and stand, moving away from her. "She will."

Nyira follows me, grabbing my upper arm, forcing me to face her. "How are you so sure? And what if she doesn't?" I try to pull from her grip, but she holds me tight. "Will you still go up against the King? And what if you succeed? Who will rule us then? You?" She grips my other arm pulling me closer to her. I look down at her, seeing what looks like panic in her eyes. "Have you thought this through, Ash? If you go against the King without Raelyn, and if by some miracle of the Fates you manage to kill him, there will be a power vacuum. The Unseelie will pounce. The Seelie will be annihilated. We're damned if we do, and damned if we don't, unless we have someone strong enough to replace Garin and drive the Unseelie from our lands."

She's right, and my emotions are swirling inside me, making me lightheaded. My shoulders slump slightly, and Nyira steps even closer. Our boots touch, and she tilts her head up, her lips slightly parted, her breath fanning across my face. "Ash, come back to the Guild."

"I can't."

"Then come back with me. We can go anywhere." Her voice is a whisper, and her chest presses to mine. Her hands slide from my arms to my shoulders and around my back. She's familiar. We've been here, in a similar embrace many times before. But that was a long, long time ago. And that was before Rae. Where Nyira's curves and lips used to ignite the fires of passion in my blood, now having her in my arms does nothing.

I push her an arm's length away. "No."

Crossing her arms over her chest, she frowns. "Do you love her?"

I do, but I've never said the words out loud, and I want Rae to be the one to hear them the first time I say them. I simply shrug. "It doesn't matter. I vowed I would be here for her, so I will stand by my word."

"How long will you wait for her?" Her words are getting louder, anger starting to redden her cheeks.

"It's only been a month, Nyira."

"That's not an answer. Will you wait six months? Six years? Six centuries?"

I will wait an eternity for her.

I don't answer, just stare her down. I might be losing my only ally here, but I can't abandon Rae. I won't.

She scowls at my silence. "I'll give you one more month, Ash. That's all I can afford."

I nod, my knees weak with relief. "That's fair."

She stalks off, but after a few paces turns, looking at me over her shoulder. "We were good together."

"We were."

"Earth changed you."

Raelyn changed me.

She turns away from my silent stare, going to where the male assassin is feeding the horses. She exchanges a few quiet words with him before stalking off into the woods surrounding the ruins. The other female assassin is already scouting and guarding our perimeter, and we don't need a second, but I assume Nyira just wants to put some space between us.

Hauling myself off the stone, I walk over to where our saddles are set aside. I grab an apple from my pack and hold it up toward the male assassin. He nods, holding up his hands, and I toss him the fruit before I grab another one and find a stone to sit on. This one seems to be the remains of a fountain or a pool of some sort.

After a few minutes, the male joins me, sitting on the ground a few feet across from me. He toes a few small rocks before calling up his air magic to float them off the ground, spinning them in lazy circles. Keeping his eyes on the stones, he says, "My name is Sylmare." I remain silent, accepting his name as the sign of trust that it is. "Nyira has her reasons for joining you, as does our other comrade." Whoever the other assassin is, her name is not his to reveal to me.

The rocks fall, his eyes lift to meet mine, and I ask, "So why did you come?"

His jaw clenches, and his eyes narrow. The clean moss color of his eyes darkens to a forest green as his hands close into fists. He doesn't break eye contact as he takes a breath. "In his quest to punish the Guild, the King killed my husband. He burned our home to ash. He dismissed my sister from her job in the castle, leaving her with no income, and if you've been dismissed by the King, no one wants to hire you for fear of retaliation. He also hunted me for months, his soldiers tracking me down relentlessly."

He shrugs, an angry smile tugging at his lips. "I guess he got bored of losing every soldier he sent after me because eventually, they stopped coming. I'm only still working with the Guild because, despite our fall from grace, I can still make decent coin—though I have to work twice as many jobs to make half of what I used to. But I'm supporting my husband's parents as well as my sister."

The rocks lift back off the ground, and the wind picks up around us, whipping his hair around his face and kicking dust into little whirlwinds. I can't hold back the ache in my chest as his show of power reminds me of Rae. Everything seems to remind me of Rae.

Sylmare's voice is low. "I honestly don't care if Raelyn takes the throne from Garin. I don't care if the Unseelie burn our kingdom to the ground. I just want to be there when the King faces his retribution."

Revenge. That's as good a reason as any. I'm happy to have him on my side.

I nod at him. "Thank you for your help, Sylmare. I am sorry for your loss. I know words don't mean much, but what I can offer you is a shot at Garin." Leaning forward, I hold his gaze. "But, so you understand, so we are clear, Raelyn has the right to claim her brother's life, so I cannot promise you the killing blow." His eyes flare at my words. "You *will* have a hand in the King's downfall. Will that be enough?"

He considers me for a moment before nodding. "Seeing the light leave the King's eyes will be enough, even if it is not by my hand. Whether we are victorious or defeated, as long as Garin suffers, that will be enough."

We fall silent, each getting lost in our own thoughts.

Eventually, Nyira and the other female join us, and we gather our supplies and saddle back up. Nyira is quiet, avoiding eye contact with me, which is just fine.

We head north at a steady pace, and as we crest a hill, I turn to look at Dorwe one last time. *We will find each other, Rae. We will always find each other.*

25

RAELYN

As I struggle to process Kem's words, I forget the discomfort of the gravel. How easy it would be to let Kem kill my brother for me. I don't care how much dark magic my brother has consumed, Kem is strong enough to face him and come away relatively unharmed. I know I'm strong enough to face Garin, but walking away unscathed is out of the question.

I stall as I try and sort my feelings. "How did you know Alek?"

He frowns at my evasion, and for a few silent moments, I'm afraid he won't answer and force me to talk about Garin, but he shifts to sit cross-legged. The position looks like it should be impossible for someone as large as him, but his shoulders are relaxed, and he looks like he could slide into a deep meditation at any moment.

His voice is low when he answers. "One of my people, a

youngling, traveled to Attolyn many years ago. He had the spirit of an adventurer and a kind and trusting heart. He loved the land of the fae." I can't help but notice he is speaking of this dragon in the past tense, and my chest starts to squeeze with sorrow. "Someone in your kingdom, or several someones, captured him, bound him in iron and magic, and sold him to the Unseelie."

I gasp at the idea that fae from my kingdom would do such a thing, but I shove aside my naive thoughts. Even the Fae of the Light have darkness within them. Just look at my brothers.

Kem's hands grip his knees a little tighter. "It's not uncommon for our youths to go traveling for months, even years, so he was not missed for some time. When he failed to return for his grandfather's Elevation, his family knew something was wrong and went to their council member, who came to me."

My brows furrow in question, so he answers, "The Elevation is a ceremony we have for a dragon who has passed. They are burned with dragon fire on a pyre at North Lake so their ashes may rise to the stars and join our ancestors."

What a beautiful tradition. It reminds me of my time in Scandinavia with the Vikings.

Kem continues his story. "Eventually, our search led us to Attolyn and then to Morthryl, the kingdom of the Unseelie." Kem's jaw clenches, and there's pain behind his eyes. "I was ready to go to war, ready to raze Morthryl to the ground, Attolyn as well if necessary. Alek sent me a message asking for a meeting."

A fraction of the tension that has slowly built in his shoulders dissolves, and a small smile curves up one corner of his lips. "I almost didn't go, but I was curious what a fae prince could possibly offer me. It turned out your brother was one of the most skilled glamour artists I've ever met as well as quite the diplomat. But what really shocked me was that he *cared*. He actually cared. He offered to go to Morthryl himself, glamoured as an Unseelie, and get the dragon out."

Kem's dark eyes meet mine, the orange glow of his inner fire burning deep in his pupils. "I didn't completely trust him, and I doubted he would survive the trip, but he insisted on trying. He was so adamant, so ... genuine in his words. All he asked was for the chance to reconstruct the relationship between Seelie and Dragon. He dreamed of an alliance between us."

With a soft sigh, Kem tilts his head at me. "You two were more alike than you think, Raelyn."

The back of my throat burns with the threat of tears as he goes on. "Your father was an honorable King, and I agreed with Alek's terms."

Kem breaks away from my gaze, looking down at his lap. "I gave him a very rare piece of dragon magic in the form of a small jewel embedded in a bracelet. Once Alek invoked the magic, I would know his exact position, and hopefully, the youngling's.

"Alek not only made it into Morthryl, but took out an Unseelie soldier, and glamoured himself to take his place. He found the youngling deep in the dungeons that lie far below their castle. As soon as Alek activated the jewel, the magic called to me, and I shadow traveled right to him."

This story should have a happy ending, but Kem's pinched eyes and flexed fingers tell me it will not.

"We almost made it out. But the Unseelie found us. They surrounded us like a swarm of insects, hungry and almost insane with the desire to capture another dragon. It was lucky they had no idea I was the King, or we might not have made it out. As it was, there were so many soldiers, and the tunnels of the dungeons were tight, leaving me no room to shift without breaking my own bones. Before I could unleash my shadows, Alek's magic erupted through the dungeons, bringing stone and earth down around us, crushing many of the Unseelie soldiers."

I rest a hand on top of one of Kem's where it clenches his knee, and he stares at our joined hands.

"Your brother fought for me, for the young dragon in my arms. Alek screamed for me to take the boy home, but I couldn't leave Alek behind. Maybe I should have. To this day, I don't know what the right answer was. Regardless, I hesitated."

Anger laces his voice, and I grip his hand a little tighter.

"I was ready to shadow travel myself and the boy home, but at the last second, I expanded my shadows to Alek, aiming the three of us for Attolyn. It was that split second that gave an Unseelie soldier an opening, and his air magic wrapped around the boy's neck, snapping his spine right in my arms."

I suck in a pained breath, no longer trying to hold back the silent tears that track down my cheeks.

"I only recall rage as my dragon shifted against my will. My body pressed to the walls and ceiling, crushing and breaking my wings. The cave around us shuddered as it started to crumble. Still, I tore the Unseelie apart. The tight confines restricted my movements, but I forced myself to move out of sheer fury. My rage was fed by the blood that ran down my throat and the bones that crunched between my teeth. I ripped limbs from bodies, clawed open stomachs, and tore heads from shoulders.

"While I was lost to the destruction, Alek cocooned the boy in a protective shell of earth, and once the smoke and fire cleared, all the Unseelie were dead, and the cave was barely standing. I forced myself back into my broken human form, but before I took the youngling home, I swore a favor to Alek."

He turns his hand over, interlacing our fingers, using his free hand to wipe away my tears, a sad smile on his face. "The youngling was Elevated with his grandfather. He is with our ancestors. He is at peace."

A sigh expands his shoulders. "Garin took the throne, and an alliance was never formed. Though we stayed in touch, Alek never called in his favor—until you."

Kem holds up his hand, his fingertips still wet with my tears. Shadows curl from his skin and swirl around his upturned hand like snakes made of smoke. When they melt back into his skin, a thin cuff bracelet sits in his palm.

He holds it out and slides the cuff onto my wrist. It's a burnished gold with a warmth to it, like dragon skin, and it warms my arm. In the center of the cuff is a round jewel inlaid so expertly that it sits flush with the metal. I turn my wrist back and forth, trying to figure out the color of the jewel, but it keeps changing color as if the colors of every dragon live within the stone.

When I meet Kem's eyes, he smiles. "It's the same bracelet I gave Alek. It is a rare dragon stone, and if you activate the magic, I will know exactly where you are."

He lifts my wrist and slides the cuff off. Holding the bracelet between his fingers, he bends the metal back.

No, on closer inspection, I see the metal turning inside out by way of impossibly tiny links. He holds out the cuff. "Flip the cuff inside out like this and put it back on. I will know you need me."

He turns it back around and slides it back onto my wrist. His fingers trail over the metal, then lift, caressing my cheek, his hand as warm as the bracelet against my skin. He smiles.

This time, the expression is bright and happy. "I will say, it looks much better on you."

I laugh as he drops his hand, and I look back at the cuff. "Thank you, Kem. This means a lot." I slide my other hand from his and let my fingers trail over the cuff, enjoying the warm feel of the metal. Every time I touch the stone, a hum of .... energy, of dragon magic, zips through me.

Keeping my eyes on the cuff, I whisper, "I wish I had known Alek better. I wasted my love on the wrong brother."

Kem rests his hand over both of mine, stilling my worrying fingers. "It's never a waste to love someone."

I inhale deeply. "Kem, Dragon's don't get involved." I glance back up. "You can't kill Garin for me."

His voice is deeper, and if I placed my hand to his heart, I imagine the gravely sound would make his chest tremble. "You're right, dragons aren't supposed to get involved, but ... maybe we should." His hand gently squeezes mine. "Let me do this for you, Raelyn. Let me give you the crown of Attolyn."

I'm so tired of goddamn crying, but here I am, tears spilling down my face once again. My throat is too tight with emotion, and I can't form words right now, so I just shake my head.

"Why, Raelyn?"

Slipping my hands from under his, I wipe my tears away. "I wish you could help, Kem. Really, I do. My people are suffering. But I was in that council meeting with you. Inchel and several of the others are just waiting for an excuse to move against you. Your people shouldn't have to suffer through another civil war, because of me."

He frowns at me, and I practically see the excuses he's sifting through to try and convince me, so I smile with a shrug. "Besides, I must be the one to face Garin. He has taken my family from me, including himself, and I need to rip that crown from his head."

"What if I promise to leave him alive for you to do just that?"

I smirk. "Tempting, but I need to do this. I need to earn the respect of my people. I can't be the princess who ran away and disappeared. I ... I need to earn my own respect. I can do this." *I hope I can do this.*

He stares at me for a few long moments before he nods. "When you say the word, I will send you home with the promise to come whenever you call."

I bite my lip and lower my gaze, absently turning the cuff around my wrist.

Kem's voice is quiet, but confident. "I am grateful our paths have crossed. I cannot wait to attend your coronation."

I exhale loudly. "If I don't die."

His warm fingers lightly grip my chin and hold my gaze. "You are strong. You are an Elemental fae, and you have the power and ability to best your brother. You are fighting for your people, for your kingdom. He is fighting for himself."

Just the thought of fighting Garin, of killing him, makes me nauseated. But I can't continue to hide out here. Garin's cruelty made me strong, even if I mistook it for affection. Fighting Ash for millennia forced me to be creative with my power, making me stronger in his own way. And being here in the Dragon's realm has unlocked magic beyond anything I could have imagined. But more than that, I've seen who Garin should have been through Kem. Kem has reminded me what a strong leader looks like.

I curl my legs under me and push myself to my feet, feeling stronger and more determined. Kem follows, towering over me as we turn toward his castle. I square my shoulders. "I don't think I will ever feel ready, feel strong enough, powerful enough. But I'm learning to trust myself again, and I have to go back." A chill steals down my spine. "Tomorrow."

I might be imagining the slight catch in Kem's stride. I swear he stumbles a little at my words, but his eyes remain forward. "Another week of preparation might be wise."

We approach the statue garden. All those stone dragons seem to watch us as we get closer. The power of my Elemental magic has snapped a missing piece into my soul, a piece I hadn't realized was absent, and I realize this is what it feels like to be complete.

I. Can. Do. This.

Still riding the high of winning the Challenge against Ziza, I call for my magic, throwing my arms forward as I release a disk of solid air at the statue on our right. There's a loud crack that breaks the silence before the dragon's stone head, right shoulder, and right wing slide down the diagonal cut that my air magic made. The side of the statue thuds to the ground, and a smile lifts my lips.

I am an Elemental. I am strong.

I turn back to Kem. "Yes, another week, another month, hell, I would stay for a year if I thought it would ensure my victory over Garin. But my people need me. I've been gone too long."

Our conversation slips into silence as we slowly make our way through the castle. Our footfalls are quiet against the stone floor and sunlight glints off the crystal walls making the air look like spun gold. I'm going to miss this place.

As we approach Kem's rooms, Syphe stands to the right, and Arvun, the silver dragon, stands to the left. Syphe bows to her King, then bows to me. I nod in return but almost trip over my feet as Arvun bows to me as well. That's new.

I'm almost across the threshold when Arvun reaches out, her soft touch halting my steps. Kem's shadows start to peel from his skin, and Arvun cuts a quick look to her King, bowing her head. "I beg a word with Lady Raelyn." Her eyes flash back to me. "Please. Just a moment."

Kem looks down at me, and I nod. He passes into his rooms, and Arvun takes a few steps down the hall away from where Syphe still stands guarding the doors. I follow the silver shifter, and once we are several yards away, Arvun turns to me, her silver eyes pinched at the edges. Her shimmering hair is pulled back in a bun at the nape of her neck, making her features appear more severe, more angular. She fidgets her hands together for a moment, and I have no idea what she could possibly have to tell me that's making her so nervous.

She drops her hands to her sides with a sigh. "Thank you for sparing Ziza."

Well, that's not at all what I was expecting.

Her gaze is on her boots as she says, "I'll be honest, I thought she would kill you easily."

"Well, thanks."

She notices my lips quirk up, and she smiles. "That will teach me. I won't underestimate you again. For such a small thing, and for someone who can't even shift, you're quite tough."

Her smile grows to a wide grin, and I chuckle, but she turns serious again. "You could have killed Ziza. You had the right, but you didn't. And I just wanted to say thank you."

"You're welcome, Arvun." I'm ready to turn and go back to Kem's rooms, but something makes me pause. I'm the victim of too much time wasted, and I hate the idea of others falling to the same fate. "Are you two ...?"

She shrugs, and at this moment, she looks every bit the

human form she wears, and not at all the powerful dragon she is.

"Arvun, tell her how you feel. She may reject you, she may not. But even for dragons, even for fae, life can be fleeting. It's cliché but true."

A shy smile lifts her lips, and she nods. "Why is facing feelings so much more terrifying than facing an enemy in battle?"

"Because there is more at stake."

I can't help but think of all the years, the centuries, Ash and I could have had on earth, but fighting was easier. What's a few cuts and bruises when your heart is on the line?

I sigh, heading back to Kem's rooms. He's waiting for me right inside the doorway, obviously keeping an eye on Arvun. Before the doors close, Syphe steps forward. "Are we training tomorrow, Raelyn?"

Kem answers for me. "Lady Raelyn is leaving tomorrow. It is time for her to return to Attolyn."

Syphe's nostrils flare, and her eyes go wide for a split second before she schools her face into a smile and nods.

I smile as well and pull her into a hug. Her embrace is strong and warm, and I realize I've started associating the smell of brimstone with safety and comfort. How odd.

She pulls back, giving me a squeeze before dropping her arms. "I will miss you."

There are tears rimming her eyes, and I swallow hard to keep my own tears at bay. "Thank you, for everything, Syphe." Our eyes lock, and we nod to each other before Kem ushers me into his rooms before the doors close behind us.

A breeze tickles my skin from the open windows, and Kem crosses his arms over his broad chest. The sun has just dipped below the horizon, and the orange and purple sky backlights him making him look like a shadow in a pastel painting. On a table in the sitting room, there's a steaming bowl of soup along with a loaf of bread and a bowl of fruit. Kem looks around the room then back to me. "Is there anything more you need?" I shake my head, and he nods, a small frown on his lips. "Then I will wish you a good night."

He slips out the doors, leaving me alone in his cavernous room. I walk to the wall of windows and stare out at the valley below. The red grass has darkened to deep purple in the fading light. A few people walk the fields or move between houses and shops down in the valley. Several dragons dot the sky, their bright colors competing with the ever-changing colors of the setting sky.

I will miss this place, and I hope the dragons will let me come back someday. I'd like to honor Alek's wish and create an alliance between the Seelie of Attolyn and the Dragons of the Crimson Plains.

But even the beauty before me can't chase away the dread that's roiling in my stomach and causing my palms to sweat. I'm going to face Garin. There's a part of me that prays to the Fates that I can find a way to resolve things without killing him. But Alek's eyes dimming into death flashes through my mind, and I picture how Ash struggled to get to me in that cave, and I know—I'm going to kill my brother.

Or he's going to kill me.

26

RAELYN

Kᴇᴍ and I are on the mountainside where he first brought me to his home a month ago. Early this morning, before the sun had crested the horizon, there was a gentle knock at the door. I was already awake. I had been up for several hours just staring out the glass wall and letting the soft breeze play with my hair. Kem pushed into the room on silent feet and nodded in greeting. There were no words, just his hand outstretched to mine, and as I slipped my palm into his, shadows curled around us and brought us here.

I had hoped to say another goodbye to Syphe, but she hadn't been outside the doors this morning. Patting the small bulge in my jacket where I placed the small tapestry in an inside pocket, I left her a note, only able to hold back my tears by telling myself I'd see her again.

I hate goodbyes. I had to say too many on Earth.

Delicate yellow flowers kiss my ankles as the soft air currents rock them side to side. The sky brightens, and the sun is moments from peeking between the mountains in the distance. I hold my breath, and Kem holds my hand, his warmth and strength buffering me against the emotions swirling in my chest. Tears well in my eyes, making my view swim and waver for a moment.

The blur in my eyes sharpens as twin tears trail down my cheeks. It's with crystal clear eyes that I watch the golden sun's rays burst into view, painting the plains of red grass in light, making the valley look as if it's on fire. My breath hitches in my chest and catches in my lungs before I let it out on a shaky exhale.

Kem's hand squeezes mine, but we keep our gazes forward, looking out over the beautiful land he rules.

His voice is deep but quiet. "Give me a minute."

I glance at him as he releases my hand and melts away with his shadows. I stand in silence as the seconds tick into minutes before the space next to me darkens and Kem reappears. "The way is clear. I will be sending you to the ruins of Dorwe."

I nod, grateful for the location. It's a secluded site in a sparsely populated area of the kingdom. I will have time to acclimate myself before ...

Kem continues, "Before I took you from that cave, I managed to get a message to Asheraht telling him to go to Dorwe. It was rushed, and I'm sure it caused him a great amount of pain, but there wasn't time for a more delicate solution. It has been several weeks since I left him that message, and I do not know of his current ... condition, but he's not at the ruins now."

My muscles bunch. A lot could have happened in the

weeks I've been gone. I steel myself, standing taller with a deep breath. "Thank you. I'll be fine."

A few seconds of silence tick by, and I feel Kem about to say something more, but I cut him off, turning to face him. "I'm ready."

He presses his lips together, swallowing whatever words he had for me, and nods, taking my hands in his and squeezes them gently.

"Thank you, Kem"—I glance at our joined hands and the bracelet that gleams around my wrist before meeting his eyes once more—"for everything."

He pulls me into a hug, banding his arms around me, and I rest my cheek on his chest for a moment. He slowly releases me, stepping back, and I immediately miss his warmth. With a final nod, his shadows leak from his skin, and the smoky tendrils reach for me. I keep my eyes on his, though, and stare into their dark depths to the glowing embers of fire at their centers.

The darkness tunnels at the edges of my vision as Kem smiles. "Farewell, your Majesty."

I smile back, taking in his beauty until the world goes dark.

I'm floating, then being sucked forward. Birdsong reaches my ears a split second before the shadows peel back, and I find myself surrounded by crumbling stone ruins. Morning sun casts long shadows. A quick glance around brings a frown to my face. I was half hoping Kem was wrong, and that Ash would be standing right here waiting for me with a smirk on his face and something witty on his lips. But it's quiet and empty. Dull.

After the bright, colorful beauty of The Realm of the Crimson Plains, Attolyn seems muted. And in comparison, Earth would feel downright colorless.

Even after all this time away from Attolyn, it's a gut reaction that has me reaching for a glamour to turn my hair silver. A pang of grief shoots through me as I remember my mother is gone, and I'll never again hear her voice chiding me about my dark hair. The tips of my hair turn silver with the start of my glamour, but then Ash's voice flits through my mind, scolding me for even thinking about hiding who I really am. He's giving me a hard time, even in my imagination. A smile lifts my lips as I release the glamour and pull my dark hair back to tie it up in a high ponytail.

My chest expands on a deep inhale, and as I exhale, I let the weight of the sword on my back pull my shoulders down. Looking around, there's not much to see—no movement besides the occasional bird flitting about. Ruins in various stages of decay lay all around this ancient, forgotten site. Stones are broken and scattered in the dirt like a giant knocked over building blocks. A few walls struggle to stay upright. An archway stands impossibly, with half of its structure tumbled to the ground.

I walk the ruins, running my hand over the worn stones, letting the rough edges ground me. After about twenty minutes, I find the first burnt circle and quickly find three more. Ash was here.

A pinch between my shoulders loosens at the confirmation he's alive. Or at least he was. I can't tell how old these marks are.

And with that uncertainty, a sense of urgency settles in my chest. I look north toward the capital, far away and out of sight, but I feel its weight nonetheless. I need to find Ash, and if the markings on the stones are an indication, he's with the New Moon Guild in the capital.

However ...

I roll my shoulders, my resolve grounding me. I used to sneak in and out of the castle when I was younger. If I can get into the castle unseen, best-case scenario, I can—even thinking the words makes me sick—take Garin out in his sleep. And if I'm not so lucky, at least in the castle there would be little-to-no collateral damage. Ash will be angry. No, he'll be furious. But he'll be alive. And it's not like I'll be going in unprepared or defenseless. I have my sword and my knives, and I have the power of the Elements.

So much magic lives within me. I still feel too full, like my power is pressing against my skin from the inside. It's uncomfortable but exhilarating, having all this magic at my fingertips.

Reaching for my power, I test my new magics, letting their energies flow through me. Instinctively, air comes first as the wind picks up, twirling through my ponytail. The stretched-out feeling within me subsides as the currents play around my body, caressing my skin. The ground trembles slightly as my earth magic surges. The sands at my feet shift at my command and carve a spiral design into the hard rock of the earth, starting at my feet and curling outward several yards.

The design continues to spin outward as I turn my attention to the power of water. There's a spring beneath me, far below the ground, and I call it up. The earth moves with my power as the fresh water rushes to the surface until a gentle bubble of water gurgles between my boots. The spring water fills the center of the spiral groove in the ground and begins to flow out and around until it arrives at the end of the enormous circle I've created. I open a small fissure in the earth at the end of the helical design to allow the spring water to fall back into the ground to rejoin itself at its origin.

My magic holds the water in this loop, making it one with the land. This spring will forever bubble in the center of this coiling design, working its way out, around, and back down into the ground.

I smile at my work, at my power, and let the magic of fire heat my blood and flare at my fingers. I feel as if Ash is with me as I send focused streams of flame to the north point of my circle. I burn the elemental sign for earth into the ground—three straight, horizontal lines, one over the other. I send more flames to the eastern point and burn in the elemental sign for air—a diamond. To the south goes the symbol for water—four wavy lines, one over the other. And finally, fire to the west—a triangle.

I walk through my creation, letting the elements flow through me, and I stand taller as I step from the outer ring. The magic of air makes me feel ethereal. The magic of earth grounds me, and I feel solid and strong. The magic of water cleanses me, the power bubbling through me like a happy brook through a meadow. And the power of fire cleanses and energizes me, snapping along my nerve endings.

My skin is glowing softly, and I know my eyes are burning brighter than normal. I feel ... good.

I feel powerful.

I *am* powerful.

My magic, the power of the elements, fills me. I understand how someone can become addicted to magic because at this moment, I never want to let it go. Flowers bloom at my feet, and fire licks my fingertips. Water condenses in the air around me, and the air currents send the droplets swirling and dancing around my body. I wonder how much power I can gather if I hold all the elements inside myself for an hour, a day, a week ...

A snap of a branch pulls me out of my thoughts, and I

spin toward the edge of the forest that lines these ruins to the east. My magic rushes from me in defense. With a blast of solidified, sharpened air, several trees at the forest's boundary slice in half, their tops falling over.

A startled deer bounds into the woods, and I let go of my magic. Shit. What if that had been Ash? I can't allow myself to get lost in my power. I need to stay focused.

Turning to the north, I start walking as I try to shake off the buzz of my magic and adrenaline. If it still exists, the closest portal is several miles to the northwest in a temple built and maintained by a religious sect that worships the Fates. Hopefully, I can slip into the temple in the dead of night, get to the portal unseen, and use it to get to the capital. Otherwise, if I'm caught, I'll have to ask permission from the acolytes to gain access to their 'holy portal site'.

My eyes roll heavily at the thought. The members of The Fated are harmless, mostly. But gaining access to what they have claimed as holy sites requires forms, delegations, and discussions. Plus, they are fae. The proceedings can take a good, long while—days, even weeks.

I don't have the time to waste. My people need me. I'm done running. No more delays. I need to get to the capital. I need to get to the castle. I need to get to Garin. I need to fix things—I clench my fists and take a few breaths—even if I have to kill Garin to do so.

I am an Elemental, and I will free my people from the influence of the dark fae and bring them peace once again. I will honor Alek's memory and form an alliance between the Seelie and the Dragons. I will do what I must for my kingdom.

The sun climbs the sky, and I walk until it's right overhead. My shadow is directly underfoot, and my air magic pushes little currents of wind against my skin. My water magic seeks out the moisture in the air to keep me cool as the sun tries its best to cook me. I've long since shed my leather jacket, unstrapping my sword to peel the heavy protective garment off, then strapped it once again to my back over my damp, linen shirt. My jacket now flaps at my side, hanging from my belt.

I could blur there in little over an hour using my fae speed but decided against it for several reasons. One, I want to wait until the cover of darkness to slip into the temple and cross the portal to the castle gardens. I could blur there and sit and wait, or I could walk to pass the time. But the second reason keeps from doing that—fae in Attolyn don't blur. We're immortal, and our extreme speed, ironically, is shunned. Why would someone with endless time stretching before them want to rush anywhere? Seeing someone blur in Attolyn only means one thing, trouble. I don't think I'll come across anyone this far south, but if I do, blurring would draw too much unwanted attention.

So, I walk.

I count my steps up to a hundred then start over to keep my mind away from thoughts of my brothers.

Seventy-four, seventy-five, seventy-six, seventy ... I can still feel Garin's arms wrapped around me in that cave, and just like when I was a little girl, I felt safe. How stupid. I shake my head as if I can fling those unwanted thoughts out of my brain through my ears. Alek paid the price for my naiveté. My eyes are now open, and I see Garin for who he is, even if my heart still weeps with pain every time I have to remind myself he's not the man I knew. He's not the brother he pretended to be.

Where was I? Seventy-one? Seventy-two, seventy-three ...

I get lost in the numbers, sometimes getting to a thousand before realizing I forgot to start over at a hundred. The southern edge of the kingdom is sparsely populated, and I have yet to see or even hear another fae, which is fine by me.

One, two, three, four ...

The sun set three hours ago, and the sounds of crickets have replaced birdsong. A slightly stronger breeze pushes its way through the branches of the trees in the forest to my right. There's a beginning of an ache in my thighs that tells me soreness will be quick to settle into my legs once I stop moving.

Fifty-six, fifty-seven ...

The grey stone of The Fated temple breaks the darkness before me, and I move closer to the treeline to hide in the shadows of the forest as I approach. There's no movement or sound, and it looks as if the temple is empty at this late hour.

I shift my weight forward toward the balls of my feet, making my steps as quiet as possible. Circling the temple, I pass column after column of grey granite, collectively lifting the domed roof to the sky. Pausing, I put on my jacket, repositioning my sword to my back. Quietly, I approach the eastern entrance and press my hands to the smooth wood door. My breath holds in my lungs as I push, and I exhale in relief when it glides open on silent hinges.

A few floating fae lights greet me as I step over the threshold into a large circular room. I rush across the granite floor, barely taking in the elaborate frescoes painted on the walls and ceilings. All I can concentrate on is the electric hum of the nearby portal buzzing along my skin.

Another closed door stands before me at the northern wall, this one made of bronze with the story of the Fates carved into its facade. I press my palms against the metal door, listening for any sounds coming from inside the chamber. Hearing none, I plant my feet and push, my fingers digging into the carved relief depicting the Fates spooling out the threads of life.

As soon as the door is open enough for me to slip through, I squeeze through and close it with my back.

I can't see it, but the portal is there, right in front of me in the center of this plain, circular room. Grey granite floors bleed into grey granite walls. There are no fae lights in here, but a faint pool of light splashes across my cheek and the western side of the room from the moonlight spilling through the glass ceiling.

Resolve broadens my shoulders with a deep breath, and I push myself off the door, standing tall. I pray to the Fates, if they are out there and if they are listening, that Ash is still alive and okay. My fingers trail a light caress over my lips as I recall our kiss and the many fantasies I've had of him during sleepless nights.

With the memory of his lips on mine and his hands touching my skin, I stride forward with even steps. Feeling the soap bubble sensation pop around me, I leave the temple and land near the stream that runs through the walled gardens outside the castle grounds.

I sigh. It's exactly as I remember it with the large white blooms skirting the edge of the water, the stone wall separating the portal from the main castle grounds, and the castle ...

I bite my lip as I take my first step toward my home. It's beautiful. Gleaming white and gold under the moonlight, the walls practically calling me forward. It's been so long. Despite why I'm here, I smile because, I'm here. I'm home.

I only get five steps away from the portal when a large hand slaps over my mouth, and an arm wraps around my shoulders and chest.

Shit!

My magic jumps to life under my skin and tingles at my fingertips. Fire coats my skin, and I snap my head back, hoping to break my assailant's nose.

There's no stopping my momentum, and I wince as I catch the scent of pine and grass.

27

ASHERAHT

THE SIGHT of Raelyn stepping through that portal stopped my heart for a moment before kicking it into a racing gallop. *She's here. She's alive.*

I'm heavily glamoured, my appearance that of a guard I killed a few days ago. I had perched in the high branches of a tree in the castle grounds, watching him 'patrol.' He was not paying a bit of attention to his surroundings as he absently kicked a round seed pod down the path and back again. On his third pass, I dropped down silently, dagger in hand. With one hand wrapped over his mouth, I slammed my blade into the base of his skull, severing his spine, and the large guard slid lifeless to the ground. After stripping him of his stinking, sweat-stained uniform, I glamoured myself into his likeness and stuffed his body into a large sack. Tossing him on a cart with a pile of laundry bags, leathers, and armor in need of repair, I hauled the cumbersome cart to the seedier part of the city where the buildings pressed together, practically holding each other up. An old contact of mine took three silver and the dead body off my hands, and I left, knowing it would never be traced to either of us. He's a good person to know.

Rae looks toward the castle with longing and determination. She's going after Garin.

Not yet. Not alone.

I blur and wrap my arms around her, slapping my hand over her mouth. Fire licks her beautiful skin, and I panic thinking my magic somehow attacked her. But no, my magic is quiet.

I barely have time to duck my head to the right to keep her from head-butting me in the nose. Thank goodness her back is pressed to my chest, otherwise, the fancy new sword strapped to her back might be lodged in my gut right now. I need to let her know it's me before she escalates and we draw attention to ourselves.

I band my arms tighter around her chest, holding her closer. "Rae."

Her struggles still, the flames extinguish, and she relaxes with a sigh into my arms. I'm unnerved by the strange fire, but my curiosity is overwhelmed by fighting the desire to lower my lips the half-inch it would take to kiss her neck right below her ear. My hands are shaking with relief that she's alive, and I'm fighting to keep them from trialing across her chest, over her stomach ... and down.

Staying close, she turns in my arms, and our eyes clash. I open my mouth to tell her it's me, but she smiles knowingly, and my heart skips a beat. "Ash." My name passes her lips on a whispered breath and my entire being responds, body and soul.

I take her hand and lead her through the garden toward

the city, but she resists, digging her heels into the dirt path. I stop but grip her hand tighter as I turn and step back into her space, her head tilting back as I press close. Her eyes travel over the face that isn't mine until she meets my eyes once again. She bites her lower lip and I'm captivated by the movement. She looks over her shoulder to the castle, and I hold my breath until she turns back to me, her lips still worrying between her teeth, but she nods.

Leaning down, I kiss her forehead and breathe her in. An emotional exhale stutters from her mouth, and I step back, keeping my tight grip on her hand and continue to take us away from the castle.

There are creeping vines bursting with sweet-smelling, white flowers bordering the path, but I barely notice. The racing of my heart almost drowns out the soft bubbling of the stream. The eastern gate comes into view, and a frown creases between my brows as the shadowed form of another guard stands lazily near the iron gate.

I drop my head, whispering, "Glamour yourself."

I don't bother to check that she has followed my order, I just keep our pace steady, aiming for the exit. The guard, an Unseelie with broad shoulders and long, black hair, looks up as he hears our approach, and his eyes flick between Rae and me. A leer curls his lips. "Ah, Thale. I was wondering where you went off to." His eyes crawl down Rae's body, and I want to stab him in the throat. "I see you found yourself a"—he licks his lips—"distraction."

His grin turns to me. I've tried to keep my verbal communication to a minimum while living as Thane since I'm unsure what his voice sounded like. I force a lustful grin and tug Rae after me. She stumbles for effect, and now my smile is genuine as she plays along.

The guard lifts an eyebrow, placing his hands on his

hips, nodding out toward the night-cloaked city. "Have your fun, Thale. I'll cover for you." He turns his gaze back to Rae, and I grind my teeth together as his arm snaps out, his meaty hand grabbing Rae's free arm. Leaning in, he sniffs her hair.

Blood drips down my palm where my nails have dug little moon shapes into my flesh. Rae appears calm, though I can feel her hand trembling slightly in mine, probably from rage, not fear. She casts her eyes down then lifts her head slightly, looking up at the guard through her silver lashes. Her glamour makes her look much smaller, petit, delicate, with shoulder-length silver hair. A pretty heart-shaped face has replaced the sharper angles of her real face. Her lean, muscled body is now all soft curves.

The guard pulls her a little closer, and she pretends to trip slightly into him while keeping a firm grip on my hand. He grins, speaking to me but keeping his eyes glued to Rae. "Once you've had your fun, bring her back here. I could use a little distraction of my own."

He finally peels his eyes away from Rae and grins at me. I swallow the rage that begs me to set him on fire and grin back, nodding. Satisfied, the guard releases Rae and slaps me on the back. "Have fun."

I walk as calmly as I can through the open gate and keep my pace steady, listening to the sound of our boots softly hitting the cobblestones. As we move silently through the sleeping city, I'm coiled tight with tension as I watch for patrolling soldiers, weaving us through side streets as necessary.

There are very few fae on the streets at this hour, and those we do pass keep their heads down and their pace quick. Five minutes later, I make one last turn and lead Rae through a little gate to a fenced front yard of a pretty house in a row of well-manicured residential houses. The grass of every lawn is trimmed, lush, and green. Roses climb the posts of the porch that spans the front of the white house. As we climb the three steps to the front door, I wonder what Rae is thinking. She hasn't said a word since the portal, but her hand is firm in mine, and her steps never faltered on the way here.

I fish the skeleton key from my pocket, the metal heavy and rough in my hand. Nyira gave me the New Moon Key last week to replace the one I left on Earth. The key slides into the lock, and I pull us into the darkened hall of the safehouse—one of a few throughout the city that Garin hasn't found, yet.

This house belongs to the Guild, but the owner is officially listed as Phran Traka—the brother of a cousin who's married to the sister of a member of the Guild.

The door clicks shut, and I turn the lock, the small sound seeming much louder in the dark silence of the house around us. I let my glamour slowly dissolve, like ice melting away to reveal the truth underneath. Rae sheds her glamour with a quick shake of her shoulders.

"Raelyn, I—"

She lunges at me, and for a second, I think she's going to hit me. Instead, her lips crush to mine, and her arms wrap around my neck. A groan escapes my mouth, and I press my hands to her back, bringing her tight against me. She licks my lips, and our tongues dance before I suck on her bottom lip, giving it a gentle bite.

Her moan vibrates against my chest as she pulls at the dead guard's jacket I'm wearing, shoving it off my shoulders. I drop it to the floor before desperately peeling hers off as well, her sheathed sword clattering to the floor with a thud.

Our lips meet again in a frantic tangle, and I back her

into the door. As my lips trail across her jaw, lightly nipping her ear, then licking my way down her throat, I grab her thigh and wrap it around my waist.

I'm uncomfortably hard for her, but I want it to last. I never want this to end.

Rae grips my shirt with a snarl and pulls it over my head before claiming my lips once again. As she grinds into my straining length, I slam my palm against the door near her head. "Fuuuck."

She throws back her head, hitting the wood of the door, and my mouth dives for her throat, skimming my teeth over the skin of her neck. I work my lips down, shoving her shirt over her shoulder.

I pause. My fingers trail along the raised flesh of what looks like a knife wound.

"Raelyn, what—?"

"It's nothing." Her muscles tighten under my touch. "I'm fine." She grips my hand, moving it up her leg until I grip her ass. "I'll tell you about it later." She presses her core harder against me. "Later."

I buck into her, and my other hand pushes under the hem of her shirt. My palm skims up the warm flesh of her stomach. I don't think I've ever touched anything more perfect ... cuts, scrapes, bruises, and all.

My fingers brush the underside of her breast, and I groan, grinding against her hips, using the door at her back to fit our partially clothed bodies tighter together. She moans and shifts, pressing her straining breast into my hand. Her nipple pebbles against my calloused palm, and I squeeze the glorious weight of her breast before pinching her nipple, drawing a soft gasp from her lips.

Her palm slides down my chest, and her breathing

comes faster between our rough kisses. She breaks away, and our eyes meet.

My world stops. She is mine—everything I've ever wanted in a mate, here in my arms. She holds my gaze as her breaths come out in sweet little pants of desire. Her fingers trail over the waist of my pants before she palms me through the fabric, pressing her wicked hand against my cock. We both moan, and her eyes roll back then close as she works her hand up and down my length.

"Fates, Rae." I wrap her other leg around my waist and pull her away from the door. Her hand continues to work my cock as her other arm wraps around my neck, pushing me closer to the breaking point as she groans, whispering my name.

There's an open doorway to the left, and I walk us through it. A quick glance around the dark room reveals a living space. I aim for the couch and press her into the cushions, lowering my body to fit against hers.

I kiss her again, and we start shedding clothes as quickly as we can. She drops her knives onto a side table, and the moment I peel her tunic over her head, I forget how to breathe. Her breasts are glorious, and my mouth waters with the desire to taste her. But I pause once again.

My fingers trace freshly healed cuts, pink and raised, over her stomach. Her hand comes to mine, pressing it flat against her skin. Meeting her eyes, I see the desire there in her wide pupils and her parted lips. Bending over her, I press soft kisses to the new scars. Her body arches into my lips with a sigh, and I move down, tasting her, relishing her, devouring her, worshiping her.

"Ash." Her moan is desperate as she pushes me up and wiggles out of her pants. I help peel them over her ankles before I kneel to draw her underwear down her legs. And then she is bare before me. I take her in, unable to pick a favorite part of her to settle on.

My pants are only halfway down my legs before she sits up and wraps her hand around my cock and squeezes. I almost come in her hand like a damn adolescent.

Her feet hook over the waist of my pants, helping me out of the last of my clothing. I grip her wrists, pulling her hand away from my aching cock with a hiss. I can't let this end too soon, not after all this time wanting her.

I pin her arms over her head with one hand, leaving my other to tease one glorious breast as I suck her other nipple between my teeth. Her scream of pleasure spears right to my cock, and she arches into my mouth and hand. In all my life, I've never known anything like this.

I lick and tease her while my other hand leaves her breast to travel down her sweat-slicked torso until I reach her wet clit. She bucks against my hand, and I chuckle with sheer male satisfaction. "So eager. So beautiful."

"Ash."

I slide a finger into her as she breathes my name—such a sweet sound. I want to hear her panting my name, over and over. I add a second finger and rub my palm against her clit, and we both groan as her muscles squeeze my fingers. I watch her body, memorizing her in this moment as she moves against my hand. I move in and out of her with her quick, shallow thrusts.

My other hand releases her wrists, skims down her arm, over her throat, and between her breasts as I slide down her body. Her breath hitches as I hook her legs over my shoulders. My gaze is glued to her flushed face as I remove my fingers from her slick heat and replace them with my mouth.

She bucks off the couch as I lick between her folds. The

taste of her arousal on my tongue is like a drug, and I'm instantly addicted. Her hands grip the couch as I hold her hip with one hand and press my thumb to her clit with the other.

"Ash! Fuck, don't stop."

"I have no intention of stopping until you have come on my hand, on my tongue, and around my cock."

She moans, and her muscles tense as she grips my hair, pressing herself harder against my face. My tongue dives deep as I flick her clit, and I growl, the sound vibrating from my mouth against her pussy. Her back arches, and her lips part in a silent scream as her orgasm crashes through her. I've never seen anything sexier, and all I can think is, when can I see this look on her face again? How soon can I wring another orgasm from her?

I'm so close to my own release, I bite my lip to keep my orgasm at bay.

Her back sinks back to the cushions with a feral grin on her face. Her leg hooks over my hip, and with a shove, I find myself on the floor with a naked, sweating, panting Rae on top of me.

She may have been a goddess, a pharaoh, a warrior, and a queen on earth, but right now, she is mine. I grip her hips, and she screams my name as I pull her down onto my shaft with one strong thrust.

"Fuck! Rae, you're so wet, so tight. You're so goddamned beautiful. I don't know how much longer I can last."

Her hips move, and I groan as her inner muscles squeeze my cock. Leaning over, her nails dig into my chest, and her dark hair tickles my neck as she whispers, "Then take me, Ash."

I roll, pinning her under my body. "Tell me what you want, Rae."

"I ... I want ..."

My fingers trail over her cheek before I press a kiss to her swollen lips. "Tell me."

"I want to let go. Just for a little while."

Of course she does. There's so much resting on her shoulders. I grin as I run my hands up her waist, skimming the sides of her breasts before teasing my touch down her arms. "That I can give you." I grab her wrists and stretch her arms over her head and wrap her hands around a leg of the couch. "Don't let go."

She bites her lip, and arches, thrusting her breasts toward me. With a wicked grin on my face, I skim my fingertips back down her arms and over her throat. "You demand I take ..." I splay my hand on her collarbone and press down, pinning her to the floor as I watch my cock slam into her then slowly pull out of her glistening sex. "But how much can you take, princess?"

"Everything." She arches as much as she can. "More."

As she half-heartedly struggles against my hold on her, my other hand grips her thigh, spreading her wider and holding her captive beneath my plunging hips. Fates, she's a glorious sight.

I roll my hips, and her hand lifts, reaching for me. I pause, holding my hips still, shaking my head. "Be a good girl and place your hand back where I put it."

Her breath catches before she tilts her head with a smile. She snaps her arm forward, gripping my hair, and pulling my face toward hers, whispering against my lips. "And what happens if I don't?"

Ah, a little push-back, seeing if I will indeed take control. The amount of trust she's putting in me is humbling. All I want is to plunge deep into her over and over, but I force myself to stay still. I move my hand from her collarbone to her throat and angle her head up and back. My lips skim her ear before I bite down.

Her breasts press up against my chest as her hand tightens painfully, perfectly, in my hair. I lick up the curve of her ear, eliciting a moan from her luscious lips. My whispered words brush across her skin. "Do you want to come again?" She tries to turn her head to look at me, but I hold her in place, kissing and biting my way across her jaw and over her throat. "Raelyn, do what you're told."

She bucks her hips, trying to break my control, and she nearly succeeds, but I press my other hand on her hip, holding her still. I pull back and angle her face so she can look at me. "Raelyn." My voice comes out deep and rumbling, and she slowly slides her hand from my hair and reaches overhead to grab the couch leg. "Good girl."

I slide out to the tip of my cock before slowly sinking deep once again. She moans but keeps a grip on the sofa as I hold her still. My palm moves from her hip back to her thigh as I spread her wide and pick up my pace.

"Yes," I growl, "such a good girl. Take all of me." I thrust harder, feeling the reverberations through the floor. "You're mine." Her beautiful whimpers and moans float around the dark room. "All I am is already yours, Rae." Her muscles clench around me, and the sound of flesh meeting flesh echoes through the empty house. I lick my lips as I lower my gaze. "Watching my cock sinking into your swollen pussy is the sexiest fucking thing I've ever seen. And now I want to watch you come on my cock."

Reaching between us, I flick her clit as I slam deep with a roll of my hips. "You're being so good for me, Rae. Come for me. Come now."

Her body shudders, and with a scream, her orgasm rips through her, tightening around my shaft as she shatters with pleasure. As she comes down, her eyelids flutter, and she whispers my name again. Like a prayer, it slides from her kiss-swollen lips, and that's all it takes. Almost unbearable pleasure explodes within me as I pound my release into her.

It takes a moment to catch my breath as the buzz of my climax slowly recedes. Gazing down at her sweat-slicked body, I slowly, reluctantly, slide out of her. I reach over, peeling her hands from the couch leg. I scoop her into my arms and tuck her against me as I lay on my back on the sofa. Her dark hair is soft against my skin, and I tuck my chin to press a kiss to her head as we both try to calm our racing hearts.

Yes, I'd die for this woman.

28

RAELYN

I STARTLE AWAKE, and Ash's arms give me a reassuring squeeze. Taking a deep breath, I mumble, "How long have I been asleep?"

"Not long. About an hour." His voice is soft and a bit raspy.

"Did you sleep?"

He shrugs, and I know that's a no. I bury my face in his chest. "I'm sorry I left you behind in that cave, Ash."

His arm tightens around my waist as his hand tilts my chin up to meet his eyes. "Kem saved you. It was the right move. If our roles were reversed, I would have done the same and not thought twice about leaving Kem behind."

I don't think that's entirely true. I mean, I'm sure Ash would have yanked me from that cave in an instant, but I don't believe he would have felt nothing at leaving Kem behind. Ash isn't as heartless as he pretends, but I appreciate his words.

I snuggle deeper into his side. "How did you know I would come through that portal outside the castle gardens?"

"I like to think I know you pretty well." An unladylike snort escapes me, and I feel his grin against my head. "I've been posing as that absurd guard for days. I had a feeling that when you came back, you'd hotfoot it to your brother."

I sag at the mention of Garin. Shit, what a downer, and after two glorious orgasms too.

Ash goes on. "I did hedge my bets, though. I have people keeping watch in the city."

Propping my head in my hand, I look around the room. "New Moon 'people'?" He nods but doesn't elaborate, so I ask, "Where are we, and why are we here?"

His hand skims down my back as he stretches under me, pressing his body a little tighter against mine. I squeeze my legs together as a rush of heat pools between my thighs. "This is a safe house of The New Moon Guild." He presses a kiss to my temple, and I smile. "I brought you here with the intention of introducing you to a few who have agreed to help."

I sit up, pressing my palms into his chest. "Ash, I—"

"You were going to go after him alone."

There's no accusation behind his words, they're simply spoken as a statement, and I shrug. "The fewer people placed between me and my brother, the better."

His grip tightens a fraction. "I understand, and I appreciate where your heart is at, but ..." The glowing gold of his eyes finds mine. "Let me help you. Let me help our kingdom, our people."

The thought of him anywhere near Garin again scares me to death, but I nod. He's right. I can't let my fears keep me from accepting help. This isn't just about me, it's about Attolyn."

Ash grins, pressing a quick kiss to my lips. "Good. Because I would have chased you down and helped you anyway."

I chuckle, amazed that I can smile and laugh like this with everything that's looming before me. My heart constricts, not with grief or sorrow as it's done so much over the past month, but with love. I drag myself up his body to kiss him again, taking my time as I memorize the feel of his lips on mine. After a long moment, I pull back and find his eyes blazing with as much desire as I feel.

Distraction. I need a distraction. "How many have agreed to help?"

His hand reaches up and twirls a lock of my hair around his fingers. "Well, you know it's not always about the size of your force ... but the skill."

I swallow a chuckle. "Ash?"

"I mean, some people have the skill of several fighters."

"Ash!"

"Three."

I try to keep my lips from falling into a frown. It's three more than I had yesterday. Ash smiles, seeing through my tight smile. "One of those three is Nyira, the leader of the Guild. You couldn't ask for a deadlier ally."

He tugs gently on my hair. "I know you are ready to storm the castle and fix things, but with a little more time, we can recruit more people to your cause. We can—"

"Ash, the longer we delay, the more power he will amass and the more the people will suffer. Besides, the more people we recruit, the more people for Garin to hurt, kill, or use against me." I meet his eyes. "We can do this."

His fingers leave my hair, and his calloused palms run

down my arms, sending a shiver up my spine. Fear of losing Ash strangles my heart. Ash is my biggest weakness, and Garin won't hesitate to hurt him to hurt me.

He must sense my unease because he changes the subject. "What was that fire? In the garden?"

Is that a hint of fear in his eyes? I sense uncertainty coming from him as he avoids my gaze, instead following the trail of his hands over my arms. Hurt and anger swell inside me, making my ribcage feel too tight against my skin, but I shove those feelings down. What else is he supposed to think? There hasn't been an Elemental fae in a very long time.

I give him a light slap on his chest before standing, gathering my clothes. "I haven't resorted to blood magic, if that's what you're thinking." He remains silent, watching me. With my shirt and one boot in my left hand, I raise my right arm and call up the tingling power of fire. A flame flickers in my palm for a few seconds before I snap my fist closed, and the fire puffs out. A potted plant near the front wall next to a window shivers as a few new leaves unfurl and large pink blossoms open, sending a light, rose-like scent into the room. Then the cleansing rush of my water magic pulls the moisture out of the air, creating a bubble of water. My air magic floats it over to Ash, whose mouth is hanging open, eyes wide, as he darts his gaze between me and my displays of power.

"I'm an Elemental."

I burst the water bubble over his head, and he sputters with a yell before leaping up, shaking the water from his hair, and I can't help but giggle.

He crosses to me in three big strides, and I yelp as he wraps his arms around my torso, lifting me off the ground. I drop the few clothing items I'd collected as the press of his naked skin against mine brings a flush to my cheeks, and the ache between my thighs starts to pulse in time with my heartbeat.

"An Elemental?" Slowly lowering me down the front of his body, my toes touch the floor, but I keep myself pressed against him. "That's ... You're ... How?"

I laugh, the move pressing my breasts into his chest, causing my skin to pebble. "The short version? I freaked the fuck out and the magic kind of, exploded from me."

His forehead creases as his gaze travels over my face, landing on the pink scars on my shoulder. "Rae, where were you?" His fingers tremble as he touches the marks. "Who did this?"

Kem's striking, dark face flashes through my mind, and I think of beautiful Syphe and lethal and elegant Ziza. A smile lifts my lips. "A dragon."

His head snaps up, and his grip tightens. "Kem did this to you?"

My brows pinch. "No!" I grab his chin, forcing his eyes to my face. "Ash, believe it or not, I was in The Realm of the Crimson Plains."

Ash goes still as his eyes search mine, a half-smile on his lips as he waits for me to tell him I'm joking. When I remain silent, his eyes widen. "Really? Kem brought you to the Dragon's realm? How did he get away with that?"

I press a kiss to the center of Ash's chest, letting my hands skim lower and lower down his torso. "A King can get away with quite a lot."

Ash's shock comes out on a sharp exhale. He grabs my hands, turning my bracelet around my wrist before shooting a glance at my new sword. A frown pulls at his lips as the edges of his eyes crinkle with what I assume is displeasure. "The King of the dragons took you to his realm, where a non-dragon has never stepped foot, where a dragon obviously attacked you, and then, what? You discovered you have the magic of an Elemental, and I assume Kem gave you this"—he lifts my arm slightly—"and that sword?"

I grin, rubbing against him. "Jealous over a piece of jewelry and some weaponry, Ash?"

He doesn't smile back, though. His eyes stay glued to the bracelet. Shit, he is jealous. My hand presses to his chest. "Yes, I spent the last month in the Dragon's realm. And yes, they were gifts ... actually, the bracelet is more of a favor than a gift."

I lift a hand and cup Ash's clenched jaw. "But, Ash, Kem is ... " Tears threaten to spill down my cheeks, and I take a few deep breaths. "He's like a brother. He showed me how ... how Garin ... how my actual brother should have treated me."

All the tension drains from Ash's muscles, and he presses his forehead to mine. "I'm sorry, Rae."

Pressing my lips to his, I kiss him once, twice, and on the third kiss, I suck his bottom lip between mine. "I missed you so much, Ash." I roll my hips against his, and his cock grows hard against my stomach as his hands move to my shoulders, gripping me tightly. I work my lips across his jaw and down his neck. "Do you know whose face I would imagine when I was feeling overwhelmed? Do you know who I would dream of and wake with a throbbing need for? Do you know who I pictured when I would slide my fingers into my pussy and ride my hand?"

He's trembling under my touch as I kneel on one knee, then both, looking up the glorious, naked length of him. His muscles are tense once again, but for a much better reason this time, and the way he looks at me has me wet and aching for him. I grip his straining shaft in one hand as I cup him with the other. His groan of pleasure is my favorite sound. I grin. "You, Ash. It was always you."

I take him into my mouth, curling my lips over my teeth as I slide all the way to his base, my hand squeezing him the entire way down. Slowly pulling back, I flick my tongue over and around the head of his cock before my lips follow my fist all the way back down his shaft. He hits the back of my throat, and I moan at the dark, salty taste of him. The sound vibrates in my chest, up my throat and down his cock.

"Fates, Rae." His fingers twine in my hair, gripping tightly, so it's right on the edge of pleasure and pain. I pick up the pace, sucking and licking him from tip to base, my hand keeping a steady stroke with my lips. His groans and curses encourage me. His thighs are trembling, and with every stroke of my tongue, his ab muscles flex. I circle the base of his cock with my other hand and squeeze, keeping a gentle pressure there as I work my lips and hand up and down his wet cock. I taste pre-cum and swallow it down with my next thrust.

He lifts me off the floor, and a second later, his lips crush to mine. He wraps my legs around his waist, and I grind against him with a groan. The wetness of his cock slides against my sensitive clit, causing my breaths to come out in strangled little gasps.

Ash carries me down a dark hall and into a bedroom in the back of the house. I see a flash of a fluffy blue comforter as he tosses me on the bed. I swallow as he stalks toward me. "I can't wait to hear the story about the bracelet." His eyes travel over my body, and I press my thighs together at the possession in his gaze. "And the sword." He stops before me. "And about how you apparently survived a dragon attack."

I grin. "Two actually."

His jaw flexes as he grinds his back teeth together. I can barely breathe at the sight of him as he practically growls, shaking his head. "But right now, I need to remind you that you are mine"—he kneels, spreading my thighs before crawling up my body—"as much as I am yours, Rae." There is a vulnerability under his feral gaze.

I grip his face, staring into the glow of his gold eyes. "I'm yours, Ash. Only yours."

His eyes hold a dark promise. His lips crash to mine, and he bites my lip before licking away the pain. "Mine." The word comes out as a deep grumble of noise, and goosebumps spread across my flesh. His hand slides down my body, and his touch has me eager for more. More of his lips, his touch, his everything.

He sinks a finger into my pussy, and I groan, "Fuck, Ash!"

A wicked smile flashes across his face before he inserts a second. "So wet. Are you ready for me again?" Pleasure is building, and I'm already close to the edge. I bite my lip and nod in desperation. "This isn't going to be gentle, Rae." I can only moan in answer. I want him deep inside me when I come.

Gripping my hips, he flips me over, lifting my ass as he grips his cock, lining himself up at my soaked entrance. I ball my fists in the sheets and shift back, sliding my aching folds over the head of his shaft, coating him with my arousal. His voice is deep and husky and makes me even wetter. "So beautiful. My Rae."

He drives into me with a savage thrust, and I moan into the bed. His grip is bruising on my hips as he slams into me over and over, hitting me deep, driving me to the brink before he stills, denying me my release.

"Ash, please."

"No. Not yet."

His hand slides up my sweat-slicked back and wraps around my shoulder. starts to pound into me from behind, pulling me back into him with every strong thrust of his hips. All I can do is hold on to the bedding.

I'm right on the edge of orgasm again, but on his next stroke, he holds himself deep within me and stops for one heartbeat, two, three ... then he draws back and slams back with a deep roll of his hips. It's torture, and I'm trembling on the edge of pleasure and pain. "Ash." My voice is shaky, and I lift my hips higher, allowing him to go deeper, harder. I bury my face in the sheets as he picks the pace back up.

"Mine, Rae." His hand leaves my hip and snakes around my waist, pinching my clit. "This is mine."

"Yes!" I scream as pleasure, more intense than all the magic in my body, erupts through me, traveling from my toes to the tip of my head. My pussy pulses with my orgasm, gripping Ash's cock as I scream his name.

A second later, his orgasm claims him, and I turn my face enough so I can see him. Watching him in the throes of pleasure, knowing I drove him there, fuels my ongoing orgasm until I'm breathless with pleasure.

We collapse on the bed, and he rolls over, bringing me with him, curling me into his chest. I smile. "That was amazing."

He hugs me tighter. "I live to serve you, my queen."

I smirk, huffing a laugh.

It only takes three minutes for Ash's breaths to deepen, and his hold on me relaxes into sleep. I flip onto my back and stare at the ceiling, noticing a crystal chandelier with globes of fae light in its center. I imagine when it's lit, the crisp, colored light dances in prisms around the room.

Ash sleeps soundly for half an hour, but sleep eludes me. Nerves flutter in my stomach as I think about Garin and what I know I have to do.

After another fifteen minutes, I can't lay here anymore, so I try to extricate myself from Ash's arms. He mumbles, and I freeze. His breaths remain deep and even, so I scoot closer to the edge of the bed, but his arms tighten around me, and his sleepy voice rumbles into his pillow. "Trying to escape?"

I look over my shoulder and see his smile, his gold eyes glowing. In this moment, I can't help but hope this is in our future—lazy mornings, soft caresses that turn desperate ... time, just time together. We squandered so much of it on Earth.

To shake off my thoughts, I sit up on the edge of the bed. "I need to pee. And at some point, I'm going to have to meet these friends of yours. We need a plan."

I feel more than see the smile slide from Ash's lips. I don't want to ruin this blissful moment, but I can't afford continued distractions, no matter how sexy those distractions are.

Without a word, Ash gets up and pads naked down the hall, and I stare unashamedly at his toned ass. A few minutes later, he returns, laying back down behind me, stroking my hair. Perfection, this man, the assassin sent to kill me, is absolute perfection, and I love him.

Staring at the ceiling, he whispers, "I've lit the logs in the fireplace and put in a charge. The white smoke curling from the chimney is the signal for Nyira and the other two assassins to join us here."

I wish Ash and I could stay locked away, just the two of

us, for a little while longer, but I stand and make my way through the darkened bedroom to the bathroom I spied earlier. Flicking on the light, I squint as my eyes adjust to the bright room. A copper sink stands to my right, the rim around the drain a mint green color where it's started to oxidize. The walls are a plain, cream plaster that blends with the cream stone floor. There's no tub, but the lack of a tub is made up for with the large walk-in shower. I could lay down on the shower floor and still have room to stretch my arms overhead. A wide showerhead comes out of the ceiling, and two more come out of each side wall. I turn on the faucet, rotating it all the way to the hottest setting. I relieve myself in the small toilet room, and when I come out, the bathroom is steamy. Stepping into the shower, I sigh as the hot water falls over my hair, down my back, over my stomach, and down my legs.

A kiss presses between my shoulder blades, and I smile. "Really, Ash? You can't possibly be ready again."

He steps closer, pulling my ass against his hard cock. "I'll never get enough of you, princess."

I suck in a breath and shake my head. "There's no time. Your friends could get here any moment." But the words come out breathy and needy as I press a little harder against his length.

One of his arms wraps around my waist and spins me around. His lips graze my neck, then my ear, and I whimper as the tip of his cock teases my entrance. The need I have for this man is overwhelming.

As his teeth scrape the edge of the sensitive curve of my ear, he growls, "Let go, Rae. Just for a little while longer." He sees me. He knows me, and I can't find the right words, so I just nod and he smiles. "We may not have much time, but I like a challenge." He grabs my ass and hauls me up, pressing me against the wall, and I wrap my legs around his waist.

I gasp as he thrusts into me, immediately starting a quick pace. His hands grip me so tightly I'm sure there will be bruises, but I don't care. I grind into him harder and harder with every thrust, and he moans. "I am yours, Raelyn." He bites my shoulder as his fingers find my clit, pressing and circling until I'm throbbing.

"Hold on." His voice rasps across my throat and I squeeze him with my thighs as my hands grip his shoulders, feeling his muscles flex with every stroke.

He drives me over the edge, and I scream his name as my palms dig into his shoulders. My legs go weak, and I'm barely able to keep myself wrapped around him as my fourth orgasm of the night rips through me. The wet sound of his hips slamming into me echoes around the bathroom as the hot water blends with our sweat. His hand lightly grips my throat as he kisses me hard and fierce. His grip tightens slightly when he moans into my mouth as his release shudders into me.

My hand runs down his muscled back. "Fates, Ash."

"I know. I just had you. I'm still inside you for Fate's sake." He presses a gentle kiss to my lips. "But I want you again."

I swallow, trying to tamp down the already-building desire his words elicit. He pulls out of me and sets me down. I run my hands through his wet hair, a small frown on my face. "I'm sorry I ran for so long."

He smiles before kissing me again, long and unhurried. "Don't be sorry, Rae. Never be sorry. We are where we are meant to be." His lips meet mine again in a quick kiss before we clean ourselves and step from the shower. My air magic floats around us as my water magic wicks the final wetness from our hair.

We scramble naked to the living room to recover our clothes, and I'm shoving on my second boot and Ash is tucking his shirt into his pants when the front door silently opens, and three people file through before the door closes with a quiet click.

The three stand like deadly shadows in the front hall, and I recall Ash's earlier words. Yes, these three are worth at least ten of Garin's soldiers.

A beautiful woman, who I assume is the leader, steps forward, dropping her hood around her shoulders, revealing short-cropped, silky silver hair. She eyes Ash, and I catch the flash of longing there before her eyes turn to me. Her brown skin, the color of an oak leaf in the fall, is smooth and flawless, and her gold, almond-shaped eyes take in her surroundings as she assesses me.

Ash steps to my side. "Princess, may I introduce Nyira, the leader of the New Moon Guild. Nyira, her Highness, Lady Raelyn."

I stand tall and unmoving, letting Nyira look her fill. After a few seconds, she bows at the waist, and the other two assassins at her back do the same. "Your Highness, it is a pleasure to meet you. I hope we can be of assistance."

As the three right themselves, I nod to each in turn. "Thank you." I turn and walk down the hall into the kitchen. I take a seat at the round wood table, and Ash busies himself making tea as the three assassins join me. A male with moss-colored eyes sits to Nyira's right, his scarf draped around his neck to reveal sharp features and pale skin with a small scar nicking his right eyebrow. The other assassin, a female, sits next to the male. Her scarf is still in place, hiding her features and her hair, only showing eyes that glow the color of lavender.

Ash passes out little glass cups with fragrant, spiced tea, then sets the pot in the center of the table before taking the last free seat next to mine. He sits close, and his nearness steadies my nerves. I wish he would touch me in some small way, but I have a feeling he's trying to be professional, letting me lead, giving me the respect of my royal title.

With a small smirk, I lift my chin and grip my little cup, and as I sit back in my chair, crossing one leg over the other, I shift just enough so my thigh presses to Ash's. His head dips slightly, attempting to cover the small smile trying to take over his face, but the three assassins don't miss a thing. The covered female ignores the gesture, the male smiles and takes a sip of his tea, and Nyira frowns, her grip on her cup tightening slightly before she relaxes her fingers and forces a neutral expression.

Holding the warm cup in one hand, I rest my other in my lap. "I have a few ideas on how to get into the castle and get to my brother, but I'm eager to hear your recommendations." I look between the three assassins and Ash. "If we can avoid a large confrontation, that's my goal. I don't want to have to fight off his soldiers. I don't want citizens to get caught between my brother and me. And I don't want to deal with the Unseelie ... until my brother has been dealt with."

I take another sip and set down my empty glass. "But I'm aware I probably won't get everything I want, and I will do what I must to end Garin's reign and expel the Unseelie from our kingdom. So"—I look at Nyira—"if you were to infiltrate the castle and kill the King, how would you do it?"

The male assassin chuckles, leaning back in his chair. The female remains unmoving, and Nyira smiles, sending a chill shivering down my spine. One simple smile reveals the assassin she wants me to see. Her smile is warm, but the way she shows too much of her teeth shows the predator within. Plus, the confidence in her posture and the gleam of mischief in her eyes says anyone should be prepared for a fight should they cross her.

I'm abundantly glad she's on my side.

29

RAELYN

WE TALKED for hours through the remaining night and into the early morning. Well, the table of assassins talked for hours. I threw in the occasional word, but I think the excitement of planning a royal takedown was too much for New Moon Guild members to contain.

The male assassin, whose name turned out to be Sylmare, practically danced in his chair as he talked about infiltrating the castle. He even made an alarmingly high bet with Ash on who could take out the most soldiers. My money is on Ash.

The female assassin remained silent the whole night. The occasional nod, shake of her head, and shrug of her shoulders, the only indication she was listening at all.

Nyira was very take-charge, and I could see what makes her a great leader. She was calm and composed, her voice never rising.

Once the talks and plans wrapped up, it took almost an hour to convince Ash that he would be better served by paving my way to the castle with Sylmare instead of sticking by my side as he desperately wanted to.

Now, standing at the back door, his hands frame my face, and I feel a slight tremor in his touch. I smile up at him, ignoring the pit of worry in my stomach, nodding that everything will be okay. His eyes bore into mine as he lowers his head to kiss me. It's sweet, slow, desperate, and terrifying. Too soon, his lips leave mine, and Ash goes with Sylmare out the back door that drops them into a shadowed alley behind the safehouse.

The female assassin leaves on her own, knowing her role and where she needs to go.

Nyira stays. She will get me to my brother.

The dark scarf is once again in placed over her head and face so only her gold eyes peek out of the cloth. She has a wicked blade at her hip, two short daggers strapped on each thigh, and has hidden several throwing knives on various parts of her body. Her dark pants hug her legs, and a tight shirt of a deep, smoke grey sits under the folds of her scarf.

I'm brandishing my dragon blade, a few throwing knives, and my magic.

"Ready?" Nyira looks back at me from where she stands at the front door.

I take a deep breath, ignoring how it hitches in my chest, and nod. A few strides bring me to the door, and Nyira cracks it open, sliding into the early morning mists.

Here we go.

Before I cross the threshold, I glance down the hall, thinking of the small tapestry I placed in the bedside table for safe keeping. I'll be back for it.

Inhaling a deep breath, I walk beside Nyira down the

short path to the little gate, I still can't quite believe I'm home. I'm really in Attolyn. With everything on my mind, the reality of being home is unable to seep through like I'm blocked from taking any enjoyment in being here. I think I'm protecting myself in case ... in case I don't survive.

I glance to my left, seeing smoke billowing into the sky from the northwest. Our plan is in motion. Two blocks over and three blocks down, the female assassin has evacuated the New Moon Guild and set it ablaze.

Nyira pauses, watching the smoke thicken and start to choke the skies. Last night, I had promised to help her find a new residence for her Guild, or funding to rebuild. Even though the building was damaged and broken, I know it's hard for Nyira to let it go. She grew up there.

She squares her shoulders and pushes through the gate leading to the street of the residential area. We step onto the sidewalk, dodging a few fae as they either run toward or away from the fire. Most are running away, either toward the commercial district and the castle beyond, or to the east where the city ends at the edge of the woods. Those few running toward the burning building are Unseelie, and I suspect they are drawn by the prospect of the blood of injured fae. I ball my hands into fists to keep from grabbing my sword and cutting down a few Unseelie right now.

Nyira leans toward me. "Focus. The diversion won't last lon—"

"Ah, sister."

I stumble then freeze, snapping my gaze across the street. Out of the shadows of the space between two houses strides Garin.

Shit. Shit, shit, shit.

Nyira steps behind me, whispering, "Draw him to the

castle," before melting into the growing rush of people in the street.

My thoughts are cut off as Garin starts a slow, stalking pace toward me. "Did you think you could come back to Attolyn and I wouldn't know?" A few fae recognize Garin and falter, gaping open-mouthed, sketching quick bows before rushing away. As people start to recognize me, whispers of the lost princess reach my ears.

My brother smiles, and flames lick at his hands. The fae scatter, not willing to stick around and possibly become fodder in the battle between my brother and me.

"Honestly? Yes. But I wasn't trying all that hard." I lie and am pretty sure he can see right through me, but I barrel on. "I'm here for you, after all."

"*You're* going to take my crown?" His steps remain painfully slow, but his jaw clenches slightly with his words. "You? You're going to rule Attolyn?"

His eyes travel over my dark hair pulled back in a braid and sneers. I inwardly flinch but hold my posture tall, fighting to keep my face impassive. I refuse to let him make me feel like I'm less-than because of my brown hair.

With a smile, he pauses. "Do you know why you have dark hair, Raelyn?"

My pulse speeds at his question, but I lift my chin. "I'm sure whatever you're about to say will be just another one of your lies, so spare me."

"Oh no, Raelyn. This is no lie. I was there. I watched our mother fall into a depression when she couldn't get pregnant. I watched our father try everything to get her out of bed, to wash herself, to feed herself. It was ... weak, and my disdain for them grew as I watched her crumble under the depression of wanting another child, and him losing himself over wanting to help her. Pathetic." He sweeps an arm out, gesturing at nothing in particular. "I mean, they had me. Was I not enough?"

His eyes snap back to mine, the dark irises boring into me, making me want to flee. "One night, I spied father with our mother cradled in his arms, heading down to the dungeons. I followed, keeping to the shadows. It was amusing to watch as father darted his gaze around, nervous and twitching at every little noise with mother laying limp against his chest, her eyes glassy."

A pit, heavy and dark, grows in my gut as Garin grins. I no longer notice the fae rushing by. My attention is completely focused on my brother.

"Oh, Raelyn. They were so despondent. It was pathetic the way father's hands shook as he fished a key from his pocket and unlocked a cell door. It was unnervingly quiet, no guards, no soldiers, just our parents, the few prisoners tucked behind the thick, wood doors, and me, hidden away in the darkness. Father carried mother inside the dark cell, but from my vantage point, I could see just fine."

Garin smirks, flicking a dagger from his belt, running the tip over his finger until blood wells. "I still remember the jolt of surprise I felt when father unsheathed his dagger. Until that moment, I didn't think he had it in him. But more than surprise, I was ... excited, Raelyn. It was a rush to watch him wrap mother's hand around the hilt, his own hand keeping her grip tight."

My brother holds his dagger in front of him, pointing the bloody blade at me accusatorially. "Together, they drove the dagger into the heart of the prisoner, murdering the earth fae. I can still hear the sound of the blade sliding between his ribs and the grunt of breath that escaped the man."

"No."

"Oh, yes, Raelyn. They consumed his blood."

He snatches out a hand, grabbing a fae rushing toward the raging fire, unaware of our life-altering conversation. Before I can blink, Garin slices his dagger across the fae's neck. The fae's eyes go wide as she reaches for the wound, falling to the street as Garin shoves her away from him.

My body won't move. Shock has taken control, and I'm horrified at my inability to do anything but stare at my brother in disgust. He brings his dagger to his lips, licking it clean. "Mmm, shame. There was no magic in that one."

He flips the blade and sheaths it. "But you know, don't you, Rae, that consuming blood magic is not enough to aid in conception. That is even darker magic." Bile climbs my throat, sweat breaks out on my forehead, and dots speckle my vision. "Yes, Raelyn. Right there, father stripped himself then mother. He laid her on the blood-soaked floor of the dungeon cell, smearing our mother's cunt with the prisoner's blood then coating his flaccid dick. I watched, fascinated, as our parents defiled themselves."

The grin on Garin's face is cruel like a serrated blade, and his eyes are practically sparkling. He's enjoying this. He's getting off on the memory, and that realization has my stomach somersaulting, shoving bile up my throat, bringing stinging tears to my eyes. But I swallow and blink away the tears.

Garin licks his lips, smearing blood over his teeth. "Father somehow got himself erect, called up the stolen earth magic, and while chanting the fertility spell, he fucked her, Raelyn. For you, our father fucked our mother with the blood of a fae."

I drop to my knees and this time there's no stopping the bile as I retch. Any food I had in my stomach vaults up my throat and splatters across the cobblestones. I heave and heave, bringing up bile, then nothing at all. Hot tears stream down my face, and I'm shaking with an intensity that threatens to topple me into the fetal position.

Garin closes the distance between us and kneels, lifting my chin and twirling a strand of my hair around his finger. "So you see, Raelyn, our parents were willing to do whatever it took to get what they wanted. I am willing to do whatever it takes to keep my throne. My little Rae of sunshine, you are not strong enough in will or magic to take what is mine."

I yank my face away from him, palm one of my throwing knives, and plunge it into his leg. I was aiming for the femoral artery but missed. Still, it sinks to the hilt, and he pushes away from me, ripping the blade from his thigh. Struggling to my feet, I let all my anger, betrayal, frustration, and rage vibrate through my body. I stand, with feet slightly spread, chin lifted. "You have no idea how strong I am."

I'm jostled as a Seelie slams into my shoulder before continuing his scramble down the street. The city is waking up, and more fae are being drawn out of their homes by the commotion. Someone steps on my foot, and I bite back a swear. The fire has spread, the orange flames are peeking over the roofs, and thick smoke climbs in a dark column up the sky. Stumbling to the side, I barely manage to keep myself upright as yet another fae, this time an Unseelie, rams into my other shoulder.

No one runs into my brother, like he's actually untouchable. He's only a couple of feet away from me, and faster than I can track, a stream of fire flares from his outstretched hands aimed right for me. Two fae fall screaming to the ground as they get caught in the crossfire. The smell of burning flesh and hair makes my eyes water.

I bury my revulsion and sorrow as I snap my air magic around the burning, screaming fae, but it's already too late.

Their deaths claw at my conscience as rage expands in my chest, trying to break me apart. While my elemental magic can't protect me from the emotional pain, it does protect me from my brother's flames, keeping his fire from touching my skin.

Garin's eyes widen a fraction as he pushes more of his fire magic at me, which is now burning white-hot and radiating from him in every direction with powerful pulses. Fae can't get out of the way in time, and I shove a couple down the street with my air magic, but three more charred bodies fall to the ground.

This is already going horribly wrong. I need to get Garin away from the people.

"Enough." Untouched by his magic, I pop a bubble of air around him, and his flames begin to stutter. I desperately grab what water I can find in the air and pull at the water from a fountain one block down. Shoving the water inside the bubble of air, Garin is submerged, his flames struggling to stay alight, even underwater. His magic presses against mine as his enraged eyes stare me down.

Time to move. I redirect my air magic, praying Garin will leave the citizens alone and focus on me. I throw my arms out in front of me, pushing a gust of wind down the street, then fling my arms wide, using the strong burst of air to shove the scrambling fae to the edges of the street.

I run.

My pulse is racing from adrenaline, magic, fear, grief, and panic. Pounding footsteps echo off the cobblestones as Garin runs after me, and the sound of his angry pursuit thumps in time with my racing heart. I continue to push fae out of the way with my air magic as I rip up cobblestones behind me with my earth magic.

The sound of Garin's steps falters a few times, but he's

still too close. I don't dare look back, but I can't help imagining I feel his fingers grazing my back.

As a ball of fire slams into me, I stumble forward but keep running. Angry, I throw my own bolt of fire back at him, even knowing it won't hurt him. The tiny look of shock on his face is worth it as my fire magic explodes against his chest. But then he laughs, and I pause despite knowing I need to keep going. The sound is so familiar. I've heard that laugh so many times. I used to live for the moments I could get him to laugh like that. Anger swirls in my chest alongside my magic. The pain and hurt will come later.

"Dark magic, Rae? Maybe you are more like our parents than I thought. I wouldn't have thought you capable. But I do understand." His stolen earth magic lifts the loose cobblestones. "The power is intoxicating." He hurls the bricks at my head. I grab them in mid-air with my air and earth magic and send them back at him. He throws up a shield of fire, deflecting several of the stones, but one gets through and slams into his shoulder. He seems unfazed, though, as he grins at me with blood-stained teeth.

I've been charging the electrons in the clouds overhead for the past few seconds, and I smile back at my brother, eliciting the briefest look of confusion on his face. Perfect. I grin wider. "The power *is* intoxicating." The hairs on my arms lift. "Especially when it's natural born." Lightning thunders from the sky, and Garin dives to the side as the white-hot electrical charge slams to the ground where he was standing just a moment ago. He props himself on his elbows and glances over his shoulder at the charred street. I yank another lightning bolt from the clouds, and Garin rolls, barely avoiding the strike but coming up with blood dripping from his ears.

Sliding his gaze to me, he stands, slapping dirt from his

pants before bringing his fingers to his ear and stares at the blood that comes away. He tilts his head with a smirk. "You want me to believe you're an Elemental?"

"You can believe what you want, but yes." I throw my water magic over him and onto the ground between us. Crystalizing the water, I freeze him to the street and turn the cobblestones into a slippery sheet of ice. I shoot him a confident grin as I bolster my courage and resolve. "I'll take my throne now."

Spinning, I blur toward the castle, and with a bellow of rage, Garin explodes with a rush of fire and follows, his flames melting the ice before him. The castle comes into view, and my relief at being out of the city is squashed when I see the ranks of soldiers barring the gates that lead to the courtyard and castle beyond.

I skid to a stop kicking up dust and gravel. I can't fight them as well as my brother. Where is Ash? Where are the assassins?

As if summoned by my thoughts, the ground cracks to my right as Nyira comes sprinting from the chaos of the city. Dozens of soldiers fall into the crevice created by her earth magic. Several soldiers break from their ranks and turn to focus their attack on her. She fends them off with her sword in one hand and wields her earth magic in fits of thrown rocks, cobblestones, tree limbs, roots, and tremors to keep the soldiers off-balance. But a few have their own magic, and she's outmatched.

I snap a protective bubble of impenetrable air around her—well, it's impenetrable for now. My attention is being pulled in too many directions as Garin throws yet more fire at me. Bolt after bolt of molten flame hits me, and while it doesn't hurt, I stumble back with each hit, driving me closer to the soldiers at my back. He shoves a blast of stolen air magic at me, and the force pushes me back another few feet.

My earth magic grabs at the roots running under the street, and the ground rumbles as they shoot upward, ripping up cobblestones before reaching for Garin. Fire erupts from his hands, burning the roots away before they get close.

My gaze catches on the glint of Garin's blade, hanging unused, almost forgotten, at his side. He's so focused on his magic, I take a chance. My air magic collects before me, leaving Nyira unprotected, but she's gained the upper hand against the few soldiers still fighting her. A whirlwind touches down, kicking up a thick layer of dust between my brother and me. I use the moment of cover to blur forward, and as I get close, I draw my sword, shove the whirlwind behind me into the line of soldiers who have been slowly advancing on me, and slice my blade in a strong downward stroke at Garin's neck.

My heart screams with sorrow, but I don't falter. My brother dodges, and my sword connects with his shoulder instead of severing his head. His fire magic erupts from him like a blast from a bomb, and it throws me through the air. I tense, angling myself to land on my back, my head thumping painfully on the ground. I'm struggling for breath, and my head is throbbing as I struggle to sit up, but I managed to keep a hold of my sword, so I'm doing okay.

A hand grabs my arm, and I wrench around to sink my sword into my captor, but Ash's face comes into view, and I suck in a sharp breath, barely managing to stop my momentum and keep from stabbing him in the chest. He hauls me to my feet, and we quickly look each other over. He has a shallow cut on his left arm, and there is dirt and leaves in his hair, but otherwise, he seems unharmed. His palm cups my cheek a quick second before he lets his arm fall to his side, and he turns to face Garin.

I lean toward him slightly. "Who's winning?"

He snorts a laugh, and I can't help but grin. "So far, I've dropped twenty-three, and Sylmare has taken out twenty."

"Twenty-one!" Sylmare yells from the courtyard. I turn and see the assassin spinning and slashing his way through the soldiers blocking our path to the castle.

"Twenty-two, twenty-three!"

"Shit." Ash strides into the melee with a grin.

I turn, knocking several soldiers off their feet with another blast of air and pin a few more to the ground in a tangle of roots. Facing my brother, I meet his eyes as he sneers, nodding in the direction of where Ash is fighting a trio of soldiers. "So sweet."

Garin's eyes look up over my shoulder, and a second later, I stumble forward. Searing pain stabs through my right shoulder blade, and I sheath my sword before I drop it. Reaching back, I feel the quiver of an arrow protruding from my back, and I fight back a scream as I try unsuccessfully to pull it out.

Garin, a smile on his face, steps to his right, and I move to my right. We circle each other until he stands before his soldiers, and my back is to the city, the castle now looming before me. He flicks his hand, and three soldiers nock and release arrows at me. On instinct, I erect a wall of air to deflect the arrows ... only, nothing happens.

One arrow flies wide, the second speeds right through where my shield should have been and sinks into the flesh below my right collarbone. I grit my teeth against the excruciating pain and brace for the final arrow. But it never lands.

The female assassin has seemingly appeared out of thin

air and holds the third arrow in her fist. I gawk at her. "Did you catch that arrow in mid-air?"

She shakes back her head, and her scarf falls around her neck. Short, shimmering hair sticks up around her delicate face. Her lavender eyes crinkle at the edges as she smiles at me. "Ellara, at your service. We can't have you taken out of the game, your Highness. Your kingdom needs you."

I'm surprised by the soft, almost bell-like tone of her voice, and before I can say more, she grips the arrow in my chest and yanks it out. I bark out a scream and take a deep breath before nodding my thanks. I shift to give her my back so she can pull out the other arrow, but she blurs to our left, engaging with a contingent of soldiers that are rushing toward us.

A glance at the arrow laying at my feet reveals a blood-coated Shungite arrowhead.

Great.

Garin smirks with a flick of his hands. "Take her."

A wave of soldiers stalk toward me, each one brandishing a weapon, several calling up their magic. I grip my sword and plant my feet. The Shungite is keeping my magic from me, but I can still fight.

"Raelyn!" Ash yells, seeing the soldiers advance on me. He and Sylmare are fighting back-to-back as Nyira tries to work her way toward them from the right, and Ellara works her way in from the left. Weapons flash, and I notice the lack of magic coming from my friends. All Garin's soldiers are fighting with Shungite blades.

Well, shit.

I blur a few feet to my right and swipe a bow and quiver from a downed soldier. I do my best to ignore the pain of the arrow in my shoulder blade, and a smile spreads across my face as I snap an arrow into position and stare down beyond the shungite tip. I inhale, exhale, and release. A soldier falls behind Ash. Another arrow is in my hand and on its way to my target with my next breath. Sylmare simply steps over the downed soldier with the arrow in his throat to swipe his sword at a soldier wielding two curved blades.

Arrow after arrow snaps from my bow.

Nyira swipes a shungite dagger from a soldier, and I see her lips moving, catching the words of the spell she's casting to extend the effects of the black blade. Sylmare rips out a Shungite dagger buried in his thigh only to plunge it through the eye of the closest soldier. The three assassins are trying to work their way toward me, but there's no way they'll get here before the soldiers before me close in.

The quiver is empty, so I drop the bow and reach for my sword. Grimacing as my back spasms with the pain of the arrow protruding from my back, I watch as the light catches each elemental symbol on my blade. The sight strengthens me, and a rush of energy tingles through my blood.

I may be an Elemental, but I'm also a fighter, a survivor.

Clenching my teeth, I swing my blade in an awkward arc behind my head and barely bite back a scream as the arrow shaft slices away. The head and a small piece of the shaft are still embedded in my skin, but that will have to do for now.

The soldiers continue to advance, sneers on their faces.

"Come at me, you bastards."

One lunges, and I tense to deflect and thrust, when he jerks to a stop. His wide eyes look down, gaping at the dagger protruding from his chest. Three more soldiers fall around him as he drops to his knees then falls back, dead.

"For the princess!" I whip around at the yells behind me. "For Attolyn!" A horde rushes from the city, blurring past me, clashing with the soldiers. Several in the crowd are wearing the clothes of the New Moon Guild, but most are citizens holding weapons of every kind. Bodies blur, magic flares, and blades flash, rending skin and felling foes. Blood sprays. The eyes of the fighting Unseelie dilate with the hunger for the dark magic spilling to the ground. Even Seelie, who have become addicted to the rush of blood magic, are pouncing on fallen and injured fae. Blood coats their mouths, and magic sizzles along their skin.

"Argh!" My head whips around at my brother's shout. "You despicable piece of fae trash." Ash twists a dagger that's hilt deep in Garin's lower back.

I catch movement to my right and duck under a pulse of air magic from an Unseelie. A citizen of Attolyn throws their fire magic on my attacker, and he goes up in white-hot flames.

My attention snaps back to Garin as I watch my brother reach back and yank the dagger from his flesh. Ash holds something in his fist, and he slams it against the open wound in Garin's back. Ash grinds his hand into the wound with a yell, "That's raw Shungite, you bastard. Cast around that!" Garin spins and grabs a handful of Ash's hair before slamming the Shungite blade into Ash's stomach. He twists the blade and shoves Ash to the ground.

"Ash!" My scream rips from my throat. The roaring in my ears drowns out everything else as I stalk toward my brother. I swing my blade, ignoring the spasms trembling through my shoulder. My sword angles for Garin's chest, and he jumps back. Still, I manage to slice into the flesh of his chest, and he hisses—reminding me of every time I made a similar sound of pain from the many injuries inflicted on me by my brother in the name of training.

Still, every time I slice into Garin's skin, my heart breaks a little more. I know that if I hope to survive, I have to kill my brother. But my heart still weeps at the idea.

I swing my blade, and Garin deflects, stepping back. I follow.

Strength and resolve punch through me as I catch a low moan to my left. Ash is alive. My people are fighting. My people are dying.

With overhead swings, upward thrusts, slashing arcs, and thrusting at any opening I can find, I push Garin back. Anger drives me, and grief gives me purpose as my world narrows to the face of my brother turned enemy. With every strike of steel, I feel the vibrations of our blades clashing together, but I can't hear them over the sounds of battle around us as well as the rage screaming in my head—rage at myself and at Garin.

The roar in my head gets louder, and I grit my teeth. Only, I don't think it's only in my head. Garin and I keep swinging at each other as everyone else around us pauses, horrified gazes turned up.

Another roar pummels my ears, and the ground shakes as something heavy lands behind me. Garin's eyes go wide, and screams erupt. "Dragon!"

30

RAELYN

As I GLANCE over my shoulder, I catch a shimmer of bronze. "Syphe?"

The beautiful dragon smiles at me, which is terrifying, but I smile back. Her voice rumbles from her chest. "I couldn't let you have all the fun, my friend." She flicks her long tail, sending several fae flying through the air.

I deflect a downward swing from a fae's sword with my own and chuckle at the enormous dragon next to me. "I thought Kem grounded everyone."

An Unseelie actually attempts to stab her sword through Syphe's foot, but the blade just scrapes across her scales and sinks into the ground. Syphe stomps on the fae with a spine-tingling squish. "Well ..." Her dragon head scans the crowd of fighting and fleeing fae. "Talk later, coup now."

I sweep a dramatic hand in front of us. "By all means, find your joy."

A laugh erupts from her, smoke curling from her lips, revealing her sharp teeth, and more fae decide this is no longer a fight worth fighting, fleeing in any direction that takes them away from the bellowing dragon at my side.

"You can't fight your own battles? You need assassins and dragons to steal my throne?" Garin's voice booms over the courtyard, through the small clearing, and into the streets beyond into the city.

Syphe turns, crushing several fae in the process. Her jaw vibrates with a deep growl as she side-eyes me. "Do you want me to eat him? I'd probably be sick for an entire day after eating someone so disagreeable, but I'd be happy to do it for you."

I smile, enjoying watching Garin's face go a shade paler. "No, thank you. I'll deal with him."

There's a shimmer of bronze light, then a woman with bronze hair and eyes stands next to me, her skin shimmering in the sun, a blade in her hand. "Okay, then. I'm going to have some fun with these Unseelie." I raise an eyebrow, and she shrugs. "Facing them as a dragon is an unfair advantage." She swings her blade. "I can at least give them a fighting chance." With a laugh, she launches herself into the fray. After training with her for a month, I can tell she's holding back, playing with her opponents, as blades and arrows slide off her skin.

I face Garin. "Yes, I have the help of your citizens, assassins, and a dragon." I gesture at the remaining soldiers. "You only have the dark fae, who I doubt hold any actual loyalty to you—them, and a few addicted Seelie. I've chosen my allies with care, brother."

I lift my sword and charge. Our blades clash, and I feel the hit in my bones. Slash, swing, thrust, block. We each struggle to find an opening to take out the other. Our blades meet again, the steel screaming a protest as we push our swords together, hoping for an advantage.

Garin smiles at me between our blades. It's the same smile I grew up craving, and I can't catalogue the flood of emotions that run through me as I look up into my brother's shining, black eyes. My arms tremble as Garin's blade continues to press against mine, forcing me to give a step, then two.

As I stare at him, I see him. I really see him. There's greed and arrogance in his eyes. Anger clenches his jaw, and his lips keep running over his teeth like he's searching for the taste of blood. This is who my brother is, and he won't stop until I'm dead. This isn't like the challenge with Ziza. I can't show mercy.

His knee comes up, trying to slam into my thigh, but I sidestep, spinning out of our hold. I follow the spin through and swing my sword behind me, catching him on the arm then stabbing quickly, piercing him high on his chest. Nothing fatal, but it's something.

He pulls a dagger from his boot and stabs it toward my neck as he swings his sword at any body part he thinks he can reach. I dodge, and we continue to circle each other, stabbing and slashing, our breaths laboring the longer we fight. My arms are tired, and my shoulder is a riot of pain that even my adrenaline can't dull, but I won't give in to the burning in my muscles. I can't.

Garin has scored a few shallow strikes, and one deep gash above my hip is bleeding quite heavily, soaking my pants. I've bled so much, my left foot is starting to squish in my boot where the blood has pooled. I'm sure there are several injuries I don't even know about, and the longer we fight, the more my wounds burn.

I have no idea how the fight is going beyond my brother

and me. I'm doing my best not to think about it. Lift your sword, Raelyn, I plead with myself. *Keep going, don't give him anything. Don't let him see how tired you are. Your people need you.* Strike and slash. *Your people need you.* Deflect, step, and thrust. *Your people need you.*

I'm exhausted. Every time I lift my sword, it feels like I'm dragging it through thick mud. I'm too slow. Garin's blade slips between my defenses, ripping across my side, scraping my ribs, pulling a scream from my lips. I press a hand to my side, trying to hold myself together and limp toward him once again, lifting my impossibly heavy sword. I'm getting really tired of being ripped apart.

He chuckles, but there's a flash of pain in his eyes as the muscles in his back spasm around the shungite buried in his flesh. Yet he still easily knocks my blade aside, scoring another slice into my skin, this time through my left bicep. "Oh, Raelyn. Give this up. Concede defeat, and I will let you live. I will even send you back to Earth if that's what you want." I swing at him, stumbling, and he sinks his blade into my already burning left thigh. He's playing with me. "Go back to Earth, Raelyn. I'll reseal the portal. You won't have to worry about Attolyn ever again. You will get to keep your life, I will keep Attolyn."

He knocks aside my blade again and steps up to me. Tossing his dagger to the ground, he grabs my throat, squeezing as he leans in. "Or, by all means, keep fighting. You were always too stubborn to know when to quit. Or maybe you're just too stupid." He stabs his sword into the ground and reaches around me, grasping the ragged arrow shaft sticking out of my shoulder blade. He twists it, driving it deeper into my flesh. Pain snaps like lightning from my shoulder to my hip, and stars dance across my vision. A scream rips from my throat as I will myself to stay conscious. My sword slides from my grip, clattering the ground.

With a smile, he licks my blood from his hand and his eyes actually flutter in perverse pleasure. "So. Much. Power." He grabs my throat with both hands, his sneering face a breath from mine. "I have a better idea." Darkness closes in at the edges of my vision as his grip tightens. My knees buckle, and Garin follows me down so we're both kneeling. "I'll watch as I squeeze the consciousness from you. I'll throw you in the dungeons, and when you wake, I'll take your blood, your magic. I'll help you pass the days by having your friends executed before you. One friend a day. And when I run out of friends"—he smiles, and I press my lips together, forcing my body to remain limp and trembling in his grip—"I'll execute citizens, Seelie and Unseelie, and you will watch as I consume their magic. I will be unstoppable. That will be your existence for the rest of your days ... *sister*."

Our bodies are nearly pressed together, and my vision is tunneling as I bring tension back into my limp body. I clamp my fingers around the hilt of the dagger strapped to my thigh. With a grunt of effort, I stab it into his stomach and twist. His eyes go wide, and I grab the hilt with both hands, yanking upwards, cutting through skin and organs, scraping against bone. He releases me, and as I gasp air into my lungs, I let myself fall to the side so I can kick him in the chest. My boot makes contact with the dagger, slamming it deeper as he falls back.

Finding my sword, I use it as a crutch, dragging myself to standing. I yank his sword from the ground with my other hand and limp over to him. Garin half crawls, half drags himself away from my advancing steps. He tries to say something but blood sprays from his mouth as he coughs on a strangled exhale.

I pity him as the first sign of actual fear crawls across his face. I've been mourning Garin for a month now, so there's only resolve behind my words. "No, brother. No more." I stab his sword through his leg and into the ground, pinning him in place.

I startle as a fae soldier falls to my right, his outstretched hand clutching a blade meant to strike me down. My blind focus breaks as I remember Garin and I are not the only ones fighting for our lives. A woman stands behind the fallen fae with a bloody hammer in her fist. Her eyes are wide, but she nods at me before diving back into the fight.

Glancing around, I take in the bloody strip of land before the castle where bodies litter the ground. I swallow back bile as I watch a few desperate fae drink the blood of the fallen, chanting spells, trying to work around the effects of the shungite. One such fae jerks back with a scream as an assassin slits their throat before moving on to their next mark.

Nyira is a shadow, her blades flashing, dealing death. I can't see Sylmare, but Ellara dispatches a soldier before her, and without breaking stride, leaps over the falling body to help a young fae fighting off a silver-haired man screaming for his blood.

It all seems to be happening in slow motion. My brain is struggling to keep up as I fight past my exhaustion and blood loss. Like in a dream, or a nightmare, I witness my people fighting tooth and nail for their kingdom, and for ... me.

My eyes fall back to my brother, who's trying to dislodge the sword pinning his leg to the ground. I take a single step toward him, and more blood spills down Garin's chin as he bellows a scream at me, like his rage alone will keep me from him.

But I don't stop. I can't.

Two-handed, I raise my sword and swing, ignoring the feeling of my heart shattering, sending anguish to every corner of my body.

My brother's head slides from his shoulders and thuds to the ground a second before his body crumples. The crown falls from his head and rolls a few feet before toppling over on the blood-soaked cobblestones with a metallic rattle that echoes through my ears.

I sink to my knees and stare at my brother's severed head. My entire body is shaking, and I'm too cold for the heat of the day. I vaguely hear the scuffle of boots behind me, but I can't move. I can't peel my eyes from my brother's bloody face.

There's a grunt, then a thud behind me as a body falls. Then two more. Garin's soldiers are still coming for me. Still, I don't move. I feel oddly empty, and I think I might be going into shock.

A hand grips my hair and starts to yank me back, but then a roar crashes through the air, and the ground shakes. A startled scream erupts from whoever has a hold on me, and I'm released before there's a familiar crunch. Then all is silent. Garin's black eyes stare at me as the world around us goes still, and the only noise is my blood rushing past my eardrums.

"Your Majesty." *Just leave me alone.* "Your Majesty." A hand lands on my shoulder, but I don't move. My chest is too tight as I stare at Garin's face. "Raelyn, you must get up."

Kem's right, I need to get up. I can't. I don't think my legs work. Why isn't Garin blinking? ... Oh.

My face is wet, and I realize I'm crying. How is it possible that my wounds seem to have gone numb, but my heart has never known such pain? I thought I had mourned Garin, but how wrong I was. This is ... agony. My entire family is gone.

"Give me a moment."

Kem's hand on my shoulder slips away as he takes a step back.

A pair of legs limp in front of me, blocking my view of my brother's face. Ash kneels, taking my face in his hands. As our eyes meet, I manage to take in a stuttering breath as I look down at his stomach. It's roughly bandaged and almost soaked through with blood. "He stabbed you. I thought I was going to lose you."

A soft smile pulls at his lips. "Nah. I'm tougher than that." His thumb traces my jaw. "Besides, it would take an outright act of god, or the Fates, to take me from you."

I attempt a smile, but it doesn't quite work. Ash leans in, lightly brushing his lips across mine, but I don't miss the wince of pain he tries to hide. He presses his forehead to mine. "I love you."

My tears are falling again. He needs to know. Before I can move forward. Before anything else, he needs to know. "Ash—"

"Shh. It's okay."

"No, it's not. There's something you need to know." I sit back, but he holds my gaze, and I swallow the fear clawing up my throat. There are people all around us, and there's a heavy silence spreading across the clearing.

Ash looks over my shoulder. "Can we have a moment?" There's no response for a handful of seconds then footsteps crunch away from us. He brushes back the stray hairs that have escaped my braid. "What is it, Rae?"

"I'm a child of blood magic."

He doesn't react. His warm, golden eyes stay glued to my face, and his silence makes me nervous.

"Did you hear me? My parents, the goddamned King and Queen, performed dark magic while casting a spell to conceive me." I pull out my hair tie and grab handfuls of my cursed, dark hair. "Blood magic created me." I tug my hair. "A dark, unnatural spell brought me into this world." My hands yank my hair again, and several strands rip from my head. "You can't love me. You can't. The people of this kingdom deserve better. You—"

Ash grabs my wrists and presses his lips to mine. My body shakes from the flood of emotions catapulting through me along with the adrenaline draining away.

But Ash keeps me upright, keeping a hold on me as he pulls away from the kiss. "I don't care. I know you, Raelyn. And I love you. Learning this information doesn't change who you are. You are the same amazing woman you were yesterday. And our people are lucky to have someone as fierce and loyal and brave who has and will forever fight for them." His hand cups my cheek. "I am yours, Rae. Always."

I let myself lean into him, resting my head against his chest, listening to the steady beat of his heart. "I love you, Ash."

"As well you should."

I giggle as he rubs a hand down my back. Even though the crowd moved off, I'm sure they're watching, but I need one more moment. We both take a few deep breaths before Ash shifts back and stands with a grunt, his hand pressed to his bandaged stomach. He holds out his free hand, and I take it.

Moving to stand, my many injuries come screaming back to life, and a strangled scream drops me back to my knees.

"Let me." A deep voice rumbles behind me as a pair of hands hook under my arms, and as gently as possible, lift me to my feet. Kem's strong hands land on my shoulders, and he leans forward, his breath fanning my hair. "Deep breath."

What?

The arrow rips from my back, and I grind my teeth together to keep myself from passing out. He whispers again, "I'm sorry." A second later, the warm tingle of healing power takes the edge off my pain, but before he can keep going, I turn, taking a step back out of his arms, and look up to meet Kem's gaze. "You came."

He grins, his shadows licking across his dark skin. "I did. We did." Looking around, I see scores of people with all manner of colored hair shimmering into existence.

The dragons. Ziza steps forward, her emerald hair perfect as always. Her bright, green eyes smile at me with a nod. Kem crosses his arms over his chest. "After you left, Syphe decided she wasn't comfortable letting you face Garin on your own." His eyes move around the clearing. "But as it turns out, you are not on your own." Kem looks at Ash before meeting my eyes again. "You never were."

I smile, though even that simple gesture seems too difficult as my strength continues to leak from me. Kem nods, then runs a hand over his tied-back locs. "Anyway, Syphe spent hours storming after me like one of my shadows come to life, yelling that it was time to stop watching the world and get involved."

"I think my words were, 'Get off your dragon ass and go help Rae, the council be damned'." Syphe strides up, a wide smile on her face, her bronze braid messy and flecked with blood.

Kem grins. "And I happened to agree with her."

Well, this is big, but it's a conversation for another time.

Syphe faces me and bows. "Your Majesty."

Oh shit, I'm going to be Queen.

One by one, the dragons kneel, and I think my own knees might give out at the sight. The gathered fae who fought for us drop to their knees, and I clench my teeth to keep the welling tears from falling. Nyira meets my eyes over the crowd, nods, then kneels as well. Ellara, supporting a wounded Sylmare, winks at me, bringing a small smile to my lips as they both struggle to their knees.

Several dragons in their imposing dragon forms, stand around the surviving Seelie and Unseelie who fought for my brother, their mere presence holding them captive. The prisoners scowl but remain silent, casting uneasy glances at the dragons.

I look over the small sea of bowed heads, not quite sure what to do, so I just stand still. We did it. We actually did it. My lips quiver, and the smallest sob bubbles from my mouth as Kem takes another step back and bows deep at the waist before kneeling. "Your Majesty." If only Garin had been more like Kem. If only …

Ash brushes a kiss to my temple, drawing me from my thoughts. He steps back, and I let him go. My tears fall as he kneels, picking up the fallen Seelie crown and holds it up to me, his head bowed. "My Queen."

Slowly, the fae and dragons stand, all eyes on me as I place the crown on my head. It's lighter than I thought it'd be, and it settles gently around my tangled hair. I do my best to project my voice, needing to sound strong, even though I'm swaying on my feet. Exhaustion is quickly taking hold, both physical and emotional, but I shove it down, ignoring it as best I can.

"There is much to be rebuilt, both in trust and structures. The Unseelie will leave our kingdom. Now. They will have one hour to leave Attolyn. After that, any

Unseelie found in my kingdom will be hunted down and executed. Without question." My gaze travels over the crowd. "If there are any Seelie who wish to continue to practice dark magic, you must do so elsewhere. Blood magic will not be tolerated in Attolyn. If the Unseelie allow it, you are more than welcome to go to Morthryl, but you cannot stay here."

The captives shift angrily at my declaration, but I keep my head held high, holding their gazes with an unflinching stare. Besides, the dragon's growling around them are keeping them in line.

I glance at Kem. He nods and addresses the crowd. "If you think to resist your Queen's orders—if you think to use your dark magic here—know that the dragons will be overseeing the banishment of the Unseelie. Do not think you can stay here, hidden away." Kem's lips lift in a terrifying grin. "We dragons do love a good hunt, though, so by all means, try your luck."

Syphe leaps into the air, shifting. The flap of her giant wings nearly knocks me back, but Ash is there, catching me, and we lean on each other for a moment. He leans in, whispering, "Do you get to ride one?"

I snort a laugh. "No."

He frowns, watching Syphe hover over the crowd. "Shame."

I shake my head with a smile, and while those around me are distracted, I steady myself, pushing away from Ash's warmth, though I almost immediately regret it as pain shoots through my shoulder and my ears pop with pressure as my body tries to shut down.

I take a deep breath as one after the other, the dragons shift and launch into the air, hovering and circling as the prisoners cringe with fearful glances at the sky. The dark fae, as well as a several Seelie, are marched toward the garden portal, escorted by the dragons.

Kem turns to me as a handful of dragons peel off and soar over the city and to the countryside beyond. "They will make sure all the Unseelie in your kingdom are returned to their home—or eaten."

His face is stern and serious, but I smile, and a tiny bit of tension drains out of me when Ash laughs. "Damn, Kemremir." His black eyes with those molten cores turn to Asheraht, and he holds up his hands. "Your Majesty. All respect intended."

Kem's lips quirk, and I laugh, but it's cut off with a grimace as pain slices through my stomach, and I grip my side. I feel myself tilt to the right as my shoulder spasms again where the shungite arrow had been.

"You need a healer," Kem and Ash say at the same time.

Ash glances at the Dragon King. "I know you have at least some healing power. I saw you ease Rae's pain earlier." He holds Kem's gaze. "Her Majesty could use your help."

I start to shake my head, but Nyira pushes her way through the crowd and carefully wraps her arm around my shoulders. "I'll see to the Queen. You boys help bring some order to the city."

Nyira starts to lead me away, and I hear the sound of footsteps following. I know it's Ash, and I dig my heels in, swallowing the groan of pain as I turn to Nyira. "Thank you, Nyira. You have proven yourself an indispensable ally. Gather your people. Bring them here. I will arrange lodging while the New Moon is rebuilt."

I hold out a hand to Ash, hoping not too many people notice the tremble before he laces his fingers with mine. I smile, holding him tightly. His eyes are filled with worry for me, even though his own face is pinched with pain. But here he stands, at my side, where he's always been, no matter how many times I ran from him. I squeeze his hand, bringing his full attention back to me as I say with a clear, steady voice, "My King will see that I'm taken care of."

I watch as his eyes go wide, and he sways slightly like he wants to take a step back. We haven't talked about this, I mean, when would we have had the time? But if he steps away from me now, if he leaves because of my dumb mouth, I don't think I'll survive.

Ash remains silent, and my heart races. I've done this all wrong. Nothing much scares Asheraht, but I think I've terrified him.

My head snaps up as Nyira laughs. "Fates save us all. Asheraht, King." I smile, not chancing a look at Ash, but I can't stop my fingers from fidgeting over his hand. Nyira looks at Ash, and whatever she sees on his face softens her laughter to a warm smile. "You know what? On second thought, the Fates do know what they're doing." She bows to Ash. "Your Majesty." I dare to flick my gaze to him, catching a small smile on his lips, and that one smile loosens the band strangling my lungs. Turning to me, Nyira's expression is serious. In her eyes, I see pride. She bows to me. "Your Majesty."

With a spin, she stands upright, whistles and strides away. Ash jerks, and I wonder if he wants to follow her call to the assassins, but he remains at my side as black-clad fae melt from the crowd and converge on Nyira's retreating form. Like wisps of smoke, they disappear into the city to gather the remaining Guild members and to call those who fled back home.

I face the Seelie soldiers who fought with me. "Is your captain present?"

Glances pass back and forth before an older fae with

actual grey in her silver ponytail steps forward. "The captain was killed early in the Unseelie occupation some forty-five years ago, your Majesty. An Unseelie was appointed captain in his place. He is among the dead today." She pauses, fighting a grin, avoiding my gaze. "I think that emerald dragon ate him."

Ash smiles as I snort a very un-queenly laugh. "That sounds like Ziza." My laugh dies off, and I tilt my head to the side. "I know you. You used to train me when ..."

"Yes, your Majesty. You were a tough fighter even then."

"I'm sorry. I don't recall your name?"

"Tial, your Majesty."

All the 'your majesties' are already getting old, just another thing for me to get used to. "Tial, please see to the people. Make sure the wounded are taken to the healer's Guild and that everyone makes it home. Make it known that the city will remain closed today as order is restored. Though if any businesses want to open, they are more than welcome to do so. I do understand the need for distraction in normalcy after a trying experience." I look over the soldiers. "I will take recommendations for a new captain over the following month. I will make my own assessments and make a decision after proper consideration."

There are a few nods throughout the ranks, and more than a few heads turn to Tial. I take notice. This woman is a leader. "In the meantime, Tial, I am placing you as acting captain. I'm trusting you with the protection of my kingdom in this fragile time."

Tial crosses her heart with her fist and bows. "I will serve with pride, your Majesty." I smile, but at that moment, my leg cramps, and I take a shaky step to keep myself upright. Tial's worried eyes shift from Ash to me. "Leave the city to us, your Majesty." She turns on her heel, issuing commands, and the soldiers scatter to follow their orders.

I slide my hand from Ash's, determined to enter my castle under my own power, but he's right here if I need him.

We pass through the castle gates, and I bite the inside of my cheek to keep from falling to my knees and weeping right here. My parents should be here to welcome me home. My father should be pulling me into his arms to ruffle my hair. My mother should be pursing her lips, telling me to wash up and put on a proper dress. Alek should be taking my hand, promising to take me around the kingdom to show me everything that has changed, and everything that has not.

My steps are getting slower, and I'm struggling to lift my feet high enough to keep from dragging my boots. I'm so tired. I'm so ... sad.

Finally, we cross the threshold of the giant doors to the castle, and two servants, worried eyes catching on each of my wounds, close the heavy doors behind us.

As soon as the loud thunk of the closed doors bounces around the large stone receiving hall, my first glimpse of home fades. Sound compresses with a rush as my body shuts down, and I sink into the darkness with the feel of Ash's arms wrapping around me.

31

ASHERAHT

Rae slumps against me, and I scoop her into my arms. Ignoring my own injuries, I race down the main hall. "Where are the healers' rooms, Rae?" There's no answer. Her head lolls against my arms, and her limbs go limp. "Healer! I need the healer!"

A large male practically jumps through an open doorway to my right. His round stomach jiggles as he slides to a stop, his gaze quickly taking us in. "This way." He blurs with impressive speed, and I grit my teeth to keep up.

He skids before an arched wood door, and without breaking stride, he shoves it open and ushers us inside. "Lay her there." He points a stubby finger to a padded table with a white sheet laid over it. Pulling his long silver hair into a bun at the nape of his neck, he shrugs into a white apron and grabs a few bottles with different colored liquids and powders.

I lay Rae down, trying not to panic at how pale she is. I hold her limp hand as the fae starts cutting away her bloody, sticky clothing. "Hastios," the man bellows, and a rail-thin fae comes barreling from a back room.

He takes one look at us and wipes his hands on his apron. "Oh Fates. Is that the princess?"

"The Queen," the healer and I say at the same time.

Hastios' eyes go wide, then turn serious as he steps up. With a screech of wood over stone, he slides over a long bench and presses a firm hand to my shoulder. "Sit. I need to see to your wounds."

"I'm fine." I don't mean to growl at him, but the words come out harsh anyway.

"You are not fine. You can keep a hold of her hand, she probably needs your comfort, but you're on the verge of passing out yourself." He shoves me, and my knees fold.

I watch as the healer cleans Rae's wounds, and I wince at every bruise and cut on her beautiful skin. I don't even register Hastios' presence as he cuts away my shirt and starts to clean and stitch my wounds. As he unwraps the crude field dressing around my abdomen, I bite back a curse as the fabric sticks to the wound, still leaking blood. Hastios has me shift enough so he can more easily access where Garin stabbed me. He grabs a bottle with blue powder and shakes it into the wound. It burns like my fire magic is consuming me from the inside out. "Fuck!" Hastios doesn't flinch at my outcry, and a few seconds later, the burning subsides. He goes about stitching me up with practiced speed.

I'm not sure how much time passes, but I watch as the healer methodically runs his hands over Rae's wounds again and again. Slowly, the shallow cuts close, and the bruises turn from purple and black to a yellowish-green. The deeper wounds, while much improved, still stand out stark and angry on her skin. Hastios does the same for me, and every breath becomes easier. I manage to peel my gaze from Raelyn to look at the thin healer running his hands over my stomach wound. "Thank you."

He nods, standing.

The healer pours a white liquid down Raelyn's throat. "It will help in the healing process." He lifts another bottle, this one with a ruby red liquid in it, the consistency of blood. Seeing my expression, he smiles. "It's not blood. It's pulverized heart root mixed with spring water and powdered mallow bark. It will help with the pain."

He pours half into Rae's mouth then holds the bottle out to me. I start to shake my head, but Hastios pokes me in the shoulder. "Don't be difficult. Take the medicine."

I grin, taking the bottle and downing the red liquid like a shot. "I thought healers were supposed to have a gentle bedside manner."

The healer grins, and Hastios chuckles. "My manner matches that of my patient."

I laugh, then wince at the pull of pain. Hastios rushes to pinch my wound together to keep the stitches from popping. "Don't ruin all my hard work. Hold your laughter."

Pressing my lips together and swallowing my laugh, I sit still, letting him inspect the stitches before he stands once again.

My thumb brushes over Rae's hand, and I watch the rise and fall of her chest. I count her breaths. My eyelids droop, and the room goes blurry. I shake my head, clearing my thoughts and my vision, but a few seconds later, my head starts to drop toward my chest.

Hastios places his hand on my shoulder, and with little effort, guides me to lay down on the bench. "The pain medication works best during sleep. Rest now. You are both in safe hands."

I let my head fall to the side, staring at Rae's profile, admiring the cascade of her dark hair spilling over the side of the table. I want to run my fingers through it to reassure her that I love her regardless of her origins. But I can't move. My limbs are heavy, and my breaths deepen as I fall toward slumber.

I hold Rae's hand, burying the panic that's threatening to close my throat any time I think about being King. I'll worry about that later.

For now, I'll hold onto Rae. I won't let go.

32

REALYN
Three Weeks Later

I STAND, head bowed in the small patch of fenced garden where stone markers memorialize my parents and Alek. There's no marker for Garin.

There were no remains of my parents, but the stones give me something to mourn over. Ash and I retrieved the charred remains of my younger brother's body last week and buried him in the small memorial garden I created with my earth magic.

Lush grass waves gently in the early morning breezes, and the soft scent of lilac kisses my senses from the blooms I created in honor of the Dragons. A silver-barked tree spreads its red leaves over the stone markers like a hug. A single tear tracks down my cheek as I watch the small flame flicker on a flat circle of stone embedded in the ground before the three graves. The flame will burn eternal, created from my magic for my lost family.

With a small nod, I turn, leaving the garden, watching my slippers peek from the hem of my dress with every step I take. I roll a shoulder, entirely uncomfortable in the gown, but today is special.

As I approach the training grounds, the grunts of punches hitting their marks, and the clang of steel meeting steel, brings me out of my thoughts. I watch as the royal soldiers, my soldiers, train in the cool hours of the early morning. The sun hasn't risen yet, and the mists capture the sounds of training, teasing the ear, making it hard to decipher where any one noise is coming from.

I shift on my feet, feeling the slight pull of lingering pain where the Shungite pierced my skin. Reluar, the healer, has done a remarkable job, and Kem sent his healer to aid ours in dealing with the many wounded. But despite the healer's skill, Shungite wounds are hard to heal. My magic returned the day after the battle, but the wounds still bother me with certain movements.

The dragon healer is still in Attolyn, fascinated by the fae and our physiology. He's been sharing dragon healing techniques with Reluar while soaking up any and all information about our life cycles, how we heal, how we age ...

Tial, the acting captain, stands to her full height after taking down yet another opponent. She helps the soldier to his feet, praising him for what he did right, then kindly going over his mistakes. She's going to be my captain; I just haven't told her yet. The soldier nods and walks out of the training ring. Tial sees me and bows. "As soon as you're ready, your Majesty, we can resume your training sessions."

"Can't wait."

"Not too soon, though." I turn at Ash's voice. He walks

toward me without a hint of a limp. By his posture and stride, you would never know he was stabbed in the gut a few weeks ago, and his back spasms less and less.

"I'm being careful, you nag."

His hands frame my face, and he kisses me, long and slow, uncaring of our audience. Pulling back, he smirks. "I'm a nag? Have you met Hastios?"

I laugh, and Ash takes my hand, leading me to the castle. "Taron just arrived."

I smile at the anticipation in Ash's voice. We'd sent a message into the city for Taron a week ago, only to learn that he and Ziza had gone back north to Dalnak, escorting the surviving fae who came to my aid, back home. Ash had worried they might encounter vengeful Unseelie during the long trek back north, but I'd reassured him that they were in good hands with Ziza. She watches over everything like a hawk—well, like a dragon.

Ash's stride quickens as we round a corner of the gardens. I know how much he's looking forward to seeing his old friend, how much he longs to thank him for what he did. And I'm just as eager.

It'd been Taron who had rallied not only the New Moon members but the citizens of Attolyn to fight for me, for their kingdom.

My heart squeezes as I recall the rush of my people as they came to my aid during the battle. They had turned the tide and given me the hope I so desperately needed at that moment.

The sun bursts over the horizon, reflecting off the shimmering green scales of a dragon standing a few yards away. Taron runs his hand over her scales before turning toward us. "Well, riding a dragon is an experience I'll never forget."

Ziza smiles as she shifts to her human form, shaking her

emerald hair over her shoulder. "Don't get used to it, fae." Her words are harsh, but a smile crinkles her eyes.

I pull her into a hug, and she holds me tight, her dragon's warmth comforting. "It's good to see you, Ziza."

"You too, your Maj—" I yank her hair, and she chuckles. "You too, Rae."

I release her and step back into Ash's hand. He wraps his arm around my waist, and I lean into him. He looks down at me, and I nod.

Ash gestures toward the castle, and we all start walking as he says to Taron, "The Queen and I—"

I nudge him with my elbow, and he exaggerates a grunt.

"*Raelyn* and I would like to thank you for what you did during the uprising."

Taron sighs, his cheeks turning red. "I thought we went over this. I did what I thought was right. I'm glad it worked out. I'm happy to see my country healing. I'm grateful to have such a kind and strong Queen ruling our kingdom once again." He pauses, and we all stop, surrounded by bright green hedges and fragrant blooms that pop red, orange, and yellow in the morning light. "I believe your parents would be very proud of you, Raelyn." Tears rim my eyes, but I swallow them down. "I'm proud to have served you in your time of need. That's all I need."

Ash smiles, resuming our walk through the gardens. "We know that, my friend. This is more for us than you. Let us thank you properly."

Taron rolls his eyes but follows us into the castle, down the long hallway. Our shoes fall quietly on the stone floor, absorbed by the intricate tapestries lining the walls. We lead Taron into the private dining area. The table and chairs have been removed from the small room, leaving the large red, blue, and cream rug exposed in the center of the room. The white plaster walls seem to glow as the morning light streams through the wall of windows that cover the right side of the room.

Lining the edges of the room are the New Moon Assassins. All of them. Each clad in their dark clothes, but they've pulled down their scarves around their necks. Every face is turned in our direction, and Nyira peels away from the wall, approaching us. She holds out her hand, revealing a skeleton key and a ring. "Taron, these are yours if you want them. I understand if you want to continue your life outside of the Guild, but if you want back in, I am asking you to be my second."

Taron's eyes skip between Nyira, her outstretched hand, and the assassins standing around the perimeter of the room. "Surely there's someone more qualified."

Nyira remains silent, as does everyone else.

Taron shifts on his feet. "I don't deserve this. I left. I abandoned the Guild."

Nyira sighs, but it's Sylmare who steps forward. "Honestly, we all should have abandoned the Guild. We made it too easy for Garin to target us."

I tense at my brother's name. I don't know how long it will be before I can hear his name without flinching or for my heart to hurt a little bit. But Ash is always here for me, and his arm squeezes around me gently, lending me strength.

Sylmare goes on, not noticing my inner struggle. "We should have fought back sooner. We should have done a lot of things. You came through when your Queen needed you, even when you weren't sure your Queen would even return." Sylmare gestures around the room. "We all agreed. The vote was cast. You are the second. If you want it."

Taron swallows and looks at Ash, who smiles and nods

at him. That's all the encouragement Taron needs. He takes the key, dropping it into his pocket and slides the ring onto this middle finger.

Ziza steps to his side, bumping his shoulder with hers. "Congratulations."

"Breakfast in the great hall," Ash proclaims, and the room starts to empty, following the scents of food.

I fall into step beside Ziza. "Are you staying for a while?"

"I'd like to, if that's okay. It's nice spending time away from the Crimson Plains."

"You are welcome to stay as long as you like." I grin and give her hip a little bump. "Will Arvun be joining you?"

Ziza blushes and swats me away. "Kem's keeping her pretty busy, but she promised that if I don't return home in one week, she'd come here to, and I quote, 'deal with me'."

"Deal with you? Hot damn, Ziza."

Her smile is radiant, making her green eyes sparkle. "I know."

We both giggle as we take a seat on one of the long benches that line the table in the great hall. Ash sits on the other side of the table, trading stories with the assassins seated around him. His eyes find mine, and he winks at me, sending an army of butterflies fluttering in my stomach.

We make it all of twenty minutes before we stand, almost in tandem. I walk around the table, and Ash takes my hand as I say, "Enjoy the food. Enjoy the day. The new roof is going on the Guild house today, so you should be able to start moving back in this evening if you wish."

Sylmare raises his cup, grinning. "Trying to get rid of us?"

"Yes," Ash says, and I shake my head.

"Of course not."

He sweeps me off my feet, yelling over his shoulder, "See yourselves out."

My giggles float around the room, and hoots and hollers follow us as Ash blurs us down the hall, up the stairs, and to our room. He kicks the door closed behind us and carries me across the room. Tenderly, he sits me on our bed, reaching around to undo the laces down my back before peeling the thin straps of my dress down my shoulders until the bodice is pooled around my waist. My skin pebbles, and my pussy throbs.

He kneels, pressing his lips to the long, pink line that travels across my ribs. "How are you feeling today?"

Through panting breaths, I whisper, "Good. I feel good." His fingers skim the waist of my skirt. "So good. Excellent. I've never felt better."

A chuckle flutters his breath over my navel. "That's good to hear"—his eyes snap to mine, and I squeeze my thighs together—"my Queen."

He peels off my dress before quickly stripping himself. He crawls up my body, and I shiver with desire. His lips press to my throat, pressing me back into the bed. A growl rumbles from his chest as I swirl my touch over the tips of his sensitive ears.

Our lips crash together as he settles between my thighs, the head of his cock rubbing my soaked entrance. I moan as I trail my fingers back down his ears, and I whisper, "Have I been a good girl?"

He slides into me slowly, drawing a prolonged groan from both of us. "Very good, my Queen." Once he's fully inside me, he starts a slow rhythm, rolling his hips against my pelvis, teasing my clit with every deep thrust. "I love you, Rae."

Kissing him deep, swirling my tongue around his, I hold

him close. I trail my tongue up his neck and nip his earlobe, whispering, "I love you, my assassin. My everything. My Ash."

Our hands touch and grope, caress and squeeze. I try to lift my hips to pick up the pace, to find that perfect position for Ash to sink deeper, to go harder. "Don't strain yourself, my Queen." The way he calls me Queen curls my toes. He holds me to the mattress, grabbing a pillow and stuffing it under my hips right above my ass, propping me up to the perfect angle as Ash rises to kneel over me. His hands grip my thighs as he watches his cock slide in and out of me, his tongue licking his lips as if he can't decide if he wants to keep fucking me or taste me instead. It's hypnotizing, watching that look of absolute pleasure, of absolute adoration on his face. It drives me over the edge.

"Fates, Ash!" My scream floats around the room as my orgasm tears through me. Pleasure pulses through my entire body as my pussy grips Ash with his strong thrusts. His abs flex, and the muscles in his arms bulge as he grips me tighter and throws back his head. His orgasm crashes through him, and I've never seen anything more perfect.

Catching his breath, he slides out of me before pressing a kiss to each of my healing wounds. "Are you okay?"

We've had sex several times since Reluar released me for 'light physical activity', and each time, Ash has worried over me.

"I'm fine, Ash, really." I press a hand to the puckered mark on his stomach. "And you?"

"Good." He smiles and reaches a hand to me, pulling me out of bed and to my feet. "I have a surprise for you."

I lift an eyebrow. "Shower sex?"

He chuckles, and I start throbbing for him again. "Sex on the balcony?"

He smirks, shaking his head. "You've got sex on the brain."

I shrug with a coy smile, running my hands over my still sensitive breasts before snaking them down my naked stomach. "Can you blame me?" I slide a finger between my slick folds and watch as he grows hard again. Lifting my hand to my lips, I lick the combined taste of our release from my finger as I rake my hungry gaze over his body.

"Fuck, Rae." He wraps his hand lightly around my throat before letting his fingers trail between my breasts, over my navel, and dips into my pussy. I buck against his hand, and he groans. "My Queen is insatiable."

I roll my hips, pressing myself into his hand, sending his fingers deeper. "I'll never have enough of you, Ash."

He growls, grabbing my hand and wrapping it around his hard cock. "Do you feel what you do to me?" Pumping into my tight fist, he continues to stroke his other hand over my clit. "How did our release taste, Raelyn?" He pulls his fingers from me and sucks them clean with a groan.

I shove him, and he falls back onto our bed. I straddle him and slowly lower myself onto his cock, enjoying every inch that stretches me in the most glorious way. Ash cups my breasts before scraping his nails over my sensitive nipples, drawing a moan from my lips. His eyes snap to where we're joined, watching as I slide up and down his length, and when I reach back and cup him, his eyes roll back, and his hands grab my hips. All it takes is one more deep thrust, and we come together. My blood sings, and my skin tingles as Ash sits up, wrapping his arms around my back and pulls me to his chest, holding me tight as we ride the waves of pleasure, bucking against each other.

His grip loosens, his fingers trailing up and down my

back in lazy strokes, and he sighs. "Fates, Rae, what you do to me ..."

I giggle. "So, what's my surprise?"

He shifts, standing once again and pulling me with him. "It's a surprise."

"What if I command you to tell me?"

"I'm your King, your commands are more like suggestions."

He's not technically King yet. And I'm not technically Queen. Yet. My coronation is in four days, and once I'm official, I can declare Ash King.

"Fine." I roll my eyes as I reach for my dress pooled on the floor.

"Nope. You'll want to wear this." He throws a pair of pants and a linen shirt at me. I catch the pants, but the shirt falls to the floor. I frown as he tosses my boots at me, and they thump on the floor at my feet.

I go to the bathroom to relieve myself, and Ash is dressed when I come out. He pecks my lips with a quick kiss. "Meet me in the garden." And with that, he walks out of our room.

Intrigued, I dress quickly, and as I leave our room, I brush my fingers over the soft wool of the tapestry hanging by the door.

"Miss you, Syphe."

Hopping down the hall as I pull on my boots along the way. As I enter the gardens, I realize he didn't tell me where in the gardens to meet him. I think about calling out to him, but I catch his scent on the breeze. I inhale deeply, drawing the smell of pine and grass into my lungs. My magic whispers to me, and I let my air magic follow his scent.

I leave the castle grounds and turn the corner into the side gardens to find him standing near the portal with a smile on his face and his hands behind his back. "What are you up to, Ash?"

"Do you know what today is?"

I tilt my head to the side, trying to think of something important I might have missed, but my mind is coming up blank.

He sweeps his arms from behind his back, and in his hands rests my iron and gold arrow. My eyes snap to his. "The competition is today?" He nods, stepping to a nearby bench. Bending over, giving me a glorious view of his ass, he lifts two bows from where they were hidden under the shrubs.

I frown, fidgeting in place. The responsibilities of the crown rest like heavy armor on my chest. "There's so much to do here. I can't—"

"Tial has the soldiers well in hand. The assassins are practically working for you, keeping the peace, which is so weird." I smile at Ash's grimace. "And Lewell has everything else under control. She knows where I'm taking you." Ash cups my face. "Trust her, Rae. It's one day. Come have a little fun with me."

It's true. Lewell, my advisor, is a godsend. She was Alek's advisor and reluctantly went into hiding at his insistence when he learned where I was and made his plans to retrieve me and take down Garin. Three days after the battle, she approached me, telling me how honored she was to have served my younger brother and would be honored to serve me in any way I found fit. It didn't take me long to learn that she's smart, funny, and competent, even if she is a little quiet and reserved, so much like Alek. I'm lucky to have her in my slowly growing court.

I nod, smiling as I let go of my responsibilities for just a little while.

Ash grins. "Glamour up, Rae." His form melts into his human form. "You're going to have stiff competition this year."

I laugh, settling my human glamour over my fae features. "Oh, it's on!" I sprint through the portal after a chuckling Ash.

I'll do whatever I need to do to keep my assassin at my side. He's my support, my adventure, my joy, my love.

But more than that, I'll use every scrap of magic and fighting skill I possess to keep my kingdom, my people safe.

I am The Elemental Queen.

ACKNOWLEDGMENTS

A big thank you to my husband for being my first reader of every draft. Working through plots and characters with you is my favorite part of the process.

To all my beta readers, thank you! You had a big hand in making this book what it is today.

To my editor, Jolene Perry. Your insight and advise added a layer of depth that I didn't know was missing.

I wouldn't have made it this far with my sanity in tact without my fellow author friends, Anna Fury and Elizabeth Brown.

And lastly, I want to thank all my friends and family for cheering me on and being as excited about my first novel as I was—I love my tribe.

ABOUT THE AUTHOR

T. B. Wiese is a military spouse, dog mom, photographer, Disney nerd, and lover of spicy fantasy. She loves animals (She grew up with dogs and working with horses, including working at the Tri-Circle D Ranch at Disney World), so don't be surprised when you find yourself reading lovable animal characters in her novels.

She has loved reading since she was little, and her tbr list is embarrassingly long, but she's always looking to add more, so if you have a spicy fantasy recommendation, pass it along.

If you'd like to keep up to date with future releases (her villain duology is coming later this year), sign up for her newsletter here.

https://www.tbwiese.com/subscribe

This will also gain you access to sign up to be one of her Advanced Readers as well as the first in line for new swag and sales.

SCAN WITH YOUR CAMERA APP FOR ALL MY LINKS